A Different Country Entirely

A Novel of The Texas Rangers'
1855 Raid Into Mexico

To
Celeta + Wally

Philip McBride

Philip McBride

ISBN: 197765777X
ISBN-13: 978-1977657770

*A **Different Country Entirely*** is dedicated to the mystique of early Texas and to the mounted volunteers who became the first Texas Rangers. Constantine Connolly, Jesse Holmes, and James Callahan are among the men from Prairie Lea and Lockhart, Texas who answered the call and inspired this novel.

My heartfelt thanks to Donaly Brice, author, historian, and friend who first introduced me to the story of enigmatic Texas Ranger Captain James Callahan. Further thanks to the members of my weekly critiquing circle, all fine authors themselves: Tam Francis, Gretchen Rix, Rebecca Ballard, Wayne Walther, and Todd Blomerth. My gratitude to Karen Phillips for another cover design that captures the spirit of the novel. And lastly, my loving thanks to my wife Juanita McBride for her ongoing patience, copy editing, and unwavering support of my compulsion to write books about the old days.

Also by Philip McBride

A Civil War Novel of the Alamo Rifles

Whittled Away

The Captain John McBee Civil War Trilogy

Tangled Honor: 1862

Redeeming Honor: 1863

Defiant Honor: 1864

Nonfiction with Joe Owen and Joe Allport

Texans at Antietam
A Terrible Clash of Arms--September 16-17, 1862

A Different Country Entirely

Chapter 1

The Guadalupe River
North of New Braunfels, Texas
June 1854

Clear and cold. The water was crystal clear and ice cold. Caroline rubbed the goose pimples on her arms as she looked down at her feet, her toes visible, but distorted in the flow of the waist-deep water of the Guadalupe River. The current pushed her thin shift into her hips as she twisted to face upstream. She reached down to futilely pull the material away, and the touch of her own fingertips sent her thoughts back eighteen hours. Just the night before, she had lain nervously in a hotel bed, her first night as Mrs. Josef Schmidt, a just married, and soon-to-be deflowered grown woman, nearly nineteen years old.

She smiled to herself. *Mama was wrong, mostly. Ja, the first time hurt, and I was frightened for a man, even Josef, to be so close—to be inside me. But, still...I liked last night, and I want to tonight to be the same.*

She dug her toes into the gritty sand and waited for her new husband to step out from behind the bushes beyond the sandbar. She eyed the brown mare that also waited, hitched to the rented buggy, where their full picnic basket was still stowed beneath the seat. When Josef came running, hopping into view, his feet bouncing high off the hot sandbar pebbles, she laughed brightly. Both his hands were cupped over his crotch, even though he wore ankle-length cotton drawers.

Josef had peered between two leafy branches and watched his bride take off her shoes, then her dress. By the time she pulled down her two petticoats, wriggling her derriere to help them along, he was beside himself. Watching her walk into the water, the sun shining through her shift, was the last straw. He pushed aside the branches and ran for the water, ran for Caroline.

When Josef's feet first splashed into the shallow water, his arms flew up, exposing his member poking out alertly between the buttons of his fly. Caroline pointed and hiccupped in laughter, then quickly put her hands over her eyes. Growing up in town, daughter of a pious Lutheran gunsmith, even after last night, the blonde teenager had never before seen a man's penis. She had seen long-necked, red-headed turtles sunning on logs along this very river, but they had been still, not waggling so, and not with only one dark eye.

At her laughter, Josef looked down at his open fly and immediately dove into the water, swimming to his new wife. Staying underwater, he reached both arms behind her and slowly ran his open palms up the backs of her legs, to cup both her buttocks through the linen shift.

She clinched, then relaxed at the touch of his hands. As soon as his lean torso erupted from below the surface, she felt the push of his manhood at her front. He blinked water from his eyes and shook his head like a wet hound. He looked at Caroline's smile, her dancing eyes, then let his gaze drop to her chest, her clinging wet shift translucent. He gasped, for even after last night, he'd never seen a grown woman's bared breasts.

She reached up and stroked his cheek, putting her other arm around his neck. They kissed, less clumsily than last night, long and deep, eyes closed. Caroline finally tilted her head back to look at her husband and tell him how happy she felt. She opened her eyes and yelped, convulsively jerking her arms tightly around Josef. She gaped in horror at the three Indians standing on the riverbank.

One of the trio of short men with broad, deeply lined faces smiled oddly, the corners of his mouth curving down instead of up. Yet the mirth in the look was unmistakable as he reached into his breechcloth and pulled out his penis, shaking it at her, yipping like a coyote. The other two pulled knives and ran into the water.

Only seconds later Josef lay on his back, dying in the shallows, blood seeping from stab wounds in his chest and stomach. The two Lipan Apaches dragged the screaming young woman to the sandbar where they held her down, spread-eagled. After laughing and poking fingers at her ivory white skin, the men took turns violating her, joking obscenely about each other's performance.

When none of them could gain another erection, they left her sobbing hysterically, *"Mein Gott, nein, nein, nein."* Turning their attention to the corpse, they severed Josef's genitals and stuffed them into his mouth. Then the leader shot a painted arrow into the chest of the mutilated body to add an unmistakable signature to their actions.

Afterwards, they cut the rented horse from its traces and added it to their string of stolen animals. One of the Apaches found Caroline's silk parasol and a leather-bound book next to her neatly folded dress and petticoats. He tossed the book of poems by Friedrich Hölderlin into the brush. After tentatively picking up the umbrella, he jerked his head back in surprise when the silk cloth ballooned open. Delighted with his find, he held the parasol above his head and quickly decided to take it to his newest wife. But he could not make it shut. He carried the white sunshade to the woman who lay moaning on the sandbar and gestured for her to do something.

In her state of shock, Caroline stared up at him, confused. He yanked her up and backhanded her cheek, no harder than he hit his wives, and again pointed at the open parasol. This time Caroline reached out and took the handle, pushed the button and pulled the silk material closed around the shaft. The Lipan Apache grunted before he led her to their horses.

He roughly lifted her onto another raider's horse, seated in front of its rider. They crossed the Guadalupe River and after two hours of hard riding west, rejoined four other warriors leading stolen stock and two captured children, one a pre-pubescent Negro girl, the other a little white boy. After a short rest, during which the other Lipan men each raped the nearly comatose blonde woman, the three captives were lashed onto one stout horse and the successful raiding party began the long arduous trek back to the Rio Grande River.

★

In the late afternoon, holding a pistol, Mr. Hoffman gaped at the body of his new son-in-law. He walked to the buggy where Josef's father leaned against a tree, vomit still dribbling from his chin. Mr. Schmidt sobbed as Mr. Hoffman patted him on the shoulder. Finally, the pair lifted the corpse onto the buggy, hitched Mr. Schmidt's horse to the vehicle and returned to town. The two men had no words for each other, for as heinous as Josef's brutal murder was, they both knew that Caroline was now enduring a hell that even an unlikely rescue could not assuage.

The next morning, both fathers, accompanied by five male relatives and a hired tracker, set off on the Indians' trail. On the second day, still north of the Nueces River, a thunderstorm pelted the pursuers with rain and hail. The violent downpour also destroyed the hoof prints they had been following, prompting the party to return to New Braunfels. All the way back, Mr. Hoffman prayed for his daughter's soul, for to him she was now as dead as Josef.

A week later, still overcome by the violent killing of their son, Mr. Schmidt sold his house and store to a cousin who'd just reached New Braunfels after a voyage from Germany. Mr. Schmidt filled three rented wagons with his family's belongings and moved his household to the new town of Prairie Lea, on the banks of the San Marcos River, thirty miles east of New Braunfels.

Prairie Lea was surrounded by black dirt fields planted in cotton, not the scrub brush hill country where hostile Indians emerged to inflict their savagery on white settlers. Mr. Schmidt tried to forget the lingering memory of his son's mutilated body by working long days to build a new house and business. He intended for Schmidt's Dry Goods and Groceries to provide tough competition to the other store in the growing town, Mr. Callahan's Hardware and General Mercantile.

Chapter 2

Austin City, Texas
September 1854

Milo McKean was at a loss. His gelding, a horse older than its twenty-two year-old owner, had lain down in its stall at the livery stable and died during the night, too worn down from the trip from Alabama to take one more step. Milo considered his saddle and bridle draped over the stall rail and reluctantly asked the livery owner if he'd buy them. The man scratched his head and said he'd give $25, but would have to deduct $5 to drag the carcass out where the buzzards and hogs could get at it without offending the neighbors, and he reminded the young man he still owed a dollar for last night's stall rental.

With the heavy gold piece in his pocket, his saddlebags over one shoulder and his blanket roll over the other, McKean walked down Congress Avenue towards the road heading south. He had a Colt cap-and-ball revolver stuffed into the waist of his filthy trousers. The soles of his boots were thin, and by the time he'd walked all day and reached the ford across Onion Creek, his feet hurt worse than he could ever remember.

The young man stopped at the creek, perched on a rock to pull off his boots and stockings, and dangled his feet in the clear, cold water. He took off his hat and pushed it under water. He poured the water caught in his hat crown over his sandy brown hair, face, and shoulders, then shoved the wet hat back on his head. He picked up one boot and fingered the sole, confirming it was down to the last layer of leather. He rubbed the stubble on his chin and over his lip. *Since I'm out of coffee beans, in the morning I'll use my tin cup to heat water and scrape my jaw clean before I started walking again. I may have holes in my boots, but I ain't going to let Jesse's mother see me for the first time with scraggly whiskers on my face. Not if I want her to take me in for a spell. Maybe I better wash my shirt and trousers too.*

McKean dug around in his saddlebag and pulled out the paper-wrapped meat and hard rolls he'd bought in Austin. It was nearly dusk and Milo knew he needed to gather some wood soon, if he wanted a fire in the evening. Instead, weary from his long walk, he sat and massaged his sore feet, lost in thought, wondering if he'd recognize the turn-off to the town of Prairie Lea. He didn't pay attention to the creaking of wagon wheels until the team of horses, still up the rocky slope from the water, saw him and snorted.

McKean jumped up, barefooted, and awkwardly reached for his pistol. Before he could pull it free, a voice bellowed, "Too late, Boy. You'd be buzzard bait by now if I thought you was a highwayman." McKean looked at the hefty middle-aged man sitting on the wagon seat, pointing a double-barreled shotgun at him. A Negro youth shared the bench seat, holding the reins.

Milo dropped his hand away from his weapon. "I'm no highwayman. Just a traveler."

"Where's your horse, traveler?"

"Played out. I been riding that gelding since I was a boy, but he laid down and died back in Austin City yesterday. I'm a foot traveler now."

The white man in the wagon grunted. "You're a tall drink of water. Maybe your old horse gave out 'cause you outgrew it. Whatever the reason, places are a far piece apart around here for foot travelers. Even the heathen redskins ride when they sneak in to steal and murder. A traveler would do well to have a horse."

"Yessir, My feet been telling me that, too. But I'm of a mind that where I'm going ain't all that far."

"That so?" The man in the wagon raised an eyebrow, but politely did not ask where that might be.

"Yessir. I'm headed to the town of Prairie Lea. I was told it's down this road, but off to the east once I get to the next river."

"That'd be a day's ride south to San Marcos, longer than a day for a foot traveler."

"Is the road to Prairie Lea marked where it forks off? I'd hate to miss it."

The man chuckled. "Nah, as I recall, there ain't no road sign."

"There a landmark? Maybe a dead tree or big rock?"

"Mister, these parts are covered in trees and rocks."

McKean slumped his shoulders. "Well, I'll get there somehow. I may be on foot and there may not be a sign, but I reckon I can follow the river."

"You thinkin' that would be upsteam or downstream? Bad Injuns upstream, not so far up in them hills."

"Downstream. I said to the east, didn't I?" Milo pointed the way the creek was flowing.

"So you did." The man chuckled again. "Just takin' a measure of your good sense before I offer you a ride. I'm headed to Prairie Lea myself. Got a load of goods to deliver to the new mercantile store. Never hurts to have another hand, 'specially one with a Colt revolver. That is, if you can get that thing out of your pants without shootin' your own pecker off." The Negro youth snorted at his master's joke.

"Shut your mouth, Thompson, or I might cut *your* pecker off," the man said without any rancor in his voice.

"I can shoot it, and I'd be obliged for a ride, that I would," McKean said, picking up his saddlebags and blanket roll.

"Climb on. All I ask is you help Thompson unload the wagon when we get there tomorrow."

"I can do that." McKean paused. "I'll help your darkie unload your wagon in pay for a ride."

The older man studied the horseless traveler. His nose was sharp, his cheek bones prominent, and his bewhiskered chin showed hints of being pointed. His blue eyes were striking, but fatigue was evident in them. He noted the fellow's wide shoulders with approval, thinking of the unloading task he'd agreed to. The older man wasn't surprised that the traveler's belly was flat, almost sunken, no different from most young men who'd recently left home and rode alone, far away from their mother's cooking.

"We're camping just over the ford and around the bend in the road. Climb up unless you want to wade across."

An hour later, McKean sat across the fire from the older man, enjoying the well-seasoned beans and bacon the young Negro had heated in a pot. "I do appreciate the hot supper. Better 'n I can do, over a fire or stove."

"Yeah, that boy ain't too bad a camp cook. The heavy man burped. "You got a name, traveler?"

"Milo McKean."

"I'm Benjamin Smith, Mr. McKean. The nigra boy there is Thompson. You just passing through Prairie Lea?"

"Don't know, sir. I'm headed there to find my friend Jesse Gunn. His family moved to Prairie Lea from Alabama last year. If there's work, I might stay. I'm a fair hand with a set of carpenter tools."

"Lots of building going on in Prairie Lea. Should be work for a man good with wood."

"Hope so."

His meal finished, the older man rose, and holding his shotgun, nodded. You can sleep under the wagon with Thompson."

"By the fire will be good enough," McKean nodded toward the flames.

"Suit yourself. But I heard some thunder earlier. There's room for two under there, and it's a roof in the rain. Thompson don't bite. I own his mammy. She's my cook and housemaid, and Thompson has been my personal servant since he was a little 'un, barely old enough to fetch me my jug for an evening by the fire. Keep your pistol close to your hand wherever you bed down."

"Highwaymen? Bandits?"

The man shook his head. "Apaches. Comanches. You just never know where the heathens might show up. This road gets lots of traffic 'tween San Antone and Austin. It's safe enough from robbers, but you never know 'bout the damned Indians. And I'd ruther face off a dozen white ruffians than even one or two of them red bastards. They don't come around often, but when they do, you don't want to be anywhere close."

"Bad, are they?"

"Boy, you can't guess how bad. They're the spawn of Lucifer. Just last summer, not far from here, a pair of Dutch newlyweds on a picnic was set upon. The first day of their life as man and wife was their last. Killed the boy. Stabbed him, shot him with arrows, stuffed his balls in his mouth. Left him layin' in the shallow water for the snappers to feed on. Took his bride. Even God don't want to know what they done to her." Smith paused to let his words sink in.

"A band of militia went after her quick enough. Tracked the Apache bastards all the way to the Nueces River, down towards the Mex border. But the trail disappeared after a thunderstorm. She's lost. Pray she's dead."

McKean lay by the fire for hours staring at the cloudy sky, thinking about wild Indians and listening to the sounds of the night with his pistol clutched in his hand. When it started raining, he gathered his blanket and canvas tarp and made himself a place under the wagon next to Thompson.

★

The wagon trip to the small village of Prairie Lea took most of the next day. Smith pulled up next to an unfinished green wood building where a middle-aged man leaned high on a ladder hammering nails into the siding.

"*Ja*, I am Schmidt," the sweating man called down. "And this is Schmidt's Dry Goods and Groceries. You have wares for me?"

"Sure do," Smith answered. "Straight from my own store stock in Austin City. You're lucky I ordered more bolts of cloth and them other things than I got shelves to put them on. I made you a prime deal, I surely did. Where you want it all unloaded? I got two boys ready to get it done."

With dusk approaching, the Negro Thompson and Milo McKean, working together, unloaded the wagon and stacked the crates of textiles, sacks of flour and boxes of other food stuffs under the newly roofed section of the partly completed building. McKean shook Smith's hand and nodded goodbye to Thompson, then walked off in search of his friend, Jesse Gunn.

Chapter 3

Prairie Lea, Texas
September 1854

Just two days after Benjamin Smith brought a single wagonload of inventory to Schmidt's Dry Goods and Grocery Store, three more wagons came from Galveston, not Austin or San Antonio. Each was loaded with goods straight off ships from New Orleans, New York, and even Europe. One wagon held bolts of printed cotton cloth along with a stack of white canvas tarps. Smaller boxes held needles, thimbles, and hanks of thread, while coils of rope filled the space under the driver's bench.

Another wagon carried boxes of tin cups, plates, pots, pans, and coffee boilers, a case of German cutlery, two sets of French dinnerware, canned food luxuries, and two dozen pairs of boots. The last wagon, pulled by four mules instead of two, hauled the heaviest load—crates of carpenter's tools, six kegs of nails, four barrels of gun powder, ten thousand copper priming caps, thousands of lead round balls and buckshot pellets, a case of ten rifled muskets from Austria, and a long crate holding ten double-barrel shotguns from England.

The wagons' late afternoon arrival caused a stir up and down Prairie Lea's main street, the only street in the settlement which was more than two dusty ruts through the weeds. Alerted by a rider an hour before that the wagons had reached Lockhart, just a dozen miles to the east, James Callahan sought out the few young men in town to unload his new merchandise, promising payment in beer, bullets, and gun powder.

Jesse Gunn, Milo McKean, who was now a houseguest of the Gunn family, and two others worked in shirtsleeves pulling every box off the wagon beds and carrying them into the back of

Callahan's store. The last hour of work was done by lantern light, and when the final wooden crate was stacked in the store's back room, the four young men gratefully followed Mr. Callahan into his taproom.

After Callahan drew them each a full mug, the quartet of tired laborers sat on the covered porch of the mercantile store where an evening breeze helped dry their sweat-soaked shirts. Mr. Callahan leaned in the doorway, wondering how much—or how little—black powder he could fairly dole out to the boys in payment. He did mental calculations weighing the value of another four mugs of good beer against eight ounces of fine-grain gunpowder.

Jesse raised his ceramic mug to his lips and blew softly at the thick creamy foam. Milo looked at his own mug. "What is this, ale of some kind?"

Callahan shook his head, "Nah, that's from the first barrel of German beer to get here from San Antonio. Fella named Menger just opened a brewery there. That's high quality brew you boys are getting."

"Damn, it's good." Elijah Harris smacked his lips. "Man, nobody makes beer like a Dutchman."

"Thought you said a German fella made it." McKean said, raising his mug.

"Dutch, German, Bavarian, all the same here in Texas," Jesse answered. "Lots of new families from little states in Europe are landing in Galveston and coming to these parts. Gets confusing, so to keep it simple, there're all Dutchmen."

Milo nodded, then took a tentative sip that turned into a long gulp. He hadn't been able to shake off visions of the gruesome atrocities done by the Apaches to the German newlyweds as told by Mr. Smith just a few days ago.

"So, are the Indians really as bad as Mr. Smith was telling me?" McKean blurted.

Again, Callahan answered, inserting his age and authority into the conversation. "Yeah, they are. I'm surprised the old boy drove his wagon down here without adding more armed outriders. I expect he was glad to come across you and your revolver before he was too far out of Austin."

"Why do they do it? The Indians, I mean," Milo asked. "Ain't there land enough? I know I just got here, but Texas seems a helluva big place to me."

"It's the livestock. Mules and horses, not beeves." Callahan grimaced. "They ride up this way from the Rio Grande valley to steal riding stock to sell to the damned Meskins. Or trade for whiskey."

"Why not cattle?" Tom Boone asked. "Beef eats a hell of a lot better than mule meat."

"Too slow to drive. Them injuns travel fast. Don't stop to sleep when they hightail it back to the Rio Grande. Ride a stolen horse to death, then switch to another one. So they just shoot the cattle on the farms they burn out. Or run 'em through with their long lances. Injun way of telling us to stick it up our arses. They'll come and go as they want, take what they want, and kill who they want. Then they cross the Rio Grande where we can't go after 'em."

"But the killing and the ravaging of women and kidnapping children..." McKean drank deeply again.

"That's just the Injun way of reminding us that they was here first," James Callahan said. "They could do a lot more devilment if they really wanted us all gone. They could burn out every damned farm from San Antone to Austin." Callahan skillfully spat far enough that the blob missed his wooden porch and landed in the dirt.

"No, what drives the raiding is our riding stock. If they murdered all the settlers, then they wouldn't have anyone to steal horses and mules from, and no way to buy whiskey from the Meskins."

Milo frowned. "Well, they sure got folks riled up. I read last night in Mr. Gunn's San Antonio newspaper that farmers are leaving their homesteads and moving into town. Sounds like maybe the redskins are trying to scare off all us white people and take back Texas."

Jesse entered into the discussion. "Nah, but, I'd move to town, too, if I lived out west or south of San Antone. Did you see the article in that same paper about the troupe of Italian harp players? They was booked at the new lyceum to do a month of performances, but have skedattled back to Galveston, scared witless the redskins were gonna attack the town, and they was

20

gonna be carved up like fat turkeys." Jesse swallowed the last of his beer and wiped the foam from his mouth.

Mr. Callahan saw all four of the young men were at the bottom of their mugs, and decided that Mr. Menger's new barrel of beer was more valuable than a keg of black powder. He stood straight and said, "Time to shut the place up 'til morning. You boys put your empty mugs on the table and come back tomorrow. I'll have your powder and lead shot ready."

"Got more work for tomorrow?"

"Afraid not, fellas. Got a clerk who has to count every piece to make sure I ain't been cheated and then arrange it all just so on the shelves. And I need to make a trip into San Antone and see Mr. Menger about buying more of his beer."

Jesse Gunn and the other two all had work to do on their family farms, but Milo McKean had never seen San Antonio and wasn't yet bound to a job. "I ain't ever been down that way. If you're taking a wagon to haul beer back, I'm a fair hand with a brace of mules—and with my Colt, should there be a need."

Callahan smiled. "I'm not taking a wagon, the beer may not be cooked yet. But I wouldn't mind your company, and your Colt, on the road. I'm going to a stock ranch on the way to buy a mule. Wesley is going with me. He's a strong boy, but he's only ten, and a stubborn mule can be a handful. We're leaving mid-morning. You meet us here."

"Yessir, but, uh, my horse died in Austin, and I sold my saddle so I wouldn't have to hump it all the way here."

"Son, a man can't be a man in Texas without a good mount, and a saddle."

"Yessir, I have the twenty dollars my saddle fetched. I'm hoping my first payday will be enough for an old nag that'll last until I can earn enough for a hardy gelding."

Callahan grunted. "Got to have a job before there's a payday."

Milo looked at his feet. "No luck so far here in Prairie Lea."

"Try Lockhart, if you can handle a saw and hammer. Things are booming there. But I'll loan you a horse and tack to go with us to San Antonio tomorrow. This isn't a real job, mind you, no pay, but you can sleep on the floor in our room at Menger's boarding house where me and Wesley are staying, and I'll make sure you don't starve. Them Mex *senoras* make some fine *frijoles* and *tamales*. Near good as a Dutchman's beer."

Chapter 4

The Ranch of Lemuel Gill
On the Salado Creek
North of San Antonio
September 1854

The three riders splashed across shallow Salado Creek and turned north, looking for the small ranch owned by a man named Gill. After following the water flow upstream for a mile, enjoying the shade of the huge trees that lined the creek, the trio stopped to stare at an unexpected curiosity. Atop a rise fifty yards from the creek, stood an arch, tall and wide enough to ride a horse through. The edifice appeared to be constructed from several ancient, wind bent cypress logs pieced together.

"What's that orange thing, Papa?" Wesley asked.

"Damned if I know. Looks like an open gateway, but I don't see no fencing," James Callahan replied to his son.

"Looks to me like a church altar, something a circuit-riding preacher would make, but giant-sized and all twisted up like it's been through a tornado," Milo said.

"Well, the man said the mule dealer had a gateway we couldn't miss." Callahan remarked.

Milo and Wesley galloped their mounts up the slope, while the older Callahan followed. Milo stopped under the wooden arch and rubbed his hand along a bent orange-tinted cypress log. All the bark had been stripped away, leaving a cool smooth surface. Limbs had been artfully arranged to appear woven, almost like the handle of a straw basket.

Milo's muses ended when he jerked his hand away, his fingers having brushed over a red-painted, palm-sized snake skull pegged to the wood, its white inch-long fangs extended. Looking closer, Milo saw more skulls of small animals and reptiles, but none so large. He shivered in spite of the heat of the warm day.

"There's the house and barn and corral," Callahan said, looking down the opposite side of the rise, not stopping to admire the odd wooden monolith, instead skirting it, ignoring McKean.

Two men in stained and mended work clothes stood talking near the empty corral, while two pre-teens took turns roping an anvil sitting on a fat stump. Introductions quickly led to Mr. Gill sending the two youngsters into the pasture to coax six mules into the pen by the barn.

While the boys were still in the pasture, Milo asked, "What do you call that wood thing on the rise? Somebody put in a peck of work to get all those logs up from the creek bed and planted and fit together like that." He didn't mention the snake skull.

Mr. Gill smiled broadly. "That, young man, is my cypress tribute to Stonehenge."

"Your cypress what?"

"Tribute to Stonehenge. Stonehenge is an ancient and mysterious circle of giant stones in England. Cabin-sized stones cut smooth, carefully stacked and arranged thousands of years ago. Very powerful magic there." Gill paused, looking up at the arch. "I don't know if my cypress gateway is magical, but it does seem to keep the hostile Indians at bay.

"So far," interjected Mr. McDonald.

James Callahan grunted. "You can have your twisted log monster. I'll keep my Colt revolver handy."

Lemuel Gill patted his own pistol grip. "I'm no fool, Mr. Callahan. Mr. Colt is my constant companion, too. I only can say that none of my mules have disappeared in the night since Bain and me and the McDonalds created *that*." Gill waved his hand at the cypress construct.

The pair of boys finally succeeded in working the mules into the corral. While Milo sat on the top rail and the older men leaned on the fence, Wesley Callahan joined the other two youngsters in the corral, where they tried to lasso an ornery black mule. Wesley fumbled with his lariat, trying to shake the loop bigger before he twirled it over his head. Lemuel Gill's son, Bain, was still coiling his rope after a failed effort at laying his loop over the mule's head.

Jesse McDonald, the shortest of the three boys, had brown skin and black hair. His hat lay in the dust, the auburn streaks in his hair catching the sun. He was confident with his rope, walking slowly several feet behind the mule, casually twirling his lariat's loop by his side. When the mule raised its head to eyeball the other boys, Jesse spun the rope once over his own head to expand the loop, and let it fly. The rope passed over the mule's long ears and settled around its thick neck. Jesse pulled the rope gently, careful not to jerk it tight and spook the beast. He slowly pulled the rope snug, and stood still, letting the animal get used to the new weight on its neck.

"That little Meskin boy has a way with animals and a lariat, don't he?" Callahan nodded in approval at the boy's skill.

Lem Gill looked straight ahead, silent.

Angus McDonald, in a thick Scottish accent, said, "The laddy's not a Mexican boy. He's a McDonald, my oldest son. That he is."

Unabashed, Callahan mused, "Well, I'll be. He's sure dark for a Scot."

"His dear mother's a Santos. My wife," McDonald answered, a touch of defensiveness creeping into his tone. "Her family came from Spain, some islands off the coast named after a wee bird, they tell me."

"Then he's European, even if he is dark." Callahan spat into the corral. "I'm glad he ain't half Mex. Too much Indian blood in a true Mex."

"You want to buy a mule, now you seen them?" Gill asked, pulling the conversation back to the reason for Callahan's visit.

"Maybe the piebald. He seems stout. He sure does look a sight odd though, with those big splotches of mottled gray on his white coat like that."

"That's because his stud was a black and white paint horse. He's in his stall if you want to see him." The three men walked into the barn to examine the mule's sire.

Coming back into the bright sun, Callahan shaded his eyes and squinted at the piebald mule. "I'll take him if the price is right, and if you've had him hitched to a plow and he ain't balked at turning a field."

"The piebald has been in a harness. My boy Bain there, he walked behind that very mule this spring putting in a new field of corn." Gill turned his attention to the corral and called, "Bain, how'd the piebald mule do plowing?"

"He done good, Pa, and there was a heap of big rocks in that field that kept bouncing the plow blade. Didn't bother the critter. But the smells coming from his thundering rear end liked to kilt me," the tall boy answered with a smile.

All three men grinned at the caveat, but Callahan was satisfied with the boy's candid confirmation of the animal's willingness to work. After a few minutes of friendly dickering, a price acceptable to both men was agreed on. James Callahan and Lemuel Gill shook hands to seal the deal, and Callahan's party left for San Antonio, Wesley leading the piebald mule.

Chapter 5

Alamo Plaza
San Antonio, Texas
September 1854

A long afternoon ride brought Milo and the Callahan father and son into San Antonio where they spent the night in William Menger's popular boarding house. After dinner in the crowded dining room, Callahan and Menger stayed at the table talking about current political events. Eventually the host proudly showed his guest--and his first out-of-town beer customer—his brewing operation and cooper's workshop. When the conversation shifted to recent Indian incursions, Menger sent his son to fetch his friend Giles Boggess, as he'd recently returned from a ranging expedition south of the Nueces River.

Boggess was in his early thirties, splitting the age gap between McKean and Callahan. He traded stories with Callahan about their days in the saddle tracking hostile Mexican bandits and Indians, both men having been active Rangers during the years of the Republic of Texas a decade earlier. They shared a strong opinion that the frequency of the Indian incursions was escalating, and both men expressed anger at how the raiders could find sanctuary just across the Rio Grande. They concluded their late night session by promising each other they'd someday take action.

As they all stood to leave, Boggess shook hands with Milo. "You're riding with a good man, Mr. McKean. James Callahan was in the thick of it twenty years back when the old boys were fighting Santa Anna. You listen and learn from him."

Boggess looked over at Callahan, winked at him, and added, "But he's a married man now with a family and a new mercantile store. If you get an itch to do some rangering, you get hold of me through Mr. Menger. I'm always open to signing on a good hand into my company of Mounted Volunteers."

The next morning the trio from Prairie Lea stood in the dust of Alamo Plaza. They'd paused in front of a vendor stall that offered squawking chickens in wooden cages and squealing piglets packed around a filthy fat sow. Plucked hen carcasses hung from a bar holding the front edge of a sagging canvas tarp. Next to the dead chickens, dangled four hollowed-out white gourd water jugs on leather thongs. On the waist-high board countertop lay piles of long red peppers, bright yellow squashes, and ears of corn in their green husks.

Other stalls and vendor carts sold hot food and Mexican versions of most of the products in Mr. Callahan's general store, along with larger items like wagon wheels, farming implements, and even livestock. The cacophony of buying and selling in two languages, the pungent aromas of spices and the sharp scents of dead and live animals, stretched all the way across the plaza to the walls of the Alamo chapel, now a U.S. Army supply depot.

"I thought it'd be bigger." Milo shifted his gaze to the limestone church façade.

"You don't think this plaza is big?"

"No, I mean the Alamo. That's the Alamo, isn't it? I've read about it and seen drawings in the newspapers. I always thought it was really big. You know, like a fortress. Where'd Davy Crockett die?"

"I'm not real sure. Most think off to the right somewhere." Callahan nodded towards the two-story edifice with the distinctive curved roof line. "And that church there is just one piece of the mission that became a fort. The fort was big, all right. Turned out to be too damned big for Travis' men to defend. Too many walls."

"Where's the cemetery?"

"What cemetery?"

"The one where the soldiers are buried. I'd like to see Colonel Crockett's grave."

Callahan snorted. "No cemetery. Santy Anna piled up all the bodies and burned 'em in a big bonfire. In San Fernando Church, not far over that way, there's a box with a few charred bones pulled out of the ashes. That's all that's left of them."

"That don't seem right," McKean said, shaking his head as they walked past more roofless market stalls.

The older Callahan led them through the busy open-air market, stopping here and there to look closely at items that caught his eye. At one stall, he unfolded a brightly colored striped blanket off a stack, and asked how much it cost.

The answer came back in rapid Spanish, causing Callahan to spit to emphasize he didn't speak the language. Instead of trying further to communicate in words, Callahan reached in his vest pocket, pulled out three silver dollars, and held his hand out. The Hispanic vender studied the three coins, smiled broadly, revealing missing front teeth, and nodded his head, thinking he'd made an easy sale to a rich *gringo*. Callahan then shook his own head, pointed at the pile of blankets, put the three silver coins on the rough board table, and held up all ten fingers. Milo watched, captivated by the silent bargaining. Callahan wanted ten blankets for three U.S. dollars.

The vender shook his head, pointed at the coins, and held up his own ten fingers--the price now a dollar a blanket. Callahan countered by dropping one more silver dollar onto the table--ten blankets for four dollars. Another head shake, and the vender held up eight fingers and pointed at the four coins—a half-dollar per blanket. Callahan nodded, and told Milo and Wesley to each take four blankets, leaving just three on the stack. Milo picked up two blankets and handed them to Wesley, taking six himself.

As they walked away, Milo, carrying three folded blankets under each arm said, "Don't you handshake to close a deal here in Texas?"

Without looking at him, Callahan said, "Not with Mexicans, I don't. I don't speak their gibberish and I don't take their greasy palm in mine."

"How much will you charge for the blankets in our store?" Wesley asked his father.

"Two dollars a blanket, and they'll all be sold by the first cold snap. My women customers do like Mex wool blankets. Must be the bright colors."

As they rounded a corner, Milo stopped and gaped at the sight of two headless rattlesnakes draped over a thick pole. One was a typical three-footer, but the other was at least twice that length. Like the chickens, they'd been decapitated and gutted, but not yet skinned, the hide left on to protect their whitish meat.

As much as the long snake unsettled Milo, the three catfish hanging next to the serpents shocked him even more. One was nearly four feet long and had a girth thicker than as his own waist. Its blue-gray skin, dead eyes, and long thick feelers protruding around its hugely wide mouth looked monstrous to McKean.

"Good God, that catfish is big enough to swallow a hog." Milo shook his head in disbelief.

"I've seen a few that size pulled out of the river that runs through Prairie Lea," Callahan said. "Not as good eating as one half that big, though. Meat gets greasy in those giant cats. But that big rattler, his meat will make fine cutlets. Some think better 'n pork."

Ten-year-old Wesley Callahan stared at the big snake and shivered as he imagined it slithering into his bedroll and burying its fangs into his neck. His father was now gazing again at the enormous catfish, the lucky catch reminding him of another big cat he wanted to learn about.

Callahan pulled another smaller coin from his vest pocket and handed it to McKean. "Milo, you take Wesley into that Mex café on the corner there. Get good meals for both of you. Ask if they have *carne guisada* today. It's tasty. After you eat, go to the stable, saddle our horses, and tie those blankets onto the mule. Be sure to put the tarp between the packsaddle and the mule's back. I want those blankets smelling like lamb's wool, not sweaty mule. I've got to go see the newspaper editor. Then we're heading home."

★

Within a quarter of an hour, back in the dining room of Menger's boarding house, Callahan shook hands with John 'Rip' Ford, the editor of the *Austin State Times* newspaper. Within a few minutes they were joined by William Kyle, owner of two large cotton and sugar cane plantations along the Brazos and Colorado Rivers. The three men had known each other since the rebellion against Mexico nearly twenty years past, and exchanged letters about politics and current events. All three had travelled to San Antonio especially for this informal meeting.

Callahan probed Ford for details of the most recent Indian depredations, a vexing topic that the veteran Texas Ranger and newspaper editor was always eager to talk about. Ford's elaborations on the continuing atrocities by the Apaches and Comanches were sobering. He enumerated eighteen confirmed murders in Bexar and Comal Counties in the past year, and put the number of stolen horses and mules as too high to estimate.

Callahan next asked for information about a Black Seminole chieftain called Big Cat. He'd heard rumors that the marauder Big Cat was the grown son of a runaway slave and a Seminole squaw. Ford confirmed stories of the half-breed's band of warriors raiding into southern Texas, and like the Apaches, taking refuge on the Mexican side of the Rio Grande with his captives, stolen livestock, and plunder.

Callahan listened closely, and urged the editor to continue printing stories about every incident of Indian mischief. Learning that Big Cat was sired by an escaped slave prompted Callahan to ask the other two men how many runaway slaves might be living in Mexico near the Texas border. William Kyle pulled out a folded paper from his coat pocket.

"James, it's a serious problem for us cotton planters, for Texas. I myself have lost eight good field hands over the past three years, all runaways who must have headed to the Rio Grande, to Mexico. That's forty acres of cotton never planted, picked, or sold every season. And my fields are a long ways east of Austin and San Antonio. I've been corresponding with other planters. Their replies to my inquiries are confirming what I've suspected. The further west a man's land lays, the more losses he endures from runaway niggers."

"How many runaways you think, William, all total I mean, are living in Mexico along the Rio Grande?

"This may sound unbelievable to you, but based on the number of runners the other land owners are putting in their letters to me, I'd put the figure at two thousand. Or more," Kyle said as he tapped his paper. Callahan nodded sagely, but was indeed having trouble accepting such a high number.

Kyle made one more point to emphasize the depth of the problem. "Bounty hunters from the border tell me there are big camps of runaway niggers within ten or twenty miles of the Rio

Grande. Safe in Mexico. Whole settlements of our niggers waiting to be put back in chains and brought back to Texas.

Ford spoke. "In my paper there are new notices of rewards for runaway nigras every week. I can believe William's estimate. But let's don't forget that four years back the census counted nearly sixty thousand slaves in Texas. Two thousand runners constitutes a sizable loss, for sure, but it's not a loss that's truly crippling to Texas as a whole."

Not liking the implication of Ford's observation, Callahan said, "Someday we've got to go into Mexico after the damned Apaches. Kill 'em all. And we can't let a bunch of niggers and half-breeds flaunt Texas laws like they're doing. Good men like you and me need to persuade the governor that those nigger settlements have got to be rooted out and a thousand or more runaway slaves returned to their rightful owners."

"James, I agree with you, but that's what the army's here for," Ford countered.

"Hmph. Rip, you and I both know the soldiers aren't going to cross the river. The treaty that ended the war in '48 has tied their hands. Nope, it's going to have to be Rangers. Rangers led by me. The people will support us. You just keep them reading about the burned-out farms, ravaged women, and dead settlers. William, if you and the other planters will keep writing the governor and senators about the financial losses caused by the runaway niggers, that'll help too. Politicians understand money."

Chapter 6

Alamo Plaza
San Antonio, Texas
September 1854

Milo and Wesley eagerly wolfed down the hot beef stew, both giving their full attention to the bowls of spicy meat. While they ate, the Mexican waiter bumped into Milo's stool, jostling his arm, which tilted his bowl, causing some of Milo's *carne guisada* to spill onto the table. Neither Milo or Wesley sensed anything amiss or looked around. Instead, both Anglos quickly sopped up the spilt stew with rolled corn *tortillas*. Neither noticed the second young man who deftly lifted three blankets off the top of the pile they'd set on an empty stool.

When Wesley reached for the blankets after the meal, he realized some were missing. "Mr. McKean, they ain't all here."

"What do you mean?"

"Some blankets are gone. I know I didn't drop any, did you?"

"No. Count 'em," Milo said as he looked around at the other patrons of the *comedor*.

"I count five. Pa's going to be smoking mad. He'll take a strap to me. I don't know what he'll do to you."

"Huh. I ain't a pup, he won't do nothing to me. And I'll speak up for you. Let's keep our eyes open and get to the livery with the rest of them. If we see anyone carrying blankets, we'll snag 'em back." Milo pulled at his pistol stuck into his trousers.

Wesley was right. His father fumed at the news. "What? Blankets don't have legs. Did you drop them or are you saying they was stolen out from under your noses?"

"We didn't drop no blankets, Pa," Wesley chimed in.

Callahan looked hard at his son, then at McKean. "The boy got it right?"

"Yessir. We had eight blankets when we went to eat. We put them on a stool by our table."

"Then some greaser stole 'em. Maybe the same old bandit who sold 'em to me. Wesley, you stay here and finish saddling the horses. McKean, you're with me. We're going to backtrack them damned blankets."

As the pair strode purposefully back to the *comedor* at the corner of the plaza, Callahan gave instructions. "I talk. You watch to both sides, and especially watch our backs. You see a knife come out, you draw your Colt and holler. You see a gun come out, you draw your Colt and cock it. If you see a Mex cock his gun, you shoot the sonofabitch. You got all that?"

"Yessir. But I ain't overly eager to shoot a man for three blankets."

Callahan spun and stabbed his finger at the younger man's chest. "You wouldn't be shooting a man for no three damned blankets. You'd be shooting a thievin' Mex who's about to shoot you or me. If you can't do that, get out of my sight. You can walk back to Prairie Lea."

"Didn't say I won't protect you, Mr. Callahan. But I won't murder a man over a blanket."

The older man sighed deeply before he spoke. "Look here, Milo. I know you ain't been around Mexicans, just coming from Alabama and all. I've been twenty years in Texas and fought Santy Anna's army when I was your age. Well, by damn, we white men won that war, and now it's our job to make sure the *Tejanos*--the Mexicans still living in Texas--remember that. San Antonio may be full of Spanish-talking Mexicans, but it's a Texas city now. And no damned spic is going to light-finger my new blankets without I kick him in the balls and get my property back. The man you paid for your meal knows what happened to my blankets. Hell, he most likely is the thief's boss." Callahan paused for breath and saw McKean's frown.

"Milo, I'll give you that some Mexes are good people. But, most of 'em will steal a white man blind if you give 'em a chance. And I ain't seen one yet who'd pull a gun face-to-face on a white man. Hell, hardly any of 'em have a pistol anyway. But they carry knives, and will stab a white man in the back. So you keep your eye out for what's behind us."

McKean nodded.

James Callahan walked into the dark *comedor* with Milo McKean two steps behind. Callahan glanced neither right nor left at the several customers eating. He went straight to the heavy-jowled proprietor who sat at a back table, chopping onions with a thick cleaver.

"*Tres cobijas, por favor,*" Callahan said softly, looking down.

"*Que?*" The man didn't stop his work or look up.

Callahan drew his pistol from its holster and repeated even more softly, "*Tres cobijas.*"

The portly man shrugged his shoulders, held the cleaver still on the table, and shifted his eyes away. Sensing that the proprietor was stalling for his waiter or cook to come to his aid, Callahan slammed the handle of his revolver down on the back of the man's chubby right hand. In the next second, Callahan jerked the table sideways with his left hand, causing the cleaver to fall to the floor.

Callahan pointed his pistol at the proprietor's groin, held up three fingers, and whispered, "*Cobijas.*"

Milo sensed movement behind him. He pulled his pistol and twirled as the waiter unsheaved a knife from under his apron. Milo shook his head sideways, cocked his revolver, and glanced at the open doorway to the kitchen. A fat bald man in a blood-splattered apron stood in the doorway holding a big knife. McKean instantly called a warning, "The cook has a knife!"

Callahan heard the loud click of the pistol hammer and Milo's shout in the suddenly silent room. He glanced at the kitchen door as the cook walked forward brandishing a knife. Callahan took a step away from the proprietor, shifted his aim to the cook's head, and said, "*Tres cobijas or seis dolares*, right damned now!"

The cook froze in place, and the proprietor scowled with his whole face. He hesitated before he slowly nodded and reached to the dirt floor for a small metal box that had slid off the table. He unlatched it and took out three silver dollars, offering them to Callahan.

"Nope. *Seis dolares,* I said."

The man's hand wavered, then even more slowly, he removed three more coins, one by one.

Callahan held out his hand and accepted the six dollars. He backed away and let Milo lead the way to the front door, keeping their weapons leveled at the waiter, the cook, and proprietor.

Once they were well away from the plaza, Milo breathed deeply before asking if they were going to buy blankets to replace the stolen ones.

"Not today. No telling what would happen back in the plaza market once those greasers talk to their *compadres*. I don't really want to kill a meskin over three blankets." Callahan glanced at the younger man to see if Milo noticed his raillery.

"Best we head to Prairie Lea now. Besides, I made my profit on those three blankets. But I sure will miss the *carne guisada* in that place."

As they were about to climb onto their horses in the livery stable, Milo said, "I thought you said you didn't speak Spanish. You sure talked it back in the café."

"Aw, I didn't say I don't know it. Hell, I been here twenty years, I've learned a word or two of their lingo." Callahan shot another look at Milo. "I said I don't speak it to Mexicans. Makes them think they're as good as we are. But sometimes, it's the only way to make sure they understand *pronto.*"

Chapter 7

El Camino Real
East of San Antonio, Texas
September 1854

Once back on the road, Callahan pulled his long double-barreled shotgun out of its leather scabbard, and rode with the weapon resting across his saddle.

"You looking for a rabbit for our supper pot?" Wesley asked his father. Callahan nodded without speaking.

"I hope you got birdshot in your shotgun, Mr. Callahan. Buckshot'll tear up a rabbit too bad to eat it," Milo said. The older man grunted in reply.

The young immigrant from Alabama still felt shaken from the stand-off in the café and Callahan's silence bothered him. *Captain Boggess said Mr. Callahan was a soldier in the revolution against Mexico. Maybe he'll talk about his war experiences.*

"Mr. Boggess said you were thick in the warrin' for Texas Independence, back when you were my age."

"Yep. I was."

"Were you at the big battle at Buffalo Bayou the day Gen'rul Houston whupped Santa Anna?"

"Nah, Milo, I was otherwise occupied that day."

"Oh. That's too bad. Were you on a scout?"

Callahan's horse took several paces before he answered. "Nope. The day General Houston whupped Santa Anna, I was still making my way across the countryside, hiding like a rabbit all day and walking all night. I'd been a captive of the Mexican army. My whole company of Georgia volunteers became prisoners after the fight at Coleto Creek."

"Don't think I know about that affair," Milo answered. *A captive? I thought you were a hero. A fighter.*

"Right after the Alamo fell, three hundred of us under Colonel Fannin were marching east to join Houston. We got caught in the wide open prairie by Mexican cavalry. Fannin formed us into a defensive square, put our cannons on the corners. We did it by the book, just like a British army square against Napoleon at Waterloo. But we were penned down. We dug in best we could. Then the Mexican infantry and artillery caught up to us. They put their cannons up a slope and fired all day. It was a hot damned day. Mexican infantry surrounded us. We ran out of water after the damn-fool artillery crewmen used all our casks of water to swab out the cannon barrels. Couldn't refill our canteens. After dark, the Mexican riflemen snuck up close in the tall grass and pecked at us all night. Come morning, Colonel Fannin gave us up, outnumbered, out of ammo, out of water."

"Fannin's whole force captured." Milo repeated. "I heard of that. Didn't know you'd fought a whole day first. But... didn't the Mexicans execute all Fannin's men at Goliad? Remember Goliad. Wasn't that Houston's army other battle cry? Remember the Alamo! Remember Goliad!"

Callahan nodded soberly. "Yep. On Good Friday morning, they pulled all Fannin's men out of the church at Goliad where'd they'd locked up the whole bunch. Marched them a ways down the road in a long column. Then the *soldados* started shooting. Murdered all the prisoners, except the ones who somehow figured out what was happening, and broke out of the column and ran. Most of them were hunted down and skewered by the cavalry. But a few hid along the creek all day and got away during the night. Just a few."

"How did you hide? Under water in the creek? Did you breathe through a hollow reed?" Milo asked, assuming Callahan had been one of the few who escaped.

"I wasn't there. I was lucky. After the battle on the prairie, the Mexican general sent sixteen of us to build a floating bridge down towards Victoria. I was the sergeant of the work detail. When we heard about the massacre at Goliad, I figured we were next. I broke out and run that same night."

"Huh. Well, I'm glad you didn't get shot while you were a prisoner. Killing captured soldiers ain't right."

"Damn right. Damn Mexicans. I hate 'em."

At midafternoon, Callahan stopped them in the middle of a wide meadow. The nearest trees were nearly two hundred yards behind them, a stand of slender post oaks.

"We'll rest the horses here for a few minutes," Callahan nodded to his son. "Wesley, climb down. Stretch your legs. Take a leak if you need to."

"Why stop here, Sir?" Milo asked. "There's no water here for the horses."

"Or shade for us," Wesley added, as he swung out of his saddle. He dropped the reins of his horse and started to take a few steps back the way they'd come.

"Go the other way, Son."

"Pa, I'm just going to pee."

"Go out ahead of us, not behind us. Now, Wesley."

Wesley looked up at his father, confused as to what difference it made. But he did as directed, walking back around the horses before he began unbuttoning his fly.

The dirt in the road erupted between the rear legs of Callahan's horse, causing the frightened animal to buck up on its front legs. Callahan stayed in the saddle by keeping his legs and boots jammed into the stirrups. When his horse's back legs came down, Callahan jerked hard sideways on the reins, twirling his mount to face the way they'd come.

"Lie down, Wesley!" Callahan called over his shoulder. "Stay down!"

Milo heard the crack of the rifle while he was looking back at the clump of trees, wondering why they hadn't stopped in the shade instead of out in the sun. He clearly saw the puff of white smoke, and reflexively ducked low in his saddle.

Callahan kicked his horse forward and galloped towards the oak trees, calling for Milo to swing around behind the trees. Milo drew his Colt revolver as he urged his borrowed horse into a run. He risked a glance to his right and saw Mr. Callahan level his shotgun as he rode, and fire one barrel. Milo heard the crack of another shot from under the trees, but not the same sound as before. Callahan's horse flinched, slowed and reared up on its back legs, this time dumping its rider out of the saddle.

Milo was about to swerve left to circle behind the little grove of trees as he'd been told, but he saw Callahan on the ground. *Mr. Callahan's down and needs my help right now!* He cut his horse to the right, going hard towards what he figured was the man shooting at them.

At the edge of the trees, Milo jumped off his horse and pushed through the screen of scrub brush. He saw a fat man holding a short rifle in one hand and a pistol stuck in his pants, trying to hook his foot into the wooden stirrup of his saddle. McKean fired, his bullet smashed into the stirrup, causing the ambusher to jump back and drop his rifle. He looked around at Milo, pulled a short sword from his belt and raised it over his head.

The blast from Callahan's second shotgun barrel knocked leaves off the bushes, but if any of the pellets struck the man, they didn't stop him. The wide-eyed attacker charged. He was only ten feet away when Milo again squeezed the trigger of his pistol. The fat man dropped his weapon and fell face down.

Callahan limped into sight under the trees, holding his revolver. He looked at the man sprawled on the ground and fired two rounds into his back. Without speaking, he nodded in approval at Milo before he rolled the body over.

The pair stared down at the face of the café proprietor. Wesley ran up panting, looked at the corpse, and gushed a string of questions.

"You shoot him, Pa? Are you hurt? Did he hit you? Your horse is bleeding, can you ride him? Who's that man? Why'd he shoot at us?"

"Whoa, Son. I'm all right. I'm not wounded. And Milo killed this scoundrel before I could even get here."

"Mr. Callahan." Milo wiped his brow with the back of his hand. "He's the blanket thief, ain't he?"

Callahan rubbed his jaw. "Well, I don't think he personally lifted the blankets off the stool. He's too old, and look at those fat fingers. But I'll wager he was *El Jefe* of the thieves. Otherwise he wouldn't have let go of six silver dollars when I leaned on him back in the *comidar*."

"Pa, are you saying he followed us out here and tried to kill you for three blankets?" Wesley's eyes were glued to the body. "Makes no sense, Pa. Six dollars worth of blankets."

"Not for the blankets, Wesley. Pride. Honor. I shamed him in front of his men. Probably his sons. He came out to reclaim his manhood."

Callahan bent down and pulled the heavy flintlock pistol out of the man's waist sash. "Here, Wesley, a souvenir."

Milo picked up the short rifle the man had fired and looked curiously at the wooden stock. The dark wood reached all the way to the end of the barrel and had a dull brass implement box imbedded into the wood near the butt. The barrel of the weapon was dark with visible patches of rust. "This musket's an old flintlock, too."

"So it is," Callahan said, taking it from Milo so he could examine the lock plate. "Thought so. See the eagle and snake engraved into the lock plate here? It's a Mexican army piece. But it's too short for a regular musket. Maybe something Santa Anna's cavalry carried. He put his finger into the end of the barrel. "And it has rifling. It's not a smoothbore. It may be a European-made rifle. I heard some of the *soldados* carried British rifles."

Callahan nudged the corpse. "I bet this old man was one of the Mex soldiers who deserted somewhere along the way. And he took his rifle. That's why he tried such a long shot at us. I reckon we were lucky his eyesight and aim weren't up to his weapon. He just got old."

"Old like you, Pa?"

Callahan snorted. "Nah, not old like me, Boy. I'm still breathing. Well, you killed him, Milo, this is yours now. Spoils of war." The older man held out the old flintlock rifle to the younger man.

Milo voiced his surprise. "Spoils of war? We're not fighting a war."

"You don't think so? You pulled your Colt twice today on Mexicans intent on slashing you. This one came at you with an army sword. What do you call it, if it ain't war?"

"I don't know. I call it duty, I reckon. But Texas is at peace with Mexico. That war's been over for five years."

"Don't matter, duty, peace, war. It's all killin' when you have to."

"If you say so. Did you mean it, that I can keep that rifle?" Milo asked as he accepted the rifle from Mr. Callahan.

"Sure, and take that sword too. I bet it fits on the end of the rifle. An old-fashioned bayonet for an old flintlock army rifle."

"We going to take the body back to San Antonio?" Wesley asked as he suddenly started shaking.

James Callahan saw his son's distress and put an arm around the ten-year-old's shoulders. "Hell, no. That would just get his whole family after us. We'll scrape out a grave right here."

Comforted by his father's strong arm, Wesley asked, "What about his nag, Pa?"

Callahan cast a practiced eye over the dun-colored horse. "Nag is right. McKean, you keep the horse and saddle, too. You need one, don't you?"

For the next hour, Milo McKean used the sword bayonet to dig a grave under the post oak trees. Wesley fashioned a crude cross from two limbs tied together with a blanket strap off the dead man's saddle. While the other two were busy preparing for a burial, James Callahan dug through the corpse's clothing, finding a small pouch with a handful of coins, which he kept. No prayers were said over the shallow grave, but Wesley hooked the man's sombrero on top of the cross.

Callahan used canteen water to rinse the flesh wound where the bushwacker's pistol round had grazed his horse's front shoulder. Then he opened a tin of foul-smelling goo and spread it over the open wound until the white salve turned pink.

Once on the road again, leading the dead man's horse and holding the flintlock rifle, Milo blurted, "Mr. Callahan, you stopped us in that field knowing we'd be shot at, didn't you?"

Callahan nodded. "I'd seen a rider in a *sombrero* way back behind us a couple of times. So, yeah, I stopped us so he'd have time to get off his horse and take a shot. If that's what he had a mind to do, I wanted him to do it from a long ways off. That's why we stopped out in the field, too far away for a musket to be a worry." Callahan rubbed his jaw, "I didn't figure on him having a rifled gun, though. That surprised me, yes it did."

"I could have been killed back there," McKean said.

"Huh. It ain't like you were by yourself. I knew he'd be aiming at me, not you. I'm the one who made him look weak in his own place in front of his own people."

Milo thought, *I bet that old Mexican couldn't see good enough to tell us apart from so far,* but he said, "Just don't do nothing like that again, without asking me first."

Callahan grunted. "You did good back there in the trees."

41

"I've never shot anyone before today."

"Bother you?"

"Yeah, it does, some."

"Well, it ain't like he was a white man, and now you have a horse."

★

McKean and Callahan rode side-by-side behind the piebald mule that Wesley led along the well-worn dirt road. Milo still rode the borrowed horse and led the buckskin gelding that the old Mexican had ridden from San Antonio. It was gaunt and covered in sores. In their easy conversation, Callahan surmised the pitiful horse had spent its days in a small pen without enough fodder. Milo hoped a few weeks of ample feed and some liniment on the sores would improve the nag's condition. Callahan recommended catfish oil, an idea that was new to Milo.

"Gawd, there it goes again," Milo said, waving his free hand in front of his nose.

Callahan laughed. "That Gill boy didn't stretch the truth none, for damn sure. That one mule has more flatulence than any three horses."

Chapter 8

Prairie Lea, Texas
September 1854

Milo McKean and the two Callahans reached Prairie Lea the morning after their adventure on the road. Milo rode the dun horse to the Gunns' farmhouse, eager to show his new mount to his friend Jesse.

When he first saw the maltreated animal, Jesse laughed loudly and told Milo if that was the best horse he could afford, he might as well walk. After Milo rushed through the story of the ambush, Jesse gently ran his hands over the gelding's ribs and immediately led the skinny horse to the barn, where he poured a bucket of oats into a feed trough. "It'll take a few weeks, but he'll fatten up soon enough. What're you going to call him?"

"He's about the color of a deer, so I reckon he's 'Buck'."

"Buck it is."

An hour later, the two young men sat on the back steps of the Gunn's dog-trot house. Jesse toyed with a lead ball from the leather pouch that came with the rifle. Milo had poured hot water down the barrel of the old English-made weapon to loosen the dried powder residue. He pulled the ramrod from its slot under the barrel, put a dry cloth patch on the end of the ramrod, and pushed it down the barrel. When he pulled it out, grunting with the effort, the cloth emerged caked black with grimy soot. Milo forced a second patch, this one wet with oil, down the barrel and it came out easier and had less grime on it. "That's enough. Don't want the ramrod stuck."

Jesse was now handling the powder horn on which some crude drawings of animals had been scratched. "Milo, that is some story. Neither one of my two trips to San Antone ended in anything but a dusty ride home. "Let's show the rifle to Mr.

Schmidt down at his store. Maybe he'll buy it from you. That is, if you want to sell it."

"I don't know, Jesse. I've been thinking about joining a Ranger company. I met a Ranger captain in San Antonio. Seems like a rifle would be a good thing to have."

"Let's go show Mr. Schmidt the gun anyway. See what he thinks about it."

"I know why you want to go to Schmidt's store. His daughter works there, don't she?"

"Well, she helps out sometimes when her home chores are done. And don't you be joshing me about that. I seen you looking at Malissa, more'n once, and you ain't been here hardly a week."

Milo grinned. "You do have a sister worth a few looks. And I can't help but see her around, me staying in your room. Let's go see Mr. Schmidt."

While Jesse saddled his horse, Milo closely examined the flintlock's firing mechanism, fiddling with the screw that held the piece of chipped flint in place. It was less than a mile ride to Schmidt's store, and the young men found Mr. Schmidt alone behind the counter. While the middle-aged man hefted and studied the weapon, Jesse excitedly related the story of how Milo came by the rifle.

"*Ja*, this is a good piece. Not as good as a *Jaeger* rifle, but good for English. Do I want to buy it from you to sell here? No. I am leaving the sale of guns to Mr. Callahan. Besides, this is a flintlock, and nobody gives specie for flintlocks when all new guns are percussion." He handed the weapon back to Milo.

"Have you shot it?" Mr. Schmidt asked. Milo shook his head. "*Nein*? Let's go out back and see if you and this rifle can hit the side of my outhouse." They all trooped out the back door.

Mr. Schmidt gave Jesse a nail and a page of used paper torn from a ledger book. "Go tack it to the near side of the outhouse, and count your strides coming back."

"Let me see your powder horn," the store proprietor said to Milo. Mr. Schmidt shook a little black powder from the old horn into his hand, brought his palm close to his eyes, and rubbed the gritty powder with a finger. "No good. Some grains are too big, but most is just dust. No wonder that bandit missed Callahan. This powder may be twenty years old. Wait here." Schmidt returned

44

with a brass powder horn. "Put fifty grains of this powder down the barrel. How many paces, Jesse?"

"Forty-seven."

"Very close for a rifled gun. You should be able to put a hole in the middle of the paper. Hand me a lead ball."

Milo handed him a marble-sized ball from the pouch. Schmidt examined it and said, "Bah. Homemade. Look at the swirls in the lead, the pits. It won't fly straight. Here, use this one. Same size. But *Deutsche*-cast."

Milo loaded the rifle, carefully replacing the ramrod after pushing the lead ball down the barrel. He stood, cocked the rifle, aimed, and squeezed the trigger. The two explosions of powder in the pan and powder in the barrel rang out loudly. Jesse immediately trotted to the paper target and called back, "Hit the bottom left, my hand length from the center."

"Give me the rifle." Mr. Schmidt held out his hand. He dropped the buttstock to the ground, poured a measure of powder down the barrel, then pushed a ball down to rest on the powder in the bottom of the barrel. He held the gun horizontally and poured a trickle of powder into the small frizzen pan. Finally, in an easy fluid motion, he raised the piece vertically, lowered it back to horizontal while pulling back the hammer, pushed the stock into his shoulder, sighted, and fired without hesitation.

Jesse ran back to the target from the side where he'd taken refuge behind a woodpile.

"Hot damn! Right in the center, Mr. Schmidt."

"*Ja*, I have victories from the *Windesheim Schützen Verein*. Your weapon is worthy. You are not—yet. You shoot ten balls a day for a month, then you might be worthy of your rifle."

Milo sighed. "Three hundred bullets. I can't afford that, and besides, it's still a flintlock."

"You take it to my friend Hoffman in New Braunfels, maybe he take off the flint part and make it use copper priming caps like new guns."

"He can do that?" Milo asked, doubting Schmidt's confidence in his friend.

"Oh, sure. Hoffman is a *sehr gut* gunsmith. But he don't work for free. You got money?"

"Only a little."

"Why you want this gun, young fellow? It's an army rifle."

"Well, me and Jesse thought we might sign on with Captain Boggess's Mounted Volunteers in San Antonio. Once my horse fattens up, that is."

"Go after Indians?"

"That's what ranging companies do, ain't it?" Jesse interjected.

"*Ja.*" Mr. Schmidt was silent as they walked back into his store. As the young men were about to leave, Schmidt held up his hand. "Wait here. I have something, two somethings, to give you." He went through the door to the family rooms and returned in a few minutes holding a small glass jar with screw-on tin lid and something long wrapped in a cloth.

He held out the jar to Jesse Gunn. "When I was young, this is what I used on my face to make those, those things go away. You take it. Mix a spoonful with water and spread it on the bad spots at night. It dries up those little red bumps."

Jesse's mouth dropped open in surprise. He put one hand to his acne-covered chin and held up the jar to look more closely at the yellow powder inside.

"I, I, ain't sure...What is this, Mr. Schmidt?"

"Sulfur. It may burn some and leave your face red, but the bumps go away after a few days."

Milo spoke up, "Ain't sulfur what goes in gunpowder? Will his face explode?"

Mr. Schmidt smiled. "Mine did not. His...who can say?"

"Why you giving me this?" Jesse asked, his face now bright red

"I see you look sideways at my daughter. But you don't speak to her. Maybe without the..."

"Pimples. We call them pimples here in America, Mr. Schmidt. And Jesse, he sure enough as a bad case of them. They move around like ducks on a pond. First they pop up on one cheek, then the other, then his chin. Thank the man, Jesse." Milo took the jar and held it up in the sunlight. "If this sulfur works, maybe you won't die a grouchy old man without a wife."

Jesse grabbed the jar back from his friend and stuffed it into the pocket of his trousers. "Thank you, Mr. Schmidt. I mean that, I really do."

"What's that under the cloth?" Milo asked, curious what else the storekeeper had brought to give them. Mr. Schmidt unwrapped the gray cloth to reveal a short arrow, painted red and black, with white feathers. He held it out to the young men.

"Take this arrow to *Herr* Hoffman in New Braunfels. Tell him if he converts your rifle to percussion, you will find and kill the Apache that shot this arrow. Tell him I will pay for the work."

"Why? Where'd you get the arrow?"

"No matter. The same Apaches took Hoffman's *wundershône tochter* away to Mexico. She and my son were man and wife one day only when the Apaches came. I'm too old, too much family, to go. Hoffman too. But we will help if you go—ranging. Bring back the rifle after Hoffman converts it to percussion. Tell him to provide you good *Deutsche* lead balls, priming caps, and powder for you to learn your weapon. I will pay."

Milo cocked his head and looked sadly at the shopkeeper.

"I understand now. It was your son that Mr. Smith told me about. And Hoffman's daughter. My God."

Chapter 9

New Braunfels, Texas
September 1854

Milo McKean and Jesse Gunn rode to New Braunfels to find Luther Hoffman, the gunsmith. Milo was pleased that Buck was filling out and responded well to even a light touch of the reins. Stopping in front of a small building, Jesse said, "I reckon we're there," as he looked at the neatly lettered sign over the door that read *L. Hoffman—Gunsmith and Locksmith.*

The Hoffman family had been among the second group of German immigrants to settle New Braunfels eight years previously. The gunsmith greeted the two young men in a reserved, but polite manner. He took the offered rifle and immediately pronounced it an English Baker model army rifle, even if an eagle and snake decorated the lock plate instead of a British crown.

He said the Spanish must have bought a contract lot of them and marked them for use in the Spanish colony of Mexico. After listening to Milo tell the story behind the rifle and their talk with Mr. Schmidt, Luther Hoffman sat still, staring silently at the Apache arrow.

Hoffman liked the two earnest young men and approved of their intent to join the Mounted Volunteers in San Antonio. *Better that wild English boys like them go into the wilderness after Indians and desperados than the good Deutsche boys of New Braunfels.* He gruffly told the young men he'd set aside his other work to take on Milo's project, since his friend Mr. Schmidt promised to pay. Hoffman still deeply mourned his child lost to the Apaches, and without saying so, like Mr. Schmidt, he would certainly help by doing what he did best—gunsmithing--in order to avenge her loss.

Hoffman could see that the old rifle had been neglected for many years, and the German craftsman could not bring himself only to change out the firing mechanisms. He would rework the entire weapon.

"You come back in one month—four weeks. Your rifle will be ready to shoot Apaches."

The next day, Hoffman took the rifle apart. He put his nine-year-old son to work scrubbing every metal component with stiff wire brushes, then with gritty cloth. The father would not approve any piece that showed any grime or rust, but almost every day the boy buffed and rubbed until just before supper, when he'd proudly offer his papa a new shiny metal part. Hoffman had a more skilled job for his eleven-year-old son, who was already learning his father's trade. The boy patiently sanded the entire gunstock and carefully filled the worst nicks and cracks in the stock with a mixture of sawdust and glue. After the stock passed his father's close inspection, the boy stained the whole thing and let it dry for a week. Then, over two more weeks, every day he methodically rubbed in a new layer of protective linseed oil.

The gunsmith himself detached the flintlock's hammer and frizzen pan before he soaked the thirty-inch barrel for a long day in a shallow pan of soapy water, kept hot by the boys' diligent effort with a tea kettle. After the soaking, Hoffman cleaned the inside of the barrel as well as he could, using small circular wire brushes attached to dowel rods.

The next step was the crux of the conversion— using a drill to enlarge the old firing channel in the top of the steel barrel, and working soft molten metal to build out a round base. When the new base was constructed and hard, Hoffman ground it smooth and polished it, before he threaded the inside channel.

Finally, *Herr* Hoffman inserted and hand-tightened a new firing cone, then attached and aligned a new hammer that fit the Baker. The project took three weeks, and when the weapon was re-assembled, small pits remained where the steel barrel had rusted while stored for two decades. Even their assiduous effort with proper tools could not totally reverse so many years of neglect. But every metal component shined, including the barrel, and the walnut stock's wood grain glowed a dull amber in the sunlight. The Mexican eagle and snake still decorated the now-gleaming lock plate which, like the Apache arrow's red and black paint, identified the weapon's origin.

The rifle was old, and the conversion work was obvious. Nonetheless, Luther Hoffman deemed the restored weapon worthy to be stamped with his personal cartouche, an ornate letter "H" emblem that his father and grandfather before him had put on the stocks of many hundreds of pistols and long-arms in Germany. This time, *Herr* Hoffman added to the family cartouche. He skillfully carved by hand a plain, but large, letter "C" encircling the "H." He did not want his daughter Caroline forgotten when young McKean fired the weapon at the Apaches that the Mounted Volunteers would soon pursue and punish.

Chapter 10

Austin City, Texas
Early October 1854

Benjamin Smith stomped angrily out of his nearly completed new building on East Pecan Street. As he climbed onto the wagon seat, he silently fumed that the cabinet maker, J.W. Hannig, was gouging him, that the price of getting anything done in Austin was just too damned high.

"Thompson, get this damned wagon rolling," Smith muttered to his young slave.

"Where to, Massah Smith?"

"You know where to, dammit. Don't play dumb with me today, I'm in a surly mood,"

"Yes, suh, We's goin' to San Antone to buy you a wagon full of beer and other things to sell in yo' new saloon and sto'. Dat's where we goin'."

"And don't get sassy with me, or I'll put you on the auction block in San Antone to pay for the damned beer." Thompson looked sideways at his owner, and prudently remained silent as he guided the wagon out of town and onto the road to San Antonio.

Thompson had been born and lived his whole life belonging to Smith, and only once had he seen a slave auction. He had driven the wagon from Mr. Smith's farm into Nacogdoches the day Smith put his field hands on the auction block and sold them. While Thompson had handled the wagon reins that day, Mr. Smith had ridden a horse behind the wagon with his loaded shotgun.

All that morning Thompson listened to the eleven men and women chained together in the wagon bed. He still remembered four of the older field hands as sullen and silent, while three excited younger men prattled on, sure their lot would be better wherever they wound up. Thompson's worst memory lay with the women. The older two remained stoic, but the younger pair sobbed and wailed, both holding small children, certain that they were about to be separated from their babies.

Driving the wagon full of other Negroes to the auction was bad, but Thompson still shivered at the vivid memory of seeing nearly naked men shackled and prodded like livestock onto the raised board platform. Even more disturbing were the women Thompson had known all his life, standing stiffly on a big stump, lewd calls coming from the crowd while the auctioneer used his stick to raise the skirts of their cotton shifts. The images burned in Thompson's head that day remained a bitter reminder to keep his master happy.

Thompson didn't know that the money from the sale of Mr. Smith's slaves, over five thousand dollars, more than the sale of Smith's played-out cotton fields, had funded Smith's move to Austin and the stocking of his new store and saloon.

★

As soon as the wagon crossed the low rocky ford over the wide Colorado River, Smith and Thompson smelled the cooking fires of Mexican peasants who were living in brush huts along the south bank of the river. Smith muttered to himself that this village of peons was a situation getting out of hand.

Smith shook his head ever so little as he thought. *Austin is a new town, a town of white people and black slaves. It's not a Mexican town, but there's more of these huts and more of these little brown people every damned week. Austin is not San Antonio, with a long Spanish heritage and ties to Mexico. This needs fixing.* Smith made a mental note to bring up the matter at his next lodge meeting.

Thompson interrupted Smith's thoughts about the Mexican problem by asking, "We gonna camp by da same crick we done befo'?" Mr. Smith liked an ample evening meal hot from the fire, an interest that kept Thompson well fed at his master's house, where his ma cooked. On the road, Thompson took over the cooking, a chore he enjoyed.

"I think so," Smith answered, his appetite, like Thompson's, wetted by the smells of the Mexican women's cooking. He pulled his shotgun up and checked to be sure a priming cap snugly topped the cone of each barrel.

Smith glanced sideways at Thompson and grinned. "Those Mex squaws sure are sending up some fine-smelling smoke. Wonder if I oughta sell off your mammy and get me a Mex cook?"

Thompson eyes went wide in sudden terror at the prospect. "Oh, no, suh, Please, Massah Smith, Don't be sayin' such a thing."

"Then you tell her she better learn to make *cabrito tamales* that smell this good." Thompson stiffened, hoping Mr. Smith was teasing, but he was never sure. Both men were silent for the next hour as the wagon bounced along the rutted road, heading south.

After camping on Onion Creek, the next day the pair reached the new town of San Marcos. Smith was disappointed to find no hotels, so they stopped the wagon at the headwater springs of the San Marcos River.

Thompson was on his knees bent over, holding an already struck lucifer between his fingers when he heard a mule braying. Without turning, he quickly pushed the flaming match under a pile of tiny twigs. He didn't look up until the spreading flames assured him the sticks had caught fire. He added a dozen slightly larger sticks before he sat back on his heels and watched his master wave and approach three white men on horseback. One led a brown mule that continued its raucous braying.

Mr. Smith held his shotgun in the crook of his arm, but Thompson watched his master reach out his other arm and shake hands with the lead rider. While the two white men talked, the slave kept putting thicker pieces of broken limbs on the cooking fire, until he was satisfied he'd added enough wood for a decent bed of coals. The trio soon dismounted and led their animals to join Smith's four horses tethered in the meadow.

"Ho, boy, you are in luck. These fellas are gonna set up their tent right near us and join us for supper. Their guide shot a nice whitetail this afternoon, so you'll have a haunch to roast on the spit nice and juicy. You go fetch it, and while you're there, unload their mule."

"Yessuh," Thompson glanced again at his fire before he stood up. The young black man approached the three men who were unsaddling their horses. The big brown mule looked at him with ears raised and snorted. Thompson studied the packsaddle that straddled the mule's back. All he could see were two large wicker baskets on each of the animal's flanks and a folded piece of canvas on top.

"Massah say I's to fetch da deer haunch and unload yo' mule. Dat's der de biggest pack I eva seen on a mule. I ain't sho what to grab onto fust."

A youthful-looking middle-age man with wavy dark hair clipped straight across the base of his neck and a thick curling mustache chuckled. "You are not the first to say that about our New York *aparejo*."

Thompson barely understood the rush of words.

The man with the clipped accent set down his saddle and asked, "What's your name?"

"Thompson, suh."

"Well, Thompson, you'll find the venison haunch wrapped in cheese cloth in the front left pannier."

Thompson nodded and walked to the right of the animal.

The man took off his hat to scratch his scalp through his thick hair. Then he sighed. "You know right from left, Thompson?"

"What you mean?"

The man shook his head in dismay and cast a glance at one of his companions. Then he walked up to Thompson and held out his gloved hand. "My name is Mr. Frederick Olmsted. My traveling companion is my brother John, and he," nodding to the third man who wore a wide tan felt hat, "is our guide Mr. Bailey."

Thompson looked at the offered hand and hesitantly held out his. Frederick Olmsted grasped the Negro's fingers and said, "Right hand. You shake a man's hand with your right hand." He let go of Thompson, and held up his other hand, "Left hand. Got it?"

Thompson nodded and looked down. "I ain't neva shaked no man's hand. But what's dat got to do wit' dat mule?"

"Mule's got two sides. Same as our hands. Left and right. Turn and face the same way as Mr. Brown here."

"What you say?"

"The mule's name is Mr. Brown." Olmsted grabbed Thompson's shoulders and pivoted him to face the same direction as the mule. We're on the mule's right side, so this," He tapped Thompson's right shoulder. "Is your right side, your right leg, your right arm, and right hand. Your other side is your left side."

Thompson nodded, and without more instruction, walked around the mule's front. "I reckon dat dis basket is where de deer meat be."

"That would be an intelligent deduction, Mr. Thompson."

"He's no mister," Benjamin Smith said as he walked up. "He's a nigger slave. I never gave him but one name when his mammy birthed him. No Mister. Misters are white men. And handshakes are between white men." Smith looked pointedly at Olmsted. "But his mammy has learned him to cook pretty fair, so after he unloads your mule, he'll skewer that haunch and roast it right nice."

"Thank you, Mr. Smith, for your clarification of Thompson's status," Olmsted answered. "I wondered if he was a freedman or not. We will erect our tent and see to our comforts while we await a 'right nice' repast."

Smith grunted, unsure if Olmsted was being sarcastic. As he turned to walk back to his wagon, he said, "Bring your own plates and cups. And I only got one chair. Didn't bring one for the nigger, and didn't expect guests for supper."

The Olmsted brothers and Mr. Bailey sat on logs, while Mr. Smith leaned a straight chair onto its back legs, picking his teeth. The four had left their dirty plates near the fire while water heated in a pot. Thompson carried the coffee pot to each man refilling their tin cups.

During supper, Frederick Olmsted continued to be the outspoken member of the trio, sharing that he had been a farmer in upstate New York, but had tired of the life, and was now a newspaper correspondent in New York City. He and his brother John, accompanied by their guide, Mr. Bailey, were midway through a tour of Texas, having just completed several months traveling through the other states of the deep south.

"I'm finding, Mr. Smith, and this may or may surprise you, that Texas is a different country entirely." Olmsted nudged a glowing coal further into the fire.

"Well, we was a republic, not a state, for ten years."

"Right. I know your state's illustrious history. Your heroes, Crockett and Travis."

"Then why do you say we're a different country? Ain't you got woods and rivers and Injuns in New York?"

"Oh, indeed we do. The red men have been pushed west, but we most assuredly have trees and rivers."

"Then what's so different?" Smith asked. "I come from Georgia way back, and Texas don't seem much different. Farms, towns, stores."

"Two things immediately come to mind, Mr. Smith. First, nearly every man I've seen since we crossed the Sabine River is carrying a pistol, and almost all of them are Colt navy models." Olmsted patted his holstered revolver. "I was leery about carrying one myself, but now I wouldn't part with my Colt. It's tough as nails and shoots straight."

"I can't argue with that." Smith smiled. "Got one myself. What's the other thing that makes Texas so different?"

"The second thing is your boy Thompson there. There are Negroes in New York. But no slaves."

"Are you sayin' you're an abolitionist? One of them fellers who wants to turn all our niggers loose?"

Olmsted sipped his steaming coffee before he answered. "I respect that the enslaved Negroes are the foundation for the plantations that grow cotton and tobacco."

Smith nodded, "Yes, they certainly are."

Olmsted in turn nodded in accord. "And I respect that the pecuniary value of the Negroes themselves is quite significant. If slavery were to be abolished in every state with the stroke of a pen, the instant loss of that value and the labor would reap instant ruin to the planters across the south. Temporarily."

"Sure would. What do you mean, temporarily?"

"I mean that my observations of the plantations along the Mississippi have convinced me that slaves work at a pace far slower than do paid laborers."

"Niggers move slow. So what?"

"They work slow because of a lack of motivation."

"Huh. Then they need a better overseer. One not shy to use the lash."

"Coercion will improve efficiency to a degree, yes. Yet, if an enslaved man brings in more cotton in a day than all his co-workers, it makes no difference to him. Only the planter sees the extra income."

"What would a nigger do with money? We give them what they need."

Olmsted smiled. "You might be surprised. Ask Mr. Thompson sometime. Nonetheless, my early calculations indicate that paid laborers can outperform enslaved workers by a factor of four. I've heard that the German farms in this area do not use slave labor. I'm eager to validate, or disprove, my four-to-one hypothesis when I visit some of those farms."

The conversation left the matter of slavery and drifted here and there, as Olmsted reflected on things he'd seen and written about in his travelogue for the newspaper. Soon, Smith was yawning and the Olmsted party excused themselves and retired to their tent.

Thompson scrubbed the tin plates in the hot water and carried them to the riverbank to rinse them. His mind was whirling. *I gots a right hand and a left hand. There's no slaves in a place called New York. I wonder if that be a fer piece off? These mens think Massah Smith ain't too bright.*

Mr. Smith decided he'd had enough of Frederick Olmsted's uppity talk about slavery and his disdain for many things southern. He went to bed in the wagon after telling Thompson to get the horse team hitched to the wagon at first light. He intended to forego a hot breakfast and continue to New Braunfels before the Olmsted party had struck their tent.

Chapter 11

New Braunfels, Texas
Early October 1854

Having rid himself of Olmsted, Smith was unusually quiet on the wagon seat with Thompson as they rolled along towards New Braunfels. While thankful for the silence, Thompson couldn't shake off one of the few things Smith did say.

"I know you was listening to that Olmsted fella last night. Don't you get no ideas about running. He's a northerner, big city man, not from around here. He has no idea how things work. I treat you and your mammy good, so don't you get no ideas about running off. If you do, I'll find you and stripe your back, then auction you off as a field hand. Don't you forget it."

Thompson couldn't forget, since he believed every word of his owner's threat.

That afternoon Benjamin Smith and Thompson reached the German settlement of New Braunfels on the Guadalupe River. Smith took a room at Baetge's Gasthaus, leaving the wagon and horses to Thompson's care. Smith spent the following long day meeting and negotiating with craftsmen in town, bristling at the hard bargaining he encountered. Even if frustrated that the Germans in New Braunfels were as proud of their work and tight with a dollar as the carpenter Hannig in Austin, Smith grudgingly admired the high quality of the goods he examined.

The man from Austin eventually agreed on a price for a dozen stout oak chairs and three tables for his new saloon. He had an easier time coming to terms on an assortment of shoes and well-made cotton dresses and shirts for his mercantile store inventory. He made arrangements to pick up everything but the furniture on his way back from San Antonio. The tables and chairs would be delivered to Smith's new building on Pecan Street as soon as the order was completed. Smith had pressed for thirty-day delivery, the wood craftsman demanded sixty, and they split the difference.

★

Back on the Austin-San Antonio Road, Smith told Thompson to pull off the road at Cibolo Creek to camp for the night. The following day, Thompson drove Mr. Smith's wagon through the center of San Antonio to William Menger's boarding house.

"You take the wagon to the livery over there." Smith pointed across the wide dusty street. "Bring my bag after you rub down the horses." Instructions given, Smith climbed down, reached back for his shotgun, and went in the front door of the boarding house.

Over an hour later, Thompson carried his master's valise and his own blanket roll around the boarding house to the open shed in the back yard that served as the kitchen. He stopped just inside the wooden fence gate and looked at the slim Negro woman who stood with her back to him at the cast iron stove. The bright yellow turban she wore over her hair caught his eye, as did the barely perceptible sway of her hips under her long dress as she stirred a pot on the stove.

"I gots my mastah's bag. Do I takes it inside to his room?" Thompson asked to her back.

The cook turned with a big wooden spoon in her hand. "Nah, puts it on de stoop. House girl come fetch it."

"There be a place fo' me to throw down?"

"Over yonder, under dat shed wit de open sides, other side of de outhouse."

"Gots anything for me to eat?"

"Comes by after de white folk eats. May be a bite left."

"Huh, not if they all eat like my mastah."

The women grinned broadly. "You dink I be born dis mornin'? Sho', der be enough for such as you and me. Dat is, after you use dat ax dere an' split me some more logs for dis stove belly."

Thompson left his blanket roll under the shed roof, noticing a thin rolled up mattress already there. He spent the next hour sawing and splitting oak limbs to fit in the stove. After stacking the split wood, he returned to the livery stable to check on the four horses.

As Thompson walked by himself across the busy street, he thought, *I could just keep walking and disappear. Not run, but just go away. Walk all night. Be long gone by tomorrow when Massah Smith calls for me. Just keep walking.* He sighed. *No, I can't. Don't know where to go, or what I'd eat. Still, maybe there come a day...*

★

Thompson and the cook ate at a worktable next to the open shed. She put food on two tin plates, but before she set them on the table, and nodded for him to sit on one of the stumps used for chairs, she said, "I's Irene. You be...?"

"Thompson."

"I say a blessin' on de food fo' we eats."

Thompson smiled, "Used to it. So do Mama."

Irene grunted as she sat, "Boy, I ain't yo' mama, but you shut dem eyes so's I kin dank de lawd fo' his blessin's on us."

The first bite raised Thompson's opinion of Irene's skill at her stove. While quickly taking big bites to work his way through the food heaped on his plate, he gushed about the meal, including asking what seasonings she used. By the time he helped her wash the dishes from the boarding house dinner, they were trading stories about their lives. After Irene dried her hands on her apron, she went into the shed that comprised her storeroom and brought out a small cloth sack of mixed ground peppers and other local seasonings.

"Don't you go an' use mo' dan a titch. Otherwise, yo' mastah be smokin' outs his earholes." She and Thompson both laughed at that thought.

After carefully putting the little sack in the crown of his hat, Thompson unrolled his bedroll, took off his leather shoes, and stretched out on his back, head resting on his arms, content in the moment. In a few minutes, it was dark enough for him to see the red coals in the stove. Irene was only a dark silhouette as she puttered about her open-air kitchen. His thoughts flitted to his mama, who shared the same habit of not seeking her bed until everything was in order for the next morning. His eyes closed.

The clinking sound of tin ware brought Thompson out of his slumber. He looked sideways and watched Irene pour water from a pot on the stove into a shallow pan, which she carried to the table where they'd eaten. She looked at the big house and saw the back door was shut, the dining room dark. She looked at the wood slat fence to confirm the gate was closed and latched. She looked towards Thompson, who quickly shut his eyes.

Satisfied that she was unobserved, Irene lit a single candle at the stove and let hot wax drip onto the table so she could set the candle upright and free both her hands. In the dim light, Irene unbuttoned her dress and let it fall to her hips. Naked to her waist, she reached for the washcloth in the pan of hot water. Thompson opened his eyes into narrow slits, his head still turned towards Irene as she ran the warm washcloth over her chest and stomach.

No, she ain't my mama, that's for damsure. Oh, Lawd, talk about blessin's. Thompson quickly again shut his eyes and turned his head when Irene looked his way before she wet the cloth again and reached inside her skirt to wash her private parts.

Thompson heard the woman walk to her sleeping pad and unroll it. He turned on his side, putting his back to her.

"Huh. So you ain't dead asleep," she said softly, not unkindly. "You like what you seen?"

"Yes."

"You never seen no woman undressed befo'?"

"No."

"How old is you, Thompson?"

"Don't know."

"Well, you chopped wood like a man. You eat like a man. An' you stink like a man. How long since yo' mama washed yo' clothes?"

"Don't know."

"Huh. Well, der be no time dis night fo' dat." She considered the young man lying stiffly on his blanket. " Sits up. Take off yo' shirt while I fetch de wash pan an' de candle."

"Ma'am?"

"I's Irene, no ma'am to you. I can't wash yo' smelly chest iffin you don't take off yo' shirt. I don't like sleepin' near no stinkin' man."

"Are you covered now?"

Irene smiled. "A little bit." Mischief crept into her soft voice. "But I hates to put on cold wet clothes in de mornin'. Now, pull dat shirt over yo head now. Keep yo' eyes shut iffen you don't wanna see a woman de way de good Lawd made Eve."

Thompson complied, squeezing his eyes shut. The warm washcloth moving in small circles across his chest brought deep sighs from the young man. He kept his eyes shut until Irene bent over to swish the cloth again in the pan of warm water. His eyes widened in the flickering candlelight to see she was on her knees, wearing nothing at all. She turned back to him and caught his eyes roving up and down her torso. He didn't even see her lips curl into a knowing smile.

"Lie back now."

Thompson again did as he was told. She unbuttoned his trousers and slid the warm wet washcloth down his pants. He gasped. She chuckled, and after wiping his private parts for just a couple of seconds, she pulled her hand away.

"Hold still, Thompson." She leaned in close, her breasts brushing his chest while she whispered in his ear. "Now pull dose trousers all de way off. You 'bout to ride a filly like you ain't ever 'magined."

The first time, after Irene guided him onto his knees and elbows, to hover shaking above her thighs, the act of love lasted just a few frantic thrusts. "Dat's good, Thompson, now rolls off. You be back fo' a longa ride in jest a bit. Reach over der and han' me de washcloth."

After quickly wiping herself, Irene cleaned Thompson more thoroughly. Soon enough, they coupled a second time, and, indeed, this time it was a longer and an exquisitely more satisfying ride for both of them.

Two hours before dawn, Thompson awoke, lying on side, his arm draped over Irene's bare waist, his hand cupping a smooth breast. He couldn't stop himself from moving his hand ever so slightly, exploring the wondrous new thing in his grasp. When Irene stirred and pushed her bottom more firmly against his loins, he immediately hardened and soon the two were again coupling in the dark.

Just before first light, Thompson felt his hand hit the ground. He opened his eyes and watched Irene stand and pull on her dress.

"Git up, Thompson. Grab de candle and fetch me all de eggs you can stuff in yo' hat from de hen house. An' don't you be lookin' at me all doe-eyed dis mornin'. We gots work to do, and den you be leavin'. Maybe yo' mastah come 'round agin sometime, but din, maybe not." She smiled down at the young man. "Either way, you 'member Irene's good cookin'."

Thompson stood and quickly pulled on his long-tailed shirt, but not before his exposed rising manhood embarrassed him. She laughed. "Boy, yo' mastah needs to buy a fulltime woman fo' you."

"Huh. Not Mastuh Smith."

"Maybe he buy a young high yella hussy fo' bo't you and him."

Thompson shook his head. "My mastuh ain't a man to share, especially with his nigger. Irene, you do this with other men like me?"

Irene wiped her hands on her apron. "Boy, you an' me slaves. We gits no say in what happens to us. I cooks, I wash. I do what de Mastah and Missus tells me to do. You come in and an' he'p me, an' say sweet dings, an' makes me smile. I give you back what I can. It don't cost me nothin', and make you and me feel close to somebody else fo' a night. Be good wit' dat."

Thompson rubbed his head, swallowed and went to gather eggs.

★

Three hours later, Thompson rolled the last barrel of Menger's freshly brewed beer up two wide wooden planks onto the back of the wagon bed. He carefully pushed the new barrel upright and wedged it in the corner of the wagon bed next to the other three. He lashed them all together, snug against the wagon's sideboards.

William Menger stood by the wagon, beaming at the sale and the prospect of his product gaining a foothold in another town. He knew more Germans were arriving nearly every month. *If my Deutsche freunde in Austin City will spend a hard-earned nickel on anything, it'll be a mug of stout beer—brewed by fellow German William Menger.*

While Menger tried not to gloat, Benjamin Smith tried not to worry. His wagon now held a substantial investment, and he wanted those four barrels secure in a storeroom in Austin. He impatiently watched Thompson finish tying the rope, then climbed onto the wagon seat. *It's going to be a long hundred miles.*

As soon as they turned the corner, Smith told Thompson to stop the horses. The slave and master watched a line of a dozen shackled Negroes, escorted by two armed white men, shuffle across the street in front of them. A door opened in a barn-sized building, and the group disappeared one by one into the dark interior.

"Know what that sign says over the door?" Smith asked his body servant. "Nah, of course you don't. Darkies don't read. It says, *J. Hart Negro Sales - Auction Every 1st Saturday.*"

Smith spat a stream of dark tobacco juice. "That's probably a string of runaways. Most men sell off a runner after the dogs chase 'em down and gnaw their legs bloody."

"I don't ever want to see the inside of a place like that." Thompson's voice was barely above a whisper.

"You just keep your master happy, boy. That's all you got to do."

The wagon reached the ford across Cibolo Creek well before dark. It was still early, but Smith told Thompson to unhitch the horses. He was already hungry and looking forward to a hot meal of the fresh beef he'd bought that morning before they left San Antonio. While Thompson worked, Smith kept thinking how easy it would be to tap one of the beer kegs. Finally, deciding New Braunfels wasn't all that far ahead, he called to Thompson.

"Put my saddle on the bay. I'm riding ahead a piece. Use the dutch oven to make biscuits to go with that beef steak, but don't put the steak on until I get back. I want it juicy and sizzling. I'll be back before dark."

In his haste to reach the tavern in New Braunfels, Smith left his shotgun under the wagon seat.

Chapter 12

Camp on Cibolo Creek
South of New Braunfels, Texas
Early October 1854

Thompson stirred the campfire and added a few sticks. Not knowing when his master may return, he'd already boiled potatoes, carrots, and onions, and had biscuits in the cast-iron dutch oven. Otherwise, except for shifting the three horses' tethers to better grazing every so often, Thompson was enjoying a rare late afternoon of inaction. He was leaning against a wagon wheel napping when a voice in his ear and the prick of a knife-point on his neck jerked him awake.

"Don't jump up, nigga. Jest set right der and looks at me."

Thompson swiveled his head to find his face just a foot from the grime-streaked face of another Negro man. "What you want? Get that knife off me."

"What I wants is somtin' ta eat. I move de knife, but lookee what mo' I gots." The man stepped back and held Mr. Smith's shotgun in one hand, pointed down at Thompson.

"Who are you?" Thompson asked, sitting up straight. He couldn't take his eyes off the shotgun. Neither hammer was cocked, and the man's thumb was wrapped around the neck of the stock, not touching the hammers. *He's never held a gun before, he don't know how to shoot it.*

"I's Philip, an' you git up and fetch me that pot of boiled tings by de fire."

Thompson pushed off the ground with both hands, but instead of rising, he threw himself at the other man's knees, wrapping his arms around them. The man who called himself Philip fell, but as he did, he hammered Thompson on the head with the butt of the shotgun. Thompson's arms went limp as he grunted in pain. Philip kicked at Thompson, pushing him away. The runaway slave sat up, pointing the shotgun at his opponent. The end of the barrel almost touched Thompson's chest, and it was shaking as Philip held it in a one-handed grip.

"Don't try to wrestle wit me, boy. I shoot you."

Thompson touched one hand to his throbbing scalp. His hand came away bloody. He looked more closely at the man holding the shotgun. He was tall, wide-shouldered, and one of the darkest men Thompson had ever seen. His wide nose flared in excitement, his brown eyes wide and lined with red blood veins.

The dark man's shirt and trousers were filthy rags and he wore no shoes. A wiry beard grew under his chin, and he stunk like an outhouse in the summer heat. Through the rips in his shirt, Thompson saw a reddish half-healed brand on the man's chest and his neck was a ring of chafed skin. The muscles in Philip's right arm bulged as he held the shotgun with one hand.

"You a field hand, and you runnin', ain't you?"

Philip nodded.

"Where you from?

The man shrugged. "Somewhere wit mo' trees."

"Where you goin'?"

"Crost a riber where brown men be."

"You mean Meskins."

"Dat's right. Old man Ezekial say African's got der own town der."

Thompson nodded. He'd overheard Mr. Smith talking angrily with other white men about such places across a river down south, settlements of runaway slaves. They'd said there were *hundreds* of runaways there living free like white men. Thompson didn't believe the talk, didn't know how many *hundreds* were, but they'd made it sound like a lot.

"It be a long run from here. You ain't even past San Antone," Thompson said.

"Done been a long run. An' now I gots a gun to shoot and a horse to ride." Philip nodded towards the grazing horses.

Thompson gasped. *If he takes one of Mr. Smith's horses, and his shotgun, the mastah will whip me, or even sell me off. I can't go on no stump wearin' chains. I can't be no field hand. I can't have no red hot brand burned on my chest, or wear no iron collar. No, hold on, hold on. Don't get all worked up. Mastah Smith not do none of that to me. He a good white man. He needs me. No, he need a nigger, and there's lots o' niggers. Maybe he just whip me. What, forty, fifty lashes. Oh Lord, I can't live through no fifty lashes.*

"Boy, you wants, I tie you to de wagon wheel der. Yo' massah know den you didn't hep me."

"No, he's goin' sell me or whip me for letting you sneak up and wollup me and thieve his belongin's. He find me tied up won't fix nothin' iffen you take his horse and shotgun."

"Den go wit me. Hep me find that riber and dat town o' Africans."

"What's that on your chest?"

"Dat where dey put a hot iron on me fo' runnin' befo'."

"But you're runnin' again?"

Philip nodded.

"You ever ride a horse?"

Philip shook his head. "Der be womens 'crost de riber."

Thompson looked sharply at the very dark man.

"You eber been wit a woman, Thompson?"

"Sure. Lots o' times."

"I mean wit' no clothes on."

"Sure. Ever now and then."

"If you likes de womens, der be womens fo' both of us crost de riber. Dat what Ezekial say."

Thompson rolled his eyes to stare at the sky. In San Antonio, just this morning, he'd realized he was too scared to run, too scared to gamble his life, to disappear on foot, on his own. *But what if I get a lashing for **not** running, a bloody back, or worse, maybe the auction block...and if I go with Philip, I wouldn't be alone, and we'd have horses and food, and even a gun.* Thompson swallowed before he spoke.

"I got no saddles. We have to ride bareback. Be hard to stay on."

Philip grinned, revealing his big yellow teeth. "No mo' jawin'. Which horse be fo' me?"

★

Benjamin Smith reached his camp on Cibolo Creek shortly before dusk, having thoroughly enjoyed several glasses of beer before riding back. While in the saddle, he'd mused over the striking contrast between the industriousness, the neat farms and homes of the Germans in New Braunfels, compared to the rundown shacks and weed-choked vegetable plots of the Scot and English immigrants he'd known around Nacogdoches in East Texas.

As he rode up to his wagon, Smith called, "Thompson, I hope you got a big pan of biscuits done nice and brown on top. Come get this nag. She'll need a good brushing."

When Thompson didn't appear, Smith looked around. *Maybe I caught the boy with his pants down behind a tree. Where're the other horses? Goddammit, where are my horses? Where's my nigger?*

"Thompson, you get your black ass out here, now!" Smith drew his pistol and walked his horse all the way around the wagon, then he went out on the circles of nibbled grass where the other horses had been grazing. The rope tethers were missing along with the horses.

Smith stopped his horse by the campfire and dismounted. The fire had burned to ashes. No smoke curled upwards. He stuck one hand over the ash and felt no heat. *My nigger's run. Hours ago. Run with my three horses. If I don't get my horses back, I'll skin him before I hang him.* Smith went to the front of the wagon and found what he expected. The shotgun was gone, as was Thompson's bedroll. *And my bedding, and the ration box is empty, too, goddammit.*

Too agitated to stay alone in his camp sitting by a fire all night, Smith left his precious beer barrels in the wagon, the wagon he couldn't pull with just one horse. He rode back into New Braunfels. He glumly rented a room at the same tavern where'd he'd enjoyed the afternoon. The proprietor pointed out a man dining in the tavern who Smith quickly hired to take a two-horse team back to Cibolo Creek at first light to retrieve his wagon. Smith had supper and another beer while he fumed over Thompson's betrayal and the chance he might lose his wagon, three horses, his slave, and four barrels of new beer. Then he went to bed.

The next morning, after seeing off the hired teamster and eating a hasty breakfast, Smith retrieved his horse and followed the tavern keeper's directions to a small neat building under a large sign that read *L. Hoffman – Gunsmith & Locksmith.* He went inside to find an empty front room, so he tapped with his ring on a glass case displaying pistols. When a slender man looking about his own age pushed through a green curtain, Smith immediately blurted out his interests.

"I need a good shotgun. No, I need a good musket."

The gunsmith waited for his agitated customer to decide what he wanted. The portly man abruptly pointed at a weapon that leaned upright in a rack behind the counter.

"Let me see that one. What is it? It looks new."

"That rifle is not for sale, Mister...?

"My name is Benjamin Smith. From Austin City. Look, yesterday my nigger body servant run off with my horses. I need to go fetch him back. He took my shotgun, so I need a musket that'll shoot farther than a shotgun will."

Hoffman sized up his distressed customer. "*Herr* Smith, with a single musket ball, fired from farther than a shotgun can shoot, you will not hit where you aim. The ball wanders. Drifts." The gunsmith moved his outstretched hand back and forth.

"You will do better with twelve buckshot balls shot from closer, or if you see good far away and have a steady hand, and much practice, then a rifled musket."

Laying a well-used weapon on the counter, Hoffman said, "This one. Twenty-five dollars, plus three dollars for one pound of *Deutche*-grade powder, one hundred priming caps, and one hundred lead balls."

"What kind of gun is this?" Smith asked, hefting the piece.

"It is U.S. Army 1841 model, perhaps ten years of age. I bought it from a soldier back from the war in Mexico. It has curving grooves in the barrel and uses percussion caps, not flints. It shoots .54 caliber round balls. The rifling--the grooves--make the ball fly straighter and farther than from smooth-bore muskets."

"Twenty-eight dollars is too much for an old gun."

"Then here is a new shotgun from New York. It's ten gauge. Twenty dollars plus two dollars for powder, caps and buckshot. Where did your Negro run to, *Herr* Smith?" Hoffman asked as he replaced the rifled-musket on the rack.

"How the hell do I know? West, I imagine, or maybe south to Mexico. I don't know."

Hoffman looked down as he rubbed the stock of the new shotgun with a soft rag.

"Which way will you go to find him? West or south?"

"I, I..." Smith stuttered, suddenly unsure of his next step.

The gunsmith spoke while Smith dithered. "Not so long ago, six of us went after Apaches. The redmen had killed a man--my daughter's new husband--and took my daughter."

Smith looked sharply at the gunsmith, saw the angst in his eyes. "Did you catch the red heathens? Get your daughter back?"

Hoffman kept rubbing the gunstock with the soft cloth, not looking up. "No. We hired a tracker. He kept us on their trail for two days to the Nueces River before a thunderstorm washed out the tracks. We came back. My daughter, my Caroline, is...gone."

"My regrets, Mr. Hoffman. Why did you tell--"

"To save you from the misery of trying to find a runaway Negro in such a vast, wild land as lies between here and Mexico. I know. I have ridden for hours and never see a tree."

"But my horses? My nigger?"

"Like my daughter, lost--for now. But, I have talked to men since my daughter was taken. Across the River Rio Grande, there is a place of...sanctuary for Negroes and Apaches. Near the town called Eagle Pass on the Texas side and Piedras Negras on the Mexican side. Perhaps your Thompson and my Caroline are both there."

"I can't go all the way to Mexico. I have a new saloon to open in Austin, a store to run."

"*Ja*, just as I have this shop to run. We are not young men without commitments. Instead of buying a weapon and entering the wilderness like an old hound searching for a scent, but confused by many scents, join me to hire two men to go to this Piedras Negras on our behalf. They will look there for my daughter and your Negro, and your horses. Are your horses branded? Burned like my cartouche?"

"You bet they are. All three of them the bastard took."

"The Negro has a name?"

"Thompson."

"Then possibly your Thompson and your branded horses can be found near Piedras Negras. As perhaps my Caroline."

Smith brightened at the idea. "You have two men in mind who can do that?"

"*Ja.*" He turned and lifted the same rifle off the rack that had caught Smith's eye. "The man who is coming back for this rifle and his companion."

"He have a name?"

"Let me see here." Hoffman looked at a small stack of papers behind the counter. "Milo McKean."

"I know that name. He a young fella, lanky, got brown hair, but blue eyes? Just got here from Alabama and talks like it."

"*Ja*, that could be him."

"Well, by damn, he'd be perfect. He's seen Thompson, would recognize him. He even slept under the wagon with Thompson one rainy night. Be just the man. He didn't have a horse, though, when I gave him a ride on my wagon."

Hoffman shrugged. "He rode to New Braunfels on a horse. When he comes for his rifle, I will try to enlist his service. How much is your Negro and your horses worth to you? How much will you pay?"

Chapter 13

Road Between Uvalde & Eagle Pass, Texas
Early October 1854

Jesse Gunn rolled his tired shoulders. "Milo, are you and me riding straight into a giant outhouse hole?"

"Jesse, we done talked about this ten times over. I need a job. You don't want to be your pa's farmhand, plowing fields all day, working 'long side his field hands. You agreed to come along. If we can bring that Thompson darkie and the horses back, we'll be in tall cotton. It's just a Mexican town we're going to. How bad can it be? You been to San Antone."

"What about the girl? We can't fight a whole village of wild Apaches."

"No, but we ain't gonna fight them. Like I said earlier, Jesse. If we can find her, we're gonna buy the girl back with whiskey."

"What's to keep them Injuns from just shooting us full of arrows and keeping the whiskey and our horses?"

"We'll find an agent to act for us with the Indians. I ain't stupid. I don't want my balls stuffed in my dead mouth no more than you do."

"Don't neither of us speak Mexican lingo. How we goin' to find this agent to the Apaches?"

"He'll find us when he learns there's someone ready to pay in U.S. coins."

The pair rode a while in silence.

"Milo," Jesse began hesitantly, " about that girl Caroline."

"Yeah, what about her? Bright yellow hair, speaks German and English. Shouldn't be hard to find out if she's in that Apache camp near Piedras Negras.

"I got that. I mean, what about *her*? Milo, them Injuns most likely have ravaged that poor girl time and again. They've had her for months now. She may be crazy as a loon, and mostly likely she's all swollen up with a redskin baby inside her."

"That won't be our problem, Jesse. That'll be for Mr. Hoffman to sort out. Besides, Mr. Hoffman said the man they killed was her new husband. If she's expecting a child when we find her, maybe it will be her husband's baby—a white baby."

"What if she can't ride a horse?"

"I don't know. We'll buy a buggy or a cart. Maybe rig up one those dragged pallets behind one of the horses. We'll figure out something."

"I bet we wind up using these." Jesse pulled the battered U.S. Army rifled-musket partly out of its leather scabbard. "Mighty considerate of Mr. Hoffman to push this on me as part of our pay."

"I'm hatin' that he thinks we may both need rifles. When we rest the horses at midday, maybe we oughta both fire a few rounds. See how good Mr. Hoffman fixed this old Baker rifle."

"And see if this one shoots anywhere near straight."

"Yup." They rode again in silence until Milo said, "Jesse, you realize how fast things are changing? How the world has shrunk?"

"What the hell you talking about? All I see is prairie grass and scrub brush. I don't see nothing shrinking."

"Think about it. Here me and you are in Texas, both born in Alabama on the other side of a mile-wide river, the widest river anywhere. We're headed to Mexico, across another wide river, into another country entirely, and I'm totin' a British army rifle made across the big ocean. And a Mexican soldier carried this rifle fighting the Texans twenty years back."

"And I'm carrying an American army rifle used to fight Mexicans just a few years back." Jesse patted his rifle. "And it was loaned to me by a German fella whose daughter got nabbed by Injuns who run to Mexico with her. So?"

"I don't know. I was just mullin' over how different pieces of things fit together sometimes."

"And we're diving into an outhouse hole."

★

During their midday rest, the two young men each fired their rifles several times at piles of rocks. Jesse shot more accurately than Milo with every round fired, even when they both missed the stack of small rocks. After they'd been back on the road for a spell, Milo stood in his stirrups staring ahead.

"I see dust over the road up yonder. Your rifle loaded?"

"Sure. But I can't tell if the dust is coming towards us or away from us."

"I think it's wagons."

It took over an hour, but the pair of riders eventually overtook the wagon train. When they were a hundred yards behind the last of the six wagons, a rider in a blue uniform cut away from the train and galloped towards them. He reined in ten yards to their front and held up his hand in a friendly manner.

"Good afternoon, gentlemen. I'm Lieutenant William Davant of the U.S. Army."

Milo took the lead, noting the lieutenant's mount was more thoroughbred than nag. "Howdy, Lieutenant. It's a pleasure to make your acquaintance. Any chance you're headed to the army post down at Eagle Pass?"

"Fort Duncan. As a matter of fact, I am. And who might you gentlemen be?"

"I'm Mister McKean and this here is Mister Gunn. We're headed to Eagle Pass ourselves."

The army officer looked at the pair's weapons carried casually across their laps. "I see you both are carrying military rifles."

"Surplus, outdated army rifles," Milo answered. "Mine's not even American. It's British by way of Mexico. Since we're going the same way on the only road around, how about we ride along with your wagons?"

"It's a public road. And the boss teamster, Senór Garza, won't mind two more friendly rifles." Davant smiled. "You are not highwaymen, I assume?"

Jesse smiled back. "Nope. We're the two most law abiding fellas you're likely to meet today."

The lieutenant nodded. "Very well. Come along."

The young men rode three abreast several yards behind the last wagon, their pace matching the slow steady tempo of the ox-drawn freight wagons. Having spent two weeks in the company of six Mexican teamsters who spoke little English and six army troopers with whom he would not engage in conversation, Lieutenant Davant didn't shy away from talking with the two civilians.

"Been on the road from Galveston for two weeks now. A man can't hurry oxen."

"I ain't had much luck hurryin' a Mexican either," Jesse added.

Lieutenant Davant coughed dust. "That too. But that's my sergeant's job. I'm not officially an officer of the garrison at Fort Duncan yet. I'm a supernumerary on this trip, just along for the ride to Eagle Pass. I still have to report to the captain before I'm part of the command structure."

"You a new officer then?" Milo asked.

"That I am. Just graduated from the academy at West Point. Fort Duncan is my first posting."

"Congratulations, Lieutenant." Milo had heard of West Point and was impressed. "What do think about Texas so far?"

Lieutenant William Davant waved his arm to encompass the horizon. "Huge. Endless. Beautiful. Different from home in South Carolina. Different from the academy in New York."

"Seen any redskins yet?"

"No, but Fort Duncan is part of the army's line of defense against hostile incursions. I expect I will encounter the red man soon enough."

"I reckon," both young Texans said simultaneously.

"And you men. Do you have families in Eagle Pass?"

"Nope, we're headed there on a business trip." Milo reached for his canteen, took a swig, and offered it to the lieutenant.

The young officer declined with a head shake. "Buying livestock, perhaps?"

Jesse snorted. "Nah. Chasing down a runnin' nigger."

"We've been hired to find and return a runaway slave owned by a man in Austin," Milo explained.

"Runaway slaves head to Mexico where they think they're safe." Milo paused. "You army boys or our Rangers can't cross the Rio Grande River, it being the official border."

"But we ain't official," Jesse added.

"Ah. I wish you success. My home, my civilian home, is Davant Oaks Plantation in South Carolina. We have the occasional runaway field hand, but our darkies have nowhere to go but the swamp. We keep dogs to fetch back those who try it."

"Woof, woof," Jesse barked. "I'm Jesse Gunn, the lean hound of Prairie Lea, hot on the trail of an African named Thompson headed to the great Mexican swamp."

Milo rolled his eyes at Jesse's theatrics. "And there's one more reason we're going to Eagle Pass," Milo said, warming to the lieutenant from South Carolina.

"What's that?"

"Last June those Indians you ain't seen yet stole a white girl, a new bride, near New Braunfels. We've heard the Lipan Apaches and Seminoles got a village on the Mexican side of the river, not far from Eagle Pass. Like with the runaway slaves, a place where you fellas won't go 'cause it's in Mexico. We're hoping to find her, buy her back, and take her home."

"A gallant quest. But, is it practical? Won't the poor woman be *ruined?*"

"Maybe, maybe not. We'll see."

Chapter 14

Eagle Pass, Texas
Mid-October 1854

After four days of breathing dust at the back of the slow-moving wagon train, Jesse Gunn spied smoke on the horizon.

"That's gotta be Eagle Pass, don't it?"

Lieutenant Davant and Milo McKean both shaded their eyes, trying to see what caught Jesse's attention. "Most likely," the lieutenant answered.

"Then I'll see you fellas later. Milo, I'll find you before dark." With that, Jesse let out a whoop and galloped ahead. He spurred his horse towards the smudges of smoke coming from the chimneys in Eagle Pass and Piedras Negras, towns on opposite banks of the Rio Grande River.

"No more holding Jesse at the back of the line any longer." Davant shook his head. "Good thing he's not a cavalry trooper."

Milo laughed at the idea of his friend Jesse Gunn wearing a soldier's uniform. "You got that right, Will. I expect by the time we get there, he'll be deep into that Mexican cactus juice the teamsters drink every night."

"Milo, you think you should go after him? Can he handle himself? Forgive my forwardness, but with those scars on his face, he will be the target of raillery. I saw it at West Point. Some upper classmen were unmerciful in their tormenting of younger cadets who had heavy pimpling, especially when drinking spirits."

Milo watched Jesse ride out of their sight. "I probably should go with him, but I ain't. Let him scout for us. As to the pimple scars, I reckon Jesse's been dealing with meanness about them for a long time now. Anyway, before we left Prairie Lea, a good man gave Jesse a jar of yeller sulfur. Jesse's been sneaking off right when we bed down and mixing a bit of sulfur salve that he spreads on his face. I think it's helping."

"You mean he looks *better*?" Davant raised his eyebrows.

"Yeah, I know. The sulfur holds back new outbreaks, but it don't smooth out the old scars. I guess he'll wear those his whole life. Heck, those gashes in his face may help him in the saloon. Gives him a fierce look. Who knows, he may learn something helpful before I get there."

"Huh. My brother Daniel is cursed with pimples. Sulfur, you say?"

"Yep, sulfur. And I've a mind to go along with you into Fort Duncan. See if I can talk to the post commander or someone who might point me in the right direction to find that Nigra boy or the Hoffman girl. Seems like a good place to start."

"Good thinking. I'll introduce you to Captain Burbank after I report in myself."

"Is he regular army? I mean, a West Point fellow like you?"

"Yes, indeed. I asked around about him. He finished in the middle of his class and fought in the Indian wars in Florida."

"Is he from the north? If he is, he might be an abolitionist, and not care about escaped slaves."

The lieutenant, who'd grown up the son of a wealthy plantation owner, shrugged. He had no answer to that query.

★

The wagon train reached Camp Duncan to cheers from the soldiers who knew the wagons held two things they held dear: American whiskey and their pay. William Davant immediately reported to the post commander's office, while Milo loitered in the shade of the wide front porch. He leaned against a post and gazed at his horse, surprised at how well the animal had filled out during the weeks since he had acquired the neglected animal. *A little daily attention, decent food, and exercise. Works with man and beast.* Within minutes, a corporal in a faded uniform opened the door and waved for Milo to come inside.

After brief introductions, Captain Burbank offered his guest a chair in front of his desk. The army officer smoothed his wool coat as he took his seat behind the desk, seemingly indifferent to the salt-colored sweat stains under both arms.

Burbank appeared older than Milo had anticipated. *He may be as old as Mr. Callahan.* The captain had a hint of gray at his temples. Bushy eyebrows dominated his round face. The post commander's dark eyes flicked from his newly arrived junior lieutenant to the young civilian who faced him. Milo thought his face looked as weather-beaten as the enlisted soldiers who had accompanied the wagon train.

"I'm offering you a few minutes, Mr. McKean, because Lieutenant Davant asked me to. He tells me you and your companion are bounty hunters on the trail of a runaway slave. I should tell you that I am from Massachusetts and I do not approve of the South's peculiar institution, and I most assuredly do not support the efforts of ruffians who seek to re-enslave the fugitives for a reward.

Milo shifted uncomfortably in his chair. "Captain, it's true we're being paid to return a runaway slave, if we can find him. And the three horses he stole when he ran."

Milo leaned forward, his hands clasped together. "But we're mainly here to fetch home a young woman taken by Indians last summer."

Milo had carried in the Apache arrow wrapped in cloth. He set it on the captain's desk and unfolded the cotton to reveal the red and black painted arrow.

Captain Burbank picked up the arrow, noting the dark blood stains on the arrowhead and shaft.

While the captain examined the arrow, Lieutenant Davant said, "Captain, it's my understanding, sir, from talking with Mr. McKean here over the past several days, that he and his friend Jesse aren't really bounty-hunters. They're aiming to enlist in Captain Boggess's Mounted Volunteers in San Antonio, a ranging company. They need rifles and the girl's pa is a gunsmith in New Braunfels. He gave Milo and Jesse each a rifle in exchange for going after his daughter."

"Huh. What type of rifles?" the captain set down the arrow.

Milo answered. "One's a surplus from the Mexican War. An 1841 Springfield. The other's a converted flintlock. An old English Baker rifle."

"Do tell. I'd like to see the old Baker conversion sometime. As for the '41 Springfield, Colonel Davis had to go all the way to the President for permission to arm his regiment with them during the Mexican War. Pushy fellow, Jefferson Davis, but I'm told that the rifles were damned effective in Mexico. Best we had. Can you hit anything with them?"

"Yes, sir. We've been practicing most every afternoon after the wagons circled up. In fact, we about went through all our lead and powder. But we've enough for this errand."

The captain grunted. "Errand? Mr. McKean, you'll find crossing paths with the Apache constitutes more than an errand. They are formidable. What about the runaway slave?"

"His owner is a friend of the gunsmith. Willing to pay for one of the rifles, and more, if we'll do what we can to find his runaway boy. A young nigra named Thompson. And his three horses, all marked with a big S brand."

"Well, I have to say, I approve of Captain Boggess and his ranging company. They make our job a sight easier when they're out doing their job. And those two rifles will give you a reach the Colt revolvers don't have."

The tension both young men had felt when Captain Burbank announced he was from Massachusetts and didn't like bounty hunters began to dissipate a bit.

"About this arrow, I'm no expert. I'll have a native scout look at it. It's no secret that the Lipan Apaches and a band of Black Seminoles both have villages within twenty miles of where we sit. On the Mexican side of the river, of course."

The captain put down the arrow and sighed. "Mr. McKean, have you been in Texas long?"

"No, sir. I came from Alabama earlier this year."

"Even a few months is long enough to be told how the Indians treat captured white women." The captain steepled his fingers together. Milo nodded.

"Then you know that this white woman has been abused. Beaten every day by the squaws. Repeatedly ravaged by the men. After several months in an Apache camp, her dignity, her whiteness, will have been ripped from her, stripped away as surely as her clothing. She may be heavy with a heathen baby by now, if the beatings haven't ruined her innards. Their intent is to turn their captives into pale-skinned Apaches. The captured women and children who cannot make that change, die."

Milo somberly nodded. "We told her father we would try to bring her home."

"If she is alive, her father may not want her home. She will be different. Broken."

"We told her father we would try."

Captain Burbank picked up the arrow. "Very laudable. If you find her in an Apache camp, how do you propose to recover her? You cannot simply ride in and ask for her. Unless you want to sprout half a dozen of these." He set the arrow down.

"If we can find her, I'm planning to buy her with whiskey."

The captain leaned back in his chair. "Whiskey. You know how strong spirits affect Indians? Makes them crazy mean, that's what it does. Even meaner, crueler than usual. And they may take your whiskey and pay you with these." He tapped the arrow again.

Milo started to speak, but the captain held up his palm. "I know, you told her father you'd try. I'll send Lieutenant Davant with word of what our native scouts have to say. Regardless what our tame Indians would have us think, I know they're in contact with the Lipans over the river. It may be easier than you think to find out about this woman--what's her name?"

"Caroline Hoffman. Eighteen years old. Long, light blonde hair. Blue eyes. German."

"Hmm. She'll stand out then. Hard to hide straw-colored hair in an Indian camp."

"Thank you, Captain. What about the Negro camp? Do your native scouts have connections there, too?"

"Perhaps. It's not an issue that's come up before. The runaway darkies don't go raiding onto our side of the river. They're relieved to be left alone where they are, safe from men like you. I urge you to proceed with caution if you cross the Rio Grande in search of your man Thompson. It's a fair assumption the Negroes there will be armed. They have strong reason and the means to defy white men who come knocking on the door of their sanctuary. They may shoot you on sight."

Milo McKean swallowed and nodded.

"Regardless, I will inquire. Lieutenant Davant will let you know what I'm told." Standing up, Captain Burbank dismissed McKean. "Now, Lieutenant Davant and I have duties. Good luck to you."

Chapter 15

Eagle Pass, Texas
Mid-October 1854

*O*KeLL*y* saLooN. Jesse read the green letters over the open double doors as he looped his reins around the wobbly hitching rail. The primitive lettering struck Jesse as a good omen that the men inside would be just the sort to know about captured women and runaway slaves. He pulled the Springfield rifle from its scabbard, remembering Milo's tale of stolen blankets. When he entered the open door to the saloon, he looked over his shoulder to be sure he could see his horse from inside.

When Jesse set down his rifle next to his leg, he noted there was no brass foot rail running the length of the bar. Nor was there a mirror or a line of bottles of various spirits behind the bar. Nor were there any other customers.

The bartender sauntered over and asked what Jesse wanted.

"Beer. Tall and cool."

"Nope. All out."

"Whiskey then."

"Nope. All out. Got tequila."

"God, that's all I've had for a week with them damn Mexican ox drivers," Jesse sighed. "All right."

"Huh." The bartender poured an inch of clear liquid from a nearly empty bottle into a smudged shot glass. "Ox drivers, you say?" Jesse nodded. "From San Antonio way?"

"Yep. Half a dozen wagons headed to the army post."

"And town. That means I'll have whiskey, and maybe even a cask of beer tomorrow. About damned time. White men'll drink this cactus juice if that's all I got, but beer and whiskey keep my door open. An army scout, are you now?"

"Nah, I ain't a scout. Never been down here before today."

"Huh. That's an army rifle. I carried one like it in the war with Mexico."

"You O'Kelly?"

"Aye. That I am. Proud owner of this little wet patch of Ireland, in the vast dry wilderness of Texas."

"Jesse Gunn, Mr. O'Kelly." Jesse held out his hand over the bar.

O'Kelly squinted at Jesse before he held out his own hand. "A hand shake don't pass for payment for that drink, Mr. Gunn."

"Never thought it would. Here." Jesse pulled a coin from his trouser pocket and laid it on the bar. "Maybe that will fetch me another, and one for my pard when he's through with his business at the army post."

O'Kelly slipped the coin into his vest pocket and smiled. "And what business would it be that attracted two young lads like yourself and your missing friend to Fort Duncan?

"A runaway slave named Thompson."

"After a bounty, are you now?" O'Kelly's smile disappeared.

"More of a favor. Been paid already with this." Jesse held up the old army rfile. "Going to join up with Captain Boggess's Mounted Volunteers in San Antone. Swapped a runaway darkie for a rifle. Now we just got to find that darkie and take him back."

"Sometimes that is not so easy, Mr. Gunn."

"Maybe, maybe not. We heard that just over the river, there's a whole settlement of escaped slaves. Hunerds of runaway darkies. How hard can it be to find them? We reckon Thompson might be there."

"Aye, I hear talk about all them escaped slaves across the river. Hundreds of them, and two of you?"

"Well, we have Mr. Colt and Mr. Springfield with us, too."

O'Kelly shook his head. "Won't be enough. Now, if you had every trooper at Fort Duncan behind you with their Sharps carbines, you might have enough guns for a fast raid. But the soldier boys ain't welcomed across the river. They stay on the American side."

"Somebody has to know where the darkies live." Jesse let his frustration creep into his voice.

O'Kelly put both his palms on the bar. "Sure they do, but they won't be guiding no bounty hunters there. You think them hundreds of darkies don't have a fair number of guns themselves?"

Jesse tilted his head back and swallowed the throat-burning liquor. He'd been worrying about that very point himself.

★

Milo McKean rode down the street looking for Jesse's horse. When he saw the animal in front of an adobe building with a badly painted sign over the door, he stopped and tied Buck next to Jesse's mount. Over the next half-hour he had two shots of tequila before O'Kelly put the bottle away, Jesse's silver coin having reached the limit of its buying power.

The two men rented a stuffy room in the back of O'Kelly's bar. As they were accustomed to doing, they tucked their stirrups under the padded saddle seats and arranged them next to the filthy mattress on the floor. With their heads resting on the make-shift leather pillows, a shared blanket under them, and boots and weapons near to hand, the pair stretched out on their backs, elbow to elbow. A single stubby candle burned on a small table by the door.

"I got an idea, Jesse, how we might smoke out Thompson. How we might tempt him to this side of the river."

"Oh, yeah?"

"Let me mull it over 'til morning."

"Sure thing, Milo. If you can figure out how to get him to come to us and hold out his hands for the shackles in our saddlebags, I'm all ears. But I ain't going to stay awake all night waiting for your vision to appear in the window."

"Now, Jesse, you know damned well that no vision of mine is going to slip past your sulfur yeller face. You shine like a haint in the moonlight."

Jesse reached up to touch the still-sticky paste on his forehead. "Seriously, Milo, you think the sulfur is working? I'd sure like for Mr. Schmidt's daughter to not look away when I come around once we get home. It ain't easy to spark a girl who won't look at me."

"It's working, Jesse. Not all at once, but I've noticed fewer new outbreaks. Keep using it. Now quiet down so's I can think about what might lure Thompson back across the river so we can nab him."

"Well, hell, Milo, what lures ever' man to the wild side of the river? Whiskey and women."

"Shut up, Jesse."

"One more thing, Milo."

"What, Jess? What now?"

"Milo, I'm not sure how to ask this, but are you sure we're doin' the right thing going after this Thompson darkie?"

"What do you mean?"

"I mean I ain't ever met Thompson and I know he's a slave. But, don't a man, ever man, even a black man, deserve a chance to make his own way? You came to Texas from Alabama to make your own way, didn't you? We're layin' on this mattress full of bugs, about to cross a river into a foreign country to make our own way as men, ain't we?"

Milo was silent for a long while before he answered. "Yeah."

"And this Thompson darkie, far as we know, he didn't hurt nobody when he ran, and he made his own way from Austin, all the way down here and across the same river. So, are we going after Thompson because niggers ain't really men? I mean, because they ain't Godly men like us 'cause they came from Africa?"

"I dunno, Jesse. I only know we're going after Thompson because we promised to. Because we need what was being offered."

"I guess so. You know, if we do catch him and haul him back to Austin, Mr. Smith will hurt him bad for running. Oh well. See you in the morning." Jesse rolled onto his side, his back to Milo, leaving his friend staring at the spider web in the corner of the ceiling, trying to sort out what makes white men Godly and Negroes not.

The next morning, as they stood next to a street vendor's cart eating stewed meat in rolled-up corn *tortillas*, Milo told Jesse his plan for capturing the runaway slave Thompson. Jesse saw a dozen holes in the scheme, but hadn't been able to think of anything better, so he kept his concerns to himself, nodding while he chewed.

★

Milo and Jesse were still on the mile-long road from Eagle Pass to Fort Duncan to enlist the assistance of their new friend, Lieutenant Davant, when they met him riding leisurely towards town.

"I've got another three days of travel time before the captain can turn me loose on my troop. The old lieutenant has them until he leaves with the wagon train heading back towards San Antonio." Davant shrugged.

"So, I thought I'd ride into Eagle Pass and see the sights. And pass along what Captain Burbank learned about the Hoffman girl."

"Oh yeah? What? Can we get to her?" Jesse immediately asked.

"Nothing. His native scouts don't know a damned thing about where she might be. Nothing. She's vanished."

"You believe that?"

"Milo, I don't know anything about the Lipan Apaches or the army's native scouts. I'd bet the army Indians do know about the woman. But..." Davant shrugged his shoulders. "Ask me this time next year, after I've spent a few months chasing them across the prairie."

"Huh." Milo grunted. "I was counting on the captain's Injun scouts telling us something. Damn. Well, there's still the darkie. Will, I have an idea how to flush him out to our side of the river. But I need your help."

Chapter 16

O'Kelly's Saloon
Eagle Pass, Texas
Mid-October 1854

The three young men sat around a small, wobbly table in the back of the saloon. Two of them were not long removed from abandoned farms in northern Alabama, sons of parents who couldn't afford slaves to till and weed and pick the ever slimmer crops of cotton. The third man hailed from a thriving plantation in South Carolina, a plantation on which scores of slaves worked the rice and sugarcane crops. Heads together, speaking in low conspiratorial voices, the three labored over a letter.

Will Davant scrawled the first line on the paper. "This sounds like an indignant slave owner. *To My Unfortunate Misguided Negro Thompson.*"

Milo shook his head. "Is that how your father would speak to a slave?"

"I bet the man in the big house don't speak to his niggers. He owns them, he don't chat with them," Jesse said.

Davant leaned back. "I fear Jesse's right. I doubt my father knows the names of any but our house servants and stable hands." He lined through the salutation. "You boys let me alone for a bit. You told me already what needs to be said. Go talk to Mr. O'Kelly about how we might find this canyon full of darkies tomorrow."

Left to his thoughts, Will Davant wrote a line or two, scratching through a single word or a whole sentence, until he finally put down the sharpened quill and studied the letter he'd composed. He read it in a soft whisper to himself, and made a few more changes. He called Jesse and Milo back to the table and read it to them in a low voice. When both nodded in agreement, Will pulled a fresh sheet of paper from his leather satchel and neatly copied the letter.

"To my runaway slave Thompson. You have betrayed the trust and comfortable position I have freely given you since you were borned in my household. I should have you brought back in chains to Austin and branded as a runner.

But the value of the three horses and shotgun you stole are of higher value to me than your skin. Hand over the animals and weapon to the man who reads this letter to you, and I will leave you be, and will not take the strap to your mammy in punishment for your cowardly acts against me.

It would grieve me mightily to inflict pain on such a loyal Negress for the sins of her young'un, but I will do it. Her back will bleed, and that blood will be as from your hands, not mine.

Signed: Mister Benjamin Smith, Austin, Texas
Legal owner of the healthy and ungrateful Negro male Who Answers to the name Thompson"

Will Davant looked at Milo. "Is Smith the sort of man who'd whip a slave's mama for his runnin' off?"

"I only met him the one time. I don't know, but he seemed to like his Negro. Would your father?" Milo countered.

Davant nodded. "He would threaten to, if he thought it would work. But then again, like I said back on the trail, in Carolina, we use dogs, not quill pens to fetch back our runaways. It's a whole 'nother place out here."

"And like I said, it ain't so different, we're just hounds with a letter of introduction. And lassos." Jesse grinned.

Milo corrected his friend. "No, not hounds. With this letter, we're more like hunters in a blind, trying to lure the game into a clearing with corn spread on the ground."

Davant rubbed his jaw. "I don't know. Why would he take this bait?"

"To protect his mammy. To save her being whipped," Jesse answered, having no trouble with the logic of the ploy.

"I don't think it's enough. I know white men who care not a snatch for their mothers. I doubt Africans are any different." Davant shook his head. "No, we've got to sweeten the pot." He picked up the quill and began to write on the back of the first draft. Milo and Jesse shrugged to each other, but sat without comment. When Will was through, he again read it to the other two.

"To my runaway slave Thompson. You have betrayed the trust and comfortable position I have freely given you since you were borned in my household. I should have you brought in chains back to Austin and branded as a runner.

Your mammy has turned worthless to me since you ran. I've taken the strap to her every day, but she just bawls like a sick cow. Her back has bled, but that blood has been as from your hands, not mine. She won't cook, won't work. Worthless.

But the three horses and shotgun you stole are of high value to me. Hand over the animals and weapon. I will leave you be, and will release your mammy to you. I send her as trade for my horses and shotgun. If you do not want her, I have instructed my agent to sell your mammy at auction.

Signed: Mister Benjamin Smith, Austin, Texas
Legal owner of the healthy and ungrateful Negro male Who Answers to the name Thompson"

"Nice words, Will. Clever. But there's just one thing. We don't have Thompson's mammy. And one more other thing. How do you know Mr. Smith owns Thompson's mammy?" Jesse said.

Milo had to grin at Jesse's response. "Your second other thing first. The one night I spent with Mr. Smith he bragged about how good in the kitchen Thompson's mammy is, and how Thompson was learning to cook from her. And to your *other* other thing, Thompson won't know his mammy is still in Austin City. The letter is to lure him close enough to rope and tie, right? We just call to him that we'll bring his mammy out when he hands us the reins to the horses. We should ride away with the whole batch--shotgun, horses, and the runaway." Will Davant looked up, his conviction in the refined plan evident on his face.

"He may have sold the horses by now," Milo said. "He may be on foot."

"No matter. You'll still get the slave himself. That's the main thing, right?" Davant asked.

Milo took the letter and wrote on the bottom

"I will have your mammy at the rocky ford a mile upriver of the big log jam. Midday. Bring the shotgun and horses."

Milo stood up and carried the letter to Mr. O'Kelly.

"You said you know a man who's been to the slave settlement across the river. He reads this letter to Thompson or gives it to a darkie who can read it. When he gets back, he gets paid half. When we get the slave, he gets the rest."

O'Kelly took the letter, saying, "The niggers call their shantytown on the other side of the river 'Eureka' for some fool reason. I know a man who'll go there for pay. He'll want half now, the rest when he comes back. But I get paid now."

Milo dropped two coins on the bar. O'Kelly walked out, saying over his shoulder. "Watch the store. Stay out of the whiskey. I'll be back shortly."

As the three men waited for O'Kelly to return, Will Davant reverted to his West Point military education. "We have to go out to the ford right away. Follow O'Kelly's messenger. Bivouac there."

"Why, and what's bivouac?" Jesse asked.

"Because our plan depends on us being there first. If Thompson or his friends get to the ford first, they can send a lookout to see we don't have Thompson's mama when we ride up." Will grinned at Jesse. "Bivouac means sleeping on the hard ground with the scorpions and rattlesnakes another night. No fire. Keeping your horse saddled. Like you'll be doing every night when you go ranging with the Mounted Volunteers."

Jesse grinned back. "Oh, just that. I can do that."

Chapter 17

The Runaway Slave Settlement of Eureka
State of Coahuila, Mexico
Near the Rio Grande River
Mid-October 1854

The white man named Weber was scared. *Damn, it's hard riding blindfolded and hands tied to the saddle horn. I sure hope this weren't a big mistake. I may have been out of coin, but I don't want to be left as buzzard meat out in the desert neither.*

He'd been confronted by three Negroes on horseback while still in sight of the river. One of them carried a long double-barreled shotgun and was the darkest man he'd ever seen. Weber had left his pistol behind, so with arms raised, holding the letter in one hand, he'd explained he was just a paid messenger, looking to deliver a letter to a young Negro by the name of Thompson. Weber handed the folded paper to them. The three Negroes passed it around, each one unfolding it and squinting at the handwriting. Weber was certain none of them had been able to read it.

They'd given back the letter before they tied his hands with a rawhide thong and covered his eyes with a grimy piece of cloth. Finally, he felt his hat jerked down over his brow and eyes. Weber could breathe, but couldn't see a thing.

After a slow ride that lasted longer than he could estimate, they stopped. A Negro untied the white man's hands and left him on his horse. Weber immediately pulled up his hat and slipped the blindfold off. He blinked and covered his eyes with hands, while he asked loudly, "Thompson? Is there a Thompson here? I have a letter for you."

A young lighter-skinned Negro approached the messenger and held out his hand. "I'm Thompson."

Weber handed Thompson the letter. He finally looked around, squinting in the harsh sunlight. *Damn, I never seen so many darkies in one spot. Damn, if ever one is worth $500 or more...damn, a man could get rich as a king if there was a way..."*

"You're Thompson and you got the letter. I done my job. I'm going now." The messenger started to turn his horse, when Thompson grabbed the reins.

"You go out the same way you come in. Tied and blind."

As the three mounted Negroes led the tied and blindfolded white man away from the community of brush and wood huts, Thompson called out, "Who can read? Can anyone read this letter to me?"

No one answered.

"Hold on, Philip," Thompson called. He walked to the white messenger.

"Can you read?"

The man nodded.

"Philip, will you let him loose again to read it?"

"Sho'. Who write you, tho'? How he know we here?"

His blindfold again lifted and his hands untied, Weber took the letter back and slowly read it out loud, stumbling over several words.

"Again. Read it again," Thompson said. Philip saw his friend was agitated by the letter.

The messenger read it a second time, without as much difficulty as the first time.

Philip spoke first. "You see any African woman wit de mens who gib you dis paper here?"

Straining to understand the odd dialect, the messenger answered, "Nope, the saloon keeper, Mr. O'Kelly paid me to bring the letter to Thompson. Just O'Kelly by himself."

Thompson looked at the other two mounted men. "Will you take the white man back to the river now? Philip, will you stay?"

"Sho'."

Philip and Thompson watched the messenger being led away, then moved to the shade of a small tree where they sat.

"Philip, I want to go to the ford. Mastah Smith ain't stupid. An' he love his money. He sees that three horses and a gun be worth more than my mama. I want to go to the ford and see. I want you to go with me."

"May be a snare to catch a hare what not payin' no mind, like one o' ol' Ezekial's stories. Yo' mama be de carrot in de snare."

"That's why I want you an' the shotgun."

"Hmm." Philip picked up a twig and drew lines in the dust. "What if we gets caught? I ain't eber goin' wear chains agin."

"Philip, it be my mama."

"It *may* be yo' mama. It may be a trick."

"You will have the shotgun."

"Yeah. I go, but I ain't crossin' de riber. No way. Not eben fo' Sweet Jesus' Mama Mary is I goin' back to Texas."

Thompson slapped his friend on the knee. "Tomorrow then."

Chapter 18

Along the Rio Grande River
Mid-October 1854

As McKean, Gunn and Davant rode along the north bank of the Rio Grande towards the big logjam, the trio fleshed out their plan for abducting Thompson.

"Look how high and fast the current is. The water's likely to be up to a horse's belly even at the ford. It'll be slow crossing, but that should help us," Davant postulated.

Jesse looked dubiously at the muddy river. "Who's going into the river? We going to draw straws?"

"Nah, it has to be you or me, Jesse. Not Will. We're the ones being paid, and I'm better with a lasso than you are." Milo slipped his lariat loose from the rawhide thong. He shook out a loop, twirled it a couple of times, and laid it neatly around a boulder.

"You better just twirl it once," Will said. "That nigra won't be sitting still when he sees the rope."

"I'm hoping he might think the rope is for the horses he better be leading."

"Well, what about those horses, and the one he'll be riding?" Jesse asked.

Milo twirled his rope in a small loop while the horses plodded along. He thought out loud.

"I'm going to put a loop over the darkie and jerk him off his mount in the middle of the river. I'll have to be quick, and I won't have hands enough for any horses. Maybe they'll just follow Buck on across to our side. Or they might turn around and go back to the Mexican side or start swimming downstream."

Milo turned to Jesse, "Jess, you fetch them out wherever they go. But the horses don't matter as much as the darkie. Mr. Smith will be happy enough to get back his slave."

Jesse butted in. "That is, if his darkie don't drown or hit his head on a rock while you're dragging him through the water to the Texas side of the river. Remember, we're being paid by the head. The runaway, sure. But three horses is a stack of cash I don't plan to leave on the table."

"Smith might even get his shotgun back too, but I wouldn't count on that." Davant said. "I bet there'll be another nigger on the Mexican side of the river pointing Mr. Smith's shotgun right at you. It's what we're going to do, after all, only hidden."

"Here's another thing," Jesse said. "Thompson's expecting someone to bring out his mammy. That'd be me, only I won't have her. I guess we could stuff a sack and I could carry it over my saddle in front of me. But I ain't got a sack."

"We can use a blanket or my oilcloth," Will offered.

"Won't work up close, but I won't be close," Jesse said. "Wonder if she's a portly darkie or a wiry one? Well, either way, once Milo tosses his lariat, I can drop the straw dummy and go after the loose horses."

"Hate to lose my oilcloth. But I suppose the army will have another one for me."

No one spoke for a while as they all tried to foresee what might happen at the ford the next day.

Chapter 19

Rock Ford across the Rio Grande River
Two Miles North of Eagle Pass, Texas
Mid-October 1854

Will Davant put the expensive collapsible brass telescope to his eye. He lay under a creosote plant on the crest of a ridge that overlooked the ford. O'Kelly had assured them that the water was only knee high. *Not today,* Davant thought. *But maybe that's better for us.* He assumed that rains upriver had caused the normally sluggish river to rise out of its summer banks. He hoped the water in the center of the wide river was no more than belly-high to a horse.

With the sun rising behind him, Davant wasn't worried about the telescope's glass lens twinkling and alerting anyone of his presence. Still, he kept the shiny brass tube covered with a dark cloth when he wasn't studying the trail on the Mexican side of the river.

Not far below Davant's hidden location, Milo sat on a rock near the bank, fiddling with his lariat, his horse tied to a bush. With a twist of his head, Davant could also see Jesse, out of sight from across the river, but ready to follow Milo into the water with the decoy.

Davant chuckled when he saw that Jesse was fooling around with the straw-stuffed oilcloth, trying to somehow fashion legs to stick out the bottom. *Jesse, you are one likable dumb-ass. Even if you shape the two limbs, they'll be straw-colored, not darkie brown. But if it keeps you busy all morning, you enjoy yourself.* Davant smiled at the memory of Jesse several hours earlier, sitting in the moonlight, carefully mixing a titch of sulfur paste in his palm and rubbing it over his newest pimples. *Poor bastard.*

Next, the lieutenant began to wipe dust off the cone and barrel of the rifle that lay lock-plate up next to him. He smiled again at the reaction of his two companions to the sight of the new Sharps he'd received as a graduation present from his father. Their admiration for the sleek new breech-loading weapon had been clear, and their envy only slightly less evident.

As Davant ran the soft cloth along the brown-tinted barrel, he pulled himself out of the moment, and pondered. *I'm all set to cover my two friends with this new army rifle. I've never shot at a man, not even a darkie on the run. Will I hesitate? No, I can't. A shot fired a second after the enemy has fired won't help Milo. Any late decision by me to pull the trigger, may kill Milo. I can't let that happen. He's depending on me.*

The morning passed with excruciating slowness for the three waiting white men. Jesse finally stopped messing with the straw legs that he'd eventually woven onto the lump of straw under the oilcloth. He was now bored, drawing lines in the sand with a stick. Milo had sat down with his legs outstretched, leaning against a boulder, holding his horse's lead, the animal nibbling at whatever tiny green weeds he could find near its front hooves. Will was fighting to keep from nodding off in the warm sunshine when he saw movement across the river.

"Ho, dere!"

Milo quickly stood up and called back, "Ho, there yourself."

Davant and Milo watched a very dark and tall Negro walk down to the edge of the water and wade in up to his knees.

Milo clambered onto Buck and nudged him into the river, stopping about thirty feet from the man holding the shotgun. Milo used his reins to signal Buck to edge upstream a few steps, making sure he didn't block Will's view of the armed Negro. Milo still held his lariat, already loosened into a twirling-sized loop.

Seeing that the tall man was not the runaway they'd come for, Milo called, "You ain't Thompson. Go get Thompson, I got no business with you."

"War be the old woman?" the Negro called in his odd dialect.

"Where's Thompson? Who are you?"

"Why, I's Thompson. And dis here be a two-shoot gun."

"You ain't Thompson. I know Thompson. And that's Mr. Smith's shotgun, I'll wager. That's part of the trade. Glad you brought it. But you call for Thompson right now. My business is with him, not some runaway field hand." Milo's mind raced. *Why the hell didn't we think that he might send someone else?*

"You gits nuttin' 'til I sees de woman. I wants to see Thompson's ma. What de rope fo'?"

"Mr. Smith's lead horse, of course," Milo answered. "And no woman until I see three horses tied together, close enough to drop a loop on." He was running out of things to say, and he worried that Jesse would ride into view behind him any second, holding the straw dummy—which he didn't think would fool anyone but a blind man.

"You send Thompson's ma into de riber. Jes' shove her out he' to me. I takes her ober and you gets de horse."

"No. You ain't Thompson. And his ma's tied up. Don't want to drown her. And it's three horses."

"Done trade one. Thompson need de udder one. You gets one and de gun."

Milo rubbed his jaw as if weighing the offer, praying that Davant had the big Negro in his rifle sights. "All right. Call for Thompson to bring Mr. Smith's one horse. I want to see him leading a big bay into the river. Don't send either of Smith's two smaller horses. I want the big bay gelding. Only a stupid man would trade that one, and you ain't stupid are you? You or Thompson."

"No, we ain't no fools. We here, dealin' wit you, man to man, ain't we?"

"I reckon you are. Now bring the horse. Then I'll wave for Thompson's ma. But first, I'm going to drop the lariat on the bay and check the brand. Don't want to take back some other man's stolen horse and lose it back to him. You got that? I'm going to check the horse's brand first, then wave for Thompson's mammy. You don't trust me, well, you're holding Mr. Smith's shotgun. All I'm holding is a rope."

The tall Negro smiled as he said, "Dat's right." He waved his right arm without looking back. Milo noted the man still held the shotgun in the crook of his left arm. That should give Davant time enough if he had to shoot.

"Good. Now, when my partner gets here, you hand him Mr. Smith's shotgun, and then you can tote the woman to the Mexican side."

Milo looked up to see the young man he recognized as Thompson walking towards the riverbank leading a brown horse.

Thompson's eyes widened when he realized he knew the man on the horse standing in the river near Philip.

Thompson stopped at the edge of the water and called loudly, "I know you, Mr. McKean. You got my mama? Bring her out now."

Milo shrugged and waved his free arm. He forgot to insist again on the big bay horse. When Jesse had seen Milo mount Buck, he had slithered on the ground to where he could watch from under a bush. He was ready to shoot his old Springfield if the big darkie in the river put his other hand on the shotgun.

At Milo's wave, Jesse scrambled back to his horse, mounted, and grabbed the decoy. He quickly arranged it across his saddle in front of his lap, careful to tuck the oilcloth over the ends of the straw and twigs inside.

Thompson saw the second white man with the dark form carried in front of him. With relief, he led the brown horse into the water. At the same time, Milo put his heels to Buck's flanks, urging him towards Thompson and the horse the Negro was leading. Philip, still holding the shotgun with one arm, pushed his way through the thigh-deep water towards the second rider, who carried 'Thompson's mama.'

For a few long seconds, the horses and men splashed through the river. Milo bent forward as if to drop his lasso over the brown horse's head as Thompson released the lead rope. At the last instant, Milo shifted his aim and neatly dropped his lariat around Thompson instead.

At the same time, Philip saw that the oilcloth hid sticks and straw, not a woman. He raised the shotgun to shoot the man holding the decoy and jerked the trigger--without pulling back the hammer.

Dropping the stuffed oilcloth, Jesse heard Will Davant's rifle fire and saw the tall Negro jerk and howl in pain. Without thought, Jesse spurred his horse hard, pushing deeper into the river.

Milo yanked his reins to turn Buck around in the swift-flowing current. Thompson fell as he thrashed in the water, frantically trying to pull the rope from around his chest before it tightened.

Will Davant calmly and quickly reloaded his rifle and put the stock to his shoulder, ready to fire again in less than eight seconds. He aligned the rifle sights on the tall dark Negro, who still held the shotgun with one hand, but bled from his side.

Davant waited until the Negro grasped the shotgun with both hands and pointed it again at Jesse. The army lieutenant squeezed the Sharps' trigger. This time the bullet ripped a deep gouge in Philip's left arm below the shoulder. The shotgun fell unfired into the river as Philip stumbled to his knees, nearly neck-deep in the current.

Jesse angled downstream to cut off the brown horse. He missed catching it, but succeeded in grabbing the six-foot long lead rope as it floated past, trailing behind the frightened animal.

The lasso tightened around Thompson's chest an instant before he was jerked painfully to one side. Milo pulled the young man through the water all the way to the river bank on the Texas side. Thompson, unable to keep on his feet, held his breath and tried to twist so his back and bottom took the punishment from the river rocks, not his knees and front.

Jesse crouched low in his saddle as his gelding swam toward the Mexican side of the river. The brown horse, now pulled by the lead rope Jesse held, thrashed frantically a few feet behind until they both reached the shallow water.

Davant stood and yelled as loudly as he could. "There's another horse on your side." He pointed up the worn trail. Still mounted, Jesse drew his revolver, and leading the brown horse, he trotted up the path. Just around the first bend he found a tall bay horse with an *S* brand on its rump.

"Come along, big fella. It's back to Texas for you," Jesse said as he pulled its lead rope loose.

Philip, hurting badly in his arm and ribs, feared being shot again, so he slipped under the muddy water. He held his breath as long as he could, letting the river take him downstream. He couldn't swim, but he was desperate not to be taken back into bondage.

Philip finally surfaced in water too deep to stand, but he was able to flail one arm and kick enough to make his way to a log protruding from the bank. He grabbed it with both arms and held tightly, hoping the white men couldn't see him.

Chapter 20

Rock Ford across the Rio Grande River
Two Miles North of Eagle Pass, Texas
Mid-October 1854

Will Davant looked at his companions. "I'm the only one who ain't wet, so I guess I'll slop around for the shotgun." He shucked his boots, trousers, and shirt and plunged into the river. He waded into the waist-deep water where he thought the dark Negro had been standing when he'd shot him. After several minutes of searching, Davant felt the smooth barrel and pulled up the weapon.

"Found it. That's two horses, one shotgun, and one escaped slave," Davant called triumphantly to the others.

"What about the other man? The one who about ripped me apart with buckshot. Where'd he go?" Jesse pulled the iron shackles from his saddlebag and approached Thompson, who lay on the sand coughing.

"Will, you hit him, didn't you? Maybe he bled out. Maybe he drowned downriver." When Jesse locked the shackles onto Thompson's wrists, the Negro looked up at the young white man.

"You better hope he drowned. If he's still alive, he'll come for you all. Kill you in your beds."

Will Davant laughed. "Boy, he didn't even know how to fire a shotgun."

"Maybe so. But, he knows plenty about long sharp knives in the dark."

Milo, still in his saddle, keeping one eye on the other side of the river. grimaced at Thompson's warning. "That was easier than I ever thought it'd be. We're half done. We got the runaway, now we just need to find the girl."

"No runaway girls in our camp," the black man on the ground said.

Jesse pulled Thompson upright and slipped the wet rope down to his feet so he could step out of the loop. "Not a nigra girl. A yella-haired German girl. Apaches took her."

Thompson jerked his head up. "You trade her for me?"

All three white men glared at Thompson as Davant said, "You niggers holding that poor girl in your camp?'"

"No. But a 'pache come in and wanted to trade a yellow hair woman—not a little girl—for my—for Mistah Smith's--horses."

Jesse snorted. "And you turned him down, did you? One white woman not worth a couple of horses?"

"Not worth three horses. He wanted all three for her. And what I want with a white woman?"

Milo dismounted and walked close to the Negro who stood dripping wet, but head held high. "Thompson, you said trade you for her. And you said an Apache came to your camp wanting to horse trade for her. That means the Apaches know where the slave settlement is, but that don't mean you know where the Indian camp is. So how do you know where the Apache camp is? Where they have this girl?"

"You going to beat me or burn me to tell you?"

"No, we ain't. We're not like that. How do you know where the Apaches have the girl?"

"Because after I turned down the white girl for all three horses, they said they'd trade one horse for a little Negro girl. Me an' Philip went with 'em to their camp."

Jesse asked, "Did you trade a nag for the nigra girl?"

"Yes, I did. Carried her in front of me all the way back to Eureka. But she'd been starved and beat up so bad, she passed on a few days later."

"She died?" Milo asked.

"That's what I said. If I take you to the Apache camp, you turn me loose on my horse with my shotgun?"

Milo coiled his lariat while he considered Thompson's offer. "No, I can't do that. You, and the horses, and the shotgun, belong to Mr. Smith, who hired us to bring you back."

"Then why you care 'bout some white girl? You got what you come for." Thompson spat in the sand.

Davant spoke while he pulled on his boots. "Her pa paid them to find her. Just like Mr. Smith paid them to find you. Boy, you are just a runaway nigger. Smith's horses are worth more than your hide. That white woman is a captive of some bad Injuns, and she's worth a hundred field niggers and a herd of horses."

"I ain't a field hand. An' if she worth so much, like I done said, trade me for her. I'll take you to their camp."

Davant looked at Milo, and tilted his head towards Thompson and raised one eyebrow in question.

Jesse walked over to his friend and whispered, "Milo, if we get the girl, if the camp is where he says, we still wouldn't have to let him go, you know that."

"Yes, we would, Jesse."

"Milo, he's a slave. And we lied to him about his mama, didn't we?"

"I know we lied, and I'm already fretting about that. Anyways, this feels different. Remember how I said the letter was like corn on the ground to lure a deer out into the open? Well, the letter was bait, like the corn. Your straw dummy was a decoy. Kind of lies, I reckon, but fair lies. But this would be a fair bargain. It'd be our word, and we're not slaves. Our word matters."

Milo suddenly decided. He looked Thompson in the eye. "Deal. But just for you. We take both horses and the shotgun back to Mr. Smith. We let you loose on foot. That's *IF* we get the white woman."

Thompson didn't answer, but walked to Milo and held out his hands in the shackles.

"Nope, the chain stays on," Milo said.

"Didn't think no different. I wants a handshake on the deal. Man to man." Thompson said. Jesse snorted. Milo hesitated a second, then reached down and shook Thompson's right hand.

Milo looked over at Will Davant. "You heard me, too, Will. You still with us?"

The army lieutenant nodded. "I suspicion that you are going to need my Sharps rifle again. And I got another day and a half before I take over my troop. We're wasting daylight sitting here. Let's get going."

Milo answered, "First thing, we've got to ride back to Eagle Pass and fetch a few bottles or a cask of whiskey if we're going to buy the girl with spirits."

This time, Thompson snorted. Milo looked hard at him and asked, "What do you know about the Apaches and that girl that we don't?"

"Nothin'. Just seems you white mens all keen on buyin' other peoples."

Chapter 21

Near Eagle Pass, Texas
Mid-October 1854

Thompson rode without effort, his shackled hands holding a fistful of his mount's long black mane. His long ride from Cibolo Creek to the Rio Grande River had provided enough hours astride a horse to learn how to stay mounted without a saddle. His horse was being led by one of the white men, so without needing to do anything else, Thompson thought about what he'd just promised to do in exchange for his freedom.

If I ride into the Apaches' camp with these white men, I'll get an arrow in my chest. We won't even get close 'fore we're shot. And if we do get into their camp, how we going to talk to the Apaches? I don't go back to Eureka unless'n that yellow-haired woman leaves with the white men.

A change in the easy rhythm of the horses' gait jerked Thompson away from his worries about the next day. He gripped his horse's flanks more tightly, squeezing with his knees and feet, as the animals began to pick their way down a steep incline to the riverbank. Looking across the river, Thompson saw three Mexican men leading burros loaded with sticks. All three of the men wore tall straw *sombreros* that bobbed with each step.

"Mistuh McKean!"

"What, Thompson?"

"See them Meskins' tall hats?"

"Yeah, so what? They all wear them."

"That's right. You mens need a way to get into the 'paches camp without bein' shot."

"We'll hold up whiskey bottles. The injuns will see we're there to trade."

"But you still white."

"Ah, I see. You're saying we should wear *sombreros* to look like Mexicans."

"Yes, suh. And rub mud on your faces. And one mo' thing."

"What's that, Thompson?" Milo asked, irritated at being questioned by a slave.

"How you goin' to talk to the 'paches? How you going to ask for the white woman? You speaks Injin?"

"No, no, I don't. I figured the Apaches would understand enough American to talk to us. You speak Injun?"

"No, suh."

"Well, that there is something to think about, sure enough."

"Yes, suh."

★

The three white men sat in O'Kelly's Saloon around the same dirty table as when they'd composed the letter supposedly from Benjamin Smith to Thompson. The recaptured slave himself sat on the floor in a corner near the table, wrists still chained.

Milo idly rolled an empty glass on the table between his hands. "I'm thinking the darkie is onto something that'll help. The *sombreros* and mud, I mean,"

"Yep, that's a good idea." Will nodded.

"We all three going into the camp?" Jesse asked. "Will done good with his Sharps back at the river. I wouldn't mind havin' him up on a hill watching over us again tomorrow."

Milo and Will Davant both nodded in agreement. Milo turned to Thompson.

"How many Apache men you reckon will be in this camp tomorrow?"

"Don't know. Maybe..." Thompson held up his left hand, all five fingers spread apart. "Five, or maybe..." rattling the links of his shackles, he held up his right hand, too, displaying all ten of his digits. "More than you and you, for sure," He nodded towards Jesse and Milo.

Jesse had been leaning his chair back on two legs. He suddenly dropped the front legs to the floor and slapped the tabletop. "I got it. I know how to talk to them redskins. Will, you got more paper in that satchel you carry? I'll draw a picture of the girl and paint her hair yellow. As we ride in, Milo, you hold up

107

the whiskey bottles, and I'll hold up the drawing of the yellow-haired woman. They'll get it if they're thirsty."

"Now that's a good idea, Jesse. But where we going to find paint? Maybe the dry goods store, but I doubt it. Don't seem to be anything painted in this town."

"I have a jar of yellow sulfur paint."

All three men grinned.

Chapter 22

On the Trail Near the Border
State of Coahuila, Mexico
Mid-October 1854

The foursome rode out of Eagle Pass at first light, Jesse and Milo wearing straw *sombreros* and baggy white cotton shirts. Conveniently, the long loose shirttails hid the Colt revolvers stuck in the waists of their trousers. In a spirit of optimism, Milo rented a saddle from O'Kelly, so Caroline Hoffman would not have to ride bareback. Milo suspected, but hadn't voiced, that they may be hauling their freight back to Eagle Pass at a gallop, and a saddle for the woman would be critical.

After more discussion, Milo agreed with Thompson's request that he go with Will Davant, thereby remaining unseen by the Apaches. Thompson had pleaded that he would be living near the Lipans after his captors left, and if the whiskey trade fell through and they took the woman with gunfire, he'd be a target for the Apaches' revenge if he were seen with the white men.

After crossing the Rio Grande at the same ford where they'd clashed the day before, they scanned both sides of the river bank, looking for Philip's body, but no corpse was visible. Thompson kept the group on the rutted road until they reached a fork a few miles south of the river. He turned north and followed a faint trail through the scrub brush for another two hours before he stopped at a sharp bend where the path veered to the right, skirting a steep ridge.

Thompson dismounted and spoke with authority as he tied his horse in the shade of a stubby tree. "Me and Mistuh Davant leave our horses here. You wait here for a good spell while we walk along the top of that hill and find a place to hide and watch. Then you two follow the trail into camp. It's a ways and the trail twists. I'd hold up a whiskey bottle all the way, so's they'll see it right off. The 'paches will have a boy up on the ridge watching, and he'll run down ahead of you, before you goes around the last bend. So the 'pache mens be waiting, ready to trade."

"Or shoot," Jesse added.

Milo scowled at Jesse and asked, "How long we need to wait here, Will?"

Davant shrugged. "Better part of an hour, I'd say. We may be crawling a ways to stay hidden. But I need to be within a hundred yards to use the Sharps effectively."

"You mean to hit an Injun and not me or Milo," Jesse clarified.

"Yep, that's it." Davant dismounted with his Sharps rifle.

"All right." Milo pulled his Baker rifle from its scabbard and slid it into the empty leather sleeve attached to Davant's horse. "No need risking a fine rifle falling into the Injuns' hands. Jesse, you leave your rifle here too."

"Nah, Milo. Some Indian or Mexican might come along and steal the horses we leave here. You think about that? My rifle stays with me."

Milo squinted at Jesse, and after a few seconds, nodded.

"Will, you want to take my rifle as a back-up?"

"Nah, I'm taking the shotgun. Two loads of buckshot is more comfort if the redskins come after me."

"All right. Jesse and me will wait what I figure is an hour."

"The shackles?" Thompson asked, holding out his hands.

"Will?"

"Don't need the sound of the links clinking together. Let's take them off and retie his hands with rawhide. I don't trust him free-handed. Wish we could hobble his legs, too."

"Thompson, hold out your hands." Milo pulled out the heavy key while Jesse found a long piece of thin rawhide. "Boy, you do anything to give us away, Will's going to shoot you dead."

"Yes, suh, I knows that. But when you have the woman, I's leaving. I ain't goin' back the way we come in. Not on foot."

Milo unlocked the iron shackles and put them in his saddlebag. "You just better have brought us up the right canyon."

Fervently hoping he had guessed right and led them to the Apache camp, Thompson rubbed his wrists before Jesse wrapped the rawhide thong around them. Davant and Thompson immediately began climbing the face of the hill. The army officer carried the shotgun in his hand and wore the Sharps slung over his back, impeding his normal athleticism. The Negro moved even more awkwardly, reaching with tied hands to grab boulders to pull himself up the steep side of the ridge.

"Jesse, you carry the picture in your hand. Not rolled up, but open so they can see it right off. And I'll hold a bottle in plain sight all the way in."

Jesse unrolled the drawing and admired it. "I may have missed my calling. This here drawing of a yella-haired lady is fine enough to decorate a parlor."

"You mean an outhouse. Look at the bosoms you drew on her."

Jesse smiled sheepishly at Milo. "Well, I want the Injuns to see it's a woman we're after, not a blond-headed man."

Milo looked at the crudely sketched portrait. "The yellow sulfur paint stands out, sure enough. Almost glows. That was good thinking. Except for her bosoms."

The two sat in the shade cast by their horses and rubbed their faces and hands with mud made with canteen water. Their faces darkened, Milo finally grunted, "Let's go."

The trail twisted along in a gulley following a dry creek bed. The scrub brush made it too narrow for them to ride abreast, so Milo led, holding up one of the four bottles of whiskey they'd brought. Jesse's right hand gripped his revolver under his shirt as he scanned the tops of the ridges on either side.

After half an hour of slow riding, rounding a sharp bend, the trail ended at the edge of a wide dusty flat. Brush huts and smoking cooking fires dotted the area. Not a tree or a horse was in sight. Jesse swallowed his fear and let go of his pistol so he could hold the paper drawing over his head with both hands. He noted an Apache warrior to their right, squatting on his haunches, ten feet up the slope. The Indian held a short bow with an arrow notched, ready to shoot.

On the opposite side of them, Milo saw a brave who was standing, arms crossed, an old flintlock single-shot pistol stuck in his waist sash. In front of the two riders, three Apache men and four women stood watching them. Two of the women had graying hair and wore loose tunics. One held a dirty white cloth parasol over her head. The other two were young and clothed only in ragged skirts. One held a naked infant on her hip and clutched the hand of a toddler, who tried to hide behind her leg.

The night before, not fully trusting in Jesse's drawing, Milo had pestered O'Kelly for a few words in Spanish that might be understood.

"Senorita el pelo amarillo aqui?" He held up a bottle in each hand, the amber whiskey visible in the clear bottles. *"Comercio!"*

A short, broad-shouldered Apache man grunted and gestured for Milo to bring him the whiskey bottles.

Milo swung out of his saddle, saying softly, "Stay on your horse, Jesse. Keep showing the picture."

The Apache held out his hand for a bottle. Milo passed one over and let his arm drop so that his hand was next to his hidden Colt revolver.

The Apache uncorked the bottle, smelled it and took a deep gulp. He nodded and walked to stand in front of Jesse, looking up at the portrait with the sulfur yellow hair. He pointed at the drawing and grunted. He handed the bottle to one of the other men and looked at Milo before he held up both hands, showing all ten fingers.

Milo answered by saying, "Show me *senorita el pelo amarillo.*"

The Apache turned his head and spoke to the two older women. The one holding the parasol said something curt back at him, but after she collapsed the sunshade, they went into the largest brush hut and came out holding the arms of a nearly naked white woman.

She wore only a short breechcloth hanging from a twisted grass rope. The filthy cloth square rode under her protruding abdomen, and her breasts appeared distended. Both her arms and legs were mottled with dark yellowish bruises. Burn scabs were visible on her chest. One eyelid was puffy, swollen shut in the center of a purple bruise. Strikingly, the iris of her other eye was blue as a robin's egg, open wide in surprise and sudden hope. And her wild, tangled blonde hair reached below her shoulders.

Jesse gaped in horror at her. Suddenly ashamed by his crude drawing of the abused woman standing before him, he lowered the paper and stuffed it under the edge of his saddle.

Milo shared Jesse's revulsion at the condition of the woman, but found his voice and asked loudly. "Are you Caroline Hoffman? Caroline?"

When Milo took a step towards the white woman, one of the Apache women picked up a heavy stick and whacked the blonde woman on the leg. The captive flinched, but she nodded before she stood stock-still.

The Apache man held out both hands, again showing his ten fingers.

Milo recovered his wits enough to hold up three fingers. The Indian spat on the ground. Milo held up four fingers, and walked to his saddlebags for the last two bottles. He lined up the three bottles on the ground.

Unnoticed, the Indian brave with the old flintlock pistol gazed at the butt of Jesse's Springfield rifle in its scabbard. He spoke in a guttural language to the other Apache men.

The Apache leader then held up four fingers, pointing at the bottles, then he walked to Jesse's horse and tapped the rifle scabbard.

Milo and Jesse looked at each other, surprised and disturbed by the silent demand for the Springfield rifle. They both well understood that trading firearms with hostile Indians was as serious a crime as horse theft or rape. Sudden indecision was evident on Milo's face.

"PLEASE!" came the hoarse, desperate cry from Caroline Hoffman. At the call, the same Apache woman swung the stick again, hitting the captive hard just below her navel. Hoffman's knees gave way and the native women let her crumple to the ground, both her arms wrapped around her abdomen.

Jesse couldn't stop himself from reacting. "Yes, dammit. Here." He pulled the butt of the Springfield loose from the scabbard, only to feel an iron grip on his hand as the Apache leader held him with one hand and freed the rifle with the other. Immediately, the Indian jumped back and whooped, pumping the rifle in the air.

As soon as the Apache released Jesse's left hand, the Texan grabbed his reins and pulled his pistol free. He jerked back the hammer and from a distance of six feet, shot the Apache chief in the chest. Jesse saw his Springfield rifle fall to the ground, but had no time to retrieve it.

Jesse spurred his horse forward as Milo pulled his own Colt and fired at one of the other braves, missing him. From horseback, Jesse pointed his pistol at the Apache woman with the stick and shot her. He leapt off his horse, next to where Caroline Hoffman lay on the ground in a fetal position. Jesse fired again, missing the second older woman who was running towards the brush hut. The young Apache woman without the children grabbed the halter of Jesse's horse, screaming for help.

Milo jumped onto Buck and spun him around, firing and missing twice more at the two Apache warriors who were scrambling for weapons. An arrow whizzed by Milo's head and he looked up and saw the bow-armed Indian fall as he heard the crack of Will Davant's Sharps rifle.

Jesse used the barrel of his pistol to strike a vicious backhanded blow to the face of the dark-haired woman holding his horse. She fell, her cheek gashed and bleeding. Jesse grabbed his horse's lead rope. He bent over and pulled Caroline Hoffman upright, using both his arms to keep her leaning against his horse. He slid his hands down to cup under her bottom and lifted her up. She grabbed the saddle horn as he grabbed her right thigh and shoved hard, forcing her leg over the saddle.

Jesse Gunn vaulted himself onto his horse right behind the saddle. He leaned forward and found the reins as he kicked the animal's flanks.

Milo saw that Jesse had the girl, as he fired again at an Apache who was lifting a bow to let an arrow fly. Both Milo and the Indian missed. Then the Apache dropped, another victim of Will Davant's marksmanship with his Sharps. The Indian with the old horse pistol shot and missed as Milo rode by, hunched low over Buck's neck. Simultaneously, Milo pointed his Colt at the Apache and fired, not knowing if his bullet hit.

The two white men thundered out of the camp, never hearing the two successive explosions from Mr. Smith's shotgun, followed by the three rapid pistol shots from the hilltop.

Chapter 23

Near the Lipan Apache Village
South of the Rio Grande River
Mid-October 1854

W ill Davant lay resting on both elbows, his hands on the Sharps rifle. Wisps of smoke curled from the end of the rifle barrel and the sour gunpowder smell permeated the still air. He'd just fired a third shot, and nodded grimly when he saw another Indian fall.

Thompson lay a yard away to the white man's left, and the shotgun rested on Davant's other side. While Davant broke open the breech of his rifle to reload, he risked a quick glance sideways at the slave. The white man's eyes widened and he flinched as the Negro thumped down on him and slid across his back to grab the shotgun. Before the army officer could react, Thompson rolled sideways to distance himself beyond Davant's reach.

The white man reached down for his revolver, intending to shoot the turncoat Negro. Thompson shouted, "Behind you!"

Davant looked back over his shoulder to see two Apaches running towards them. Before the army lieutenant could unholster his pistol, Thompson sat up, reversed the long shotgun and rested the stock on the V made by his feet pressed together in front of him. With hands still tied, Thompson cocked one barrel, pointed it and fired. He missed.

The two charging Native Americans came on, knives raised. Thompson cocked and discharged the second barrel. The chest of the shorter, younger Indian, now just a few yards away, exploded into a mess of red pulp as he was punched backwards by the buckshot tearing through him.

Davant sat up and fired his revolver three times, his thumb pulling back the hammer with practiced speed. The second

Apache collapsed. The lieutenant stood, glanced at Thompson and nodded a thanks. He confirmed that both Apaches were lying still, then looked back down the steep ridge to see that Milo and Jesse were out of sight, hopefully pounding back down the dry creek bed.

He picked up his Sharps rifle and waved with his pistol for Thompson to come along. The slave held onto the shotgun and started trotting, angling away from Davant, not following him.

"Hold it, Thompson!" Davant called, cocking and pointing his revolver at the slave.

Thompson stopped, turned, and spoke clearly. "You kilt my friend in the river yesterday, but I just kilt one of them two Injins for you. Now you let me go like Mistuh McKean say."

"Dammit," Davant muttered, exasperated at being reminded by a Negro of a binding agreement. "All right, but give me the shotgun. It doesn't belong to you. It goes back to Mr. Smith."

"Nah, it do belong to me. It be back pay from Mistuh Smith for all them years of fetching and working for him for nothin'. I lost a horse, an' a good friend at the river, but I'm keepin' the shotgun."

William Davant was the son of a South Carolina plantation owner and graduate of the US Military Academy. He had held his own during many nights of heated debates with northern cadets about the merits of slavery. For all that, he was flummoxed by Thompson's resolute manner and honest logic.

After a few seconds that seemed longer to Davant's whirling mind, he simply said, "Here." He pulled a small leather pouch from his belt and tossed it to Thompson. He then stooped over and picked up the knife carried by the Apache he'd just shot. He flipped the sharp blade to land at Thompson's feet. "Cut your own wrists loose. There's powder, caps, and buckshot in the pouch. You may need it to stay alive. Git."

Without further comment, both men ran off in opposite directions.

Milo, Jesse, and the rescued woman reached Mr. Smith's and Will's tethered horses before the lieutenant could run the mile along the rim of the high ground. Davant finally saw the horses below, and slid down the steep side of the plateau, causing a small avalanche of loose dirt and rocks as he went.

Milo had slipped off Buck and accepted Caroline Hoffman in his arms just long enough to carry her a few steps and push her up into the saddle of Mr. Smith's horse. Milo tried without success not to gawk at her bare chest and hips. Jesse immediately pulled off his white cotton shirt and handed it up to the woman. She winced with the pain of raising her arms, but quickly slipped the shirt over her head, covering herself. She had yet to speak since her plea of *"Please"* had jolted the two men into violence.

Will Davant landed in a rush of pebbles around his feet. He wordlessly climbed into his saddle so the four could resume their flight back to Eagle Pass. For half an hour the three men and the injured woman pushed their horses as fast as the terrain would allow. Finally, Milo finally held up a hand for them to stop.

"I don't know if we're being tailed, or even if those Indians had horses we couldn't see. This here's a good spot for me to wait with my rifle and stop anyone following us. Jesse, you and Will take Miss Hoffman on as fast you can."

A low voice interrupted. "It's Mrs. Schmidt. My name is Schmidt. I'm a married woman." She suddenly sobbed and shook violently. "A widow."

Jesse pulled off his *sombrero*. "So you are, Ma'am. Here, put this shade over your head. Now, Mrs. Schmidt, let's you, me, and Will here, get going."

Davant blanched, seeing the young battered woman up close for the first time. "I'll hang back with Milo. His Baker won't knock down but one hostile, if he can hit one, that is. But my Sharps will take care of several."

"Thanks, Will." Mention of the Sharps rifle reminded Milo of Mr. Smith's shotgun—which he didn't see. "I reckon Thompson lit out—with the shotgun." Davant nodded, suddenly looking sheepish. Milo let it go and looked at the ridges surrounding them. "I think up there to our left, Will. We'll have a good view of our back trail."

Jesse Gunn and the widow Schmidt trotted away, side-by-side, the men not realizing that the pregnant young woman had begun to leak blood and fluid onto the seat of the saddle.

The two riflemen climbed the hill where they lay down to watch. After five minutes of silence, Davant spoke in a near-whisper. "The nigger saved my ass up there. Rolled over me, grabbed the shotgun and shot an Apache running up behind us. All with his hands tied. Damnedest thing I ever saw. So I let him take the gun." They both kept their eyes on the trail, Will embarrassed, and Milo glad his friend couldn't see his grin.

After another ten minutes of silence, the pair remounted and galloped down the trail. When they reached the rutted road south of the ford half an hour later, they found Jesse working to lash together slender branches from the scrub brush to make a crude travois. Mrs. Schmidt lay groaning on her side atop Jesse's blanket.

"Milo, she's bleeding from her woman parts. She can't ride no more. Says the bouncing hurts her insides worse than the beatings did. We got to get her to the doctor at Eagle Pass."

Will Davant dismounted and took his rifle up a small hill to watch back the way they'd come. Milo saw the small tree branches, the only material around them, weren't long enough or thick enough to make a functional travois.

"Jesse, we'll use Will's oilcloth again. We'll bunch the ends and tie them to our saddle horns and make a hammock. We'll carry the woman between our horses that way."

Jesse nodded and scrambled to retrieve Davant's painted canvas oilcloth from his saddle. It was a very small hammock, but they wedged the suffering woman in, her head forward against the top of the cloth, her calves and feet dangling out the back. The two horses seemed to sense their shared load and walked together, almost as a hitched team. Will Davant rode behind, leading the fourth horse, and turning repeatedly to watch for the dust of pursuers.

By the time they reached the rocky ford, the woman was unconscious and pink droplets were seeping through the stained oilcloth.

Chapter 24

Fort Duncan
Near Eagle Pass, Texas
Mid-October 1854

Lieutenant Davant galloped ahead, bypassing Eagle Pass and going directly to Fort Duncan. He found the surgeon, Captain Walter Doss, who quickly agreed to treat the rescued woman, even if she wasn't a member of a military family. From what the lieutenant told him, the doctor suspected the woman was in labor, so he sent for his wife who had some experience delivering babies. Both were waiting in the post infirmary when Milo and Jesse arrived with Mrs. Schmidt, who now lolled in the makeshift hammock in a puddle of her own blood and amniotic fluids.

When the two young civilian men laid the unconscious woman on the table, the doctor's wife grabbed her husband's arm and squeezed until he pried her clutching fingers away. He curtly dismissed everyone but his wife and cut away the bloody shirt, grass rope belt, and blood-caked breechcloth.

Before his wife could even start wiping the patient clean with warm soapy towels, the doctor put his stethoscope on Mrs. Schmidt's abdomen and listened for a heartbeat. He kept still, kept listening for at least a full minute. He heard no faint heartbeat. He felt no faint movement.

He raised his head and looked at his wife of eighteen years. "Abigail, the child is dead."

She wiped the patient's brow with a wet towel as the tears ran down her cheeks. "I know. And the mother hangs to life by a thread."

The doctor slowly examined the woman starting at her scalp beneath her filthy matted hair and her bruised and swollen right eye. He gently pried her mouth open, looking past her severely cracked lips, grateful to find no broken teeth or open sores inside. He let his fingers probe her arms and legs beneath the worst of the purple-yellow bruises, feeling for broken bones. The patient flinched at the pressure of his touch over her bruises. He held a magnifying glass above each burn circle that dotted her chest, and asked his wife to sniff each one, seeking signs of infection.

"Walter, I need to examine her private area to learn if we might extract the fetus. Will you hand me the forceps and hold the lantern behind my head so I might see her birthing canal?"

"Of course." The physician pulled out his handkerchief and wiped the cold sweat from his face.

After a short examination, Mrs. Doss stood up straight and told her husband, "She's bruised and bleeding internally as far as I can see. The degree of abuse is beyond belief. Reaching in further with my hand or forceps might burst more arteries. She may well bleed to death if I do that. I'm sorry, Walter."

"Abigail, we can't let the baby remain inside the poor woman. She'd die of infection from the oncoming decay of the fetus. I have to cut it out. I'll need help. Are you up to it, or should I call a soldier?"

"Walter Doss, you just tell me what to do. I'm not leaving this table." A tiny smile crept into the corners of the physician's mouth as he looked in the eyes of his resolute and beloved wife.

"I will make a transverse incision, here," He ran his finger across Mrs. Schmidt's distended abdomen just above her pubic bone.

"But, Walter, she's half conscious, delirious. Won't the pain of your scalpel fully awaken her? She's suffered enough."

"I'll use ether first. Put her into a deep sleep."

"Is that safe, my dear? Is she strong enough?"

Doctor Doss somberly studied his patient. "Abby, she's survived months of inhuman cruelty. As battered and broken as she looks, I think she's strong enough. Regardless, I must use the ether."

"God's will be done," Abigail prayed. She watched her husband insert a rubber tube into one of the girl's nostrils and wait while potent gas ran through the tube from a covered bucket into which he'd poured a small amount of liquid ether.

The patient now fully unconscious, Doctor Doss made the long incision. Mrs. Doss held the cut open and sopped blood with towels. The physician whispered his own silent prayer, reached in with both hands, and pulled the fetus out, trying not to flinch at the sounds of ripping tissue. Mrs. Doss snipped the umbilical cord so he could gently set the bloody whitish bag in a pan on the floor. He then held together torn and severed tissue where it seemed needed, as his wife sewed tight stitches with dark thread and a curved needle. Both husband and wife barely breathed during the operation.

When they were done, Dr. Doss stretched a large bandage across the sewn together incision. The doctor's wife, a stickler for cleanliness, glared with disgust at the thick layer of dirt that covered the young woman. She blinked back a tear as she realized that the patient appeared no older than her own first child, long dead, would now be. *Do those heathens never bathe in the river?* Using clean towels, Mrs. Doss gently washed Caroline Schmidt from her matted blonde hair to the grimy, calloused soles of her feet. Finally, after her white towels and wash pan of water turned brown, Mrs. Doss pulled a sheet up to the patient's neck. With a satisfied sigh, the doctor's wife gently patted the girl's shoulder. *There, I have washed away the Apache filth. You're a white woman again—oh, that it could really be so easy.*

Doctor Doss went to the door and ordered a sergeant to have an infant's grave dug immediately. Before he wrapped the fetus in a sheet and placed it in an empty artillery shell box, he parted the embryotic sack enough to see matted ebony colored hair covering the top of the tiny skull cap. When he returned to Abigail and their unconscious, but breathing patient, he remarked to his wife, "You may tell her when she awakes that her daughter had blonde hair."

Abigail looked him in the eye. "Blonde, you say? A little girl?"

Walter nodded. "I've ordered a grave dug immediately. You and I shall offer prayers to the stillborn Schmidt girl who now is sealed in her casket. That will be sufficient," the captain said, his military demeanor creeping into his voice, cutting off further discussion.

"Yes, Walter. I understand."

Chapter 25

Near the Town of Piedras Negras
State of Coahuila, Mexico
Mid-October 1854

Juanita Garcia enjoyed her daily trips to the riverbank. During most of the year, when the river was sluggish and stayed within its normal banks, she rolled up her long skirt and walked through the mud, enjoying the cool silt squishing between her toes and over her feet. On those days, the young woman would meander up and down the river gathering sticks for the cook fire. After tying them into a bundle that would balance on her head, she'd put on the crude wooden yoke from which two large ceramic water jars hung in rope webs.

Rolling up her full skirt even further and tucking it into the strip of rawhide that served as her belt, Juanita would wade into the river until the water reached her thighs. She would squat and tilt the jars until they were full of the cleanest water the river had to offer. Finally, on most days she would clear her bowels and let the water current wash her clean before leaving the river. She would settle the bundle of sticks on her head for the long uphill walk back to the small brush and mud hut where she and her younger brother and sister slept and cooked.

Juanita was not a weak woman. Her shoulders showed a pronounced ridge of muscle from carrying the full water jars nearly a mile for over six hundred consecutive days. The daily water collection began the day after their mother died, the morning walk to the river having been her parent's duty, a chore on which Juanita and her sister Theresa usually accompanied her. Their father went away the same night he'd buried the children's mother in a shallow grave, and he had not returned.

Juanita had immediately taken charge of the tiny family, assigning her brother the job of goat herder and putting her small sister in charge of tending the corn and bean patch that grew near the hut. Every day, the contents of one jug went to the crops, the valuable water carefully dipped and poured at the base of each individual plant at dusk.

If asked, Juanita could not have said how many years she had lived. In fact, she was barely sixteen and in full bloom of youthful womanhood. At two inches over five feet tall, even with rough hands and wide flat feet, her legs were firm and shapely. Her short waist was without fat, her bosom full and inviting. Ebony hair framed Indio facial features that were broad, brown, and unblemished. Her dark hair shined because she washed it in the river and at night stroked the long strands with the gummy sap from aloe vera leaves.

On this October day, the river was flooding. The current strong. Juanita reluctantly waded forward until she stood in calf-deep water, already having to brace her feet against the swift current. She knelt in the cold muddy water, holding the jars below the surface, looking downstream as she felt the yoke grow steadily heavier.

While the young woman idly wondered if the sameness of her days would go on forever, she heard an unexpected voice. The words were gibberish to her, but she had no trouble recognizing his panic. She looked back over her shoulder, upriver, searching for the man belonging to the voice. What she saw in the one-second glimpse alarmed and amused her simultaneously.

A tree trunk awash in the flooded river had drifted into a protruding boulder and stuck, the long piece of driftwood now bobbing, but no longer moving downstream in the current. At one end of the trunk a very black man clung tenuously to the stub of a broken limb, just his head, shoulder, and one arm above water. At the other end of the log, a thick black snake lay coiled, opening and closing its jaws, exposing a pearly white mouth and fangs. The man's eyes were huge and pleaded to the woman he'd just seen for help.

Juanita stood and quickly left the river. She set down the jars and yoke and grabbed up the biggest driftwood branch on the bank. She walked upstream and waded back into the water until it reached her knees. She extended one end of the branch out to the man who had stopped shouting, but still shifted his gaze back and forth from snake to rescuer.

Juanita saw that the black man could not use the arm that was underwater and seemed afraid to let go of the branch stub he gripped with his other hand. She too warily eyed the thick black snake, recognizing the moccasin as the poisonous type that often swam in the river and was best left alone.

She hesitated, fearful of going further into the current and fearful of the snake leaving its perch and swimming towards her. The man suddenly seemed to understand her concern, for he nodded to her and grunting in pain, he released the branch and swung his arm out, reaching for the end of the driftwood limb she held. He found a grip in the small branches at its end and left the safety of the buoyant tree trunk.

As soon as the floating wood was free of his weight, three things happened at the same time. The power of the current dislodged the tree trunk, again shoving it downstream. The moccasin slid into the water and began swimming towards the man and woman, who held opposite ends of the limb. In a sudden panic, Juanita began to back out of the river as fast as she could, pulling the man who clung to the small branches five feet behind her.

The snake won the race. It slithered onto the limb, wrapped itself around a finger-sized branch and turned toward the black man. Juanita looked back, to see the moccasin between them on the limb. She let go and picked up a three-foot long stick as she waded back into the water. She threatened the thick snake with the extended stick while she tried to edge past and reach out her other arm to the injured black man.

Now in waist-deep water, he let go of the limb and found the girl's fingers with his. The limb began to drift downstream, and again, the moccasin abandoned its perch and slipped into the river, disappearing under the muddy water.

Juanita dropped her stick and pulled the man's arm with both of hers, backing up to the shore. She had dragged his torso onto the bank when she stumbled. As she regained her feet, the man grunted and jerked before he pulled his legs up, both man and woman seeing the moccasin hanging onto the man's dark flesh, fangs embedded just above his bare ankle. She tightened her grip on his arm and yanked backwards with all her strength.

The Negro man slid further onto the bank as the snake let go and quickly disappeared under the water.

The man sat up and tried to bend forward to grab at his snake-bit ankle. Juanita saw the bullet wounds in his upper arm and side. She gently pushed his chest to force him to lie on his back. When he complied, she wrapped her leather belt twice around the Negro's calf and tightly tied it. With the small knife she always carried, she cut an 'X' over the bite marks and pushed down on the skin around the bite, hoping to push out some of the snake's poison. She did all this just as she'd watched her mother do when a large rattlesnake had bitten her older brother on the arm while the whole family was harvesting cotton. Even though her brother had died, her mother explained that the heart had to be protected from the blood infected by the snake's poison.

She looked at the man's other two wounds, but she didn't try to bandage them. She left the man lying on the sand to stash her yoke and water jugs under a bush and cut a few green branches to better hide her precious belongings.

With some difficulty, she pulled the Negro to his feet and draped him across her shoulders. The long uphill walk that normally took less than an hour, took two hours. Twice she had to kneel and let the man slip off her shoulders so she could rest. By late afternoon she knelt with her burden a last time, just outside her hut.

The Garcia children lived in sight of several other dwellings scattered across the wide plain on the outskirts of Piedras Negras. Two women grinding corn and an old man weaving a grass rope had watched Juanita carry the Negro like a young goat across her shoulders, but no one ventured forward to assist or ask questions. They would all know soon enough.

By morning the man's lower leg and foot were grossly swollen. Juanita had taken off the leather band before she slept and didn't know what else she could do. His bullet wounds had stopped bleeding, so she didn't bandage them. Later in the morning, Juanita was visited by Isabelle Santos, one of the old women who'd seen her carrying the Negro. She looked at the man, left, and returned with a handful of shredded willow tree fiber. Gesturing for the groaning half-delirious man to chew it, Isabelle told Juanita that it should lessen his pain. She also probed at both his bullet wounds, causing him to flinch, then pass out at the sudden pain of her touch. Isabelle found that the bullets had passed through arm and waist, having missed his arm bone and ribs. She told Juanita that his enemy was a poor shot as she brought out a small horn container and used her little finger to spread a smelly goo on the entry and exit holes.

At dawn on the third day, the man was more lucid. While Juanita spooned a goat and corn stew into his eager mouth, he repeated the word *Thompson* several times. When Juanita pointed at him and asked, "Thompson?" he shook his head. He pointed at himself, uttering, "Philip. You must get Thompson." The exchange meant nothing to her, except maybe the man's name must be Philip.

That morning, Juanita made her daily trip to the river, grateful that the day before she'd found her yoke and jars unmolested. As she filled her water jugs, she saw another Negro man walking down the riverbank towards her. He was shorter and lighter in color than Philip, and the sight of the long gun he carried frightened her.

He stopped when he saw her and called, "I'm looking for a man, a tall black man."

She shook her head and shrugged as best she could under the weight of the yoke.

Seeing that the young woman didn't understand, he called, "Negro," and held his hand above his own head. "His name is Philip. He's shot." The man shook the gun. "And in the river." He pointed at the water.

Juanita thought perhaps he meant a tall black man named Philip and something about the river. She didn't know why he'd shaken the gun. She nodded and called back, "Philip, *aqui*," pointing at the water. Then she remembered the other word.

"Thompson?"

"Yes, yes." He jabbed himself in the chest with his finger, grinning broadly, "I'm Thompson. *Dondé* Philip?"

Chapter 26

O'Kelly's Saloon
Eagle Pass, Texas
Mid-October 1854

Jesse Gunn refused to leave the porch of the infirmary at Fort Duncan. He slept the night leaning against the wall, his long legs stretched out in front of him. At dawn he began pacing the length of the porch, continuing until Mrs. Doss let him inside. She made a quick visit to Mrs. Schmidt's cot and confirmed the patient was sleeping. Standing next to Jesse in the doorway, she allowed the young man to look briefly at the sleeping woman. Then the doctor's wife shooed him out, promising she'd let him know when Mrs. Schmidt awoke.

Exhausted, Milo had returned to Eagle Pass and slept fitfully in the stuffy mattress room in O'Kelly's Saloon. The next morning, he bought two envelopes and paper and wrote two copies of the same letter, informing his and Jesse's employers of the outcome of their efforts to recover the slave Thompson and the captive Caroline Hoffman Schmidt.

October 21, 1854

To Misters Luther Hoffman of New Braunfels and Benjamin Smith of Austin City,

We (Jesse Gunn and myself) are now in Eagle Pass after riding across the Rio Grande River to meet the terms of our contract to recover Mr. Smith's fugitive slave and stolen property and Mr. Hoffman's taken daughter.

I am most gratified to write that we returned to Texas ground with two of Mr. Smith's stolen horses—the big bay and a smaller sorrel—and also with Caroline Hoffman Schmidt. Mrs. Schmidt is in the infirmary at Fort Duncan under the care of Dr. Walther Doss and his wife, now recovering from her mistreatment by the hostiles. I do not know her condition as I write, so I cannot say if her recovery will be complete or partial, but it appears she will live. When she is able to travel, we will bring her to New Braunfels, and then deliver the two horses to Austin City.

To Mr. Smith, I regret that we were not successful in locating your slave Thompson. We acquired the two horses with your brand from a Mexican in the town of Piedras Negras who claims to have bought them from a Negro. Since the horses carry your brand and the Mexican had no bill of sale, we relieved him of the animals to return them to you. He said the Negro rode another horse with the same brand. I regret we were unable to locate your man even after undertaking several dangerous journeys into the Mexican hills in search of the darkie.

To Mr. Hoffman, with information acquired in Eagle Pass we were able to locate a Lipan Apache camp and succeeded in trading ten bottles of whiskey for your daughter. You will need to pay us an additional $10 for the ten bottles of spirits and $5 we paid for the information about the location of the Apache camp. With the return of your precious daughter, I am convinced that you will accept that small added cost to your contract.

Regrettably, Mr. Gunn's Springfield rifle was lost in a shoot-out with the hostiles following the exchange for Mrs. Schmidt. This is a difficulty because myself and Mr. Gunn are to soon enlist in

Captain Boggess's Mounted Volunteer Ranging Company in San Antonio, and Mr. Gunn will be in need of a long-reaching weapon. With that requirement in mind, we are willing to accept a replacement rifle from your stock, instead of specie for the ten bottles of spirits and the information fee.

As to the gunfight with the Apaches I can confirm that at least six Lipans were shot to death by our party when the extent of the abuse to your daughter became known.

I will send another letter to Mr. Hoffman when we are told that Mrs. Schmidt is able to travel again. I hope we will remain in Eagle Pass no more than a week, but I am no doctor.

Your obedient Servant,

Milo McKean

Milo addressed and sealed the envelopes before he took them to the general store where the post rider left and picked up mail. He then returned to tell Mr. O'Kelly more about their adventures across the river. The saloon keeper listened politely and probed for details in regards to the value the Apaches placed on a bottle of whiskey. Yet, he never asked the whereabouts of Thompson, the captured slave. Satisfied that he'd met his immediate obligation to their employers and that he'd been reasonably forthcoming with his new friend O'Kelly, Milo returned to Fort Duncan to wait with Jesse.

As he rode to the fort, the young man from Alabama suffered no pangs of guilt that he'd omitted any mention in his letter, or during his conversation with the saloon keeper, of their capturing Thompson at the river, and his own subsequent agreement to free Thompson for guiding them to the Lipan camp. Rather, Milo was somewhat smug about the omission of Thompson, especially in the letter. *I'm preventing a likely feud between our employers over a conflict of interest, that's what I'm doing. After all, Mr. Smith is getting back two healthy horses, while Mr. Hoffman's poor daughter is damaged goods. Neither man will be fully pleased with the outcome of our contract, but neither is being left empty-handed. It could've gone a lot worse.*

Chapter 27

Fort Duncan, Texas
On the Rio Grande River
Late October 1854

Caroline Hoffman Schmidt opened her eyes twenty-four hours after her surgery. She immediately put her hands on her abdomen to feel the sutures. Although she was alone, she called out asking about her baby, prompting the doctor's wife to drop her knitting and hurry into the room. Holding Caroline's hands in her own, Abigail Doss told Mrs. Schmidt that her beautiful blonde baby girl had been stillborn and was already buried. They cried together until the doctor's wife left to warm a pot of soup.

Jesse Gunn came to the door while the grieving mother was still sobbing softly. After a moment, when Jesse's boots scuffed the floor when he shifted his weight, she noticed him and quickly wiped her tears with the back of her hand.

"I know you. You shot the chief's wife and threw me on your horse. You brought me here." The woman blinked away more tears. "*Danke schön.* Thank you."

Embarrassed, Jesse bobbed his head up and down before he retreated to sit on the porch of the building.

★

The next morning, Caroline Schmidt asked Mrs. Doss, "May I have a book?"

"A Bible?"

"Yes. A Bible would be good. So would a novel or poetry, any book. I want words to read. I want to hold a book. I want to turn pages. I can do that lying on my back." For the next three days,

Mrs. Schmidt would read for a few minutes, then fall back to sleep, repeating the process time after time.

Doctor Doss insisted that Mrs. Schmidt remain in the infirmary for a week. On the fourth day, he allowed her to walk around the room, supported by him or Mrs. Doss. On the fifth day, the recovering patient took Jesse Gunn's elbow so he could escort her to the covered front porch, where they sat together through a thunderstorm. It was cool, and Mrs. Schmidt kept a wool shawl, loaned by Mrs. Doss, wrapped snugly around her shoulders. She wore thick knitted wool socks under her borrowed dress. Her long hair had been washed and combed, parted in the middle, and pulled into a tight bun that rested on the nape of her neck.

Jesse desperately wanted to start a conversation, but was wholly at a loss of how to do that. Finally, he awkwardly said, "I imagine sittin' out a storm like this in a brush hut ain't such a pleasant experience."

"It dripped." The woman spoke in a low monotone, not looking at Jesse. "I'd move around, and set clay pots to catch the water. But the others just ignored the drips." She watched the heavy rain splashing on the muddy parade ground in front of them.

After a few minutes, she went on. "Mr. Gunn, the Indians are different that way...different in many ways. Drinking cool rain water seemed no better to them than lapping up a puddle of mud, like those puddles out there." She grew silent, pensive, again. Jesse figured it was a good time to wait without speaking.

"Personal comfort is not important. Their lives are without...niceties. Every day is harsh. Perhaps that is why they are so savage."

Still not knowing what to say, Jesse asked if he could get her a cup of coffee.

"Oh my, yes. Coffee. Coffee would be...*sehr gut*."

When Jesse returned with two steaming tin cups, she deeply inhaled the fragrant aroma. "They can't boil water. The Indians have no metal pots. When they trade with the Mexicans, it's for whiskey or guns, so even if they had coffee beans, they wouldn't be able to boil them."

Jesse shook his head. "Glory be. No pots. No coffee. No boiled spuds."

She snorted. "No potatoes at all, just roots baked in the ashes, gnawed like dogs with a bone." Caroline Schmidt then asked, "Are you going back with me to New Braunfels?"

Jesse spilled coffee down his front before he could reply. "Yes ma'am. Me and Milo are going with you all the way."

She took a first sip of the coffee, seemingly immune to the burning hot rim of the tin cup. "Mr. Gunn, when we leave here, if the Indians...if the Indians come, do not let them take me again. Do you understand? Shoot me if you must. Will you promise that?"

Jesse sat through a flash of jagged lightning and roll of thunder before he replied. "Mrs. Schmidt, I'll shoot every Apache in Texas, and take arrows meant for you until I die. But, no ma'am, I couldn't put a bullet your way."

Caroline Schmidt turned her head and looked at the slim man with the pocked face and unruly dark hair. She reached out and gently touched his acne-scarred cheek. "You were there. You saw. But you just don't know."

★

Milo fretted over how to transport Mrs. Schmidt until Will Davant solved his problem by purchasing a small wagon.

"Sell it and send me the money when you're done," was all that Will said when he'd peeled off the bills to pay the wagon dealer. Milo thanked him as he reflected how helpful it was to have wealthy friends.

Mrs. Doss appropriated an army mattress to arrange in the bed of the wagon. Two later, Mrs. Schmidt and her two escorts joined a small group of wagons going to San Antonio.

On the day before their planned departure, the rescued captive prevailed on Jesse to borrow money from Lieutenant Davant in her father's name and purchase a small two-shot pocket pistol for her to carry as a last resort.

Lieutenant Davant's first patrol was to lead the cavalry escort north as far as the Nueces River, allowing he and Milo to spend more hours in the saddle talking. Jesse drove the wagon, pulled by Benjamin Smith's two horses. On the second day out, Mrs. Schmidt abandoned the mattress in the wagon bed and joined Jesse on the driver's bench seat.

"My stomach hurts as much when I'm lying down as it does when I'm sitting up."

Most of that day she said very little, instead reading a thick book given to her by Mrs. Doss. It was a novel by the popular British writer Charles Dickens.

Late in the morning on the third day on the road, Caroline Schmidt closed her book and broke their morning silence by asking, "The day you rescued me, was I horrible to behold, covered in bruises and filth?"

Shocked, Jesse shook his head. "No, ma'am."

"That's very kind, Mr. Gunn, and I'm younger than you, I'm no *ma'am* to you."

"Yes, ma'am."

She smiled, and in an instant of impulsive sauciness asked, "Had you never seen a woman without her clothes before?"

Jesse swallowed. "Certainly not." Then, with what he hoped sounded as humor, "Unless you count me and my sisters bathing in the creek when we were little 'uns."

Caroline Schmidt replied without any trace of mirth, "No more outdoor bathing for me. Not ever." Jesse stared ahead, his eyes locked on the wagon in front of them.

After a long moment, Caroline added in a halting voice while looking away from Jesse. "I'm sorry your first glimpse of...Eve, was during such a dramatic moment, and I regret that I--she-- appeared no better than an aborigine."

Flustered, Jesse tried to assure her otherwise, but only a garbled stutter came out.

Throughout the rest of the long slow days on the road to San Antonio, Caroline Schmidt's demeanor remained unpredictable. She would read, then close the book and talk of her childhood, of her parents, of her family. Jesse could hear a wistfulness in her voice during those times. Then she would lapse into long quiet spells.

She would only rarely mention her captivity, and never so candidly as she had spoken to Jesse when they'd sat through the thunderstorm on the infirmary porch. She did not speak of her dead husband. Jesse took her behavior in stride, assuming she was trying to push the bad memories deep down, lock them away, and resurrect whatever pleasant memories she could.

★

Jesse guided the wagon, following Milo's horse, until they reached the livery stable across the street from Mr. Menger's boarding house. Milo planned to stay two nights, allowing Mrs. Schmidt to rest before they finished the journey to New Braunfels. Jesse thought she was healing, both physically and emotionally. Yet, he also detected what he figured was a growing apprehension that her parents and family would not welcome her home. Jesse correctly thought she feared that her debasing captivity had forever tainted her. The idea she may be right made him grind his teeth in anger.

At the dining room table, Milo and Jesse ate with six other travelers, leaving Caroline Schmidt in her room, at her request. She did not want to explain, or listen to her escorts explain why the three were traveling together. She did not want to see the looks of pity on the faces of strangers when they learned she'd been taken by the Apaches. She didn't want to listen to any bombastic rhetoric about stamping out the Indian threat.

Irene knocked gently on the door, after she set the supper tray on a hall table. She heard a soft, "Come in," before she opened the door to see a thin, blonde white woman sitting in a chair by the window, reading. Irene put the food tray on the table next to the woman, and said, "It be good beef stew. I be back fo' de empty plate."

The woman looked at Irene and nodded her thanks. Then she surprised the Negro cook by asking, "Are you a slave?"

"Yes 'm."

"Until just two weeks ago, I was a slave. For months. Taken by the Apaches. Tell me, do children throw rocks at you for sport? Irene shook her head.

"Do the women beat you with clubs?" Irene shook her head more vigorously.

"Do the men...do the men just take you whenever they want?"

"No, ma'am."

"No? How fortunate for you that you are a servant, not a slave. I hope you are grateful for your blessings."

"Yes, ma'am. I is." Irene left the white woman staring out the window.

★

During Caroline Schmidt's day of rest, Milo and Jesse went in search of Giles Boggess, finding him at his home.

"We're ready to enlist in your mounted volunteers," Milo said for both of them.

"Dandy. Very fine, indeed." Boggess, a round-faced man starting to bald, shook both their hands vigorously. "We muster in front of the Alamo on December first. That's when the governor has commissioned the company to form."

"Do we get paid?" Jesse quickly asked.

"Twenty-five dollars for the thirty days service. You provide your own weapons, your own horses and tack. I'll have a mule packed with cornmeal and other rations as I can manage. You boys have any experience fighting Indians?"

Milo and Jesse looked at each other. "A little," Jesse answered.

The two friends signed forms making official their enlistment for a thirty-day stint as privates in Captain Boggess's Company A of the San Antonio Mounted Volunteers.

As they were walking back to Menger's boarding house, Milo said, "Mr. Callahan will be pleased."

"I need a rifle," Jesse answered. "I hope Mr. Hoffman agrees with your letter."

"How can he not? We're bringing his daughter back."

Chapter 28

Luther Hoffman's Gunsmith Shop
New Braunfels, Texas
November 1854

Jesse Gunn glanced at Caroline Hoffman Schmidt sitting next to him on the wagon seat. "Do you want me or Milo to go in first and let him and your ma know you're here?"

She patted Jesse's hand on the reins. "No." The swelling around Caroline's eye was gone, but the skin still had a yellowish pall from the bruise that hadn't fully healed. She wore a long-sleeve, high-neck dress bought in San Antonio, covering the bruise marks on her limbs and the burn scabs on her chest.

Before Jesse could help Caroline down from the wagon, Mr. Hoffman flung the door open for his wife. Mrs. Hoffman rushed through with both arms extended, joy in her face, embracing her daughter as soon as Caroline's feet hit the ground. Jesse stepped back, and as the mother hustled her daughter into the building, Caroline glanced back and smiled her thanks at her rescuer. Mr. Hoffman followed his wife and daughter inside, leaving Milo and Jesse alone.

"Jesse, I do believe that the widow has developed an affection for you."

"And me for her."

"Yeah, I can see that. What about her dead husband's sister back in Prairie Lea? I thought you was planning to spark her now we're back for a spell."

Jesse gently stroked the acne scars on his cheek. "Maybe I'll find some work here in New Braunfels 'til we report to Captain Boggess in a couple of weeks."

"Maybe that's a good idea. Me, after we deliver Mr. Smith's horses in Austin, I'm heading to Prairie Lea where a girl named

Malissa Gunn lives, somebody else's little sister." Milo tied his horse to the hitching rail. "Since we're heading off ranging next month, I don't want Malissa to forget me."

The two young men found Luther Hoffman behind the counter in his shop, waiting for them. His wife and daughter had continued through the shop to their living quarters behind the storefront.

The gunsmith spoke first, his face betraying confused emotions. "*Danke*, for returning my daughter. I did not truly expect you to find her."

Milo replied, "We took on the job intending to get it done."

"Finding her weren't so hard, Mr. Hoffman." Jesse stuck his hands in his trouser pockets, wedging his left hand past the grip of his pistol. "It was the few minutes after we found her that got...exciting."

"*Bitte*—Please, tell me everything." Hoffman stepped to the door and locked it, setting a neatly printed *Closed* sign in the window.

Leaning against the wall, Milo recounted their story as he had written it in his letter to their two employers. Jesse listened without interrupting, his instinct telling him to stay quiet, while Milo wove fact and fiction together in regards to how they found Caroline Hoffman Schmidt.

When Milo told of the fight with the Apaches in their camp, he told it straight, saying the sight of the Apache woman clubbing Caroline caused Jesse to react, turning the trade into a shooting rescue. Milo stressed Jesse's role in bravely riding through the camp, firing his Colt right and left, and physically putting the injured Caroline on his horse before carrying her to safety. He spoke with praise of Lieutenant Davant's role as their cover marksman, how he saved their lives with his fast-loading Sharps rifle. Finally, Milo reluctantly admitted that he shot several times without hitting any Apaches.

Luther Hoffman listened without questions until Milo finished. Then he simply asked, "How is my daughter now?"

"Sir, she was heavy with a baby when we found her. The blow to her stomach and the fast gallop away from the Apache camp, well, it killed the baby. The army doctor at Fort Duncan had to perform surgery to take the dead child out of Mrs. Schmidt."

"And this dead child, was it..."

"Mr. Hoffman, the doctor said it was a tiny, blonde-haired girl."

"*Mein Gott. Danke shön.* And Caroline, she knows this?"

"Of course, sir. The doctor's wife told her as soon as she woke up."

"And, in other ways, is she..."

Jesse spoke. "Mr. Hoffman, your daughter is healing. I drove her wagon all the way here, and Caroline—Mrs. Schmidt—was better every day. She is weary, and, sir, she's frightened you and her mother might not welcome her back, since..."

"Bah!" Hoffman flapped his hands in derision. "Her mother is at this moment smothering the child in affection. Did Mary not rejoice at Jesus' rising from the tomb? I too will squeeze Caroline in my arms. She is still our beautiful daughter, now returned from the dead. Glory to God."

Milo nodded. "We figured you'd feel that way, sir. Now, about that letter I wrote."

The gunsmith answered with an unexpected question. "Mr. McKean, do you read well?"

"Well enough. Why?"

Mr. Hoffman held up a finger indicating for them to wait. He pulled six small pieces of wood from a cabinet drawer and arranged them to lean against the wall. "Stand by the door, *bitte.*"

Milo did as asked, while Mr. Hoffman turned the boards over, revealing a different printed letter on each one, the size of the letters decreasing on each successive board.

He tapped the first board. "What letter is on this board?"

"E."

"And the letter next to it?"

"M."

"And the next?"

"G."

"Are you sure?"

Milo answered, "Yes." Jesse saw that it was not a G, but was an O.

"And this one?"

"D." Jesse and Mr. Hoffman shook their heads.

"It's a B, Milo," Jesse said.

"And the last one?"

"I, I can't tell. It's too small."

"Can you read it, Mr. Gunn?"

"Yeah, it's an N."

"Mr. McKean, you did not shoot any Apaches because your eyes are weak. You do not see well at a distance. Even a short distance."

"Well, shit." Milo crossed his arms and looked at the ceiling. "I thought I saw things like everybody else."

"Try these." Mr. Hoffman set a box on the counter. Inside were four pairs of wire rim eyeglasses. "Put on each pair and look at the letters again."

Milo fumbled with the first pair of glasses until they perched on his nose. "No help." He tried on the other three pairs, and went back to the third ones.

"With these I can read the damned N."

Mr. Hoffman smiled. "Take them. I do not expect you to wear them often. Men here in Texas seem to laugh at those who wear spectacles. But, when it matters that you hit at what you shoot, I suggest you remember them."

Milo was speechless, but he nodded in gratitude and put the folded glasses in his shirt pocket.

"Mr. Hoffman, how'd you come to have a box of spectacles in your cabinet? Ain't you a gunsmith and not a, a spectacle-maker?" Jesse asked.

Hoffman chuckled. "Sometimes a man buys a gun and brings it back. He will say the sight is attached off-center, that the weapon does not shoot straight. Sometimes I sell that man a pair of spectacles instead of repairing a gun that is not in need of repairs."

"You're a clever old coyote," Jesse grinned in admiration.

"Now," Mr. Hoffman said, "Tell me more about your army friend's Sharps rifle. I may have something for you, Mr. Gunn."

While Jesse described Will Davant's new breech-loading rifle, Mr. Hoffman reached under the counter and pulled out a short carbine that smelled of clean oil.

"I thought so. The lieutenant has the infantry model. Here is a cavalry model Sharps carbine. Also breech-loading. Just put on the market. I ordered this one after a fellow riding through from New York showed me his." Hoffman put two cardboard boxes of cartridges next to the weapon.

Jesse picked up the carbine, surprised at its short barrel and light weight.

"This, Mr. Gunn, along with Mr. McKean's spectacles, is the last of your payment for my daughter's return. I doubt Mr. Smith will be so generous. Only two horses. No shotgun." Hoffman paused. "And no Negro to fetch him another beer and empty his night soil."

Milo thought he detected the slightest hint of sarcasm in the German gunsmith's voice, but he wasn't sure.

Chapter 29

**Pecan Street
Austin City, Texas
November 1854**

Benjamin Smith's new saloon, the *Musket and Mug*, was now open on Pecan Street, just a block off the Congress Avenue, the main street in Austin. The large two-sided sign over the boardwalk hung from hooks and moved gently in the breeze, the professionally painted red letters outlined in white on a black background. In the front window, a second sign announced *Menger's Fine German Beer*.

Late in the afternoon, Milo and Jesse tied their mounts and Mr. Smith's pair of horses to the hitching rail. They went in, each resting a dirty boot on the brass rail below the ornate wood bar, and ordered beer. Milo didn't recognize the bartender, so he asked, "Is Mr. Smith in the building?"

"Nah. This time of day he's still at his mercantile store."

"Where would that be?"

"Around the corner. Go to Congress, turn left. Can't miss it. *Smith's Merchandise*."

"Obliged. And this is good beer."

"Glad you like it. Brewed by a Dutchman in San Antone. That'll be a nickel each."

★

Benjamin Smith was busy with a customer when Milo and Jesse entered his store. At the sound of the tinkling doorbell, he glanced up to offer a polite welcome. His merchant's smile sunk into a frown, and his normally cordial greeting of a new customer came out sour. "Oh, it's you. Take off your hats and don't touch anything. I'll be with you when I can."

Jesse shot back without thinking, "If we're too much trouble, we'll just go sell your horses at the livery stable and take our pay out of that."

Smith narrowed his eyes at the pair of young men while Milo scanned the store merchandise.

"Don't worry none about Jesse, Mr. Smith. I made him gulp down his beer at your new saloon, and the boy gets prickly when he's rushed. We'll wait. With our hands in our pockets. I might even find a new shirt, since I'm going courtin'."

Jesse fingered the frayed placket on his own shirt, thinking maybe Milo had a good idea. He'd worn his only shirt sitting next to Caroline Schmidt all those days on the wagon seat, and he suspected it was too filthy to wash with much success. And it wouldn't hurt to have both a working shirt and a new shirt for the evenings, which he hoped might be spent at the Hoffman household.

He followed Milo to the counter where men's shirts and trousers were neatly stacked. While they waited for Mr. Smith, Milo looked back and forth, deciding between two nearly identical white cotton shirts, one having thin green stripes and the other thin red stripes. Jesse pawed through another stack and pulled out a bright multi-colored calico print shirt.

"Those striped shirts are seventy-five cents each, and the calico print is one dollar." Mr. Smith walked his lady customer to the front door.

Once he'd closed the door behind her, and they were alone in the store, he continued. "You men know I'm deeply disappointed that you did not return with my boy Thompson."

"Yes, sir. No more disappointed than us. We were both counting on the $100 you were willing to pay for him." Milo paused. "But we brought back your best horse and one of the others. They've been eating good, look real healthy."

"Where are they? I want to run a hand over them before I pay."

"Right out front."

Outside, Smith walked around each horse, checking for split hooves and scars. Smith straightened up and looked hard at Milo. "You boys sure you didn't sell off my other horse?"

Jesse bristled. "You callin' us liars?"

Smith shook his head. "No, just double-checking, that's all."

Jesse shot back, "Then why don't you ride down to the Piedras Negras and double-check with the pissed-off Mexican who ain't got these horses, or the pesos he paid your darkie for them?"

Smith held up his hands palms out. "No offense intended. Come back in the store with me, and I'll pay you what's due."

Back inside he led Milo and Jesse to his small safe and told them to turn around while he worked and spun the combination lock to open the heavy door. He took out eight ten-dollar bank notes and relocked the safe. "Here's forty dollars for each horse."

"The agreement was fifty dollars, payable in coins, not bank notes," Milo said, his voice hard. "I've got the contract out in my saddlebag, written and signed by all of us."

"All right. But specie is scarce. I don't keep that much in my safe. I'd have to go to the bank depository for it. And since you like those shirts, how about you each find ten dollars of merchandise to go with the bills to fill out the fifty."

Jesse was about to agree when Milo answered. "We don't know what you paid for the shirts or anything else in your stock. So, make it twenty dollars each of merchandise, and we'll go with you to the bank for those twenty dollar gold pieces."

"You're a horse trader, Mr. McKean, so you are. You've come a ways since I gave you a ride on my wagon back in the spring. Here's what I'll do. The twenty dollars in goods, as you ask, but the rest paid in these bank notes."

Milo shook his head. "We're almost there. We'll settle on the twenty dollars each in merchandise at your regular store prices, and we'll split on the money. Twenty each in gold, and twenty each in bank notes. I'll wager you have two screaming eagles in your safe."

Mr. Smith sighed deeply and nodded, already thinking prices were not marked on most of his inventory, so it would be easy enough to up the costs of whatever the men chose.

Jesse stuck with the calico shirt and impulsively added a pair of dark brown trousers and two pairs of cotton socks. With half his credit committed, Jesse shocked Mr. Smith by asking help in selecting a Sunday dress for his sister. When Milo looked oddly at his friend, Jesse winked.

Once a five-dollar dark gray dress was agreed upon, Jesse picked out a tin boiling pot with an attached lid, a small sheet steel frying pan, a pound of ground coffee beans, and a small sack of mixed salt and pepper seasoning,

Milo first considered following Jesse's lead in all his purchases, but quickly decided a new sunbonnet for Malissa would be far more appropriate a gift from a suitor than a dress. Jesse's decision to buy a dress for his *sister*, met Milo's approval, only because he considered Mrs. Schmidt unique in regards to her widowhood and Jesse's already-familiar relationship with her. Plus, the bonnet for Malissa was a fraction of the cost of a dress. That left Milo credit enough for two black-painted canvas ground-cloths that would protect both him and Jesse from the cold wind and rain during their coming ranging expedition with the Mounted Volunteers.

They stuffed the new cooking ware and sacks of coffee and seasoning into their saddlebags, and wrapped the new clothes in their rolled-up black ground-cloths, tied to the backs of their saddles. Within minutes they were on the road south to San Marcos where they would camp. The next day, Jesse intended to go on to New Braunfels and Milo would take the side road to Prairie Lea.

"Milo, Did it strike you as peculiar that Mr. Smith never mentioned Caroline Hoffman. Never asked about her, even when I bought a dress."

"I did notice. I believe Benjamin Smith doesn't think of much besides Benjamin Smith. Since you mentioned the dress you bought for your *sister*, don't you know widows wear black during their mourning years, not dark gray?"

"I do know that, Milo, but does Caroline know it? She has a new life ahead, and she can't keep looking back."

"Didn't I see Mrs. Schmidt reading a Dicken's novel while you drove the wagon?"

"Yeah, so what?"

"Jesse, Charles Dickens is a famous English writer. People trust him to write the truth, the way things should be. Books that thick, there's gotta be lots of dying going on and lots of grieving widows—wearing black dresses."

"How do you know that? Have you ever read a Dickens novel, Milo?"

"Hell, no. I'm not a nancy boy. But I've seen your mother and my mother reading them. And in England, widows wear black mourning dresses for two years."

Jesse twiddled the end of his reins for a while before he replied. "Well, first of all, we ain't in England, we're in Texas where things move faster. Folks ain't got time for two years of grieving what with the Apaches and all. A woman in Texas can't afford to push away men who take a shine to her for two whole years after she becomes a widow."

Milo took off his hat and scratched his scalp, thinking about that one.

"Second, the Hoffman's and Schmidt's are Germans, not English. And third, I reckon Caroline Hoffman's months of mourning her husband while she was a captive should count as double time at least, so she's been mourning for a year now."

"But that still leaves her a year more to wear black," Milo said.

"Unless she's in Texas, like I said. Besides, dark gray is nearly black. Close enough to black for Texas. That's how I see it." Jesse nodded his head in satisfaction that he'd well defended his choice of a gray dress.

"It's not too late to turn around and exchange that gray dress for a proper black mourning dress," Milo suggested.

"Nah, I'm giving her the gray one. I really like that bit of white lace around the collar."

"Huh, and I suppose when you give it to her, you'll be wearing that new calico shirt."

"Yup, that's why I bought it instead of a workaday shirt like your new one."

"You'll look like a strutting yard rooster with all those mixed-up colors."

Jesse crowed like a rooster before he added, "And glass buttons. Did you see the glass buttons on my shirt?"

"What am I supposed to tell Mr. Schmidt when I get to Prairie Lea? I've got to go see him and tell him we brought back his son's widow."

"Aw, Milo, I don't know. Just tell him I'm working in New Braunfels until we report to Captain Boggess in a couple of weeks. That'll be the truth enough. No need to burden the man with complications."

"You know that Mr. and Mrs. Hoffman may well turn you away at the door. Not even let you see their daughter. Really, Jesse, she's *IS* a grieving widow."

Jesse considered Milo's warning before he reached over and patted his friend's knee. "I'll just have to rely on my strikingly handsome face and charm. And the calico shirt."

Chapter 30

Alamo Plaza
San Antonio, Texas
December 1, 1854

Jesse Gunn's new 1853 model Sharps carbine drew attention. Half a dozen other young volunteers for Captain Boggess's ranging company clustered around Jesse, watching him demonstrate how to load the linen cartridges.

"Boys, you see that the trigger guard is welded to this slanted steel block that sits right on top, so when you pull down on the trigger guard, it acts as a lever to pull the slanted steel block down too. Then all you gotta do is slide the cartridge in nice and easy." Jesse held up a cartridge.

"Slide it in nice and easy, huh?" smirked Isham Jones, a farm boy from Prairie Lea.

Tom McKenzie, a friend of Isham's, and also from Prairie Lea, picked up on the joshing. "Now don't that there cartridge look a whole lot like that thang I been sliding into that darkie girl what works on yo' daddy's farm? Cain't say my thang goes in nice and easy, though."

While the crowd of young Rangers snickered, Jesse shoved the lead-tipped, finger-size cylinder back into the cardboard box of ten cartridges and dropped the box into his jacket pocket. He tried to ignore the profane banter that made him uncomfortable.

Jesse went on. "When you pull the lever up, the sharp edge of the steel block nips the linen cartridge to loose the powder for the priming cap."

Jesse modeled the loading procedure as he talked.

"The thing is, I can load and shoot half a dozen times while you fellas are still poking your ramrods..." Everyone around Jesse hooted and slapped each other on the back. Red-faced, Jesse gave up and stomped away to slip his new carbine into the custom leather scabbard that Mr. Hoffman had made for him.

"What's wrong, Jess?" Milo walked up, leading Buck.

"Ah, nuthin'. Just, well, the boys from Prairie Lea, they was making light of my new carbine."

"From what I saw, they was hoorahin' your foot in your mouth about loading it."

"Yeah, I know." Jesse looked down and rubbed his boot toe in the dust. "Milo, after, after seeing up close what the Apaches done to Caroline, I just can't joke about that stuff. Them boys just don't know."

"Yet. They're likely to find out once we get out on the prairie, if we come on a burned-out farm or a family caught out in a wagon by themselves. They may see a dead woman looking worse than Mrs. Schmidt did."

"I hope so. I mean, I hope not. I mean, well, hell, I don't know what I mean. But I do know I hope to put one of those cartridges into the belly of ever' Apache we can catch."

"You do that, my friend. I'll be right beside you."

"How did Malissa like the sunbonnet?"

Milo grinned. "She thanked me, and when your ma turned her head, your sister leaned over and kissed me real quick-like on the cheek. Yes, she did."

Jesse punched Milo on the shoulder, "Go on! My sister did that? To you? I thought she had better sense."

"She is a very sensible young lady, in spite of her bird-brained brother. Now, tell me about New Braunfels. Did you and your gray dress get tossed out on your ear?"

"Not quite. Mr. Hoffman took the dress package, but he told me his daughter wouldn't be receiving company for a fortnight or two. Hell, what's a fortnight, Milo?"

"Beats me."

"But I got a surprise when Mrs. Hoffman invited me to Sunday lunch a few days ago. I ate with the whole family. They put me next to Mr. Hoffman at the head of the table, and Caroline was across from me wearing a black dress."

"I'm sorry about that Jesse, but I ain't surprised."

"Well, you told me about the mourning dress, you did."

"But you got your foot in the door, I'd say."

Jesse nodded. "When she was showing me out on Sunday, Mrs. Hoffman told me my calico shirt was just the thing for a brave man like me. I think when we get back from this month of rangerin', I'll make another visit."

The pair, along with the twenty-six other volunteers, waited with their mounts saddled and gear packed for Captain Boggess to arrive.

"Milo, did you talk with Mr. Schmidt?"

"Yup. I thought he'd never stop pumping my hand up and down in thanks. I showed him my spectacles, and he made me go out back and shoot a few rounds with the Baker while I was wearing the eyeglasses. Damn, if I didn't hit the target every time. Jesse, I been shootin' blind."

Jesse thumped Milo on the shoulder.

"And look here at my new wool vest." Milo pulled back his coat lapels to show a gray vest with brown stripes, lined with a thick cotton flannel. "Your ma give me this and sent one for you, too. Her and Malissa did all the cutting and stitching. She told me her boys need wool over our hearts at night. Your ma's a dandy."

Jesse took the rolled vest Milo handed him. He quickly shucked his jacket and put on the hand-sewn sleeveless garment, immediately feeling the new layer of warmth close around his chest. For the next twenty-nine days, he didn't take the vest off, not even unbuttoning it.

"Oh, I near forgot." Milo reached back into his saddlebag and pulled out a small package he handed to Jesse. "I told Mr. Callahan about our fight with the Apaches, and how you got so mad when the old woman whacked Mrs. Schmidt in the stomach, that you shot the chief and turned our swap session into a shooting war."

"I did that, didn't I?"

"Yeah, you did. But I don't think that old heathen was going to give us the woman without a fight. You just started the dance before he could." Jesse tried to look contrite, but failed.

"Mr. Callahan told me he's chased some Indians in his day and what you did was worthy of a token. So he sent this to you."

"What is it?"

"I dunno. I ain't opened it. It's to you, not me."

Jesse untied the string around the brown wrapping paper and held up a small soft leather pouch. He opened the draw cord and pulled out a piece of paper, unfolded it, and in an audible voice, read the writing on the note.

Good work, Mr. Gunn. You performed a meritorious service for all the white people of Texas. This pouch will be a fine place to carry the lead balls for your Colt revolver. It's made of the tanned tit skin of a Lipan squaw that was kilt a long time ago. You earned it.

Jesse dropped the note and the leather pouch as if they were on fire. As the two young men stared down in horror at the pouch, a voice called out, "Mount up. There's the Captain!"

Privates Milo McKean and Jesse Gunn of Company A of Captain Boggess's Mounted Volunteers, swung into their saddles, the leather pouch soon trampled into the dust. As the last rider rode out of the plaza, a six-year-old Mexican boy picked up the soft leather sack and ran off to show his newfound treasure to his mother.

Chapter 31

On the Prairie
Southwest of San Antonio, Texas
December 4, 1854

The first few days on the prairie were warm, the air just brisk enough for pleasant riding. During the nights, the temperature dropped, the early morning hours cold, but without the bone-chilling bite of the winter months ahead. A tired man could still button up his vest and coat, cover his ears with a knitted scarf, wrap up in his wool blanket, and sleep for a few hours without shivering.

The Rangers well knew of the Indians' uncanny ability to slip unseen among their tethered horses in the darkest hours of the night, cut them all loose, then start a stampede of the animals they weren't stealing. Captain Boggess intended to prevent such an occurrence by keeping four mounted sentries patrolling the camp perimeter on three-hour shifts. Two more guards walked among the horses.

Jesse and Milo drew the midnight to three a.m. watch. Orders were for two sentries to each ride alone in a slow counter-clockwise circuit around the camp, while the other two men eased along in the opposite direction. Each sentry was to keep a weapon in hand and to stop and listen every minute or so.

The hours dragged along, Milo fighting sleep when a voice from his left softly announced himself.

"Ho, to the sentry. This is Lieutenant Jackson. Don't shoot me."

"Glad you spoke up right away, Lieutenant, or I might of done just that. This is Private McKean. You bring my relief?"

"Nah, you got another hour. I'm just making sure you're awake."

"Wide awake, sir. Since you're here, you able to tell me where we're headed tomorrow? I seen the courier ride up late this afternoon. He bring any news that'll point us at some hostiles?"

"As a matter of fact, he did. Reports of more horse-thieving and a drover and his herd sprouting arrows up near D'Hanis. At sunrise I'm taking half the company north to find the hostiles' trail. Captain Boggess is taking the first platoon farther west towards the most likely pass through the hills. The plan is to catch them between us."

"Sounds good to me, Lieutenant. We're all ready for some action."

"Me too, Mr. McKean. I'll make my way on around to the next man now."

"Well, the next fellow behind me is Private Gunn. Don't let him give you fright if he's glowing like a haint in the moonlight."

"McKean, I've no idea what you're talking about, but I'll be watchful of glowing spirits. Fact is, I could use some spirits in this cold. Carry on."

★

Lieutenant Jackson sought out Private McKean the next morning as he led his fourteen Rangers north. While their horses walked during a break from loping at a faster pace, the lieutenant pulled up and waited for McKean and Jesse to reach him.

"Private McKean, I've been told that you and Private Gunn just returned from a foray into Mexico after a captured white woman. A successful foray, that is. Not just wandering around in the hills, but finding the Lipan camp, taking the woman, and shooting your way out. I'd say well done."

"Thanks, Lieutenant," Milo answered, unsure where the Ranger officer was going with the compliment.

"I'm of a mind that our company needs two Indian fighters like you to inspire the other, less-experienced, men."

"Huh. I'd say your men are plenty inspired. We're all volunteers, ain't we?"

"True enough, but you two have actually engaged the hostiles, something my other volunteers have not yet done. Or me, I regret to say."

Jesse spoke up, "It ain't all you're cracking it up to be."

"Maybe not, but it's enough for me to name one of you as corporal of the second platoon of Captain Boggess's Mounted Volunteers. An extra five dollars pay goes with it."

Milo looked at the lieutenant. "Captain Boggess know about this? He approved it?"

"Yes, he did. This morning, he'll be naming his own corporal for his first platoon. We waited a few days to watch and see how all the men handle themselves. See which men the others appear to respect, before we selected our corporals."

Jesse asked, "Just what does a corporal do, I mean, besides inspire the privates?"

Lieutenant Jackson smiled. "He reports to Sergeant Lewis. In camp, he'll take over running our night sentries and making sure the water and firewood details get things done. When we're on the trail, he keeps tabs on the privates. Uses his eyes to make sure every man's gear is squared away, and uses his ears to catch the first signs of any malcontents who might be tempted to sneak off back to San Antonio."

"You mean be your snitch?"

"No, I mean be my second non-commissioned officer, who is responsible for the welfare of the men. Under Sergeant Lewis."

"Five dollars more pay?"

"Yes, and for that, when we encounter redskins, you'll lead the way right behind me—inspiring the men. Riley, Sergeant Lewis, that is, will bring up the rear, making sure none of them youngsters lose their nerve."

"Sounds like a job for Jesse," Milo said.

"Nah, not me. Lieutenant, My face may glow in the dark like you seen, but Milo here has the brains."

The lieutenant raised his eyebrows towards Private McKean, who reluctantly nodded. "So be it. Corporal McKean it is. I'll add your new rank to the roster."

★

The next day, Jackson's platoon of Mounted Volunteers reached the homestead of the Batot family in the settlement of D'Hanis. Jean Batot, a French immigrant from the Alsace region of France, led them to the spot where he'd followed circling vultures to find the mutilated body of the cattle drover. Batot and his son

Christian had buried the hired hand, leaving the rotting carcasses of a dozen or more cattle surrounding the shallow grave.

While the best trackers in the company circled the area in search of the Indians' trail, Lieutenant Jackson confirmed from Mister Batot that there were supplies available for purchase in D'Hanis. The immigrant from France also noted that the empty buildings in abandoned Fort Lincoln would make a decent campsite for the company when they returned.

The platoon of Rangers set off on the trail at a trot, three days behind the raiding Apaches. They rode generally south, the trackers out front having little trouble following the signs of a large number of horses and mules. When they stopped at a spring, Lieutenant Jackson waved for Corporal McKean to join him.

"No need to remind you to check that every man's canteen is full when we leave here. Now, tell me, Corporal, when we catch up to these hostiles, will they cut their stolen stock loose and run, or will they turn and fight us?"

"Can't say, Lieutenant. I weren't in Texas when the militia caught up with the big Comanche war party that came through where I live now in Prairie Lea. But my friend James Callahan was there. Older man. Hates Indians. Hates Mexicans. Fought in the revolution against Santa Anna. Led many a ranging company chasing Mexican bandits and Indians since then."

"I've met Captain Callahan. Good Indian fighter. Good man."

"Yes, he is. Owns a store in Prairie Lea now. Promised his wife he'd settle down now that they have a passel of young'uns."

"Huh. He sure never struck me as the kind of man to run a store, not with all the Indian raiding still going on."

"Well, he's trying. But, I agree with you, he don't seem to be taking to a harness well at all. The captain's a mustang, not a plow horse."

"Yeah, that fits." Jackson grinned.

"Anyway, he's told me that it was hundreds of Comanche warriors, and they were driving hundreds of horses and mules they'd stolen along the seacoast. The militia finally caught up with them along Plum Creek when the Comanches were nearly back in the mountains. Mr. Callahan, and some others who were there, they all say the Comanche braves both fought and ran. Some turned and fought like savages. Others stuck with the horses and mules and ignored the fight, just tried to get the animals to the safety of the hills."

"That sounds like a preconceived battle plan. I didn't know the hostiles were so well organized." Jackson replied.

"Nah, they ain't. More like ever Indian doing what was best for him. Some chose the glory in fighting and counting coup, and some chose the stock they could sell to the Mexicans. Mr. Callahan said there were maybe a dozen chiefs, each leading a few dozen braves, all doing whatever the hell they wanted."

"I trust the band we're trailing are no more than a dozen or two braves. I believe with our Colt revolvers we have the firepower to handle that many, but more than thirty or so...?"

"Me too. Lieutenant, me too."

★

Around midday, the mounted volunteers were on foot, leading their mounts to give them a moving-rest. Corporal McKean drifted back to walk next to Private William Clopton, a young man who Milo hadn't talked to very much.

"Where you hail from, Clopton?" Milo asked to start a conversation.

"Curry Creek. On the Blanco River in the hills."

"I'm from Prairie Lea, east of San Marcos. Flat farm land. I hate it when we walk to rest the horses."

Clopton cut a quick glance at the corporal. "Not me. Feels good to get my legs straightened out for a spell."

"Huh. Your boots must have thicker soles than mine. Is this your first rangering patrol?"

"Yep."

"Like it?"

"Don't mind it. But I'd like to catch up to some Indians. Make the saddle sores worthwhile."

"Got a job back in Curry Creek?"

"Just keeping up with the livestock on Pa's spread. That's why I'm here. We keep losing mules and finding dead cattle. Figured it was time to do what I can to slow down the redskins. And the twenty-five dollars. Don't see much cash money out our way."

"Two good reasons, I reckon."

"You?"

"Well, my pa's in Alabama. I don't own any land to farm or raise cattle on. Yet. So far, rangering is the best job to come my way. When we get back, I aim to work as a carpenter. Lots of building going on around Prairie Lea and Lockhart."

★

Late on the second day of trailing the hostiles, Jesse spied a faint dust cloud ahead and off to their left. He pointed it out to Lieutenant Jackson, who immediately waved for his troop to form a single line abreast. They all watched the dust for several minutes as the haze steadily took on a bubble shape above the ground. Finally, the lieutenant called for the men to draw their revolvers. Without further delay, Jackson rode out in front of his platoon and signaled for them to change their course and ride at a gallop straight at the dust cloud.

Milo was at the left end of the formation, next to Jesse. Sergeant Lewis rode by himself behind the center of the line of Rangers, his eyes sweeping back and forth, alert to any trooper whose mount might lag behind the others.

Leaning forward in the saddle, pistol in hand, Milo glanced to the side and noted Jesse's grim face. *He's thinking about Caroline Hoffman. That's good, my friend.* Looking past Jesse, Milo saw Billy Clopton, wide-eyed, but keeping his horse in line and his Colt revolver held high. *He'll do.*

As the dust cloud ahead quickly grew larger, the lieutenant was sure the hostiles had chosen to challenge their pursuers in battle.

"Steady men, steady!" Jackson shouted as he cocked his revolver and peered hard into the roiling brown wall of dust, eager to spot and shoot the chief who would be leading his warriors.

No horse slowed, no young Ranger faltered. Fourteen pairs of squinting eyes probed the dust for targets. Fourteen sweaty hands held revolvers, trigger fingers tightening, prepared to fire five lead balls each.

Finally, the first dark shapes emerged from under the thick dust, still too far away for a pistol shot. The two groups of mounted men quickly closed on each other. Then, Lieutenant Jackson cursed and held up his arm, as he reined in his own horse. He realized his half of the company and Captain Boggess's men had been charging each other. The hostile raiders had eluded both platoons of Rangers.

Chapter 32

Abandoned Fort Lincoln
D'Hanis, Texas
December 18, 1854

Lieutenant Jackson sat by himself in the abandoned headquarters building that no longer had a roof. He perched on a straight chair which no longer had a woven cane seat. Jackson had laid a few sticks over the hole and sat gingerly, holding his hands out to the blazing fire in the middle of what had been a room. He thought it must be midnight, at least, because the temperature was dropping, and his backside was feeling cold. He remained seated by the fire only to delay the necessity of walking several yards into the darkness to relieve himself before rolling up in his blanket

Sergeant Lewis approached and saluted formally. "Lieutenant, Private Gunn out on sentry duty just beyond the fort says he's hearing gunfire south of us. He says it sounds like pistols. Permission to take a squad to see what's going on. Could be Mexicans."

Jackson briskly rubbed his warmed palms together. "Riley, there are just fourteen of us here, since Captain Boggess headed south again with the first platoon. That's a slim number of guns to face an unknown enemy. And didn't you give permission for half of our privates to go to the saloon in D'Hanis?" Sergeant Lewis nodded.

"If I've learned anything as a Ranger, it's that the Injuns and Mexicans always seem to know where we are, and go somewhere we ain't to do their devilment. That's why we're always chasing them *after* their depredations."

"Yessir, but those gun shots..."

"I'm betting those pistol shots are our boys liquored up and letting off some steam."

"Maybe, but..."

"Sergeant, if you take a squad out in the dark chasing random pistol shots, which, as I said, are our own drunk Rangers, I'll be left with just one or two men here. And should I be wrong, and a rider shows up with a report of hostiles in the immediate area, I'd have no force to respond with until you got back."

Sergeant Riley Lewis didn't agree, but he nodded and returned to his own fire where Milo McKean waited with their saddled horses.

"No go, Corporal. We might as well unsaddle them."

★

Before dawn, six hung-over Ranger privates straggled into camp. Two of them carried huge bloody pork hind-quarters. By dawn, the hams were skinned and roasting on an iron spit, two of the recovering Rangers dozed while the other four sipped bitter coffee from their tin mugs.

An hour after dawn, Mr. Batot arrived with two other angry men from D'Hanis. While Lieutenant Jackson remained seated on his chair frame, enjoying the smell of the roasting pork, the trio encircled the officer and berated him with their complaints.

Jean Ney began. "Two dead hogs. My animals, one mutilated and now cooking over that fire right there." He pointed where the quartet of young men stood around the cook fire.

"Sir, my boys swear that hog was roaming wild. I resent your implication that one of my command is a thief," Jackson replied with forced indignation.

"The sign to my store, the store where I sold you supplies, lassoed and pulled down. The boards broken apart," added Henri Moreau.

"Maybe someone thought your prices were jacked up," Jackson suggested.

"And the mailbox in front of the new Post Office, torn down and the mail, the letters and newspapers, scattered all over the road and trampled," Jean Batot concluded.

Lieutenant Jackson took a last sip of his coffee, before he stood up. "What's your name again?" he asked the farmer whose hogs had been shot.

"Jean Ney. I demand five dollars apiece for my lost property."

"Ney, weren't he a French general? Sure seems like my daddy's regiment in Wellington's English army fought on the Continent against some fella named Ney."

"*Oui*, I'm proud that Marshall Ney was a member, a distant member, of my lineage."

"That so? An' there was another French general named Woll, who led a pack of Meskin soldiers up to San Antone, years after we whupped Santy Anna. Just wouldn't let it go. Wouldn't admit Texas ain't part of Mexico no more. We had to beat his bunch of bandits back across the river." Lieutenant Jackson spat into the fire.

"I never got that. Why would a Frenchman lead a Mexican column into Texas? But the Frogs seem to have a hankerin' for Mexico, so they do. But let 'em try for Texas. Oh, you men are Frenchies, ain't you?"

Mr. Ney ignored the insult and persisted. "Lieutenant, my swine?"

"And the Post Office?" Jean Batot added.

"Write the governor a letter. Maybe he'll see fit to settle with you. But me, I got no proof my men kilt your hogs or tore down any signs in D"Hanis. You should be thankin' me and my boys for being here, not whining at me about some mischief last night."

"But..."

"An' which one of you French gentlemen sold that whiskey to my boys? What did you think they'd do when you didn't cut' em off the bottle before they got their blood up and decided to have some fun?"

"But..."

"Mr. Batot, we got lots more ground to cover looking for hostiles. We'll be riding south as soon as we pack up. I expect you good French gentlemen of D'Hanis will see to the safety of your town, your Texas town. Now, if you'll excuse me, that roasted pork..."

★

Three days later, the two platoons of Captain Boggess's ranging company reconnected. During the first night's camp, stories of the barely aborted blind charge at each other dominated the talk.

"Just one more second, and I would'a plugged you, sure 'nuf."

"I had my eye on one ugly fella almost hidden in the dust. I coulda swore he was wearing a buffalo horn bonnet. Damned if those horns weren't your big ears stickin' out."

"I was 'bout to loose both barrels at a big black horse. Yourn."

Now the whole company was strung along a trail that looped around south of San Antonio, hoping to intercept tracks of unshod horses. As he rode, Jesse Gunn gummed a dirty ship's cracker, one of the last ones from his saddlebag. *I wonder where and when this damned rock was baked. Sure wish it was saltier. But it's better than a sucking on a pebble like the Injuns do.* After a few seconds of softening the cracker with his saliva, Jesse nibbled gingerly on the edge, working to break off a small chunk. He made sure to keep the brittle dough away from the upper tooth that he'd loosened by taking a big bite of an apple from the basket they'd "bought" from the store in D'Hanis.

Billy Clopton, riding next to Jesse, looked wistfully at the piece of cracker Private Gunn held. "Uh, you got any more of that?"

Jesse slowly bit down, finally snapping the cracker, grimacing at the sharp crunch. He tossed the remaining brittle dough to Clopton.

"It's rock hard, Billy. Go easy."

"Shoot, Jesse, my middle name is Easy."

Jesse grinned as he looked at Clopton tonguing the cracker around in his mouth.

"So be it, *Easy* Clopton." Jesse twisted in his saddle, to see who might be listening.

"Hear that, Milo? I'm now ridin' next to Easy. No more Billy."

From two files back, Corporal McKean cautioned, "Just so's he don't go easy on the Apaches."

★

Captain Boggess's company of mounted volunteers spent the last nine days of their thirty-day ranging patrol crisscrossing a fifty-mile stretch of scrub brush without encountering any hostiles. A cold, wet storm plunged the temperatures to the freezing mark, causing Boggess to abandon their futile search two days early and return to San Antonio.

★

After the company disbanded in the Alamo Plaza, Jesse and Milo turned their tired, muddy horses towards Prairie Lea, foregoing even a single night in a boarding house. Their arrival at the Gunn farm prompted the family to bring out Christmas gifts held back for the occasion and for Mrs. Gunn and Malissa to roast a goose and bake a peach pie. But before the bird was caught, killed, plucked and put in the oven, water was boiled and the two Rangers each took a turn standing in the washtub in the corner of the kitchen behind a curtain, scrubbing themselves with lye soap.

On the last day of the year 1854, Milo and Jesse spent a single day of rest in the warm kitchen sipping coffee. Both young men sat at the table, the parts of their revolvers spread out on a rag on the table, while they scrubbed and oiled each piece, removing any trace of rust or grime. Milo tried not to stare at Jesse's sister as she puttered around the room, helping her mother cook. Regardless of his attempt to be discreet, when Malissa mixed a big bowl of biscuit dough, her hips swaying ever so faintly as she stirred the thick batter with the wooden spoon, he quit trying to mask his interest. Jesse noticed and winked at his friend as he went on embellishing the bare facts of their weeks of discomfort and frustration, weaving the drudgery of their long days in the saddle into tales of adventure.

On New Year's Day, 1855, Jesse turned to the winter maintenance chores that had been set aside during the fall harvest season, and Milo rode to Lockhart to seek work as a carpenter.

Chapter 33

Lockhart, Texas
April 8, 1855

Eighteen year-old Malissa Gunn enjoyed the ten-mile buggy ride from the Gunn's farm near Prairie Lea to Lockhart. Wide swaths of red and blue wildflowers carpeted the gently sloping ridge that set Lockhart above the river plain where Prairie Lea was located. Only a few small clouds dotted the sky, cause for Malissa to wear the yellow sunbonnet that had been a gift from Milo McKean.

On this Easter Sunday morning, her brother Jesse drove the rig, his horse tied behind. Malissa and her mother had made a substantial lunch which filled a basket right behind the buggy seat. The aroma of freshly fried chicken nibbled at Jesse's nose. The pair planned to meet Milo in time to attend service at the newly built Methodist church and then enjoy a picnic near the springs that bubbled up in Plum Creek, not far from the church.

As the buggy followed the winding road that climbed the flower-strewn ridge, Jesse broke the silence.

"You know, your green dress and yellow bonnet make you look like a giant daisy. It's a good thing you're so skinny, since I ain't seen many daisy stems very big around."

Malissa swatted him with her folded fan. "And when did you start noticing flower stems?" Yet, she suspected he was right, as only a brother can be. She made a mental note to not wear the dress and bonnet together any more. And just in case Jesse was hinting she was gaining weight, maybe she'd eat only one piece of chicken and refuse a slice of the pecan pie she herself had baked.

Malissa was pleased that Milo had labored for the past several months as a carpenter working on several construction projects around the booming new town of Lockhart. When he'd begun, he secretly told her that he intended to save enough of his wages to secure a loan for at least eighty acres of farm land west of Lockhart. Milo hadn't proposed, exactly, but he'd been clear that once he was a landowner and not just a hired hand, he'd ask for *her* hand. And that pleased Malissa Gunn mightily.

"When are you going back to New Braunfels?" Malissa asked, looking to change the subject away from her attire.

"Oh, I don't rightly know." Jesse had ridden to the Hoffman's house for lunch on the first Sunday of every month since the new year, but Mrs. Hoffman continued to politely refuse Jesse any more time with her widowed daughter. He was frustrated, but still hopeful.

"Her mourning period just seems to go on and on."

"What, four months now, and no grey dress yet, huh?"

"How'd you know about that? Does Milo have to tell you everything?"

Malissa coyly answered, "I doubt he does that. But he did tell me it was you, not him or that Lieutenant Davant, who saved the woman."

"Hmph."

Malissa slid her arm through the crook in Jesse's elbow next to her. "Brother, I think that you are a man worthy of a Greek story. I've not seen Caroline, but perhaps she is a modern Helen. 'Was this the face that launched a thousand ships, and burned the topless towers of Illium?'"

Jesse rolled his eyes. "You're just showing off now. But, yes, I believe she could. And I remember Mother reading that story to us, too. I'm no Paris, but I'm sorely tired of waiting to talk to her again and maybe take a walk together."

"Be patient, Bubba. Your time's coming. Healing, forgetting, takes longer for us girls than for you men."

"Too long."

"Jesse," Malissa tried to make her voice sound old and wise like their mother, "You came upon Caroline in the middle of any woman's worst nightmare, except her nightmare was real. You laid eyes on her when she was practically naked, beaten and bruised and filthy to the bone."

"How do you know that?"

"Milo, of course. Now listen to me, Brother. You saw Caroline like no woman ever wants a man, any man, to see her. Part of her hopes never to see you again because you've seen her, body and soul, laid bare. You came into that Indian camp and saw her in that den of slavery, abused and stripped of all decency. Part of her hates you for that."

"But I didn't do anything bad. Hell, I saved her. I killed Indians to save her."

"And bless you for your heroism that day. That's why another part of her wants to hug you tight for rescuing her, for ending her real nightmare."

"Could you talk to her about getting along to the hugging part?"

Malissa laughed. "Oh that I could. I pray her sisters and mother understand and are guiding her away from her horrible memories. But, time, Jesse, you just can't rush the healing hands of time."

Jesse was silent for a few seconds before he answered. "Malissa, I spent more time with Caroline on that wagon seat coming back to New Braunfels than I've ever spent around any woman, except maybe you and Mother. I believe all you say, but those stairs she's on go two ways. With me, there's nowhere for her to go but up."

Malissa hugged her brother's arm.

"And, Sister, you know what else? She was sitting right there on that wagon seat, close as you are now, and she reached out and touched my cheek. My ugly scarred cheek. She didn't turn away or blush like other girls have done."

Jesse flicked the reins. "I can wait for her. Oh, yeah, I can wait."

★

The church service was not brief. It was mid-afternoon when Jesse threw the quilt on the ground in the shade of a giant pecan tree near Plum Creek. The fried chicken, even in a covered metal pot, held no heat but the crushed green peppers that Mrs. Gunn had sprinkled into the batter.

Warm or not, Jesse and Milo plowed through the eight pieces of chicken, not even noticing that Malissa restricted herself to a single drumstick.

"Do you boys know that Father is talking about buying a slave family after he sells this year's crops?"

Both young men looked at her and shook their heads.

"I'm not sure I like the idea. Is it safe to have a bound family living just a few yards away?" Melissa said, collecting all the chicken bones onto her plate.

Milo ran his fingers through the pie crumbs on his plate. "I'd worry more about your pa's investment. Darkies around here run for Mexico. Like Thompson. Texas ain't like Alabama where they didn't have nowhere to go."

Malissa sat up on her knees and smoothed her skirt. "I've never talked to a Negro. Milo, what was it like talking to that Thompson slave?"

"Like to talking to a big boy who ain't been to school. Thompson knew things and he was quick to catch on, but he was sorta stunted, too."

"Stunted? You mean like a dwarf?"

Jesse laughed. "No, he was tall enough."

Malissa looked sharply at Jesse. "How do you know, Brother? I was talking about the very first day Milo got to Prairie Lea and worked with the Thompson slave unloading Mr. Smith's wagon. They must have talked some. But I thought you two never found him when you went after him and the captured woman. When did you see him?"

"Uh, well," Jesse looked at Milo for help.

"Go ahead, Jess, tell it true. If there's one other person in Texas you and I can trust, it's Malissa."

Jesse looked relieved. "We caught him in the river. Milo lassoed him. Then we let him go after he showed us the way to the Apache camp."

"Did you now? Just let him go and lost the reward for him?" Malissa tilted her head and raised her eyebrows in doubt.

"Yeah, Milo promised him tit for tat," her brother confirmed.

Jesse reached for another slice of pie. "Caroline's family don't hold with slavery. Hardly any of the Germans do. They seem to get along just fine doing their own chores."

Malissa cast an eye towards Milo and asked, "What do you think about that, Milo? When you save enough to buy land, will you keep doing carpentry work and rent slaves to plant and harvest your crops?"

Milo swallowed the pie in his mouth before he answered. "I think a man should be paid for his work. The man himself, not his owner. Even black men. So, I reckon my answer is either I'll walk behind the plow, or I'll kidnap Jesse and chain him to the plow handles."

Jesse sat up straight. "That ain't funny, Milo. Them leg irons we put on that Thompson runaway, they were serious business."

"That they were, Jesse. I'm glad you and me are through with keeping shackles in our saddlebags."

Malissa smiled. "I'm glad. And I'm going to persuade Father not to buy any Negroes."

While the two friends stayed seated finishing the pie, Malissa wandered to the edge of the creek to toss in the chicken bones. She threw a leg bone into the water, then took an involuntary step back when she saw a thick black snake stretch its jaws wide open. The long fangs reached out from its pearly white mouth before it slithered into the water from the opposite bank.

"Milo, Jesse, bring your guns, please," Malissa called, taking another few steps away from the bank.

The pair pulled their Colt revolvers and hurried to the creek. Malissa pointed at the S-shaped black shape that was swimming towards the floating chicken bones. Jesse raised his pistol, but Milo stopped him by saying, "Wait, we'll shoot together."

Malissa forced herself not to giggle or even smile as Milo reached into his shirt pocket. He used both hands to settle the brass rimmed spectacles over his ears and the bridge of his nose before he aimed.

Malissa started a count. "On three...one, two--"

Jesse squeezed the trigger of his weapon, hitting the moccasin in the thickest part of his body. Milo fired an instant later, putting a bullet into the water close, but not quite through, the snake's V-shaped head. It twisted and flailed in the clear creek water for a few seconds before going still. As soon as it quit thrashing, both men shot it again, both hitting somewhere on the target.

"I don't think I'll go wading today," Malissa said.

"I'll take a rattler any day over one of those black boogers," Jesse said. "At least a rattler announces himself when you get close."

"I'm with you," Milo said. "Don't seem fair for a scoundrel like that cottonmouth to get between a man and a cool drink of water."

Malissa studied Milo's face. "You look older with those eyeglasses. I like it."

Milo snatched the spectacles off and stuffed them in his vest pocket.

"They're just for shooting."

"Why don't you wear them for a whole day sometime? You might be surprised at what you see," Malissa suggested.

"I see fine up close. I don't need them to saw and hammer." Milo walked away.

Jesse put his arm around his sister. "Don't you go sounding like a wife. Not yet, anyways. Weren't you preaching to me about *time* in the buggy this morning? Milo's time with full-time spectacles is coming, but he ain't ready for those days yet, not by a long shot."

"I thought you told me he needs them for a long shot." Malissa elbowed Jesse and followed Milo back to the picnic quilt.

Chapter 34

The Callahan Farm
Between Prairie Lea & Lockhart, Texas
Late May, 1855

James Callahan gazed at the long scars that crisscrossed the back of the slave. He looked at George Johnson who owned land to the south of Callahan's farm. "George, why would I want to rent a nigger who runs? He might take off again, this time on one of my horses."

"Because those stripes on his back taught him a lesson. Didn't they, Edward?" The dark man nodded, his bloodshot brown eyes cast down.

"How far did he get when he ran?"

"A few miles. The hounds sniffed him out the next day hiding in a pecan tree along Plum Creek."

"Huh. Can he handle a plow?"

"He's been working my fields for two years now."

"Until he ran. Well, he looks strong enough. A dollar a day is what I'll pay. No rent for Sundays when he don't work. Wife won't let the niggers work on the Lord's day. Never understood that myself."

Mr. Johnson rubbed his boot toe in the dirt. "I was planning on a dollar two-bits a day."

"Hell, Johnson, a dollar a day is how much a Ranger private makes chasing Indians. I can't pay more for a day's work by your nigger than the state of Texas pays a white man to protect us from the savages."

"All right, a dollar a day. I'll need a guarantee of three months," Mr. Johnson said.

"Three months is good. And another month in the fall when we pick the cotton."

Mid-June, 1855

Six long days each week, Edward walked behind the plow pulled by Callahan's piebald mule. For twenty-four days, the slave thought about cutting the mule out of its traces, climbing on its back, and lighting out for Mexico. *If I'd been on a mule, the dogs wouldn't have catched me. This mule can git me gone, but not 'til the sun go down. An' not afta a long day pullin' this plow. Afta the day o' rest comin'. But I be needin' food. Have to find some at night an' stash it.*

On Thursday night after the lamps went out in the Callahan farmhouse, Edward lay still until he couldn't hold himself back any longer. He had been gathering and saving pecans and wild onions, but he knew he would need more food when he ran for Mexico on the mule. He left his pallet in the barn and ever so slowly walked to the back door of the kitchen. He froze when the step board creaked under his weight. Edward pulled on the door handle, not surprised to find it latched from the inside. He waited several minutes considering if he should climb through the open window. Finally fear and prudence prevailed. Rather than risk pilfering food from the family kitchen, Edward decided to just save the bread and meat Mrs. Callahan gave him each morning. His mind made up, he stepped down and returned to his blankets.

James Callahan stood barefoot in the doorway from the kitchen to the parlor. At the first noise from the back of the house, he'd silently risen. He held his revolver and listened. After a moment, he eased around to his left where through the window, he could see the barn in the moonlight. Sure enough, there was Johnson's slave, his back to Callahan, walking slowly towards the barn. *If he's using our outhouse, I'll chain the bastard at night and make him lie in his own shit.*

The next morning Callahan told Edward he'd watched him walking in the yard the night before. He gruffly warned the slave not to use the family outhouse.

On Friday night, Callahan lay awake next to his softly snoring wife, his hands linked behind his head. He had been thinking back twenty years to the days when Captain Ward's company had been holed up fighting Santa Anna's *soldados* at

Refugio. *We held out just fine until we finally ran out of bullets, but then...*

With no ammunition, Ward's company had surrendered and suffered the indignity of being taken prisoner and marched to the fortified stone church at Goliad. There they endured awful days of captivity, crammed elbow-to-elbow in the stuffy sanctuary. Callahan had the incredible good fortune of being chosen for a work party, sent to build a bridge for the Mexican army near Victoria.

How lucky I was not to have been among the massacred men at Goliad. Damn, I about starved during those days of hiding and nights of running, living off pecans and wild onions. God, I hate the Mexicans. Papists and horse thieves, all of 'em.

He smiled in grim satisfaction as he remembered executing the wounded *bandito* they'd caught hiding by a spring on one of the patrols he'd led years ago. *Just because that stupid greaser had a bullet in his leg, he thought we were going to bandage him and take him home instead of shooting him. Dumb shit.*

Already stirred up by his memories, Callahan immediately left the bed when he heard an outside noise through the open bedroom window. He saw the barn door move and a shadow go through the door. *That damned darkie of Johnson's is prowling around again. I'll deal with him in the morning.*

Just after dawn, Wesley Callahan came into the kitchen with the basket of eggs he'd been sent to gather. As he put the straw basket on the table, he remarked to his parents. "Mr. Johnson's darkie is behind the barn filing an old piece of steel from a barrel or something. Looks like he's working it into a long knife blade."

"Is he now?" James Callahan pushed back his chair and swallowed the last bite of his biscuit. He shoved his pistol into the waist of his trousers before he strode purposefully out the door with Wesley at his heels.

Callahan rounded the corner of the barn and saw Edward seated on an upturned stump near the stack of split firewood. A foot-long thin piece of steel was wedged into the crack in another stump and Edward's full attention was on making firm strokes with the file along one side of the steel. Callahan could easily see the shining sharp edge of the half-finished knife blade.

"Edward, what are you doing there?"

"Making me a knife fo' choppin' weeds, Mastuh Cal'han."

"We got hoes for that. An' you still got acres to plow before any hoeing."

"Yassuh, but dis be a knife I can carries when I's plowin'. Come on big ole snake or eben a possum, I kin kilt it wit dis knife. Good fo' de stew pot."

"You put down the file and go get the mule. I'll take that knife blade."

When Edward didn't answer or stand up immediately, Callahan said, "Wesley, fetch me the shotgun." The boy turned and sprinted back to the house.

Edward stayed seated on the stump facing away from Callahan while he moved the steel bar back and forth until he freed the crudely curved point of the blade. He stood up, holding the bar in front of him by the squared-off end, looking the white man in the eyes.

Callahan said, "Nigger, I told you to leave the knife."

"Nah,suh, you said you'd take it. I's gonna give it to you."

"You challenging me? Are you that stupid?" Callahan held up one hand, his thumb and forefinger not quite touching. "Boy, you are about this far from being tied to a wagon wheel and the lash put to your back again."

Neither man moved, both staring at the other.

"Here, Pa." Wesley panted as he held out the long shotgun to his father. Callahan took the weapon in one hand, keeping his eyes on Edward.

"Set the knife on the stump. You got plowing to do."

The Negro kept staring at Callahan as he raised his arm and hurled the knife point first into the ground between the men.

"Why you defiant black bastard!" Callahan raised the shotgun. Edward spun around and broke into a run. The first blast caught the Negro in the legs and buttocks, sending him sprawling onto his stomach on the ground. Callahan held out the shotgun for Wesley to take. Then he walked to stand over Edward, pulled his Colt revolver and shot twice more, killing him.

"Wesley, take the shotgun inside and reload it, while I get a wagon tarp to cover this mess before your mother sees it. I'll send your little brother to tell Johnson to come get the carcass. Then you're going to have to spend the day plowing."

That morning at his store, James Callahan penned a short note to George Johnson. He wrote that he'd been forced to shoot the Negro Edward when the slave had threatened him and his son with a long knife before trying to run away. Callahan sent his younger son, Jimmy, to deliver the note to his neighbor.

Later the same afternoon, Johnson arrived in a wagon at the Callahans' farm, furious and demanding eight hundred dollars for the dead Negro. Callahan bluntly refused, retorting that it was common practice to put down mad dogs, no matter who owned them, and Johnson was at fault for leasing out a dangerous slave, a known runner. Johnson left threatening a lawsuit.

The owner of the *Seguin Mercury* weekly newspaper heard about the conflict in Prairie Lea, involving one of the founding fathers of Seguin. He rode to Callahan's store, interviewed his old friend over a pint of Menger's beer, and printed the following story in the next edition of the Seguin newspaper.

A NEGRO KILLED

We understand that a negro, the property of Mr. George Johnson, of Caldwell County, was killed by Capt. Callaghan, at his place near Prairie Lea, a few days ago. We learned that Capt. Callaghan had been molested several times, for two or three nights, by persons attempting to break into his house. The noise he made in arising scared them away, and each time he found the negro man in question near the woodpile. This probably excited his suspicion. In the mean time he learned that the negro was armed. He therefore ordered him to give up his arms—a six-shooter, and an unearthly, long, sharp steel blade. The negro refused to do so. The captain then drew his six-shooter and told him he must give up his arms or be shot. The boy drew his pistol, and told him to shoot, and seemed careless of his life. The Captain then sent his little son to the house for his shot gun, and as the little fellow approached with the gun, the negro broke and ran towards a horse he had staked out, with a view to mounting him and escaping. The Captain discharged his fowling piece at him without serious effect, and the boy still running, he plumped him in the back with his six-shooter, and that was the last of "Poor Old Edward." The Captain's experience with the "Injins" doubtless assisted him in this affair.

When James Callahan read the newspaper article two weeks later, he grunted in satisfaction. When George Johnson read the article, he loudly swore, "Callahan's a damned liar."

Chapter 35

Near the Farm of Pendleton Rector
Cibolo Creek, North of San Antonio, Texas
Early Morning, July 4, 1855

The nine raiders rode slowly and quietly along dry streambeds and ravines, staying out of sight. Every half mile, one man dismounted and crept up to high ground and scanned for pastured horses and mules. When they spied the dark-skinned girl climbing the path from a flowing creek with a water bucket balanced on her head, the men grinned to each other.

Wild Cat saw his companions were eager for the amusement of a young female, but he was nervous about their nearness to so many settlements. Her screams might be heard, and her body would be quickly found. The chief had been on enough raids to know the whites would pursue his band with much more commitment if they left a ravaged corpse behind, even a black woman, than if they only stole riding stock.

Nonetheless, he saw he would have difficulty forcing the others to ignore her. Wild Cat reluctantly nodded his consent to his men, but tapped his lance, then shook his head as he pointed at his own groin. His younger half-brother, who displayed the dark skin of their Negro mother, spat in disgust, but lowered his lance as he kneed his horse forward. Four braves galloped towards the girl, who saw them and screamed, dropping the bucket. The Lipans and Seminoles slowed their mounts to a walk as they formed a ring around her, tormenting her with their spear points, stabbing, but not piercing her skin deeply, Two warriors dismounted and ripped the girl's clothing away as they forced her onto her back.

Wild Cat growled as he nudged his horse between two others. He leaned down and thrust his lance through the girl's chest, impaling her to the ground, stopping her frantic struggling and shrieking. He looked at his braves and said, "No time for fun. We came for horses and are too close to the white villages. Come." With that he rode away, confident they would follow.

The band of raiders made their way along a dry gulch, traveling barely a mile from the Negro girl's body. As they rounded a slight bend, Wild Cat and a gray-haired white man simultaneously spotted each other, maybe a hundred yards separating them.

"There." the leader pointed and the whole band surged forward, whooping in the excitement of a new chase.

"Dammit to hell!" Pendleton Rector cursed. He jerked on the reins to turn his mare. Fourteen-year-old Jouette McGee looked ahead and saw the Indians galloping towards them. He kicked his small mule in the ribs, but the animal balked.

"Mr. Rector, help me!"

The farmer looked back at the oncoming Indians and looked at the mule, recognizing the obstinate animal wasn't likely to run anywhere. He also instantly decided if he took the boy onto his mount with him, they would not outrun the Indians. Rector shouted, "Kick him harder!" as he spurred his mare and galloped away.

Jouette kicked with all his might, but the mule simply laid back its long ears and brayed.

The Indians reached the mule and laughed at the boy who sat on its back. Jouette bit his lips to stifle the sobs that tried to escape his mouth, but he couldn't hold back the tears in his eyes. He raised his hands up high in surrender.

Wild Cat joined the circle of warriors who surrounded the white boy. The Black Seminole chief was still irritated over the others' defiance when they'd come upon the black girl just a few minutes earlier. To reassert his authority, he slid off his horse and walked to the boy on the mule. He pulled him off the animal and shoved him out of the circle of mounted warriors. He pointed up the gully and said something the boy didn't understand. Whatever the Indian meant, Jouette ran blindly up the wash away from his captors.

One of the braves thought Wild Cat had released the boy for sport, so they could skewer him in the back like a running buffalo calf, so he turned his horse to be first among the pursuers. Before he could kick his gelding into motion, Wild Cat grabbed the horse's long mane and shook his head. He was letting the young white boy go. The young brave glared down at his older chief, but didn't challenge him.

In his flight, Pendleton Rector reached the end of the wash and veered his mare to climb the side. He was nearly at the top when the horse lost its footing in the loose dirt and slowly fell sideways. Rector barely had time to pull his feet from the stirrups and push himself away from the panicked beast. The farmer frantically crawled on all fours to the top of the slope and disappeared into the thick brush growing there.

Three braves had galloped past the boy on the mule and chased the white man on the tall horse. The strength and speed of the Rector's mare kept the prey ahead of the predators. They weren't able to catch him before his mount stumbled and fell. Two warriors dismounted and followed the white man into the scrub brush, while the other brave scrambled up the side of the wash to secure Rector's horse, which appeared uninjured from its fall.

Leaving the two dismounted warriors searching for the white man hiding in the brush, the Lipan leisurely rode back towards the others, leading the captured horse. He was surprised when a white boy ran into view just ahead of him. Without hesitating, the warrior lowered his lance and drove the point through the boy's breast. He stopped only long enough to dismount and quickly use his skinning knife to peel off a swatch of hair-covered skin from the top of the dying boy's head.

The two braves soon abandoned their search for the white man hiding in the brush. Neither really wanted to be the one to discover him and risk being shot by the pistol he was sure to have.

Assuming that the two corpses would be discovered that day, Wild Cat cut his raid short. As soon as they came upon half a dozen horses in a nearby pasture and lassoed them, the Indians started with the stolen animals back towards the Rio Grande.

Chapter 36

The Magnolia Hotel
Seguin, Texas
Late Afternoon, July 4, 1855

Merchants, lawyers, physicians and politicians in dark suits sat knee-to-knee in the rows of straight chairs that filled the dining room of the Magnolia Hotel. Farmers and stockmen leaned against the walls, holding their sweat-stained hats, shifting from one foot to the other. The attendance at the Independence Day gathering reflected the thirst for news and political direction in Seguin, a town on the edge of civilized Texas.

The main speaker of the day, Reverend James C. Wilson, part-time Methodist itinerate preacher, had been introduced by another Methodist circuit-rider, the Reverend John McGee. McGee, a Kentuckian with a large family, was newly assigned to Texas and exhorted his flock in Seguin three times a month. Even if introduced by a preacher, Wilson had left the Lord's word in his pocket today, and spoke as a senator who had served in the most recent session of the Texas Legislature. Today his message was political, and held the attention of the packed house.

Nearly half an hour into his speech, Wilson paused. For going on thirty minutes, his oration had focused on the increasingly dire state of the American Union. He'd given examples, some documented and some questionable, of how the fat politicians in the north were shredding the sacred Constitution and over-extending the power of the central government far beyond the intent of the Founding Fathers. Perspiration ran into Wilson's eyes, blurring his vision. He theatrically wiped his brow with his sweat-soaked linen handkerchief, sipped warm water from a small glass, and hooked his thumbs in his vest pockets.

He scanned the audience to assure himself that they would willingly endure another half-hour of his wisdom before he lost them to the barbecue beef roasting outside. Wilson opened his mouth to offer more good reasons why southern secession from the old New England states was a good idea, and inevitable.

The thirty-five year-old with the stentorian voice did not like interruptions once he was deep into his flow of words. He scowled darkly at the dust-covered man who didn't even slow down as he hurried through the open double doors and pulled everyone's attention away from the speaker.

The man quickly snatched his hat off his head and called out, "Is Captain Callahan here? I have a message for him."

Wilson knew Callahan and hadn't seen him in the meeting, so he replied in his penetrating public speaking voice, "Young man, the captain is not here, but since you have interrupted my time at the podium, bring me the message, so we can all learn what is so important."

"Sir, it's Ranger business, for the captain..."

A man in the middle of the third row stood and announced in a loud voice, "Son, I'm Rip Ford. You can hand that message over to me, and I'll deliver it right away to Captain Callahan."

The young messenger recognized Captain Ford and complied by leaning over several seated men to pass the message to Ford who was a veteran Ranger, past state senator, and now a newspaper editor in Austin. Ford silently read the message, squeezed his way into the main aisle, and walked briskly towards the podium. Instead of handing the note to Senator Wilson, he stopped at the first row of seats, tapped Reverend McGee on the shoulder, and pointed they should go into the kitchen.

Ford wordlessly gave the note to Reverend McGee and left him alone. Back in the dining room, the old Ranger slipped up behind Senator Wilson and whispered a condensed version of the note's contents. Wilson swiveled his head to confirm by sight what he'd just been told. Ford held his gaze and nodded.

James Wilson instantly and seamlessly shifted from Senator to Methodist preacher as he lowered his head and raised his hands above his head, palms up. The expectant silence in the room was palpable.

"Gentlemen, there has been yet another tragedy. Bow with me as I address the Lord." Wilson waited while men glanced at each other, then lowered their heads. Finally, Wilson closed his eyes.

"Most High God, Creator of All Things, it is my solemn Christian duty to commend to thee the soul of young Jouette McGee, son of your devoted earthly vessel, the Reverend John McGee." Wilson swallowed and let a catch be heard in his voice as he continued.

"Mighty God, we have just learned that young Jouette has been murdered on this very day, this celebrated Day of Independence. This morning, the poor lad became another victim of Indian depredations, a pestilence loosed upon Thy world by demons in this place we call Texas. The savages are a hideous scourge that rival the great Biblical plagues of ancient Egypt." Wilson opened his eyes to see the expected angry reaction among the crowd. In an even louder voice meant to stymie any murmuring between members of the audience, he went on.

"We pray now for the soul of young Jouette, an innocent boy cruelly lanced through his breast, his earthly remains mutilated by heathen barbarians who year after year torment Thy people. Barbarians who ravage our women, kill our children, and steal our livestock before they scurry like cockroaches to hide in the dark wastelands across the Rio Grande."

Many in the all-male audience now raised their eyes and look around at each other, many letting their hands rest on holstered pistols.

Now thundering in his passion, Wilson prayed, "Great God in Heaven, I stand before thee in this gathering of patriots and Christians to beg Thy hands rest on the shoulders of the good men, who even as I humble myself before Thee, are in pursuit of the foul heathens."

Wilson paused, letting the grim news sink in. His next words come out in softly. "Lord, we remain mindful of the blessed teachings and sacrifice of Thy son, Jesus of Nazareth. Yes, Lord, we remember that in Thy holy book, your New Testament, we are taught that He is the way, the only way."

The preacher turned politician took a deep breath before he almost whispered, "But today, Lord..." In a voice growing louder with each word, "Today, we remember that your inspired voices on earth wrote another Testament, an older Testament. So, in accord with the actions of your chosen leaders in the Old

Testament, bold actions taken by your chosen ones like King David, today, we seek Thy blessings for retribution." Wilson waited a heartbeat. "Swift and terrible retribution against the savages who are not Thy sons, but the spawn of Satan, Thy eternal enemy. Amen."

Chapter 37

A Pasture Belonging to James Callahan
East of Prairie Lea, Texas
July 8, 1855

Milo slapped at the blue fly that lit on his hand which rested on the saddle horn. James Callahan took a pull from his pocket flask and offered it to Milo.

"Early, ain't it?" the younger man said, but to be polite, he accepted the flat glass bottle and tilted it up for a sip.

"Sunday mornings don't count." Callahan corked the flask and slipped it back into his coat pocket. The pair sat on their horses in the shade of a weathered old live oak tree, the time still shy of mid-morning. Before them lay a wide grass-covered plain.

"Why'd you ask me to ride out here with you, Mr. Callahan? We could'a shared a snort on the porch of your store." Milo grinned. "You're cutting into my courting time with Malissa. I only get to see her once a week, and I'm out here with you, instead of back at the Gunn's place with her."

"Huh. I'll try to make it worthwhile. What do you think? Two hundred acres, prime virgin crop land. Never seen a plow blade." Callahan waved his hand expansively.

"I think it's a mighty fine sight. Are you offering me a job?" Milo shifted in his saddle, suspicious of the older man's motives. "Are you asking me to farm your land for you? I thought you just hired a slave from Mr. Johnson to do your farming."

"I did, but that nigger didn't work out. No, I have something else in mind for this field."

"Well, I hope that plan don't include me. The only land I aim to farm is going to be mine. Until then I'm keeping to the carpentry work."

"You're good with a hammer and saw, huh?"

Philip McBride

"Mostly I'm good at measuring and making things fit tight together."

"How long is it going to take you to save enough to buy a pasture like this?"

"A while."

"How much you make with your tools?"

"Two dollars a day. I save half, a dollar a day."

"A year of carpentry work for a down payment, plus a big loan. Then building a house and a barn. Fences for livestock. Putting together a farm weighs a man down with debt."

"No way around it, unless a man's born rich," Milo countered.

"How about three month's work for fifty dollars a month, no expenses? Save it all."

"Sounds good. But doing what? All I know is carpentry for two dollars a day, and rangering for half that."

"Governor Pease authorized me to raise a new Ranger company to go after the Apaches. Regular army strength, over eighty men. The first sergeant will make fifty a month."

"You offering me the job of first sergeant?"

"Yup, that's why I brought you out here."

"Three months at fifty dollars a month. Why me? Sir, you've led Minute-Men and Ranger patrols since I was a babe in Alabama. Why not one of the men who's ridden with you before?"

"You've ridden with me, Milo. It wasn't a rangering patrol, but I ain't forgot that ride to San Antone and the Mexican bushwacker you killed. Besides, you've been across the Rio Grande River after that captured white woman. Fought Indians and brought her back. You earned a lot of respect doing that. And Captain Boggess tells me you were a good corporal on his patrol last winter. You looked after the other men."

Milo tried not to let it show, but he was flattered. "That's a tempting offer, Mr. Callahan. But even a hundred and fifty dollars in my pocket, if and when the government ever pays, don't get me any closer to land like that there." This time Milo waved his hand over the prairie before them.

"That's where you're wrong, Milo. You serve as my first sergeant. Go with me into Mexico after the Indians, maybe round up a few runaway niggers. You've done that before. You keep my--our--men in line, make sure they follow my orders. When we get home, I'll carry the note on this piece of land for as long as it takes you to pay me. No down payment. When your Ranger pay comes through, you keep it."

"Why don't you farm it, Mr. Callahan? Rent a few slaves to work it, grow your own cotton. Maybe open your own gin."

Callahan stroked his graying beard. "I'm moving west, Milo. I ain't cut out for minding a store or farming. I aim to raise cattle out on the Blanco River. Already found a spread with a house. Got a buyer for the store. New immigrant from England, landing in Galveston soon."

"Why not run those cattle here, on this land? Stay in Prairie Lea."

"The dirt here is too good to waste on cattle. Cattle can live on a rocky hillside. No, this patch is screaming for cotton, or maybe grain."

"Why not move back to Seguin? Gosh, Sir, you started the town. You know most of the people who live there."

"Used to know most of them. Not any more. That was twenty years back. Too many new faces now. Nope, I belong out on the edge."

"What about your wife and family? Is Mrs. Callahan ready to move again?"

"Milo, I know you are smitten with young Miss Gunn, but don't you ever forget God made woman from Adam's rib, to serve man. Mrs. Callahan will move where I say we're moving."

Milo had no reply, wondering if Malissa would follow him if he said they were moving into the hills where the Indians still raided.

"Well, how about it? Is it a deal?" Callahan asked. "You up for being Sergeant McKean?"

Milo got off his horse and walked twenty yards into the pasture where he knelt down and pulled up a tuft of tall prairie grass. He massaged the clump of sticky black dirt clinging to the grass roots, letting little clods trickle through his fingers.

Looking up at Mr. Callahan, he brushed his hands clean on his trousers.

"Shouldn't we talk about price first?"

"Three dollars an acre. That's two-bits an acre less than a land dealer from Galveston offered me."

"I seen you riding with a lanky fella in a city suit. Wondered who it was."

"That was him. John McBee. I fought Indians with him fifteen years ago at Plum Creek."

Milo squinted up at Callahan, "Seems a good offer. Why didn't you take it?"

"Because I wanted to talk to you first."

"That's six hundred dollars. Too much for me. Jesse told me a cousin of his bought two hundred acres just two years ago near Stockdale for fifty cents an acre. I might be able to afford a dollar an acre. That's twice what he paid." Milo turned around and studied the field again.

"That was two years ago, Milo. And Stockdale ain't near the good farm land as this plot. That part of the country is half rocks and half scrub brush. Look at that black gumbo you pulled up. Holds water like a clay pot. Cotton and corn take to it like pigs to slop. Besides, you can see times are changing fast. More new settlers than land now. Nope, can't go that low, Milo. I'll go down to two fifty an acre. That's a fair price."

Milo walked back to his horse and climbed into the saddle.

"A dollar, seventy-five cents an acre. There'll be expenses. I got no mule, no plow. Have to buy seeds."

"Two dollars an acre and not a penny less. You're robbing me at that price." Callahan grinned. "But I don't give a shit. I want you as my sergeant, and I want you to have this land. Hell, the Republic gave me six hundred acres for my soldiering during the rebellion against Santy Anna. Is it a deal?"

Milo nodded his head, disbelieving what was happening. "Damn. Two hundred acres of prime cotton field. Captain, I'm your man. It's a deal at two dollars an acre. I ain't forgotten you bargaining down that Mexican selling blankets in front of the Alamo. You taught me good. And you treated me more than fair when you let me keep Buck and the Baker rifle last year. You keep your mind on our mission, and I'll make sure not a man lags behind. But one thing, there's no telling what might happen to either of us while we're rangering. I want a written contract of sale for the land before we leave."

"Wouldn't have it any other way, First Sergeant McKean."

The two men shook hands, and on their way back to Prairie Lea, they talked about how best to recruit a hundred men for a three-month enlistment. Callahan was confident he could persuade Governor Pease to pay for recruitment announcements in the four regional town newspapers: The *Seguin Mercury*, the *New Braunfels Zeitung*, the *Lockhart Watchman*, and the *Austin Gazette*. That was fine and good with McKean, but he still opined that personal recruiting would bring in more enlistments.

"Captain, I'll be wanting a voice in who serves as the other sergeants and corporals."

Callahan looked hesitant. "Normally the men elect their own lieutenants and non-commissioned officers at the company muster."

"That ain't what happened in Captain Boggess's company last winter when he and Lieutenant Jackson asked me to be corporal."

"Milo, I agree with Boggess, but we're aiming to recruit nearly a hundred volunteers, not twenty-five. That many men will expect elections."

"What about me as first sergeant? Do I have to run for election?"

"Nah, your appointment is my command decision."

"It'll be a help if I already know my sergeants and corporals. I work with some good men from Lockhart and Prairie Lea who I trust.

"Hmph. Then recruit them and campaign for them to be your sergeants and corporals. Twist some arms. Buy votes with whiskey. Hell, I don't care."

"A tapped barrel of Menger's good beer on election night would be even better."

"Milo, I swear, you do know how to push a man to his limit." Callahan smiled broadly. "Maybe a small barrel."

Chapter 38

Campground by the Springs
San Marcos, Texas
July 20, 1855

C allahan's big piebald led the mule train and wouldn't be hurried. It seemed to Milo that the odd-colored beast was testing his handler's resolve to maintain a respectable pace.

"Private Clopton, do you need help getting that spotted mule to quit sleepwalking and move his ugly ass faster?"

"Aww, Milo,"

"It's Sergeant." Milo sharply popped the end of his reins on the mule's haunch. Instead of speeding up, the piebald passed wind, brayed and kicked out both rear legs, smashing a hoof into the chest of the black mule that trudged along next in the line. That mule hee-hawed and stopped until the lead rope jerked him forward.

"I was going to say he don't respond real well to anything but rotten fruits. An' I'm out of them." Billy 'Easy' Clopton held up the empty sack

Behind the last mule, Private Gunn watched, amused at Milo's futile efforts to speed up the line of pack animals. Not one to let his friend's frustrations slip by without comment, Jesse called, "Maybe he has a throbbing head from them rotten peaches. It's hard to hurry a man—or a mule—in his cups. We're almost there, anyway."

Milo trotted Buck back to the front of the column where he resumed the first sergeant's position, riding next to Captain Callahan. The pair led the twenty-three volunteers from Caldwell County. The majority came from Prairie Lea, but several hailed from Lockhart and rural homesteads along Plum Creek. Most were young unemployed men in their early twenties, the sort who filled out every ranging company. Three of the mounted volunteers were forty years old, rivaling the age of Captain Callahan. Two had served as youngsters in the war against Santa Anna, but now, twenty years later, were still poor enough to respond to the call for volunteers. The third middle-aged man, Samuel Arlidge, had years ago lost his wife, children, and farm to the Comanches. He'd yet to quench his thirst for vengeance against the Indians, even after a decade of joining every ranging company he could.

Without looking at his first sergeant, Callahan asked, "Have you picked out who you want for your other sergeants and corporals?"

"Yessir. I have. And Jesse and me spent a whole evening next to a lantern writing out eighty copies of those names to hand out to the men before the election. You plan on tapping that beer barrel that's strapped onto the piebald?"

"Yep, I said I would, didn't I? How many of your choices are from Prairie Lea and Lockhart?"

"All of them. I don't know anyone from anywhere else around here. William Word and Joe Sanders as sergeants. Ben Elam, Tom Boon, and Bill McMurrain as corporals. All steady hands."

"What about your friend Gunn?"

"Jesse? He won't let me add his name. He's not much for telling other fellas what to do."

"Some men are like that. Don't make him any less a man. Add Riley Lewis from Seguin to your sergeants list. I want him as my aide-de-camp."

"I thought you'd bring along a darkie to handle the mules and be your body servant."

"Nah. We're most likely going into Mexico. Too easy for a slave to slip away."

"You going to have the election tonight?"

"Depends if the recruits from Curry's Creek and Seguin have reached the muster ground. Maybe wait one more day. But there's no need to dawdle in San Marcos. Hell, I half emptied my store inventory making sure we have enough food, coffee, and horseshoes. Don't want to break into those supplies before we even start west."

189

Suddenly curious, Milo asked, "How many horseshoes? I hadn't thought about that."

"Hell if I know. A lot. We got what, nearly five hundred hooves to keep shod for three months of riding over rough ground? You'll have to ask Jake Roberts. He's a decent enough farrier, but damned if he didn't bring a whole mule load of iron shoes and nails. And a little bitty anvil and a hand-pumped bellows and hammers and a sledge."

"Hate to be the mule humping all that iron."

"I made him spread it out."

"Well, the piebald won't have a beer keg to carry after the election."

"Come on, Milo, I'm paying you to think. Water. We'll put our emergency water in the empty beer keg. That's mainly why I brung it. Not to ensure your pals are elected sergeants and corporals. Although that was a fine idea. When the beer's gone, it'll hold clear, cold water from the springs at San Marcos."

"Yeah, I should've thought of that. Wonder if that spring water will taste like beer later on when we need it?"

Callahan barked a laugh at the idea. "By then, it'll probably taste like pond scum."

Milo thought so too. "I'm mighty impressed, Captain, with your outfitting the company from your own store stock. Mighty generous."

Callahan barked loudly again. "That's a good one, Milo. Rest assured that every damned item was priced fairly and put on a list, and that list is on its way to the governor right now. I'll get reimbursed about the time you get paid."

"Even the beer?"

"Well, the barrel of beer might have turned into a barrel of flour on the list."

★

At the San Marcos Springs campground, just off the road connecting Austin City and San Antonio, dozens of volunteers lounged in the shade, sitting around small campfires drinking coffee. Their tethered horses dotted the field, grazing. More than a few young men swam in the river, some swinging into the water off a lariat tied to an overhanging oak limb.

Captain Callahan's right foot was barely out of the stirrup when he saw William Kyle, Jr., who'd recently moved to San Marcos. Callahan had offered Kyle the second lieutenant's position, even though he was only twenty-five. He knew the young man's father, who was the influential owner of two plantations and nearly two hundred slaves. Beyond that, Callahan was impressed with Kyle's self-confidence and good handwriting. As the Second Lieutenant, Kyle would serve as the company's adjutant—the keeper of paper documents and correspondence that Callahan found burdensome, but vital.

"How many men have showed up, William?"

"Nigh on all of 'em, Captain. Sixty-two by my last count. How many with you?"

"Twenty-six armed men. You scare up any good boys from around here?"

Kyle smiled. "Not many folks live around here. But I found a handful of willing men. Me and my cousin Polk. Ed Burleson and his brother and cousin. Five or six others. More from up Austin way. A good number from Curry's Creek and the Blanco River settlements. Most of the volunteers are from south of us, though. Seguin, farms along Cibolo Creek and the Guadalupe River. I'm surprised at how easy it's been to get our full complement of guns."

Callahan nodded. "Yep, word of the McGee boy's death riled up folks. Thank God. It's past time to settle up with the damned Apaches."

Captain Callahan handed his reins to a Negro boy who worked for the Burleson family at their new house in San Marcos. He and Lieutenant Kyle walked to the tent fly serving as the headquarters for the gathering company. When they were both seated on stump stools and holding tin mugs of steaming coffee, Kyle spoke.

"Captain, we all know you've been commissioned by the governor to chase down and kill as many Apaches as we can find, even if that takes us into Mexico." Callahan sipped the hot coffee and nodded.

"I don't know if crossing the Rio Grande will be needed, William. My orders are to keep the Apaches out of Bexar and Comal Counties. But that's a tall order. You know that even if I split the company, we can't watch over every farm and homestead. But when we do get word of the next damned Apache raid, we'll follow those bastards wherever the trail takes us. Even into Mexico."

"We're ready for that, Sir. The men are primed and loaded, ready to ride."

Callahan nodded again.

Kyle looked down at the steam swirling up from his mug and jumped into the issue that had suddenly dominated the volunteers' conversations that same day. The lieutenant wasn't sure how the matter had become a hot potato in just a couple of hours, but it was now a subject that had seized the attention of almost every man.

"Sir, what about the fugitive slaves along the Rio Grande on the Mexican side? Rip Ford's newspaper is printing that there may be two or three thousand runaways along the river. It's hard to imagine that many nigras, one or two million dollars worth of darkies, living just over the border. It makes my father furious."

"I believe editor Ford is right about that, Lieutenant. Those runaway niggers are a huge loss to the planters like your father. They need 'em back in the fields."

"Yessir. I wonder why Governor Pease hasn't done anything to fetch 'em back."

"William, he's a politician, that's why. He sees the runaways as the plantation owners' problem, not a public matter. I bet your father has told you that a couple of emissaries from the planters delivered a letter to Mexican Governor Vidaurri.

"Yes sir, Father mentioned a letter, but didn't say much about it."

"Well, it was a letter asking Vidaurri to look the other way, like a good neighbor would do, while the planters' men crossed the fence into his pasture to retrieve a stray bull."

Lieutenant Kyle raised his eyebrows waiting for Callahan to relate the governor's answer.

"The letter didn't work. Governor Vidaurri rebuffed the emissaries. And that's not all. A few weeks later, Captain William Henry led a filibustering company into Coahuila. He'd heard and believed there was a faction ready to break away from Mexico, form their own republic like Texas did."

"And?" Kyle asked.

"Henry was run out of Mexico. Hell, he should of known better."

Kyle nodded in agreement. "I hear Captain Henry is a pugnacious sort."

Callahan snorted at the description. "You heard right, but then, so am I. Huh. Pugnacious. I like that." Kyle grinned at Callahan's joking candor, admitting what others already knew.

"That's why the men keep volunteering for your company, Captain. You hit hard and don't let up. That's why the governor's willing to let you lead us into Mexico."

Kyle took a breath and eased into his concern. "But sir, a rumor is spreading among the boys like wildfire. A rumor that we're not only going south to punish the Apaches, but also to round up as many fugitive Negroes as we can catch. Bring the darkies back to Texas and turn 'em over to the plantation owners."

Kyle watched Callahan take another sip of coffee before he answered.

"Lieutenant Kyle, would you object if that rumor were true?"

Kyle let his gaze drift up at the tree branches behind the captain, as he formulated his response. After a few seconds, he brought his thoughts together and looked at Callahan.

"I'm not sure, Captain. My worry isn't the idea of rounding up fugitive darkies. We could do that easy enough, I imagine. That would certainly please my father and the other planters."

Callahan nodded and waited for young Kyle to tell him why he was hesitant.

"Although, if we were to bring back a hundred runaways, the boys should share the reward for every runner we can return to its owner and the profit from auctioning the others."

"I get that, Lieutenant Kyle. None of our volunteers are rich men, and they wouldn't abide just giving over such valuable recovered property to the planters. Not after they risked their hides to catch 'em and bring 'em back. So what's making you uneasy?"

"Captain, it's the idea of having two missions. Two missions that might tug us in two opposite directions. There might be an Apache encampment upriver and a Nigra settlement down river. Sir, there ain't all that many of us. Less than a hundred. We don't know how many Indians we may find over the border. I can't see that we have the manpower to split our force and take on two jobs."

"I see. Don't you worry none about that, Lieutenant. I may be pugnacious, but I ain't a stupid captain. I know our strength is in our massed firepower, our Colts. I'm not one to water down our ability to punch through a bad spot with the pistols of eighty rangers, all together, not divided up. If we get into Mexico, our aim is to punish the Apaches." Callahan stood as he tossed out his coffee grounds.

"After that, only afterwards, if we have an opportunity to sweep through a nigger settlement and round up a few dozen runaways, I won't hold the men back. Put some cash money in the boys' pockets. But runaway niggers ain't our mission if we do get into Mexico. We'll go to kill enough Apaches that they'll quit raiding into Texas."

"Yessir."

"Lieutenant, you let the word seep out. Apaches first, then maybe a coon hunt to sweeten the payday for the boys. But only if we can do it without endangering our mission or our men. And between you and me, and this is important, anything besides killing Apaches would be unofficial. Off the books—the books you're going to be keeping."

★

During the late afternoon, Sergeant McKean and Private Gunn circulated among the campfires announcing that anyone wanting to run for a corporal or sergeant's spot needed to go see Second Lieutenant Kyle to get on the ballot. The pair also distributed the handwritten list of Milo's recommended sergeant and corporal candidates.

The men were told they were all due a tin mug of Menger's beer from the keg that was cooling in the springs. It was also mentioned that they could sign the little paper square of names and use it as a ballot for the non-commissioned officer election. After Milo walked away, Jesse would quietly mention to every group that if they dropped the signed ballot in First Sergeant McKean's upturned hat while their tin mug was under the tap of the beer barrel, the wooden faucet might be left open a bit longer.

The vote tally turned out to be a clean sweep for McKean's ticket, with the addition of eighteen-year-old Charley Taylor of San Marcos as fourth corporal. Taylor was a short, slim young man who frequently won horse races on his father's exceptionally fast chestnut filly. Burleson planned to use the young man as the company's courier.

Only one corporal candidate groused about the outcome of the election, and he only grumbled about it to the friend who'd enlisted with him. Twenty-year-old Luther Blessingame from Seguin had counted on his father's old friendship with Callahan to win him a corporal's extra pay.

Captain Callahan started a brief motivational speech, but cut it short when he saw that the men were more interested in the whiskey, beer, and slabs of hot roasted pork sliced off the whole hog carcasses. Callahan quickly saw his words weren't penetrating many skulls. He muttered to himself, "To hell with talking. They know why they're here," and shut up.

By midmorning the next day, the eighty-eight mounted volunteers of Captain Callahan's ninety-day company were riding southwest, many of them nursing throbbing heads from the beer and whiskey drunk the night before. Two loaded wagons followed the Rangers, headed to the town of Bandera where Lieutenant Kyle had rented a house to store the food needed to keep the Rangers on patrol for ninety days. Among the sacks of cornmeal and barrels of salted pork was a heavy wooden crate that had arrived from Galveston and contained four dozen sets of steel shackles—leg irons.

Chapter 39

Near Bandera, Texas
Northwest of San Antonio
August 1855

After a month on the ranging patrol, Private Gunn had grown accustomed to the rhythm of the days. The volunteers left their bedrolls an hour before dawn to boil coffee and eat what rations were available. Horses were watered and saddled in the growing light and the men's canteens filled as the last chore before mounting. Jesse gazed around, enjoying the early morning play of light among the cypress trees that lined the river. He and 'Easy' Clopton squatted on flat rocks in the shallow water and held bubbling canteens under the surface. Their horses stood next to them, noses down, mouths sucking up water.

This day, Gunn and Clopton were part of a small detachment from the company, on an overnight scout to the west of Bandera, a new settlement built around a water-driven mill on the Medina River.

The crack of several gunshots startled the pair of Rangers. Both instantly scrambled onto their horses, leaving their canteens and drawing their revolvers, scanning all around for the white smoke of gunfire. Within seconds, First Sergeant McKean thundered past them on Buck, his dun-colored horse.

"With me!" Milo shouted as he disappeared into the brush, seemingly riding away from the gunfire.

The three Rangers pushed their horses through the thick growth, making a wide circle away from the river to emerge on the edge of a field. They heard more gunfire and saw a figure on the far side of the clearing on horseback, between them and the river. He was holding the reins of four other animals.

As more gunfire continued from the riverbank, Milo leaned towards Jesse and whispered. "Use your Sharps."

Jesse holstered his Colt pistol and slipped his new carbine from its scabbard. He quickly cocked it, aimed and fired. The man fell from his mount.

"Now, let's go!"

The trio kicked their horses forward as four figures ran from the tree line, climbed onto their mounts and galloped off. The Rangers ineffectively fired their revolvers at the receding targets nearly a hundred yards away. Two Rangers on foot appeared out of the tree line, one limping and holding a hand pressed to his thigh.

Milo glanced at Private Clopton. "Easy, you ride like hell back to Bandera and tell Captain Callahan we've found the hostiles."

"They found us, you mean," Clopton answered as he turned his horse.

"Just git gone and bring them back *pronto*." Milo dismounted and knelt by Private Luther Blassingame, who had plopped down to get off his wounded leg.

"Luther, let me see it." Blassingame, a twenty-year-old from Seguin who was the son of an old neighbor of Callahan's, grimaced as he moved his hand tentatively away from the bullet's entry wound. Milo poured canteen water on it and wiped blood away with his dirty fingers.

"It's not real bad, Luther. I think. We'll get you to Bandera though." Milo looked up at the other Ranger who'd appeared with Blassingame.

"Sam, where's Danny? Is he with your horses? Is he hurt?"

Private Sam Durham looked nervous. "Sergeant, I think he's dead. He was off in the trees doin' his business when the Injuns started shooting. I never heard his pistol fire."

"Shit. Jesse, stay with Luther. Sam, show me where he was." All four Rangers kept their weapons in their hands. No more than thirty yards away, Milo and Sam found Private Daniel Shuler face down, trousers around his ankles, an arrow in his back.

★

Two hours later, several Rangers stood in a circle around the fallen hostile. Corporal Tom Boon nudged the jaw of the corpse with his boot toe.

"Look at his lips. Them's thick African lips, not Injun. And look at his kinky hair. I heard of black redskins, but didn't believe it."

"Are we fighting runaway slaves or Indians?" Corporal Bill McMurrain squatted on his heels by the body and ran a finger over the dead man's shirt.

"He ain't dressed like no Apache I ever seen. Look at the fancy tin gee-gaws on his shirt and those red cloth bands around his knees. What was he, a nigger or a foreign Injun?" Still mounted, Captain Callahan approached the group.

"That there is a black Seminole. Way back 'bout the time Texas was fighting Santa Anna, the Seminoles were nearly wiped out by the army in Florida. Andrew Jackson saw to that. The Seminoles that weren't killed were resettled somewhere west of Florida. But a bunch of them escaped from the reservations and trekked to Mexico. Now, twenty years later, here the bastards are, helping the Lipans raise hell on our side of the Rio Grande."

"But he's gotta be a breed, Captain," Corporal Boon said.

Still on horseback, Callahan agreed. "Sure looks it, don't he? Young looking, too. I been hearing that runaway niggers in Mexico have been taking Seminole squaws as wives since hardly any women slaves run for Mexico." Callahan spat on the corpse. "There's your proof. Maybe we should send his head to General Smith to show him the niggers and redskins are now allies. Hell, this boy proves we're up against a whole new kind of hostile. Who plugged him?"

"Private Gunn got him with his Sharps, from way over yonder on the other side of the field."

Callahan twisted in his saddle and gauged the distance. "That was good shooting, Jesse. Sure wish more of us had Sharps carbines."

With the marauders having a lead of only a few hours, Captain Callahan split his ninety-man company into three segments. He personally led fifty men following the tracks of the raiders who'd attacked Sergeant McKean's scouting party. He sent a small ten-man patrol under Second Lieutenant Kyle with the two corpses and the wounded Blassingame back to Bandera with orders to patrol south of the town every day until the rest of the company returned.

Callahan selected a third group of thirty Rangers who rode the strongest horses. Under First Lieutenant Burleson, they would ride with all haste south along the Medina River, skirting the rugged mountains until they emerged out of the hills. They would then head west to the Rio Hondo River. Once they intercepted the Rio Hondo, Burleson's patrol would then turn and ride northwest along the riverbank. The plan was to catch the raiders on the south side of Bandera Pass in a pincer movement by the two groups of Rangers.

In spite of the nearly immediate response and the effort to trap the hostiles between the two Ranger contingents, the raiders once again eluded their pursuers. After two days of hard riding, the whole company camped on the Rio Hondo for four days to rest the horses while Callahan sent a courier to communicate with Governor Pease. The governor replied promptly, informing Callahan of more far-reaching Indian raids. In the dispatch, he relayed that Judge Jones of Fredericksburg estimated one hundred hostiles were actively raiding in the counties west of San Antonio.

In response, Callahan next sent Burleson's thirty men north towards Fredricksburg, noting the governor's mention of new depradations in that region. Finally, he reluctantly split his fifty remaining Rangers again, sending twenty troopers back to Bandera to reinforce the ten men patrolling that more southern region.

Callahan would lead the last thirty Rangers further west towards the Frio River, hoping to intercept the tracks of Apaches or Black Seminoles raiding parties.

Watching the two parties ride away, Milo shook his head in doubt at dividing the company into three parties. Captain Callahan surprised Milo when he spoke from right behind the first sergeant.

"I don't like it either, Milo. Not one bit. To cover all the places where the redskins are raiding, we need two or three more companies the size we mustered in San Marcos. And I've written that to Governor Pease. But money's tight. Ain't it always? But maybe the governor can squeeze out one more company. We'll see."

★

The two far-flung Ranger detachments rejoined Callahan's core company in mid-September. Each of the three Ranger patrols had fought skirmishes with small parties of Apaches or Comanches. Yet, an aggregate of only three hostiles were confirmed killed. More positively, due to the fleeing Indians' willingness to release any stolen stock that might slow their flight when pursued by the Rangers, fourteen horses had been recovered.

The corpse of one Indian warrior was clothed in a well-made collared and cuffed white shirt of a size to fit a teenage boy. The shirt displayed a faded bloodstain around a hole in its front the size of a lance point. Captain Callahan sent the shirt to the governor as tangible proof of his company's diligence, and as a reminder. Callahan did not want the governor to gloss over the need for more volunteer companies to patrol the vast frontier if they hoped to prevent Indian depredations, rather than futilely pursuing the Indian raiders after they'd done their damage.

Callahan's three-month company of mounted volunteer Rangers only had one more month of service. Throughout the first sixty days of patrolling, the captain had remained determined not to let the company's mid-October expiration date pass without fulfilling his promise to himself and others like newspaper editor Rip Ford.

From the time of the governor's first authorization of this, his newest, and likely his last, command of a Ranger company, forty-year old Callahan intended to follow the Apaches across the Rio Grande to attack them in their safe haven in Mexico. Callahan, the governor, and the citizens of Texas all realized that fruitlessly searching for small parties of hostiles in Central Texas was not going to impede the Apaches' ability to continue raiding. They needed to follow the raiders into their own den and clean it out.

In early August, Callahan had written the governor requesting authority to buy more supplies to provide for an expedition to the Rio Grande and perhaps cross the river to attack the Apaches in Mexico. The governor agreed and Lieutenant Burleson had been sent to secure those provisions and store them in the rented house in Bandera, a house that also served as a hospital for wounded and sick Rangers.

More importantly, as Callahan had requested weeks ago, the governor agreed to disengage Captain Nathaniel Benton's small company of Rangers from patrolling around Seguin, east of San Antonio. Surprising Callahan, the governor also contacted Captain William Henry, who with his company of volunteers had just been released from jail in Mexico, having been incarcerated during his ill-advised filibustering adventure. The governor offered to accept Henry and his men as official Rangers if they would attach themselves to Captain Callahan's company.

James Callahan didn't like William Henry personally, but he was still elated, for now he would command a battalion of two fully-manned mounted companies, a force of sufficient strength to confront any size group of hostiles—in Texas or northern Mexico.

Chapter 40

Camp of Captain Callahan's Rangers
West of San Antonio
Mid-Day, September 25, 1855

The day before, Captain Nathaniel Benton and twenty-six volunteers from Seguin had reached Captain James Callahan's company. This morning, another fourteen men under Captain William Henry's command arrived from San Antonio. As the recruits greeted each other and sought out old friends, Callahan conducted an informal officers' meeting, the three captains perched on rocks, clumped under a square of mildewed gray canvas stretched between thorny mesquite trees.

Callahan scratched at a fly bite on his neck. "Well, William, glad you caught up with us. I counted fourteen men ride up with you. More coming? We can't wait much longer before we head south."

"Nope. This is it. These boys were all with me in Mexico. They're the determined ones, the ones with sand in their bellies. The soft ones have gone home."

"Sure could use more. I was thinking you'd show with sixty guns. Well, nothing for it now, except we need to consolidate yours and Nate's companies into one--with just one company commander."

Nate Benton frowned deeply, but nodded. For his part, Henry scowled and said, "I reckon that'll be all right. We'll let the boys decide whether they want Nate or me leading them."

Captain Benton sat up straight. "What? I got years of seniority on you. The consolidated company will be Benton's Company."

Captain Henry looked at Callahan. "James?"

"Ah, hell, Nate. I agree with you. But the men are used to electing their leaders when there's a consolidation. An election will make the boys happy."

Captain Benton muttered something under his breath, but did not further protest Callahan's agreement to hold an election for captain of the consolidated company.

Now smugly confident from that small victory, Captain Henry said, "That's settled then. Now, what about the battalion commander? There's three of us. We going to hold that election first?"

James Callahan's brow furrowed, his eyebrows came together and his eyes narrowed. "Captain Henry, you are misinformed. *I'm* commanding the battalion."

"No offense, James, but do you have a written order from Governor Pease appointing you to battalion command?"

"No, Captain Henry, I do not. But what I have is a roster of eighty-eight volunteers in Captain *Callahan's* company. They serve under me. Only me."

"Yes, I see you brought a lot of men, James. Still, it's standard practice, isn't it, for volunteers in three different companies serving under three different captains to elect their battalion commander?"

Captain Benton looked up and tried not to grin. "James, I don't like it either, but William has a point. If I have to stand for election as company commander, even though I have seniority, it's only proper that all the men, all three companies, vote for the battalion commander."

Callahan stared hard at the other two captains. "All right. So be it. Damned waste of time, but it'll make the men feel important. Now tell us, William, how'd you find things on the other side of the Rio Grande?" Captain Callahan pulled his flask and offered it to Captain Benton.

"Hot. Hostile. You know that chickenshit Mexican governor locked us up for a while. He was too scared to use our firepower against the *Federales*. James, Coahuila is a state in shambles, just waiting for a strong leader to break away from the government in Mexico City and go it alone, like Texas did. Like we oughta be doing now, instead kowtowing to the damned abolitionists in Washington City."

Nate Benton sipped from Callahan's flask, while William Henry continued on about his aborted filibustering adventure across the river. Finally, Henry took a breath and reached for the flask, letting Benton slip in a word.

"William, you've been beating that drum about a weak Mexico for a long time, and it's about played out. Hell, you got thrown in prison. What did you really think you'd do with just a few dozen volunteers? Did you think all them Mexican *caballeros* would rally around a damned *gringo* come to save them from their own rulers? Ain't you learned nothin'? You're lucky you weren't put in chains, and marched south to prison like Meier and them others."

"Nate, you sound like a *weak* sister. I'm telling you northern Mexico could be part of Texas. I know it in my bones."

Benton shook his head as he took the flask back. "William, I'll let that weak sister crack pass by this one time because we got work to do, but say such again, and I'll demand satisfaction. Hell, man, you were in the Mexican War. You should know the Rio Grande border is a deal that's done. The river ain't a piece of rope on the ground you can wiggle around to get where you want it."

Captain Henry stood up, stepped towards a mesquite tree, and urinated in the dust. As he stood with his back to the other two captains, he asked Callahan a question.

"James, you've been in touch with Governor Pease. Has he heard back from General Smith? Is the damned army going to send back any of the soldiers they sent up north where some fool thinks the *real* Indian threat is?"

Callahan patted a folded paper in his vest. "Governor Pease wrote me. Seems that in July, what, eight weeks ago now, he got a letter from General Smith saying the army would release a company back down here only *after* they have successfully completed their current assignment."

Benton spat in the dirt. "Shit. They took two thousand soldiers from our frontier forts to go fight Indians in Kansas or Minnesota or some damned place, and now those fat bastards in Washington are promising to send a hundred soldiers back— when they can."

"I told you," Henry said as he sat down again. "It's just us now. Won't be any U.S. army blue jackets helping us turn back the heathens in our part of Texas."

Callahan put his palms on his knees and pushed himself upright. "All right. No sense bawling like babies over spilt milk. Let's get on with it." The other two captains stood.

"Sergeant McKean! To me, if you will," Callahan called. "Gather the men together."

Milo heard the captain and trotted to find First Bugler John McCoy. When he didn't see McCoy, he collared Second Bugler Isaac Tanner. "Grab your horn, Ike, and blow 'assembly.'"

"Don't think I know that one yet."

"Well, just play something to get the men together. And tonight you get with Johnny and start practicing the calls you ain't learned yet."

"Ah, Milo, I can play as good as Johnny, he's just a kid. He's barely sixteen."

"It's Sergeant. And how old are you, Ike?"

"Seventeen--Sergeant."

"You're both youngsters, that's why you're both buglers. Now toot!"

Bugler Tanner tooted, badly, making him the instant butt of good-natured ribbing from the men lounging nearby.

"Ike, is that noise two calico cats fighting over the black queen of the barnyard?"

"Sounds more like a mama cow birthing a big ole bull calf."

Before he walked away, Milo patted young Tanner on the back. "Stick with it, Ike. You'll get there. But I was dead serious about you and Johnny practicing together ever free minute you get. The battalion is going to need both you fellas before long. When we're galloping towards the Indians, your calls will be the only way to reach all the men at once. Your bugle is even more important than that Colt revolver in your holster."

Tanner wasn't too sure about that, but he vowed to practice more.

Within a few minutes, nearly one hundred and fifty volunteer Rangers formed a rough semi-circle around their captains.

Captain Callahan stepped out front and center. "Boys, you can see there's three captains, but only enough rangers to form two decent-sized companies. So, Captain Benton's and Captain Henry's companies are going to consolidate into one company and you are going to elect who will lead that second company. We're going to do that first, then all of you, my boys included, will vote to officially decide who's going to lead the battalion."

Milo scanned the men's faces. Callahan had their full attention.

"Here we go. For the command of Company B, you got two choices: Captain Nathaniel Benton from Seguin who arrived yesterday with twenty-six men, and Captain William Henry who rode out from San Antone today with fourteen Rangers. Now I'm going to call on each captain to speak to you before you vote."

Callahan turned to his old friend Nate Benton and pointedly used his first name. "Nate, you first."

Forty-four year old Captain Benton stood up, squared his hat, and buttoned his coat, ignoring the heat. "Most of you fellers ain't ever met me. But, I've been around. Twenty years back I was part of Sam Houston's army that freed Texas from Santa Anna's iron grip. I hail from Seguin now, and I can tell you that I believe in the sovereignty of Texas. I believe in securing our borders against all hostile elements. I believe that it is our Christian duty as husbands and fathers to punish the savages who've been depredating upon our lands." Benton went on in the same manner for several more minutes before he politely asked the men for their votes and sat down.

Callahan walked back to the center of the gathering. "Thank you, Captain Benton. Now, here's Captain William Henry."

Captain Henry stood, spat in the dirt, and walked out to stand next to Captain Callahan. Henry was ten years junior to Captain Benton, but his swagger was evident.

"I ain't a grand speechifier like my grandpap Patrick Henry, who stirred up a war when he said, 'Give me liberty or give me death.' I can't match words with Governor Pease, or General Houston, or even Captain Benton. I was too young to fight with General Sam against Santy Anna, and I take my hat off to Captain Benton for carrying a gun for Texas back then. It's too bad, though, that he shot his own self in the foot and missed the fray at San Jacinto." Henry lifted his hat and cast a glance at Captain Benton. "But you can see he's better now. No more limp."

Captain Henry set his hat on the back of his head before he resumed. "I'll just say that if you boys elect me as captain of Company B, we'll kill Apaches and any other damned fools who get in our way, on this side—or the Mexican side—of the Rio

Grande. The so-called *border* ain't nuthin' but a muddy creek, and I—we—aim to root out the damned heathen Indians and send them straight down to Lucifer, whether they be hiding in Mexico or Texas."

The captain's words brought a chorus of cheers, mainly among the men who'd ridden in with him, but other volunteers scattered through the audience whistled and clapped as well. Encouraged by the response, Henry continued.

"Hell, I just come back from south of the river, and I'm telling you, with so many brave and fearless Rangers riding together, those greasers will scatter like goats wherever we go." Henry pulled out his massive Walker pistol.

"You all have seen these. This one is the same Walker .44 caliber revolver I've carried for over ten years, including during the Mexican War. I can't remember how many *soldados* and *peons* have been on the receiving end of its gifts. I am a generous man when it comes to sharing lead balls with the enemies of Texas." More men hollered in support.

"Cast your vote for William Henry, and we'll avenge every poor ravaged woman and murdered settler in Texas." To put an exclamation point to his speech, Henry raised his pistol.

Captain Henry threw a quick, pointed glance back at Captain Benton. "Don't worry Nate, I'm not going to shoot your foot." With a grin, Henry fired a round into the air before he holstered his big revolver. Several men shouted in support and all across the semi-circle of dust-covered volunteers, heads nodded in approval.

Captain Callahan looked sour when he resumed center stage. "All right, men. No more electioneering. Time to vote. We don't have paper ballots, so we'll raise hands."

"Wait a minute, James," Captain Henry interrupted. "I happen to have brought along a San Antonio newspaper I've cut into pieces. They'll do fine for ballots."

Callahan turned to Henry and replied loudly enough for the men to hear, "You did, huh? You thought ahead and just happen to have a stack of paper to use for ballots. So tell me, Captain Henry, just how the hell are they going to mark the ballots? You bring sixty quills?"

Henry barked a laugh. "Nah, no need. Simple, each man uses a little stick to poke one hole in his ballot for Nate, or two holes for me."

Callahan tried unsuccessfully to stare down Henry who returned his glare with a fixed smile. Finally, Callahan shook his head in dismay. "Sergeant McKean, get the damned newspaper ballots from Captain Henry. All you men in Company A, Callahan's Company, *my* company, sit down. Sergeant, give a newspaper *ballot* to each man standing."

Milo distributed a four-inch square of newspaper to each man who stayed on his feet. He stopped and pulled back the ballot when he glanced up at the face of Private Billy Clopton.

"Dammit, Easy, set your skinny ass down." Milo growled, then said more loudly, "If I see any more of you boys in Captain Callahan's company still standing, I'm going to wallop you."

"I was just joshing, Milo."

"Now ain't the time, Billy."

Callahan fretted as he watched Benton's and Henry's volunteers sticking twigs through the newspaper squares. *Too damn many are punching two holes. That arrogant prick may win.*

"When you're done, fold the ballot and Sergeant McKean will collect them in his hat."

Milo and Callahan sat under the tarp and pulled out the ballots one by one and put them in two stacks. Benton and Henry stood right behind them, watching closely.

Benton was the first to protest a ballot. "That one goes in my stack, not Henry's! That ain't two holes, it's one."

"Nah, it ain't," Henry countered. "Can't you see it's two holes that were punched real close together before the paper tore."

"That's one hole, dammit."

Callahan sighed. "Set that one aside, Milo. We'll see if it matters to the outcome."

Four more times Callahan directed Sergeant McKean to set a ballot aside when the intent of the voter seemed unclear.

When Milo's hat was empty, Callahan picked up the stack of one-hole ballots and slowly counted them.

"Nineteen."

He repeated his count with the undisputed two-hole ballots.

"Seventeen. All right, we gotta decide on the other five ballots. Milo and I will study each one and decide which stack it goes on."

"Hell, no!" Captain Henry protested. "You two already know the tally, and it's plain you want Nate as the second captain."

"Dammit, William, you are a royal pain in my arse. All right, my two lieutenants-- who don't know the vote tally--will take the five ballots over there and decide on each one. Will that satisfy you, William?"

"Yes. I trust Burleson and Kyle. Go ahead."

"How about you, Nate?"

"Get on with it. Your lieutenants are honest men."

"Captain?" Milo asked quietly.

"What now, dammit?"

"Captain, we got forty-one ballots and only forty men came in with the other two captains."

"Sergeant McKean, you mean you gave a ballot to one of our own men?"

Milo nodded. "Or I accidentally gave a man two ballots that were stuck together and someone voted twice. Either way, what do you want to do?"

Callahan looked with raised eyebrows at Henry and Benton.

"This ain't the damned Congress. Just count the five votes," Benton grumbled in disgust. Looking smug, Henry nodded in agreement.

Chapter 41

Camp of Callahan's Ranger Battalion
West of San Antonio
Late Afternoon, September 25, 1855

Captain Callahan again stood before the assembled battalion. "Men, the results for the captaincy of Company B are: Captain Nathaniel Benton—nineteen votes. Captain William Henry—twenty-two votes. Captain Henry will command Company B. That's all. We'll be breaking camp and heading south tomorrow. The battalion is dismissed."

As the murmurs from the dispersing men grew, Captain Henry approached Callahan. "You forgot the election for battalion command. Conveniently."

Callahan crossed his arms and faced Henry and Benton. "No, I didn't forget. We'll get that out of the way in the morning. It won't take long, and we ain't using any damned newspaper ballots. Nate, I already got two lieutenants for Company A. Will you accept second-in-command of Company B? Keep your captain rank, of course."

"Hell, no, I won't serve under William Henry. And I'm betting my men won't either. You heard them growling when you announced Henry would lead Company B. There's no telling what shit Henry will stir up when we get into Mexico."

Benton scowled at Henry, who glowered right back, but stayed quiet. Henry had thought all along that three captains in one ranger battalion was like the damned Comanches—too many chiefs.

Captain Nate Benton turned his glare to Captain Callahan. "James, I'm riding out in the morning. I'm going back to Seguin, with as many of *my* company as want to go with me."

Leaving a flustered Callahan and smirking Henry behind, Benton stalked off to where his men had gathered. For the next several minutes the sound of a heated discussion pervaded the camp. About twenty of Callahan's volunteers clustered a respectful distance from Benton's group and tried to listen in.

Private Lafayette Stokes, one of Callahan's older volunteers, owned a farm near Seguin. He'd ridden on patrols with Captain Callahan for a decade, but preferred Benton's easy-going manner to Callahan's irascibility. After eavesdropping for a few minutes, he walked up to the circle and caught Benton's eye. The two took a few steps away from the others.

"Captain, I just overheard you say you're leaving tomorrow."

"That's right, Stokes. What of it?"

"Well, sir, the battalion needs your steady hand. I'm of a mind to approach Captain Callahan and offer to transfer to a third company led by you. I'm thinking a dozen of Captain Callahan's men from around Seguin would be willing to go with me."

"Huh. You'd do that? James might not agree. He does get testy sometimes."

"Yessir, he does. But, it ain't like we'd be leaving the battalion. I think he's counting on commanding a three-company force. Captain Callahan may be too stiff-necked to admit it, but he needs you."

Frustrated at the prospect of William Henry leading the consolidated company and not wanting to lose Benton's twenty-six guns, Callahan had quietly walked close enough to stand unnoticed in the dark and hear the conversation. When Private Stokes quit talking, Callahan spoke up.

"Dammit, Nate, Stokes is right. I am stiff-necked, and I do need you, and your men. And having a third company will allow me more options when tough decisions have to be made. You stay and lead that third company—your men from Seguin."

Benton looked with a raised eyebrow at Callahan, who answered by calling for his first sergeant.

"Sergeant McKean!" Suspecting the business of company organization was still unfolding, Milo had been waiting not far away.

"Sir?"

"Pick out fourteen of my men to transfer into Captain Henry's Company B." Callahan pulled Milo close enough to whisper in his ear. "You personally pick out the fourteen who are at the bottom of your list of good troopers, or men whose horses are likely to play out on the trail. You've had nearly two months to learn who that is."

Milo smiled. "Yessir, I have, and I do indeed already know exactly who's about to be transferred to Henry's company. I'll have you a list real soon."

The next morning, Captain Callahan announced what everyone had already heard around the campfires the night before, that Captain Nate Benton would lead a third company of his own Rangers. The transfer of fourteen men from Callahan's company to bolster Captain Henry's fourteen guns didn't improve Henry's sour attitude. Callahan ignored his morning bristling, just as he'd ignored his protests the night before.

Callahan next proposed a vote by acclamation to confirm himself as the battalion commander. He didn't offer a second name as an alternative to his own, so if any man wanted to vote for Benton or Henry, he would have had to shout out the nomination. No one did.

Firmly ensconced in his position as the unchallenged leader of the one hundred and thirty mounted volunteers, Callahan quickly dispensed with a final administrative detail—determining and recording the dollar value of every man's horse for reimbursement by the state should the animal be killed in action against the hostiles. The first sergeants of each company queried each man as to what he'd paid for his mount, then the lieutenants made adjustments, usually downward, to ensure a degree of consistency.

Milo valued Buck, his own dun-colored horse, at one hundred dollars. Callahan put a value of seventy-five dollars on each of his pack mules. The commander was the only Ranger who'd brought two horses, one a dependable sorrel gelding, the other a tall high-spirited bay-colored stallion with a white face, which Callahan called his war horse. Lieutenant William Kyle, the adjutant who maintained the battalion's documents, did not question that the commanding captain placed the stallion's value at one hundred and fifty dollars, the most of any horse in the battalion.

When all was ready, the three companies of volunteer Rangers mounted their horses and arrayed themselves in double ranks in a U-shaped formation. Companies B and C faced each other and Callahan's large Company A formed the base of the U. Callahan rode his black war stallion into the open center of the formation. He pulled off his hat to reveal his sandy, but now graying, full head of hair. In his other hand he held an envelope. Holding his battered tan slouch hat high over his head, Callahan reveled in the rapt attention he held. He had lobbied the governor and button-holed newspaper editors for a year to reach this moment.

"Men, it is my privilege to lead you. You are the Rangers in the biggest damned battalion of mounted volunteers to serve the great state of Texas since the rebellion from Mexico twenty years ago! During the next month you are going to be the wall that stands between the heathen red barbarians and our families. You will be the wall that stands between those same barbarians and civilization itself. You yourselves will be the dreaded sword of vengeance that guts the heathen red barbarians when they dare to cross the Rio Grande River. You yourselves will make the heathen red barbarians tremble when we ride them down." The men cheered enthusiastically.

"A month ago I sent a good man, August Schmidt, on a scout into Mexico to find where the Lipan Apaches hide after their raids. August risked his neck to track a band of the red bastards right up to a big camp. He snuck up close enough to eyeball pitiful white women captives in that camp."

Callahan put his hat back on and held up the envelope.

"This is our authorization from Governor Pease to pursue and punish the damned Apaches wherever they run, to pull them out of whatever rabbit hole they try to hide—on either side of the Rio Grande. And now we know where that rabbit hole is. August found it in the hills of San Fernando de Rosa in northern Mexico." Those words brought more cheers. Callahan lowered his arm and his voice, now speaking as quietly solemn as he could.

"If the idea of crossing the Rio Grande gives you pause, don't worry. I've assured the governor that we will only enter Mexico if we are in pursuit of hostile Indians who have sought sanctuary across the border. And if we do enter Mexico, we will leave harmless the lives and property of the Mexican people. It's the damned murdering Apaches we aim to hunt down and chastise, not the peaceful citizens of another nation." Callahan raised his arm and swept the assembled Rangers with his pointed finger.

"If any man among you expects to disturb Mexicans in life or property, unless with the enemy, you must quit the ranks right now, or hereafter suffer the penalty of disobedience." Callahan lowered his arm and turned to look straight at Captain Henry's company.

"We ain't setting out on any damned filibustering expedition. We ain't going to foment insurrection among the Mexican peons. We ain't going to plant the Texas flag anywhere on the other side of the Rio Grande. Our mission, our only mission, is to find and punish the Apaches, wherever that takes us. That's all."

Callahan sat back in his saddle for a dramatic pause. "Captains Benton and Henry, Lieutenant Burleson, take command of your companies. We will adhere to this order of march: Company A, my Regulars, will lead and send out scouts and an advance patrol. Company B, who Captain Henry calls his Esquimaux—God knows why--will provide outriders on both flanks and protect the mule train if attacked. Company C, to be known as Benton's Mohawks, will provide our rearguard."

Chapter 42

Near the Uvalde Settlement
The Texas Frontier
September 27, 1855

The long column of Rangers wound their way through the pass near the Leona River. Milo had been this way the prior month when Callahan's Company had split to unsuccessfully pursue the band of raiders who'd killed Private Shuler. As first sergeant, Milo rode at the front, first in line behind Captain Callahan and Lieutenant Kyle. The command elections having created a rift among the trio of Ranger captains, Captains Benton and Henry rode at the head of their respective companies farther back in the column.

Next to Milo, First Bugler Johnny McCoy bounced along in his saddle. The teenager was not an experienced horseman, and even after several weeks of long days in the saddle, he still rode stiffly. Nonetheless, he was the better musician of the two young buglers, so he rode up front near the battalion commander, ready to use his brass horn.

Private Jesse Gunn rode near the back of Company A, his left stirrup occasionally knocking against Private Billy Clopton's right stirrup as their mounts negotiated the rugged trail. When the head of the column reached the crest of the pass, Captain Callahan let his horse slip back to walk next to his first sergeant.

"Milo, what do you think about your other two captains?" Callahan asked.

"I think that I'm real glad you're in command, Captain. I'm goin' to make a point of keeping you alive, just so I won't have to take orders from Captain Henry."

"I'm relieved you've seen I have some value," Callahan answered, his genial sarcasm evident.

"I mean it, Captain. Henry's still mad as a ground hornet over those weeks he and his men spent in a Mexican jail last month. He's too eager to get revenge."

Callahan smiled faintly. "He does act like he has a burr up his bum hole, don't he?"

"Yes sir, that's how I read him. On the other hand, Captain Benton, well, he don't seem to have the grit I want in the man who's charged with getting us all in and out of Mexico alive. And, since we're goin' after this Chief Wild Cat, I want a hellcat leading us. Hellcat Callahan."

"Milo, you just showed me again I chose the right man for First Sergeant. Now, you drop back and let Benton and Henry know that once we clear the pass, and get on the plain, we're going to drill the battalion before we stop for a midday break."

"Thought you said earlier that we were done drilling, Captain."

"Remember we're three companies now, not just one. Benton and Henry's men haven't had even an hour of military horseback drill. It'll be the same things you've been doing with our boys since we mustered at San Marcos. Mainly getting from this long snake of a column into a line where we can charge. You remind Benton he's to form on our left, and Henry on our right. We'll use our buglers, so you make sure they know what we're doing."

"Yessir."

"One more thing. After the whole battalion makes a single line. I'll give the order to right wheel by company, so we're in four lines, one behind the other with about a fifty foot gap between each line. That means you and Lieutenant Burleson will need to split my company in the middle to wheel in two platoons."

"Yessir. Captain. I'm not a trained cavalryman, but I think I understand what you want. I don't know why we might want to be in four ranks going sideways, but I get the picture."

"We may start sideways, but those four lines will be a maneuverable flying column that can bust through a thin line of hostiles. We punch a hole in their line with the first two lines, and then the two rear lines turn out to either side and roll'em up. I saw the damned Mex lancers do it to our boys more than once during our rebellion against Santa Anna."

"We ain't got lances, though."

"No, we have Colt revolvers and shotguns, all the better. Now go let Benton and Henry know what to expect. We've talked about this, so they shouldn't be surprised." Instructions given, the captain nudged his horse forward, returning to the head of the column.

The Ranger battalion cleared the pass and entered a more open landscape. Soon the mounted drill began, the men in the two newly arrived companies surprised by the expectation that they learn formal cavalry drill. Their first efforts at wheeling and changing formation were ragged. Hardly any of the privates and most of the sergeants did not recognize the bugle calls. The air was filled with shouted curses by officers and confused sergeants. Yet, after two hours, and the fifth or sixth energetic repetition of responding to the bugles, each company began to perform with a degree of competence.

Captain Callahan finally proclaimed it enough for one day, and ordered a noon break. He conferred with all the officers and promised that they'd repeat the drill tomorrow to insure the men didn't forget the bugle calls overnight.

The column moved on towards the South Texas savannah, an arid plains region, much of which was most covered with thorny mesquite and other scrub brush. Only one road crossed the area, a rutted path called Woll's Road. Once on the road, Milo pulled off to the side to satisfy himself that every horse in the company had made it through the drills without injury. When the last rank of Company A men was abreast of him, he swung Buck in next to his friend Jesse, who immediately started talking.

"Milo, this road don't seem the same as it was last year. We went both ways, going to and from Eagle Pass. Seems like I'd remember some landmarks."

"That's because it ain't the same road, Jesse. Last year, we were on the army road that runs further south from Eagle Pass to San Antonio. This road loops north, goes west of San Antone."

"So we're on the Injun trail."

"Captain Callahan told me it's got two names. Used to be called the Smugglers' Road and now it's Woll's Road."

"Don't look like a wall, looks like a road."

"Woll was a French general who the Mexicans hired. He led a Mex army into San Antonio about a dozen years ago."

"How you know that stuff? You just come to Texas last year."

"Your sister reads a lot and tells me things, and Captain Callahan likes to talk about Texas before it became a state. He's fond of remembering those ten years when Texas was its own country."

Late in the afternoon, a hard-riding courier intercepted the column. The young messenger swung his sweat-lathered horse into line next to Lieutenant Kyle.

"You gotta be Captain Callahan's Rangers. I ain't seen so many mounted volunteers all together before. You look like the U.S. cavalry, except you ain't wearing uniforms."

Kyle nodded. "You ride all the way out here to chat about clothes or do you have a message for the captain? Is there Indian trouble back in San Antone? You have news?" Callahan watched with interest, but didn't speak.

The courier reached back into his leather saddlebag and pulled out a large envelope sealed with red wax. He held it close and said, "This here is to be put in the hand of Captain Callahan himself."

"That's me. Pass over the damned thing." Callahan reached across, snagged the envelope and tore the seal loose. While he continued to ride, the captain silently read the one-page missive twice before he handed the paper to Lieutenant Kyle.

"Milo, halt the column. Dismount the men. Tell them we'll rest the horses for half an hour. What's your name, young man?" Callahan asked the courier. "Aw hell, your name don't matter. Get off your horse and straighten your legs for a minute." As if to model for the young messenger, Callahan swung down from his horse and stretched his arms and back.

"Lieutenant, write a reply right now to the governor. Tell him I am distressed at learning of the most recent Apache raids, and that I am immediately responding to the good citizens of San Antonio and New Braunfels who met to send their collective pleas for Ranger protection from the Apaches. Tell him, as he instructs, I'm pulling fifteen men under a good sergeant to patrol Bexar and Comal Counties while the battalion continues south. Milo, fetch Sergeant Sanders."

Callahan watched Lieutenant Kyle write the message, and as the captain signed it, he told Kyle, "This just proves Pease is a politician through and through. His thoughts flap like a flag in the wind, changing direction with every new gust. He sent me two

Ranger companies to bolster our numbers, then within a few days, tells me to give back half the new men so they can patrol close to home, where they were in the first place."

Kyle took the signed missive back and folded it while Callahan continued to grouse to his adjutant.

"Wish I could get away with sending Captain Henry to command the detachment that's staying around Seguin, but he'd refuse and the argument would just rile him up more than he already is. Better I send a sergeant."

Within half an hour, the courier started back to Austin with Callahan's written reply to the governor. Sergeant Sanders led his newly formed patrol back towards San Antonio, heading to the scene of another burned-out farm and murdered family.

The whole battalion was sipping hot coffee, boiled as soon as the men learned they were resting the horses for a spell. Lieutenant Kyle and Sergeant McKean squatted around the small fire with Captain Callahan. Kyle closed his small notebook that contained the rosters of each company.

"Captain, detaching the patrol under Sergeant Sanders puts us down to fifty-eight men in your company, and twenty-six and twenty-eight in the other two—a hundred and twelve Rangers."

Callahan rubbed his neck. "Hated to dispatch Sanders' bunch, but we should still be the biggest dog along either side of the river. We just can't lose no more guns. Milo, you keep a sharp eye out for any more couriers from Austin. Shoot the next one before he reaches me."

Milo nodded his head, half believing the captain was serious.

Callahan glanced at Milo, "Sergeant McKean, is that a pair of brass spectacles sticking out the top of your jacket pocket?"

Milo stiffened. "Well, uh, yes."

"You have trouble seeing near or far?"

"Far, but it's not trouble, it's just that things way out there get a little fuzzy."

"How are you going to spot the Apaches, or another damned courier from the governor, if you're not wearing your eyeglasses? Put them on, son. They ain't doing you any good in your pocket, and you ain't doing me any good half-blind."

"But, Captain, the men..."

"Milo, you're the first sergeant of the company. Don't you dare take crap from anyone but me. First time some fella says something about your spectacles, you may have to bust a nose or two, that's all."

Milo sighed and settled his eyeglasses onto his nose. He blinked as he looked at a mesquite tree not too far away. *Dammit, the trunk ain't fuzzy, it's sharp like a knife edge. Shit.* He pushed up the nosepiece on the spectacles then flexed his right hand into a fist a few times. *The captain's probably right about me reminding one or two men not to mock their first sergeant. Might as well get to it.*

Milo got up and approached a group of privates who grinned when they saw their first sergeant wearing brass eyeglasses. When Private Zachariah Bugg, a tall young man from San Marcos who talked a lot, cracked a joke about the spectacles, Milo wordlessly popped him in the face. Bugg's swollen black eye reflected a clear message sent and received. Not another word was uttered about the first sergeant's eyeglasses.

Chapter 43

On the Woll Road, South Texas
North of the Nueces River
Mid-morning, September 28, 1855

The two riders pounded up Woll Road, approaching the column. Captain Callahan rode a few paces forward and held up his hand, but kept his horse at a steady walk. The pair reined in their exhausted horses in front of him and turned their mounts to walk next to their captain's horse.

"Well?"

"We found their crossing place on the Nueces."

"How many tracks?"

"Too many to count. Lots. Mostly unshod. Indian ponies, I'm betting."

"How long ago?"

"A couple of days. Maybe more. No more than a week."

"Is it near this road?"

"We're two or three hours to the ford on Woll Road. The tracks are maybe another hour's hard ride upriver."

"Why wouldn't they use the ford at the road?"

"Dunno, Captain. Maybe there was a wagon train or an army patrol on the road. Maybe they had too many stolen horses and mules to want a fight."

"Maybe they were too thirsty for Mexican liquor to risk a fight. Don't matter. We're going to run them down now. Let's go." The battalion commander kicked his horse into a trot.

As soon as the Rangers crossed the Nueces River and followed the tracks of the Indian ponies along the river for a few miles, Captain Callahan called a halt. He checked his small brass compass to confirm the direction the tracks led. Callahan unfolded the map he'd bought in San Antonio that traced the route of the Rio Grande River where it defined the Texas-Mexico border. Cross-referencing the location of the Woll's Road ford across the Nueces River and the compass heading of the Indians' trail, he calculated that the hostiles were vectoring to cross the Rio Grande about twenty miles north of Eagle Pass. The only settlement on the border river in that region identified on the map was a village on the Mexican side called Quemado. Callahan suspected that's where the Mexican horse-buyers met the Apaches and swapped horseflesh for strong liquor.

As much as he'd relish arriving at Quemado in time to interrupt that exchange, and make a point with the Mexicans, Callahan concluded they were too far behind to close the distance in time. His column still had cross the Nueces Strip, the thirty-mile wide swath of badlands that formed the practical border between civilized Texas and Mexico. *Those stolen Texas horses and the Mexicans will be long gone by the time we reach the river. That's too damned bad. But, I ain't letting these redskin raiders slip away. Not this time. Just like I knew all along, we're going into Mexico after the bastards. I know where you're going, Mr. Wild Cat, or whatever Apache asshole is leading this bunch. You don't know it yet, but you are now Hell Cat Callahan's meat.*

Studying the map, Callahan saw that the closest ford over the Rio Grande from their current position was near the mouth of Las Moras Creek, ten or fifteen miles downriver from Quemado. *That's where we'll cross, and that will put us within a day's ride of the Lipan villages at San Fernando de Rosas.*

Chapter 44

On the Texas Bank of the Rio Grande River
The Ford at Las Moras Creek
Late Afternoon, September 28, 1855

Sergeant McKean's horse stood placidly on the edge of the sandy embankment next to Captain Callahan's mount. Both horses nipped at the big biting flies that landed on their sweaty withers. The battalion commander paid no attention to his fidgeting gelding as he watched a volunteer edge his horse into the swift-flowing water. Still in the saddle, Milo held his eyeglasses in one hand and with his other hand rubbed the raw skin behind his left ear. Jesse Gunn eased his horse up on the other side of Milo.

"Milo, that river is flooding. It's even higher and flowing faster than last time we was here. Weren't we here about this same time of year?"

"Yeah, we were, and yeah, it is."

"I sure hope we ain't about to swim across it."

"We'll know in a minute. There goes Tanner Solomon. He volunteered to test the current."

Loops from two lariats encircled the neck of Solomon's horse. Its rider also had a rope tied around his chest. The mounted Rangers holding the other ends of the lariats waited at the river's edge, slowly feeding out rope as Solomon's horse took each step. When the rushing water was higher than the horse's belly, the animal lost its footing. Solomon slipped his boots out his stirrups and left his saddle, flailing his arms as the current sucked him under water. The Ranger who had the other end of the lariat wrapped around his saddle horn quickly pulled Solomon to the bank, where he lay in the mud coughing up water and gasping for air.

The two Rangers who held the horse's safety lines weren't as successful. Their own mounts didn't have the strength to keep Solomon's panicked horse in place until it could regain its footing. The current worked against them, pushing the thousand pounds of thrashing horse downriver. They soon released their safety lines when their lariats popped taut and threatened to pull over their own two animals.

"Shit." Captain Callahan shook his head in frustration. "One less horse. One more Ranger who'll have to stay back with the mules."

"The drowned horse is too big to wash down very far. It'll snag up somewhere and we'll save his saddle and tack. Then he can ride a mule, Captain. Put him on your piebald," Milo said as he resettled his glasses.

"Maybe. If he didn't bust a rib or bash his head on a rock during that rescue. All right. Milo, relay the word we'll make camp here. Maybe we can cross tomorrow morning. Double the sentries around the stock tonight."

"On it, Captain."

"And Milo, get somebody to cut a tall pole and plant it deep right it next to the river, right on the water's edge. We'll know at dawn if the river's rising or falling."

September 29, 1855

The next morning Captain Callahan cursed loudly when he saw that the tall stake now stood in the river, over a foot from the bank. The Rio Grande was still rising. The three captains, six lieutenants and First Sergeant McKean gathered around Callahan's campfire and sipped bitter coffee from their steaming tin mugs.

Knowing that the lieutenants wouldn't broach the topic of the flooding river, and not wanting to play second fiddle to Captain Henry, Captain Benton blurted out, "What now, James? Wait here for the river to fall? Times short. Our men's enlistments run out in a couple of weeks."

"Nate, you think I don't know that? We ain't sittin' here all day watching no damned river. Here's what we're going to do." Callahan swiveled his head to be sure all the men were listening.

"I'm go downriver to a town on my map on the Mexican side called Piedras Negras. It looks to be about a mile or two the other side of Eagle Pass. I'm going to hire as many boats and skiffs as I can find on the Texas side. This afternoon, while it's still daylight, Nate and William will take the battalion downriver and find a nice deep ravine to wait out of sight for dark. Then you'll take the whole battalion in a wide loop around Eagle Pass and Fort Duncan, down to Piedras Negras where the boats will be."

"And just how are you planning to pay for those boats at Piedras Negras? A credit voucher from Governor Pease?" Benton was shaking his head in doubt.

"As a matter of fact, Nate, yes, that's exactly what I plan to use for currency."

Benton voiced an even bigger concern. "James, what about the horses? They can't ride in a skiff. And if we swim them behind the boats, we may lose half our mounts. You saw how easily the current took Solomon's horse in belly deep water. No telling how strong the current is at mid-river."

Captain Henry threw out another idea. "Why don't we take the whole battalion into Eagle Pass and commandeer the two big wagon ferries there. Each one can take across maybe ten horses and riders at a time."

"William, I've thought of that too, and it's just what I'd like to do. But there's a problem. Fort Duncan is less than a mile downriver from Eagle Pass. If the fort commander decides we're provoking an international incident by crossing into Mexico, he might trundle out a damned cannon battery and try to stop us."

"We got Governor Pease's authorization to go into Mexico after the Apaches. That's all we need. Besides, the American army wouldn't dare fire on us," Captain Henry insisted.

"I wouldn't bet on that, William. We *are* going into Mexico to punish the Apaches. But we can't risk a stand-off with a U.S. Army artillery battery. Governor Pease was emphatic that his approval to cross the Rio Grande is contrary to U.S. law, and like it or not, we're a state of the United States. And Washington City makes international law, not Austin City. The governor's blessings won't matter a damn if the commander of Fort Duncan wants to be stiff-necked about us crossing. And if we use the ferry in Eagle Pass, right on his doorstep, he won't have any choice but stop us."

"Shit. Texas should still be a different country entirely. We'd be better off," Henry muttered, prompting nods from every man in the circle.

"But we ain't," Callahan said as he tossed his cup to the ground. "And I'm headed to Piedras Negras to hire boats. Quietly. We'll take the boats downriver, well past Fort Duncan, where we can start crossing the men. We'll swim the horses between two skiffs, one at a time if we have to."

"I'm going along to Piedras Negras," Benton said.

"Me too," Henry added.

Callahan sighed deeply. "Suit yourselves. Our lieutenants can take our men downriver to wait until dark. Lieutenant Kyle, bring your office satchel, you'll be writing payment vouchers. Sergeant McKean, you're with me."

★

On the ride downriver to Piedras Negras, Captain Callahan motioned for his first sergeant to come alongside him.

"Milo, I'm thinking back to your story of rescuing that German girl last year."

"Yes, sir. What of it?"

"Didn't you say that you had help from a young officer stationed at Fort Duncan?"

"Right. Lieutenant Will Davant. Him and his Sharps rifle. Couldn't have gotten out of the Apaches' camp without his cover fire. He's a real marksman."

"He don't wear brass and glass spectacles, huh?"

"Captain, you saw me give Private Buggs a black eye for sayin' less."

"I know. That was a good punch. You earned the men's respect without saying a word. I like that sort of eloquence. Now, that shoot-out where the army lieutenant saved your bacon, that was across the Rio Grande, right?"

Milo nodded. "But he wasn't wearing his uniform. In fact, he hadn't even taken over his duties yet. The man he was replacing was still at Fort Duncan."

"Think your friend has any sway with the commander of the fort?"

"I dunno. He was a brand new officer last year when we met. But he and Captain Burbank are both graduates of the academy at West Point. I hear they help each other out when they can."

"Well, that's something to think about if we can't avoid the soldier boys all together. You meet Burbank?"

"Yes sir. He said he was from Massachusetts and didn't care for our *peculiar institution*. He meant..."

"Milo, I know what the damned abolitionists call our owning Africans."

"Yes sir. Captain Burbank fought the Seminoles in Florida. When we brought Mrs. Schmidt to the fort's doctor and the captain saw her condition, he got really mad. He don't like Indians."

"Well, that's something. Glad he ain't soft on redskins." With those words the captain returned to silence.

★

The Ranger leaders met with no success in hiring the three skiffs they found tied to a ramshackle dock on the American side of the river in Piedras Negras. The Mexican oarsmen flatly refused to take their crafts downriver, gesturing at logs and debris that streamed by them in the swift current. When Captain Henry began to berate the men in crude Spanish, Captain Callahan pulled him aside.

"Yelling at them in Mex-talk won't do no good, William. Tonight right after dark, you come back with your company and persuade these greasers to help us out. You can figure out a way, can't you?"

Henry grinned. "Damned right, I can."

★

Half a mile downriver from Piedras Negras, the five Rangers stopped where Elm Creek flowed into the Rio Grande on the Texas side. Captain Henry then rode straight back to the battalion so that right after dark he could lead his company back to Piedras Negras for the three boats.

Lieutenant Kyle and Sergeant McKean used the afternoon to scout the wide loop around Eagle Pass and Fort Duncan so they could lead the other two companies unobserved to where Captain Callahan waited downriver near Piedras Negras at Elm Creek. They'd cross the Rio Grande in the boats here, far enough away from Fort Duncan to escape the army's attention.

★

The battalion reached the confluence of Elm Creek and the Rio Grande around midnight. Shortly thereafter, Captain Henry arrived from Eagle Pass and found Captains Callahan and Benton on the river bank.

"Well?" Callahan growled as Henry swung down from his horse.

"I got riders with lines attached to the bows of all three skiffs and Rangers with cocked pistols sitting in the stern of each boat watching the oarsmen work."

"Huh. How'd you persuade them?"

Henry snorted. "It weren't too hard. Just had to shoot one, but he had a helper who took the oars without another word of protest. The other two decided right off that rowing in the black water was a better bet than a slug in their bellies."

Neither captain asked if the Mexican oarsman was alive or dead.

"One more thing," Henry said. "Someone on the Mexican side took a couple of shots at us while we were bringing the boats downriver. Somebody knows we're here."

"Anybody hit?"

"Nah. It was real dark, but I saw the muzzle flashes myself."

Callahan rubbed his beard stubble. "I ain't real surprised. It's hard to hide as many men and animals as we got. How many men can fit in each boat?"

"Maybe four and the Mex oarsman."

Callahan stared into the dark, listening to the rush of the water, thinking how to best proceed.

"All right. You load up all three boats with a dozen of your men and row across. Tie a rope between the boats so you'll all land at the same place. Set up a perimeter with your first nine men and send the boats back for more men until your whole company's on the other side. Leave your horses and mules here. Keep a guard in each boat all the time."

"That fits my own thinking," Captain Henry said. "My company will protect the landing spot, but we won't be able to move beyond the river without our mounts, and I didn't come here to just sit and guard a few boats while the rest of you go after the Lipans."

Callahan put his hand on Henry's shoulder. "William, you know I wouldn't venture even a mile into Mexico without you and your company. We'll get your stock to you in the daylight when we take the rest of the battalion across."

"I'll need a lantern in the lead boat."

"Fine, but just in the first skiff."

Callahan and Milo watched while the first three boatloads of Henry's Rangers pushed off from shore.

"Hello ahead! Don't shoot, I'm coming in," called a male voice with a heavy southern drawl. A dozen Rangers pulled their pistols as a slender man in civilian clothes approached on foot, leading his horse.

"I'm looking for Captain Callahan."

"I'm Callahan. Who the hell are you?"

The man, still a dark silhouette, stepped close enough to Callahan to lower his voice to a whisper.

"To your men, I'm a new volunteer. To you, I'm Captain Burbank's eyes and ears. He knows you are determined to cross into Mexico, and he sent me to observe."

"The army's spy, huh? You saying Burbank ain't going to oppose our crossing?"

"I'm here alone, Captain. That should answer your question. But Captain Burbank told me if you show up in Eagle Pass to use the ferries, you'll force his hand. He'll stop you."

"Huh. Pretty much what I figured. You got a name?"

"Will Davant"

Callahan smiled unseen. "You bring your Sharps rifle, Ranger Davant? I hear you're a marksman with it."

★

Will Davant wasn't sure whether he more glad to see Milo or see Jesse. His adventure the prior year with the two remained his favorite memory, the months since then having been consumed with arduous and generally fruitless patrols on the Texas plains.

Only twice had he led his troopers into horseback engagements with small bands of hostile Indians, and neither action compared to the day Milo, Jesse, and he—and one Negro slave--had rescued the abused white woman from the Apache camp.

The pleasant surprise that Milo held the rank of first sergeant was offset by Davant's irritation as a professional soldier that Milo's company of wildly dressed and armed Rangers called themselves the 'Regulars.' To West Pointer Davant, regulars wore uniforms and understood army discipline, two important traits not visible among the Rangers. Nonetheless, he believed the stories reflecting the eagerness of Ranger companies to unleash the brutal firepower of their Colt revolvers. They might look like a bunch of cowboys and clerks, but their reputation belied their appearance.

Around midnight, after the three boats had delivered the last wave of Captain Henry's men across the river, Callahan found Davant with Milo and Jesse. "Sergeant McKean, why don't you take Ranger Davant and introduce him to Captain Henry."

"You mean take a boat across the river?"

"Yep, and tell the captain that since he ain't been attacked, starting at dawn we'll cross the whole battalion over in the boats, swimming the horses beside the skiffs. Once Benton's company is across, Henry can bring his men back to this side to fetch their horses. The Regulars will follow Benton's company and Henry's bunch will go last with their horses."

"Yessir."

"And Milo, detail four men from our company and two each from Benton and Henry's companies to stay with the mules on this side. It wouldn't do for a damned raiding party of Apaches or *banditos* to swoop in behind us and steal our mules."

"Yessir." Milo elaborated to let Callahan know he understood the need for guards, but also share the captain's reluctance to further diminish their fighting force in Mexico. "I know we got a couple of injured men and one with the trots real bad. They won't mind staying here as mule guards. You want to leave all the mules on this side?"

"I wish we could, but I expect we'll be on the Mexican side for a few days. How many mules in our pack train altogether?"

"Around forty. I'd have to check for an exact count."

"Put Solomon on my piebald, he's too good a man to leave guarding the stock." We'll take a dozen other mules. Six for the Regulars and three each for the other two companies. No tents, no heavy stew kettles. Rations and stock fodder for a week."

"Captain, that ain't enough mules. We got nigh-on sixty men in our company. One mule can't carry grub and grain for ten men and horses for a week. And we can't count on much grazing. The hills I seen last year on the other side of the river ain't covered in grass, it's scrub over there."

In the moonlight Milo couldn't see Callahan glaring at him in irritation at his decision being questioned.

Milo plunged on. "Aren't we going straight to the hostile's camp? In and out. A raid, not an expedition. How about three days of supplies instead of seven?"

"Dammit, Milo, I hate it when you out-think me." Callahan grimaced in the dark. "You're right. We gotta go light. Three days of horse feed packed on the mules, that's all. No cooking gear at all. Corn cakes and cooked bacon in the men's saddlebags. Get the cooks and muleskinners to work right away."

After Milo made the rounds relaying Captain Callahan's orders, he and Davant walked to the boats and clambered into one of them. They sat uneasily on the front bench, both gripping the gunwale tightly, with the Mexican oarsman between them and the Ranger guard in the stern holding his pistol.

To keep his mind off the swift current and the fact he couldn't swim, Davant whispered to Milo, "Captain Callahan treats you more like the battalion sergeant major than his company first sergeant."

"What's a sergeant major?"

"The head sergeant among all the sergeants. Reports directly to the battalion commander."

"Yeah, I reckon that's me."

"And he listens to you more than he does to the other captains."

"Sometimes. Mostly though, he bulls ahead without taking anyone's advice."

Chapter 45

Near Piedras Negras
State of Coahuila, Mexico
October 1, 1855

The battalion had spent a second restless night on the river bank, this time on the Mexican side, under the high bluff that paralleled the river. The whole of September 30th had been consumed with getting most of the nervous horses and mules across the Rio Grande. The swimming animals were kept between the small boats which were loaded with saddles and supplies. Early in the day, Callahan had sent out scouts who returned with two stolen cows which were butchered and roasted over a dozen campfires.

An hour after dawn the delegation from the village of Piedras Negras appeared. The Ranger sentries stationed on the lip of the bluff watched the four men slowly cross the wide plain that separated the border town from the Rangers' landing point. The church bell tower was the only building in Piedras Negras that was visible to the Texans. The only horse in the approaching group, a striking black on white spotted appaloosa, carried a portly gray-haired Mexican man dressed in cleaner clothes than the other three men. His companions looked much younger, two of them carrying ladder-back chairs, and one holding a sturdy stool.

The Mexicans stopped twenty feet in front of the Ranger sentries. The stool was placed next to the horse, and the rider clumsily dismounted to stand on the footrest. Two of his companions provided supporting shoulders as he stepped to the ground with a grunt. The heavy man sat down on one chair that faced the river and the other chair was positioned facing him a few feet away.

The seated man then called in barely understandable English, *"Por favor, Capitan Callahan?"*

Rufus Hynyard, a thirty-year-old Ranger from Cibilo, had been married to a Mexican woman for a dozen years. As a result, he spoke Spanish better than anyone else in the battalion. He walked next to Callahan as they climbed the embankment. Behind them, Lieutenant Davant, in civilian clothes, and Sergeant McKean kept a respectable five paces back.

Once at the top, Davant leaned in to whisper to Milo, "I've never seen a horse with those markings, what is it?"

"Appaloosa. Bred by the Sioux Indians way up north, I'm told. Valuable horse flesh this far south. That chubby old Mexican must be important."

Callahan inspected the fat Mexican sitting on the chair and his companions standing several feet behind their leader. None of them appeared to have any weapons. The seated man nodded and gestured to the empty chair. The Ranger captain smiled.

"Must be the town *alcalde*. Looks like he wants to sit and chew the fat. Now ain't that mighty white of him," Callahan said to Hynyard.

Davant heard Callahan and asked Milo, "What's a *alcalde*?"

Callahan glanced back at the pair. "It's Mex talk for the town mayor. Well, that old greaser ain't going to out-do me with his spotted horse and damned chairs. Now I wish I'd ridden my warhorse up from the river. Somebody bring me two mugs of coffee. Be quick about it!"

The Ranger captain and his interpreter walked forward and Callahan sat on the empty chair. He leaned back and crossed his leg, his left boot and spur resting on his right knee. Hynyard stood right behind him. Another Ranger approached them carrying two tin cups of coffee.

"Him first, then me," Callahan instructed.

The Mexican accepted the offered coffee, smiled broadly and nodded his thanks.

"Rufus, ask him what this parley is all about."

For the next few minutes Hynyard interpreted for both men.

The *alcalde* began humbly. "My people are very nervous that so many armed Americanos are crossing the river. We live in a peaceful village."

Callahan assured him they meant no harm to the residents of Piedras Negras. "We are not here to make war or do injury of any kind to your people. Our sole purpose is to chastise the Lipans for their many crimes committed on Texas soil. They cross the river and kill our cattle, take our children, ravage our women, and steal our horses."

The *alcalde* sagely nodded his head during Hynyard's recitation of the Lipans' depredations. Then he sadly shook his head.

"But the Lipans are not here. They stay in the hills, many miles from Piedras Negras."

"We know that. We tried to cross at the ford upriver, but the water is too high. We needed boats. Piedras Negras is the closest town to where we were."

The *alcalde's* response surprised Hynyard and Callahan. "Captain, pardon my correction, but last night you rode wide around Eagle Pass on the Texas side of the river. There are two ferry rafts in Eagle Pass, much larger than the boats you have *borrowed*. Rafts big enough for your horses. Why not use them instead of swimming your animals?"

Callahan put his foot down and tossed out what coffee remained in his mug. He brusquely told Hynyard to tell the fat greaser that was none of his damned business.

Hynyard tried to soften his captain's visible irritation. "*Señor*, that is not important. We are here now."

The *alcalde* nodded again without asking further questions.

Callahan stood. "As soon as all my soldiers and animals have crossed the river, we will leave here. If you can provide us more boats, we would cross faster and leave sooner."

The *alcalde*, still seated, nodded and turned to his companions. In a flurry of Spanish that Hynyard barely understood, he told them to bring two more boats to the crossing.

Callahan thanked the *alcalde* and said he had two questions. "How did you know my name?"

The *alcalde* shrugged, looked up at the standing American, and said in slower Spanish, "Colonel Langberg, he told me you were coming. He directed me to confirm your intentions, and if you offer no threat to my people, to welcome you to our country, and wish you good fortune in your mission to punish the Lipans."

Captain Callahan rubbed his jaw at this news, mulling over the possible implications of the unexpected message. He knew that Colonel Langberg was a mercenary European army officer, the commander of the region's military.

If he already knows me by name, he has spies on the Texas side of the river, and he knows how many Rangers I have. Maybe he doesn't have the guns to stop so many of us. But it was his soldiers that captured Captain Henry and his boys just a month ago. But Henry only had two dozen men, I got over a hundred. Besides, Governor Vidaurri let Henry go after a few days in jail. I bet Vidaurri and Langberg really are welcoming me as an act of good will. Or maybe the welcome is a stall while they wait for more troops. It don't really matter. Fact is, either way, we're going to San Fernando de Rosa to kill Apaches.

Callahan reached into his vest pocket and pulled out a cigar. "One last thing, *Señor.* That's a fine looking appaloosa mare behind you. You want to sell it?"

The *alcalde* shook his head when Hynyard interpreted.

"Why not? Because you got it from the Apaches? Or maybe from Big Cat himself, that Black Seminole bastard? You afraid of taking Yankee dollars for a horse your Indian friends stole in Texas and sold cheap to you?" Callahan looked at his interpreter.

"Private Hynyard, don't wash my words this time. Repeat it like I said it."

Before Hynyard could speak, the *alcalde* stood and replied in heavily accented English, "*Sí, Capitan.* I do not wish to be gutted like a river fish by the Apaches for selling you a gift I had no choice but to accept. The Lipans pay generously for my good will, which is more than I expect you to do. *Adios.*" He turned to walk back to the appaloosa where his companions helped him mount.

To the *alcalde's* back, Callahan muttered, "You mean they pay generously for your damned whiskey, Injuns don't care spit about your good will."

The parley completed, Captain Callahan lit his cigar and called for his adjutant.

"Kyle, I want to send a message to Governor Pease. Write that we have crossed the Rio Grande. Tell him that I have received a message written in Spanish from Colonel Langberg of the Mexican army, assuring me and Captain Burbank at Fort Duncan that I have Langberg's permission to pass into Mexico in pursuit of the Apaches."

Kyle innocently asked, "You want me to transcribe Colonel Langberg's letter and include it?"

"No, Lieutenant, I don't. The letter has information in it that I don't want out yet. My word will be sufficient." *Don't probe any more, Kyle. You've been watching and haven't seen me receive a damned letter. Now be a good junior officer and just do what you're told.*

"Whatever you say, Captain. I'll have a draft of the message for you to read in half an hour."

★

The two black men squatted, squeezing in next to the bell at the top of the church tower, shielding their eyes from the morning sun with their hands. When an old woman had come to their hut and told Juanita that an army of *gringos* was crossing the river in boats, Thompson and Philip had hurried into Piedras Negras to see for themselves. They'd heard rumors of a huge posse of white bounty hunters planning to cross the river to recapture the hundreds of runaway slaves in the region.

"I see four or five boats haulin' men and sacks of somethin'," Thompson said. "An' horses comin' out of the river by the boats."

Philip looked up where the church cross was invisible to them on top of the tower. "Lawd, de Pharaoh done sent anoder army into de riber. Now be a fine time to make a big ole wave and smite dose wooden boats to splinters."

Thompson smiled at his friend's fanciful prayer. "I wish He would. But we ain't the Israelites, are we. The sacks got to be grain for the horses. Means they going somewhere."

Philip flexed his stiff leg, trying to ignore the lingering soreness from the water moccasin's bite last year. He squinted at the growing number of distant specks he took to be white men and horses. "Then where they goin'? After you an' me? Again?"

"Too many men to be after just two."

"Maybe they goin' to Eureka, put de whole camp in chains."

"Huh. Philip, that's it. How many guns in Eureka?"

"Not dat many. What we gonna do?"

"One of us will go to Eureka and warn them that an army o' white men is comin' for them."

"Thompson, what de peoples at Eureka gonna do afta we tells 'em?"

"Fight, or scatter and hide."

"Better run, dan fight wit no guns. But we got no horse."

"Look there, the *alcalde*'s comin' back. He's on a horse. We got the shotgun. We borrow his horse."

"Thompson, you go to Eureka. I ain't leavin' Juanita an' de baby. Ain't no white soljer gonna have his way wit' my wife while I'm livin'."

Thompson agreed. "Philip, the baby is nearly dark as you are. Bounty hunter see the baby, he'll take him back to Texas. Same with you. Maybe the whole family should go up in the hills 'til the white soljers leave."

Philip nodded at the wisdom of his friend's urging, but grimly said, "No. We got de corn and beans growin'. Got de goats. Got Theresa an' Antonio an' Tomàs. I ain't runnin' no mo'."

★

The *alcalde* vehemently shook his head at the pair of black men. "*No, Señors, Lipans. Apaches. No Negroes.*"

"Thompson, do he mean the Texas soljers here to fight Injins? Not us?"

"I think so. I wish Juanita was here to talk to him. But he may be wrong or lyin'. Philip, you go on back to your family. You want the shotgun?"

"Nah, you keep it. If I shoots, mo' white men wit' mo' guns come to see. I gots my long knife."

"All right. I'm borrowin' the *alcalde*'s horse and goin' to warn them at Eureka, don't matter what he says."

The *alacalde* shook his head. "No horse. Horse stay *aqui*."

"So you do speak more than Mexican. I'm just borrowing your horse. I have to ride to Eureka, you understand? I have to warn the other Negroes. Right now."

"No. Horse stays."

"Sorry, *Señor*. My gun and his knife say I'm borrowing your horse. I'll be back before dark."

As the day passed, the noise of the hundred *gringos* crossing the river just outside of town caused a wave of alarm to wash over the thousand residents of Piedras Negras. In spite of the *alcade's* assurances that they were safe, the road soon filled with families going further into Mexico, away from the frightening *Americanos*. Many of them also saw the lone black man holding a shotgun and galloping through the streets on the *alcalde's* prized appaloosa. More than a few viewed his flight as ominous, causing even more town residents to leave their homes that night and hide in the hills.

Chapter 46

Near Piedras Negras
On the Rio Grande River
State of Coahuila, Mexico
October 2, 1855

For the second morning, the five skiffs continued to ferry men, saddles, and supplies across the Rio Grande. Horses and mules swam alongside, halters held tightly by their owners sitting in the boats.

Around midday, Captain Benton stumbled getting out of the boat that had just brought him across. Captain Callahan had been waiting for him and grabbed Benton's hand to help him out of the shallow water.

"I sure hope the river's gone down when we come back," Benton gasped. "How soon are we moving out towards the Apache camp?"

Callahan waved towards the skiffs in the river. "The damned boat crossing is slow as molasses. It's taken us two damned days to cross every man and animal. It'll be close to dark by the time we're done, so we ain't moving out until dawn."

Benton then broached a topic at the request of his first sergeant. "Sergeant McKean said for the boys to empty their saddlebags of everything but food for three days."

"Right, those're my orders," Callahan declared.

"What about shackles for any slaves we find? Most of my men brought them."

Callahan stared at the river for a moment. "Nate, you know the planters want us to bring back a herd of runaway slaves."

"Yup, and my boys want to collect some bounty money."

"So do mine. Keep the shackles in the saddlebags."

Sergeant McKean approached the two captains, his stride fast. He interrupted without hesitation.

"Captain, I've got a few boys on horseback patrolling almost to the edge of the town. One of 'em says he just saw the *alcalde's* spotted horse galloping away from town."

Callahan smiled mirthlessly. "So the fat man is either reporting to Colonel Langberg, or he's hightailing it to somewhere safer. Either way, I ain't surprised. Rats and politicians take care of themselves."

Milo shook his head before he reluctantly corrected Callahan. "Well, sir, here's the thing. Corporal Elam said a black man was riding the *alcalde's* horse. A darkie holding a musket or shotgun across his saddle."

Callahan snorted. "Now that does surprise me. Even in Mexico, niggers with guns on high-dollar horses ain't right. I wonder if he's part of Big Cat's half-breed bunch. Speaking of niggers, Milo, do the Regulars have leg irons in their saddlebags?"

"Captain, I told them to empty out everything for food, like you said. That we're riding light and fast."

"Pass the word for the men to carry the chains. First, we're going to hit the Apaches hard. And on the way back to the river, we'll sweep the region, picking up ever' runaway slave we can find. That way the men will earn a nice bonus back home."

Milo nodded without reply and dutifully went to detail a few men to re-cross the river and bring back the four dozen sets of ankle shackles. He didn't mention that he'd heard of a runaway slave settlement called Eureka back in the hills. Fighting Apaches was an honorable thing. But after months of mulling over his and Jesse's adventure in Mexico last year with the black man Thompson, Milo wasn't happy about hunting runaway slaves again.

On the Road to Eureka
Late Afternoon

Out of sight of the town, Thompson pulled the reins to slow the spotted horse. He marveled at the beast's ability to keep running, but he was scared of falling. He knew the route from Piedras Negras to Eureka since he'd walked it every few days, going to look in on Philip while his friend's snake bite and gunshot wounds healed. He hadn't been surprised when Philip told him he was staying permanently with Juanita, that she was going to have a baby—his baby.

Thompson had spent hours on the dusty path to Eureka thinking about his new life in Mexico. *Yes, I'm free, no man owns me now.* Yet, with that freedom came hardship, The people they'd met at the collection of mud and brush huts known as Eureka were all gaunt black men, no black women. Almost all of them had reached Mexico with nothing but the rags they wore. Most still had nothing and drifted in and out of the settlement between stints of doing whatever work they could for Mexican ranch owners. Hunger was the accepted norm. Philip and Thompson had immediately learned that the three horses, shotgun, and mercantile goods taken from Mr. Smith's wagon made them wealthy men in Eureka.

During their first hour in the primitive settlement of ex-slaves, three black men with knives stuck in their belts challenged them. The leader of the trio demanded food. Philip agreed and reached for their food bag. He pulled out several ears of corn and casually flipped them at the group. His slashing knife blade at the end of his long arm came right behind the corn. Philip sliced a long gash in the forearm of the leader and put his shoulder into the man nearest the leader, making him stagger backwards. He grabbed that man's shirt, stepped in close and put his knife point to the man's throat, pricking the skin. The third man had caught one of the ears of corn and hadn't moved.

"I changed my mind. Thompson, point the shotgun at them while I fetch their knives."

Philip's quick violence immediately elevated their place in the pecking order at Eureka. When they made a circuit of the huts offering a bit of cornmeal, a potato, or an ear of corn, their status rose even further.

Since Philip had been living in the Garcia's hut, Thompson had begun learning Spanish, mostly taught to him one word at a time by Juanita's younger sister while he helped her tend the crops. He also watched the goats some days, freeing Juanita's brother so he could fish in the Rio Grande. Thompson refused to go to the river, even armed. It was too close to Texas and shackles.

Even though he was now spending more time at the Garcia's than in Eureka, Thompson wasn't sure about this new connection with the Mexican family. He was pleased for Philip and Juanita, but Thompson didn't feel any particular manly attraction to Theresa, even though puberty was quickly changing her appearance from a thin girl to a rounded woman. Instead, his thoughts kept returning to his one night in San Antonio with slender Irene, the cook at Mr. Menger's boarding house. Not only had she shown him the magic of a man and woman lying together, she was a Negro like him.

During his first few months in Mexico, Thompson often daydreamed about how he might bring Irene to Mexico where they could open a café as a free couple. When he'd still possessed the two horses brought from Texas, he kept gnawing on the idea. He'd sorted out that there were three pieces to fit together: Distance, transportation, and money. Since the two horses were transportation, and he couldn't change the distance, he needed only the money for an agent to buy Irene, or to convince her to run with him on the horses to Mexico. Who such an agent might be, Thompson had no idea. A Mexican, he supposed, but Thompson had no money and foresaw no way to get any. Then the day at the river ruined what little hope he held. After he'd lost the two horses to the three white men, the black man well understood that he might as easily flap his arms and fly to the moon.

The sight of Thompson on the appaloosa mare caused someone in every hut to come out and gather around the horse. Without dismounting, Thompson loudly addressed the crowd of several dozen men and a few Mexican women.

"With my own eyes, just outside of Piedras Negras, I saw over a hundred armed white men on this side of the Rio Grande River. The *alcalde* says they are in Mexico to punish the Indians who raid in Texas. But those white men with all their guns could also ride in here and put every one of you in chains and take you back to bondage in Texas."

"How soon, Thompson?"

"Not today. They was still crossing the river in little boats when I saw them from the church bell tower this morning."

"Tomorrow?"

"They could, if they know how to get here."

"But you said they goin' afta Injuns."

"I said the Mexican *alcalde* told me they're here to fight Indians. The *alcalde* may be wrong. Or the white men may be here to fight Indians *and* capture us. There's a bounty in Texas for every escaped slave."

"Thompson, what do we do?"

"What are you going to do, Thompson? Did you steal that horse to run?"

"You gots de shotgun, is you goin' to fight de white men?"

"No, I didn't steal the horse. It's the *alcalde's*. I borrowed it to come warn you'uns. I'm taking the horse back, then I'm going to go to ground and hide. How many of you have a gun?"

Seven hands went up.

"Not enough to fight. You better hide in the hills. If I was you, I'd go now. Away from the river. Walk all night. Hide tomorrow."

Thompson left the crowd milling about, a few going to their hovels to retrieve what food, water, and possessions they had before they took his advice to flee.

Back on the trail, Thompson decided not to risk going to the *alcalde's* house. Instead he resolved to return to the Garcia's hut on the prairie near Piedras Negras. As he rode, he once again wondered why God put a single muddy river between a country where all Negroes lived free of chains, from a land where there were no free Negroes, a land where the very law forbade free Negroes.

The Confluence of the Rio San Antonio & the Rio Escondido

The eight long lances stood upright in a neat row, a yard between each one. The brass-tipped butts of the ten-foot shafts were pushed into the soft dirt, the steel spear points winked in the sunlight.

Seven of the eight Mexican cavalrymen sat in the shade of the embankment, their saddled horses grazing next to the narrow river just yards away. The *soldados* were of the Morelos Company and constituted one of four patrols sent out by Captain Miquel Patino to give advance warning of Callahan's Rangers.

The eighth lancer stood wedged into the fork of a live oak tree, twelve feet above the ground, watching the road that connected Santa Rosa and Piedras Negras, fourteen miles to the southeast.

In the quiet of the late afternoon, the drumming hooves of a loping horse came from the wrong direction, causing the lookout to twist and nearly fall from his perch in the tree. He shouted for his companions while the approaching spotted horse was still a hundred yards away. The relaxing men immediately mounted their horses, each one riding by the row of lances to retrieve his before they hastily formed a line across the road.

The blue-uniformed soldiers blocked Thompson's way, forcing him to pull hard on the reins, halting his horse in the road. His shotgun lay across his saddle, tied with a strip of rawhide. Seeing he was armed, the Mexican sergeant spoke quietly to his men. Three of the lancers lowered their long spears threateningly, while the other three slung their lances and aimed their cocked carbines at the lone rider. The seven Mexican *soldados* walked their horses forward, all of them surprised to see a Negro on the horse.

Thompson raised both hands high.

In broken English, the sergeant asked where he stole the horse and shotgun.

"Not stolen. The *alcalde* at Piedras Negras loaned me the horse. I'm taking it back now. The shotgun used to belong to my master in Texas. I took it when I ran for Mexico."

"Why would the *alcalde* do that? That horse is valuable and rare, such markings." Their sergeant's disbelief in what the Negro had said was evident to his troopers. Fingers tightened around triggers.

"He was nice enough to let me use it so I could beat the Texas soldiers to Eureka to warn the other black men, to tell them to go hide in the hills. Hide before the Texans put them back in chains and take them to Texas. Back to being slaves."

The sergeant grunted and prodded his horse forward. In spite of his skepticism, he decided to pass the problem along to the captain. Additonally, he did not doubt that the beautiful unusual horse would soon be the mount of Captain Patino, or maybe even the colonel. He only hoped they would remember who delivered the animal into their hands. Telling Thompson to keep his hands high, he pulled the shotgun from the loose loop holding it in place across the saddle.

"I doubt the *alcalde* is so concerned for the fate of you Negroes. You will go with two of my men to tell your story to *Capitan* Patino."

★

An hour later Thompson stood before the Mexican captain having told his story from spying on the Rangers from the top of the bell tower, to his capture by the army patrol. Captain Patino was in a good mood, relishing the prospect of action against the constantly meddling Texans. Through his interpreter, he told the black man he was not in danger. Patino didn't believe the Negro's story about the *alcalde* of Piedras Negras loaning his prized appaloosa, but he didn't much like the overweight *alcalde*, finding him pompous.

"However," the captain continued, "I cannot release you to return to Piedras Negras. The *alcalde* will have to wait a bit longer for his appaloosa to come home. It would not do for you to encounter *los diablos tejanos* on the road today or tomorrow. At least not by yourself. Not when Colonel Menchaca has such a surprise awaiting this *Capitan* Callahan." The captain waved his arm to encompass the large camp of Mexican soldiers.

"You will stay with us tonight as the corporal's guest. Tomorrow you may rejoin Sergeant Marroquin and ride with his men. Perhaps you will have a chance to use your shotgun against those who would re-enslave you and your people in Eureka."

Thompson nodded and muttered, *"Gracias,"* having no idea how else he could reply.

"I suggest you take good care of the *alcalde*'s appaloosa. I know the man, and I suspect he would not be easily satisfied should his spotted horse be returned injured, or found dead on tomorrow's battlefield. *And I expect Colonel Menchaca would look with favor on the officer who gifts him with such a steed after the battle tomorrow."*

Patino dismissed the Negro and his guard, saying, "Corporal, return *Señor* Thompson's shotgun and offer him a blanket, *por favor*. It is chilly tonight."

Thompson repeated, *"Gracias,"* but this time added, "You think the corporal might have some *frijoles* and a *tortilla* to spare? I ain't et since yesterday."

The captain laughed. *"Sí,* and I smell *cabrito* on the fires. You arrived at a good time for eating."

Chapter 47

State of Coahuila, Mexico
Mid-Day, October 3, 1855

The battalion of Texans had been in the saddle for five hours when they stopped for a mid-day break. While the Rangers ate, the forward scouts escorted a thin Mexican with deep-set eyes to the three captains who were sitting in the shade of the same oak tree that the Mexican lookout had climbed the day before. The barefoot man first asked for food. Hynyard relayed his request in English and Milo tossed him a corn fritter. The peon bobbed his head up and down before he spoke in rapid Spanish.

Hynyard rubbed his jaw and spoke softly to Captain Callahan. Without invitation, Captains Benton and Henry leaned in to hear.

"He says Mexican soldiers are waiting for us a few miles ahead."

"How many?" Callahan asked.

Hynyard asked, and listened to the one-word reply.

"Hundreds."

"He lyin'." Callahan stated. "He's lyin' for food. There's no reason for this one sorry greaser to warn us. Hell, he's a Mex."

Captain Benton seemed less convinced. "I don't know, James. Maybe he's mad because some Mex soldiers stole his pigs. I've seen our boys do as much back in Texas."

"Ask him why he's warning us," Callahan instructed Hynyard.

After listening for a moment, Hynyard interpreted to the captains.

"Not pigs. Goats. A patrol of Mexican army lancers skewered all his goats and carried them off."

Captain Henry spoke up. "When?"

Hynyard and the man again spoke in Spanish.

"Two days back. He's been following the soldiers since then. He says he wants to slice the throat of the sergeant who killed his ram. He said without his rutting billy, he can't grow another herd, he can't live. The man is some kind of mad. He wants revenge. Captain, I believe him."

"Hmph." Callahan looked at Benton and Henry.

Benton went first. "We came to punish the Lipans, not fight Mexican cavalry. And where there's a patrol of lancers, there's a passel more behind them."

"*If* he's telling the truth," Callahan replied. "Remember the *alcalde* said Colonel Langberg won't oppose us as long as we leave the Mexicans alone."

Henry took off his hat and slapped his thigh with it, dust rising. "I ain't turning tail at the first hungry little bastard to come wantin' to trade a pack of lies for a handout."

"Agreed, William." Callahan stood. "Fact is, we don't know if that peon is lying or not. But another fact is, we're here today with over a hundred well-armed Rangers, who all are spoiling to punish the damned Indians. And so am I. We're just a few miles from the Lipans' camp, and we ain't going back to Texas until we put the fear of God--and us--in those heathens."

Callahan popped the last of his corn fritter in his mouth. "Milo, get the men back in their saddles."

★

The Ranger battalion began its march again, the road gradually vectoring away from the Rio Escondido. The river became little more than a shallow stream which meandered a few hundred yards off to their right, angling away from the road. Milo drifted back in the column to ride next to Jesse and Billy 'Easy' Clopton.

"Boys, a Mexican peon just told the captain that there's a big bunch of Mexican cavalry ahead. He may be lying. Or he may telling it straight."

"I thought you said the Mexican town mayor back at the river said different. That the Mexican colonel gave us a pass to go after the Apaches." Jesse looked worried.

"That's right, he did. But he may have been lying too, to lure us away from Fort Duncan. To get us out where they can cut us off from any help."'

Clopton spoke, "Don't worry, Milo. We're ready."

"Damned right we are, Easy." Milo then looked hard at his best friend.

"Jesse, your Sharps carbine is one of the best rifles in the battalion. If I know Captain Callahan, before this day's over, we'll be using our Colt revolvers for close work."

"That's why I borrowed a second pistol from one of the sick fellers. It's just a pocket pistol, but it's comforting." Jesse reached around to pat the small of his back where he'd stuffed the little pistol.

"That's good, Jess. But don't jump the starting gun. If you have a chance, get off your horse and take a few good shots with the Sharps."

"Milo, getting off my horse sounds like a good way to get left behind."

"Well, at least hold your mount still and get off a couple of shots with the Sharps before we go in. Aim for a Mexican officer showing lots of brass. Easy, your shotgun don't shoot far, so you save your loads and help Jesse pick out the brass. Help him find targets before you charge."

"Sure thing, Milo."

Milo grinned, "That's 'sure thing, *Sergeant.*'"

Milo nudged Buck ahead, but heard Jesse calling, "Clean your spectacles, Sergeant McKean. They're so smudged you might shoot *me.*"

First Lieutenant Burleson, the twenty-nine year old from San Marcos who served as second in command of Callahan's company, rode next to Will Davant. They were right behind the two buglers, who rode behind the trio of captains at the head of the column.

"How long you been stationed at Fort Duncan, Lieutenant?" Burleson asked Davant.

"So you know I'm an army officer?"

"Sure. Everyone does. And we're glad you're with us. But I hope you'll do more than observe when the shooting starts. If there really are Mexican soldiers ahead, we may need every gun."

"Don't worry about that. And I've been at Fort Duncan for about a year now."

Before Burleson could ask anything else, Captain Callahan raised his arm and the battalion halted on the road.

They were riding through a grassy prairie of low hills, but several hundred yards ahead, off to their right, stood a large grove of oak trees, surrounded by a thicket of scrub brush. A cloud of dust was hanging above the oak trees.

Callahan, Benton, and Henry gazed in that direction.

Ever more cautious than the other two Ranger captains, Benton spoke. "The dust may mean that thicket is full of Apaches."

Callahan rolled his cigar in his mouth. "Nah, we're still too far from where Schmidt said their camp is at San Fernando."

"Who's Schmidt?" Benton asked.

"He's my scout who found the Apache camp at San Fernando."

"Then it could be Mexican soldiers in there," Benton replied.

Captain Henry answered, "Look at the cattle grazing between us and them trees. The damned cows are stirring up the dust. There may be a few Mex drovers in the mott taking a siesta or hiding from us, but that's all."

Callahan nodded in agreement and waved for the column to resume its march. The battalion commander kept the horses moving at a brisk walk, saving their strength for the upcoming fight with the Apaches, which he fervently hoped would occur before dusk. The Rangers were holding in their excitement and nervousness, masking any apprehension with jokes and jovial talk. Lieutenants Burleson and Davant resumed trading stories of the army officer growing up on a South Carolina plantation and Burleson's teenage years on the frontier during the days of the Texas Republic.

Captain Benton's company was detailed to guard the twenty pack mules at the back of the formation. When the mules were opposite the grove of trees and the head of the column a hundred yards beyond, four riders appeared behind the last of the Rangers.

Private Brent Shiller was riding drag behind the mules. He spotted the riders as they topped the embankment that masked the riverbank and called for his sergeant. Together they watched and quickly noted the head feathers and painted designs on the horses that marked the riders as Indian warriors. The sergeant called for more of Benton's Rangers to gather around him.

Two of the hostiles remained near the river, coming no closer. But soon, the other two galloped forward until at about a hundred yards, the pair released arrows towards the Rangers. Both missed. One of the Indians reined in his horse and whooped, notching and firing a second arrow. This missile pierced a mule's haunch, causing the beast to buck and disrupt the pack train. The other warrior continued riding towards the Rangers, firing his second arrow from seventy yards. Private Shiller flinched as the feathered shaft whirred past his ear.

Even though the sergeant ordered the rear guard not to shoot yet, Shiller reacted to the near miss of the arrow by raising his double-barreled twelve-gauge shotgun and firing a round of buckshot. Two of the small pellets hit the Lipan's horse, prompting the warrior to turn tail and ride out of range.

Captain Callahan heard the shot, stopped the battalion, and with Private Hynyard and First Sergeant McKean, he galloped back to see what caused one of his men to shoot. He was certain any riders would be either Mexican *rancheros* or, just maybe, a small party of Mexican cavalry sent to shadow his Rangers. Callahan began to mentally phrase his assurance that Colonel Langberg himself had consented to the Rangers' expedition to locate and punish the marauding Lipans.

Callahan pulled up next to Lieutenant King, Benton's second in command, at the front of the nervous cluster of pack mules. King pointed towards the four mounted warriors near the river.

"Well, I was wrong about the Lipans not coming out to meet us." Callahan gazed at the Indians for a few seconds. "Here we go."

Callahan stood in his stirrups and bellowed as loudly as he could, "Battalion, right face!"

Sergeants and lieutenants relayed Callahan's order along the fifty-five pairs of mounted Rangers in the long column on the road. Within half a minute, the Texans had shifted to a single rank of over a hundred Rangers, knee-to-knee, weapons in hand, facing the four Native American warriors who now sat stoically on their ponies near the river. The two buglers, Captain Benton, and Captain Henry spurred their horses to join Callahan.

Callahan then loudly ordered, "Privates Gunn and Davant! Dismount with your Sharps and shoot those red bastards!" Jesse Gunn and William Davant passed their reins to their file mates and dismounted, Gunn with his Sharps carbine and Davant with his long Sharps rifle. Without further orders, they prepared to fire towards the four mounted Indians.

Davant took a kneeling position, braced his left elbow on his knee, and aimed carefully at the figure with the most feathers showing on his headdress. He squeezed the trigger of his Sharps. The warrior's horse fell and the rider leapt off and disappeared down the embankment. Jesse then fired, without seeing any effect. Milo had slipped behind the single rank of Rangers and was too occupied watching their flanks and rear to notice.

After a minute of peppering fire from the pair of dismounted marksmen, Captain Callahan ordered Gunn and Davant back into their saddles. The whole battalion sat immobile on horseback in their battle line, holding their shotguns or Colt revolvers at the ready, cracking jokes about the mighty war band of three hostiles in front of them. When three dozen more Native American riders suddenly climbed the river embankment to join the first three Indians, the Rangers hooted in derision and anticipation of an easy fight.

Callahan gauged the strength of the Indian war band and turned to his two buglers and unexpectedly ordered them to sound the notes for the entire line to turn about and withdraw.

"What the hell?" Captain Henry shouted at Callahan. "We can't run from that little bunch of Indians! We must outnumber them five to one."

"Settle down, Captain Henry. We ain't running. I'm feigning a retreat to draw out the rest of the hostiles that gotta be waiting out of sight. They wouldn't confront us like this outnumbered so badly. There's more either in those trees or down by the river."

Henry sighed in exasperation and waved for his company to turn their horses.

With a fair amount of shouting by the sergeants, the battalion followed the bugled directions. All three companies turned and in good order retired a hundred yards. Then they faced the river again and waited.

Callahan's ploy worked. While the Texans watched in disbelief, the entire river embankment filled with horsemen. On either side of the Apaches and Black Seminole warriors, hundreds of uniformed Mexican cavalry appeared.

In an exhibition reflecting years of rigorous duty and training, the blue-uniformed cavalry turned outward and trotted forward to extend their lines past both ends of the Rangers' single rank.

Captain Benton muttered in alarm, "Dear God Almighty."

Captain Henry drew his revolver. "Goddammit."

Private Easy Clopton's bladder betrayed him, but the young Ranger never noticed.

Milo instinctively wiped at his eyeglasses' lenses with his shirt cuff and swallowed.

Captain Callahan chomped down on his cigar, biting it in two. He spit out the pieces and called Benton and Henry to him.

Benton blurted out, "We can retire in good order and reach the river and the cover of the artillery at Fort Duncan if we go right now."

Henry growled, "Hell, no. I ain't gonna be chased for fifteen miles then get jammed in and trapped next to the river. Let's charge the left wing of the Mexicans and then roll up the middle."

Callahan shook his head. "Nah, the other wing of lancers would be right on our tail and catch us from behind."

"Then let's get out of here. Head to Piedras Negras. Now!" Benton urged.

"Nah, Henry's right about being chased, then penned to the river. They'd line the top of the bluff and shoot down on us. We'd be fish in a barrel. And our horses have been ridden fifteen miles today, their mounts have been resting by the river. We'd get caught and skewered all the way back. I ain't dying with a damned greaser's lance stuck in my back."

"What then?" Benton asked, a growing desperation clear in his voice.

Callahan, alarmed himself at the numbers of enemy before them, but determined not to show it, growled at his old friend. "Get a grip, Nate. You've been in tight spots before. You two remember the drill where we go from one long line, like we're in now, to four ranks?" Both captains nodded.

"My Regulars will form the first two ranks. Then William's company, and Nate, you follow in the fourth rank. We'll head straight at the redskins in the middle. They'll likely break and skedaddle when we get close."

"What about the mules?" Benton wanted to know.

"Let 'em go when we charge. Push 'em out to our left. Maybe they'll get in the way of the Mexican cavalry."

"After we bust through, which way we go?" Henry asked.

Callahan raised up in his stirrups scanning right and left. "To our right. We'll keep the river to our left and fight our way back to where we had our nooner. We'll dig in there and hold until sunset. They may have us outnumbered, but we got the firepower. After dark we'll slip away if we have to."

As the Ranger commanders made their hasty plans, a line of Mexican infantry wearing red coats and white pants emerged from the thicket and formed a two-rank firing line to the right of the mounted Native American warriors. The Mexican cavalry, mostly lancers wearing blue uniforms and flat brimmed black hats, moved farther to the Rangers' left flank to make more room for the musket-armed foot soldiers. The red-jacketed *soldados* quickly attached gleaming bayonets to their long muskets and stood shoulder to shoulder.

Jesse and Billy Clopton caught each other's eye. "You good, Easy?" Jesse asked in a voice that sounded more strained than he wanted He ignored the dark spot in the crotch of Billy's trousers.

Clopton thumped his chest with his revolver while he rolled his tongue around his dry mouth before he answered, "H-hell yeah, Jesse."

A group of forty or more Mexican horsemen dressed in the rough civilian clothes of *rancheros* emerged from behind the thicket and eased up behind the Native Americans, leaving a gap between them.

"Damn," Will Davant exclaimed to Milo as they both checked the loads in their revolvers. "I see Injuns, I see Mex cavalry, I see Mex infantry, and I see Mex irregulars. Must be hundreds of them. Is there anybody in this part of Mexico that ain't out there in front of us?"

Unseen by Davant or any of the Rangers, an appaloosa ridden by a black man carrying a shotgun lurked behind the Mexican lancers.

The Rangers efficiently performed the formation change more quickly than Milo would have guessed possible. As a first sergeant, Milo knew his position was properly behind the second rank, his duty to keep the men in Callahan's company going forward in formation. Regardless, he shoved Buck into the space between Lieutenant Kyle and the corporal at the end of the first rank of Callahan's Regulars. He glanced sideways and saw Clopton in the first rank, Jesse and Will Davant right behind him in the second rank. Captain Callahan paraded out front on his black war horse, hat in hand. Callahan's countenance was alive with excitement and an intensity like Milo had never seen before. The captain faced his battalion, his back to the enemy. He stood in his stirrups and shouted.

"Men, the time is now. Remember the barbarities done to our women by the red heathens who are right there in front of you!" He waved towards the Apaches and Black Seminoles ahead.

Callahan then pointed his finger at the Mexican cavalry.

"See those Mexican lancers? Remember the massacres of your fathers and uncles at the Alamo and at Goliad! Remember Houston's grand charge at Buffalo Bayou!" Callahan dropped his hat and drew his pistol.

"Now, boys. Remember the bloody son of McGee, and charge with me!"

Callahan pulled up hard on his reins, rearing his stallion onto its back legs, crashed down, spun and spurred the beast into a gallop towards the Indians. Milo and the entire battalion followed. Within their horses' first strides, the four-rank formation of drilled Rangers dissolved into a mass of a hundred and ten angry Texans, each one holding a cocked revolver or shotgun. They kicked their horses' flanks and yelled curses as they raced forward eager to kill the hated Apaches.

Chapter 48

On the Fields Next to the Rio Escondido
State of Coahuila, Mexico
Early Afternoon, October 3, 1855

Big Cat and the Lipan chiefs grew apprehensive watching the Rangers on the ends of their formation move towards the middle. Instead of a single rank that stretched out in front of the Mexican lancers on either side, all the Rangers were now clustered directly opposite their warriors. Before the chiefs could decide to leave and let the Mexican army engage the Texans, the Rangers' leader kicked his black horse straight towards them

All the Rangers galloped right behind him, screaming and firing their revolvers. A few of the Native Americans, seeing they were the main target of the madly charging white men, made their own decisions to retreat beyond the river. Most accepted the white men's challenge and kicked their own mounts forward, howling their war cries, shooting arrows and muskets, waving tomahawks.

The Rangers' mules, once released, ran bucking and braying back down the road, straight away from the fight, providing no interference that might disrupt the charging Mexican cavalry.

To the left of the Indians, Captain Patino ordered his cavalry forward. His well-disciplined troops held lances upright for the first hundred yards as their horses trotted in tight single rank. On his next order, they spurred their animals into a gallop and lowered their long spears, aiming for the juncture where the *Tejanos* would meet the lancers' Apache allies.

On the other side of the Rangers, Colonel Menchaca ordered the carbine-armed cavalry to shoot into the knot of charging enemy. The ineffective volley delivered, Menchaca ordered sabers drawn and released his troopers to crash into the flank of the enemy. One of the few carbine balls to hit a Ranger found Captain Benton. The ball smashed into his left arm just below the elbow, was turned by the thick bone and tore down his forearm, mangling flesh and cartilage before it erupted out at his wrist.

Benton dropped his reins but tried to stay in his saddle while blood covered his empty hand. His yell of pain reached Lieutenant King's ear. Before the lieutenant could twist his mount through the chaotic melee to aide his captain, a Mexican cavalryman's saber slashed down on King's shoulder. The heavy blade sliced through King's coat and shirt, finally stopped by the lieutenant's collar bone.

Captain Benton's son, eighteen-year-old Private Eustace Benton, shot the Mexican swordsman as the trooper jerked to free his embedded saber from the lieutenant's shoulder. A second later a Mexican corporal, only yards away, aimed an old flintlock pistol at Eustace's head. The weapon's powder was damp and most of it failed to explode. In a fizzle rather than a flash, the bullet flew forward with a tiny fraction of the expected velocity. The ball entered Eustace's eye socket at an extreme angle, and lodged against the inside of his skull, next to the young Ranger's ruined eye. Eustace immediately lost consciousness and fell from his horse. A friend from Seguin, Private Wesley Harris, jumped off his own horse and pushed Eustace across his saddle and remounted, determined to take his dying friend home.

Captain Madero, the foot soldiers' veteran commander, knew to keep half his *soldados* holding loaded weapons when confronting cavalry. He restricted his single oblique musket volley to his front rank, even though he doubted the *Tejanos* would charge into his hedgerow of bayonet points.

The unseen irrigation ditch was wide enough that four horses in the Rangers' front line were caught off-stride by the unexpected chasm and failed to leap all the way across. Other horses saw the danger in time to gather their legs under them and jump successfully. Most of the horses behind followed the first ones across, even though some yawed to the right to avoid the obstacle.

Private Gunn's brown horse made the leap, and plunged ahead, still right behind Captain Callahan. Jesse had fired his revolver three times. The last shot hit an Apache who was about to swing his war club at Callahan's head as their horses passed each other.

Private Clopton was the first rider whose horse thudded into the far wall of the ditch, throwing him over the twisted broken neck of his mount. Clopton held onto his revolver, but landed on his shoulder and neck, stunned, but conscious. He lifted the arm holding his pistol, trying to find a target through his blurred vision. A few seconds later, an arrow from a charging Lipan's bow punctured the young Ranger's neck, killing him.

The lancers on the right thundered toward Sergeant McKean and Lieutenant Kyle. They both shouted for the Rangers around them to face the threat. Milo emptied his Colt, unseating one lancer. He fumbled with his empty revolver trying to holster it until it dropped to the ground. He pulled his Baker rifle. With no time to aim it, Milo grabbed the barrel to use the stock butt as a club. He clumsily parried a lance thrust with the rifle, managing to deflect the spearhead so it passed beyond his ribs, but pierced his flapping jacket, the lance shaft hanging up in the wool. As Milo urged Buck forward, the wooden shaft snapped, the spearhead fell, and Milo bashed the Mexican trooper with his rifle stock.

The Mexican cavalry's charge onto both flanks of the Texans was blunted by the firepower of the Colt revolvers and buckshot from the Rangers' double-barreled shotguns. Most of the lancers veered away from the mass of white men, choosing to lessen their risk of death by not directly confronting the Rangers' rapidly firing pistols.

Captain Callahan passed through the last of the Apaches and paused to sweep the field with his eyes. He noted the Mexican *rancheros* and a scattering of Indians milling around across river. To his left and behind him the melee raged on. He jerked his war horse to the right, bellowing, "With Me! With Me!," exhorting his men to push through the thin line of lancers remaining along the riverbank.

Jesse Gunn was about to follow Captain Callahan when he saw a hatless Ranger on the ground. Recognizing the fallen man as Billy Clopton, Jesse twirled his horse and rode past other Rangers until he reached Billy's side. As Gunn slid off his skittish horse, he saw the arrow in Billy's neck. Intending to lift his friend's body onto his horse, Jesse holstered his pistol and stooped down. As he did, a pinto horse appeared next to him, the dark rider swinging a thick club that crashed into the Ranger's chest.

Jesse fell backwards, the force of the blow emptying his lungs of air. The rider, a Black Seminole with a wide flat nose, barked a laugh and kicked his paint horse forward, intending to come back and take the white man's scalp, whether he was dead or alive. The warrior hoped the man would still be breathing when he returned, so he could both take his trophy hair and kill the white devil again.

Captain Callahan rallied his disordered command around him and led the whooping and exultant Rangers along the river, scattering the few Mexican cavalrymen who confronted them. The battalion, moving as a disjointed, but still somewhat effective unit, crossed another irrigation ditch that branched from the river.

Captain Benton's company instinctively formed the Rangers' rearguard. They surrounded their two wounded officers while Private Harris carried their captain's unconscious son across his saddle, holding a dirty handkerchief against Eustace's mangled eye socket.

After going three hundred yards downstream, the river flowed twenty yards below the Texans, at the bottom of a rocky bluff. Callahan nudged his horse forward to slide and bound down the steep slope, followed by his troopers. Dismounting without orders, his men with rifles climbed back up to the lip of the embankment and began firing at the closest Mexican lancers.

Seeing the strong defensive position that the Rangers now held, Colonel Menchaca withdrew his cavalry out of rifle range and ordered the musketeers under Captain Madero to advance in a skirmish line and engage the Texans. The Mexican commander glanced up at the sky, estimating he had four hours of daylight to root out the damned *gringos*.

Menchaca noted that the Apaches and Black Seminoles were hovering around the far end of the Texans' position. He could make out that a few chiefs were vigorously waving their arms and gesturing towards the river. The colonel supposed they were working up their warriors to charge the opposite side of the ravine where the Rangers had fled. He doubted the Indians would succeed, but their presence on the far side of the ravine would draw fire from Rangers who otherwise would be shooting at his *soldados*. Menchaca had never believed that the Apaches and Big Cat's Black Seminole warriors would be a decisive factor in the engagement, but he welcomed them as allies, nonetheless.

Milo had been the last Ranger to reach the safety of the bluff by the river. He'd hung back, letting the other Texans pass him by as he searched with rising despair for Jesse.

★

Spellbound, Thompson watched the Rangers, Indians, and Mexican cavalry across the river all dash towards each other and clash together. Dust from the churning horse hooves filled the air, quickly limiting what Thompson could see. But the shouts, gunfire, and yells of anger emerging from the chaotic scene were beyond anything Thompson had ever imagined.

To Thompson's eyes and ears, the melee seemed to go on and on. The discharges of the Texans' Colt revolvers were a rolling thunderstorm as they shot hundreds of bullets in the confusing swirl of horses and men. The cries of dying soldiers and the bellows of wounded horses undergirded the staccato gunfire. The raucous shouts of men impaling, shooting, or slashing enemies punctuated the other sounds.

Yet, the intense melee was brief. Horses and riders passed by each other, the first vicious engagement ending as the hammers of Colt pistols fell on empty chambers. The Texans had burst their opponents' thin ranks, and needed time to reload revolvers for another round of close combat. Thus, the initial violent collision ended quickly as the white men pushed through the lancers and braves in front of them, turned downriver and galloped away, leaving the ground littered with the fallen.

Thompson saw the uniformed Mexican horsemen milling about. Officers and sergeants shouted to reform a line of battle. A large number of riderless horses stood on the abandoned battleground, some already grazing, reins hanging down. *Horses are as good as hard coins, and there they are waiting for me to lead one or two away.* He nudged the appaloosa into the shallow river.

He guided the spotted horse among the bodies, passing by animals with Mexican trappings, looking for those with Texas saddles. *I best stick to the white men's animals or the soldiers will just take their army horses away from me.* Thompson stopped and leaned down to grab the reins of a brown horse standing dutifully over a still figure. He looked at the fallen white man's pock-scarred face. *I know you! Gettin' kilt here is what you get for tricking me at the river last year.* Then the body groaned and its fingers fluttered.

Leaving his shotgun tied across his saddle, Thompson dismounted and knelt by the white man, trying to remember his name. *One of the men in the river was called Milo, another was...Jesse. That's it, the ugly one, this one, was Jesse.* Not seeing any visible wounds on Jesse, Thompson was thinking furiously when a paint horse stopped next to him. A young dark Indian holding a long knife slid off the animal.

The two men, gazed at each other's complexion. The Black Seminole warrior nodded as he reached out and touched Thompson's chocolate-colored cheek. He then spoke in a combination of Spanish and a Native American dialect that made no sense to the runaway slave. The Indian pointed at the white man on the ground and touched his own hair, holding up his knife.

Thompson shook his head and reached for Jesse's arm to pull him upright, blocking the Indian. The Black Seminole, standing above the supine white man and the Negro, grabbed Thompson's shoulder and pushed him sideways out of his way.

The Negro from Texas didn't think about his next act. He picked up the Colt revolver that lay under Jesse's hand. The dark Indian pulled up the white man's head by his long hair and put his knife blade against his victim's hairline. As the knife slid across Jesse's skin, Thompson cocked the revolver and shot the Indian in the chest. The surprised warrior fell backwards, revealing the long bloody cut he'd just made across Jesse's forehead. Thompson quickly wedged the smoking pistol under his belt, hidden by his shirttail, telling himself, *That's for the little black girl you Injuns beat and starved so bad she died.*

He quickly glanced all around, peering between the legs of the three horses that surrounded them. None of the other men who were riffling the bodies for valuables seemed interested in him. More gunshots sounded as scavengers killed those of the wounded who protested being robbed.

With great effort, Thompson lifted Jesse onto his shoulder and draped him across the saddle of the brown horse, which he supposed was Jesse's own animal. The slice across the Ranger's forehead stopped bleeding, but not before streaking his face in ruby rivulets. Thompson mounted the appaloosa and leading the brown horse, grabbed the reins of another grazing horse that wore a Texas saddle. Holding his shotgun upright, defiantly, the black man made his way off the killing field.

Looking straight ahead as if he were following an order, Thompson directed the appaloosa towards the nearest hill. He broke into a trot as he skirted around the base of the high ground, leaving the scene of the fighting as rapidly as he dared. After clearing the first bend, Thompson smiled broadly. He was headed back to Eureka with good news, two valuable horses with saddles, and a bleeding hostage.

Chapter 49

Along the Rio Escondido
State of Coahuila, Mexico
Mid-Afternoon, October 3, 1855

First Sergeant McKean made his way up and down the ravine, peering over the edge just often enough to mark the positions of the red-coated Mexican musketeers. Their locations weren't hard to see as the muskets belched white smoke with every ball fired. Since the Mexican foot soldiers were shooting at extreme range at mostly hidden targets, the Texans felt little danger. Still, Milo reminded every man to shift his position after he fired because the white smoke of their own weapons marked their positions as well.

Twice Sergeant McKean eased his Baker rifle to his shoulder and shot at a figure who wielded a sword rather than a musket. As he squinted through the smoke of his second shot, Milo thought he saw the man jerk before he dropped out of sight.

At Captain Callahan's orders, Milo told those with shotguns to save several cartridges in case of a cavalry charge. That was fine with the first sergeant, because he worried intensely about the cavalry making a determined attack. Since the Rangers were now dismounted, lining the rim of the steep ravine, their horses were tethered in the bottom of the gully. Milo feared that the Texans would be trampled and easy victims of the long Mexican lances and sabers if a cavalry charge reached them.

As Milo moved from man to man, he also asked each Ranger if he had seen Jesse in the fight. He'd been told that Private Clopton's horse crashed into the wall of the irrigation ditch early in the battle and Clopton had fallen. Another Ranger had seen Private Jones, the son of a prominent judge, fall from his mount. But no one remembered seeing Jesse after their charge began.

Milo borrowed Lieutenant Davant's telescoping spyglass to scan the area where the melee was fought. He carefully folded his spectacles and put them in his coat pocket before he put his eye to the telescope. The battlefield was slightly elevated above the ravine, so the ground was visible through the telescope. He saw both Indians and Mexicans walking among the fallen. Several horse carcasses blocked his view of small areas of the field. Most of the bodies he could see were clothed in blue uniforms, but some were identifiable as Indians, and Milo could tell that two wore brown coats.

A bare-chested Indian squatted next to one of the bodies before he stood up and brandished a bloody scalp in one hand and his long knife in the other. Milo bent over and vomited. He was wiping his mouth when a single pistol shot echoed from the battlefield. Milo looked through the telescope again. *Not Jesse, please God, not Jesse.* Then Milo remembered Billy Clopton and felt a pang of guilt for leaving him out of his silent plea to God.

As he scanned the figures prowling among the slain, Milo saw a Negro pushing a body wearing civilian clothes over a saddle. Transfixed, Milo watched the black man tie the limp form's hands and legs together under the horse's belly. It looked like a white man, so Milo assumed it was a Ranger casualty from the melee. *Is that Jesse or maybe Billy Clopton?* Then the Negro mounted a horse he couldn't see—until the black-on-white spotted horse emerged into view. *The alcalde's appaloosa!* He focused his view through the telescope and again inspected the hatless Negro rider. Milo watched him set a long-barreled shotgun upright on his thigh. With a start, Milo recognized him. *That's Smith's runaway slave, Thompson.*

What? Were the runaway slaves fighting alongside the Mexicans and Apaches? Who was draped over the horse? Why would a Negro take the body of a Ranger? Was he taking a trophy to show other runaways that he'd killed a Ranger? Dammit! I'm watching something really bad and I can't stop it.

Army lieutenant Will Davant lay next to Milo watching the same vignette, but without the aid of the telescope.

"Look, Will, that's Thompson the runaway slave on the white spotted horse. Shoot him. I think he's taking Jesse or maybe Billy."

"Milo, I'm a good shot, but that appaloosa is too far away. I might just as easily hit the body draped over the brown horse as the nigger on the appaloosa."

"But he's taking a wounded Ranger, it might be Jesse!"

"It might. You say that's the nigger Thompson?"

"Yeah,"

"You know Thompson saved my life last year. Shot an Apache that was charging me with a big knife. Shooting at him doesn't seem a Christian way of repaying him for his kindness. Maybe he's taking Jesse or whoever that is, to save him from being scalped."

"I can't just lie in the grass and watch my friend get kidnapped. Will you go with me after him?"

"Milo, we're soldiers in a war here. Neither you nor me can just go off by ourselves. Besides, there's hundreds of Mexican cavalry out there who'd snag us right away."

Milo pounded his fist against the ground, and rolled over to stare at the sky. "Will, I ain't a real soldier, and Jesse's family to me. What the hell kind of mess has the captain gotten us into?"

Davant took the telescope and scanned the area, stopping to study three mounted Mexican officers. "I might just hit one of those bastards." He aimed and fired his Sharps. A tuft of dirt flew up in front of the three horses. As he reloaded to fire again, the three officers turned their mounts and withdrew behind the hillcrest, out of sight.

Davant rolled onto his side and studied Milo's drawn face.

"Milo, you may be a Ranger first sergeant for only three months, but you are the key Ranger in Callahan's company. I'm real sorry about Jesse and Billy. I am. But that's war. Now get your ass down to the captain and let him know how things look up here."

Milo looked back at Davant. "They teach you to be such a tough guy at that military academy?"

"Yeah, Milo, they did."

"Well...you're right. My duty's here. But I'm going after Jesse when this is all over. I ain't leaving him in Mexico."

Still distraught over Jesse and Billy Clopton, Milo slid down to the bottom of the ravine to report to Captain Callahan what he'd seen through the telescope. Everything except that he knew the black man on the *alcalde's* appaloosa horse.

Captains Callahan and Henry were listening to the first sergeant's report when voices from the rim of the ravine interrupted their conference.

"FIRE! They's settin' the grass on fire!"

Callahan responded first. "Dammit! Milo, get a blanket party ready to beat out the flames if it burns this far. And if we got any buckets on the mules, let's get 'em filled up with river water."

Henry answered, "We only got three mules, James. The rest bolted and the Mexicans got them now."

Callahan spat. "That means we got no grain for the horses. All right. If the flames come too high and fast, we'll retire back towards Piedras Negras under the cover of the smoke."

"Hell, No!" Captain Henry blurted out. "We came to attack the Lipan village at San Fernando. We can't turn back now."

Milo said, "Captain, there ain't hardly any wind. I don't imagine the fire's going to be much of a bother."

Callahan nodded to both men. "William, I'm as eager to reach that Apache camp as you are. But right now there's three hundred Mexican soldiers blocking our way there. Milo, you get with the other two first sergeants and do an ammunition check. I want to know exactly how many rounds we have for our Colt revolvers."

"Yes, sir." Milo moved away to carry out his orders.

"William, with both Nate and Lieutenant King wounded, I'm putting the men in the third company under your command."

"Right. But what are we going to do now? Which way are we going?"

Callahan looked at the sky, thinking. "Neither way, not as long as it's daylight and as long as the damned Mexican cavalry outnumber us and stay close."

"Hell, they're mostly lancers. We can shoot our way through them again."

"Maybe. Let's see what our cartridge count is before I decide."

Milo came back after a busy hour. "Sir, we have seven wounded too bad to fight. Four dead or missing. That leaves us with ninety-seven men who can shoot."

"About what I figured. How about bullets for the revolvers?"

"Seventeen men reported to me that they lost a pistol during the fight. Mostly trying to switch guns, or change cylinders in the saddle."

Captain Callahan noted his first sergeant's empty holster. "You one of them seventeen with a lost Colt?"

Milo nodded. "Dropped it while a lancer was trying to stick me." Milo held out his ripped jacket. "But he only stabbed my coat, and I knocked him out of the saddle with the butt of my Baker."

"Huh. You never were worth a shit with a pistol. Does every man have at least one revolver now?"

"Yessir. I made sure of it. Had to encourage three men to pass over their second piece to a friend."

"But not for yourself. That won't do, Milo. I got a spare revolver in my saddlebag. You go get it when we're done. How's our ball and powder count?"

Milo looked down at the tally sheet he'd written as the numbers had come in. "Thirty-six caliber balls for the Colt Navy's—1,434. Forty-four caliber balls for the Walker's—216. Didn't measure the powder, but it's a safe bet there's enough. Same with priming caps."

Callahan looked over at Captain Henry. "That's a titch over two full cylinders per Ranger. One cylinder to shoot up in a charge and one cylinder in reserve for the ride back to Texas. Ain't much."

Henry nodded, but added, "Don't forget the shotgun loads. I bet seventy-five of the boys have double-barrels, too."

"I ain't forgot the shotguns, but they're a man's back-up when his Colt's empty." Captain Callahan checked to see how high the sun was above the horizon.

"Let's wait until sundown and see what the Mexican cavalry does. Maybe they'll just go away and leave us be. Then Gus Schmidt can lead us in the moonlight to the Apache camp. He's been there. He can find it again, even in the dark."

"Captain, Ranger Schmidt was one of our casualties. He's missing. I got a report he was lanced."

Callahan looked hard at Milo. "Anything else you ain't told me, Sergeant McKean?"

With as much assertiveness as he could muster, Milo replied, "No, sir," even as he thought about the Negro Thompson.

★

Philip McBride

Lieutenant Colonel Menchaca listened impatiently to his subalterns' reports. The casualties among Captain Patino's lancers were far higher than he'd expected--fourteen deaths and thirteen with wounds too serious to continue. Menchaca's own dragoon company suffered six troopers killed and eleven wounded. The Mexican commander scarcely listened to Patino's explanation that the Texans attacked toward his lancers, while riding away from the dragoons. Captain Madero's infantry sustained light losses, the worst being a lieutenant who was fatally shot while overseeing the skirmish line after the Texans hid in the ravine.

No officer mentioned the involvement or the casualties taken by their Indian allies. The Apaches and Black Seminoles had disappeared after briefly threatening the dug-in Texans at the river. Roughly thirty Mexican *Rancheros* remained, but Menchaca knew their commitment to combat would be negligible.

The sergeants' ammunition reports revealed a shortage of musket and carbine cartridges. When Menchaca reprimanded the infantry commander for wasting powder and balls, Captain Madero reminded the colonel that he himself had ordered the infantry to force-march to the Rio Escondido.

"Without our supply carts, my men carried only one full cartridge box per man—twenty paper cartridges. Oxen cannot be hurried, but they will arrive tomorrow, or maybe the next day, with more cartridges and more rations."

Colonel Menchaca chose to ignore the insolence. "I do not imagine that the Texans will be here when the sun rises tomorrow. Their supply mules are now in our hands, and they carried no ammunition. The saddlebags of their fallen horses held no ammunition. They must now be almost without powder and balls for those damnable pistols. No, they cannot stay in place by the river. They will ride away in the dark. The question is will they return to Texas or push on to San Fernando after the Apaches?"

"And do we challenge them?" Captain Madero imprudently added.

Colonel Menchaca pursed his lips as he made his decision. "We punished the Texans today. We will withdraw a few miles towards San Fernando and wait to see if they continue in that direction."

The commanding colonel caught the eye of both his sub commanders. "We have them. If they do march towards the Apache camp, we will ambush them again tomorrow. If they return to the Rio Grande, we will follow and attack if they stop or veer away from the road back to Texas."

★

Thompson reached Eureka at sunset. Many residents, but not nearly everyone, had fled the settlement the night before at Thompson's urging. Enough people remained that a small crowd immediately gathered around him.

Thompson swiped down with the long shotgun, waving it like a broom. "Get away from them saddlebags! If there's food, I'll share it. Now get away from them horses."

His menacing shotgun and commanding tone of voice had the desired effect, a circle of open space grew around him as the crowd backed up.

A tall Negro asked, "Who dat white man? He daid?"

"I don't know if he's dead or still with the living. He was breathin' when I loaded him on the horse. Now, two of you lift him off that saddle and lay him on his back."

Another man pointed at Jesse. "Look at his face. It be cut an' covered in blood. Can I have his boots? He don't need 'em no mo'."

A man with a stutter asked, "Wh,why you bring a white man here? M,maybe some oder white mens come lookin' fo' 'm."

"Be quiet." Thompson knelt by Jesse and put his ear to his chest. He heard breathing.

Thompson still wondered what caused the white man's injury, so he unbuttoned the front of Jesse's shirt. He saw a huge dark bruise in the middle of his captive's pale white chest. A voice interrupted Thompson's inspection.

"What 'bout food? You said you'd share."

Thompson scanned those around him, seeing pleading eyes and sunken cheeks in every face. He went to the brown horse and opened the nearside saddlebag. Inside, he found a cloth sack full of fried corncakes and two chunks of barely seared slab bacon, the Ranger's rations for two days. He pulled out the sack of corncakes and gave half of one to each of the hungry people who surrounded him.

Thompson returned the nearly empty sack before he walked around the horse to the other saddlebag. He grunted when he opened the flap. The runaway slave pulled out a set of iron leg shackles and tossed them on the ground near Jesse's feet.

"Put those on my prisoner."

"What you want a white man prisoner for, Thompson? Ain't no bounty on white mens, just on us'ns."

"No, but he's got a friend named Milo, and I'm goin' to trade that white man there in chains for a slave woman named Irene. She's gonna be my wife."

Chapter 50

Near Piedras Negras
State of Coahuila, Mexico
Night of October 3-4, 1855

Buck's gait felt uncertain to Milo. Maybe it was the darkness, maybe the horse sensed his rider's nervousness as he kept twisting in the saddle, looking behind and to both flanks.

"Dammit, Milo, quit flopping around like a fish on a hook," Captain Callahan growled at his first sergeant. "You can't see in the dark, even with them specs, and neither can the Mexicans."

"I bet they're following us."

"Of course they're tailing us. And it takes about three seconds to pull our Colts and put out a wall of lead between us and them Mex bastards. You ain't going to get skewered by a lance out of the dark."

At sunset, the Rangers had watched the Mexican cavalry form columns and ride away, going south in the direction of San Fernando. The red-jacketed infantry soon followed. The Indians and the *rancheros* had already left. Grudgingly acknowledging their shortage of ammunition and the need of their wounded for medical treatment, Callahan ordered his battalion back to the site of their crossing the Rio Grande. They had begun their ride back to the town of Piedras Negras before midnight. Callahan and Milo rode at the head of the Ranger column.

"So Jesse Gunn is missing, along with Billy Clopton. I'm sorry, Milo. I know they were both good friends," Callahan said. "They were good Rangers."

"Yeah. I don't know how I'm going to tell Jesse's sister or parents."

"Huh. You're sparking his sister, right?"

"Yeah."

"Well, promise to name your first son after her brother. She'll like that."

"I suppose so. Jesse's why I came to Texas. Why I left Alabama. He wrote me how good things are here."

"That boy was smarter than he looked."

"Yeah." Milo smiled to himself in the dark. "Couldn't paint worth a damn, though."

Callahan grunted, no longer listening. As the expedition's commanding officer, he was striving to appear calm to those around him, to display the confidence his men expected of him. Yet, Callahan was seething with anger. The captain, a veteran of the Texas Revolution and two decades of leading Ranger companies against Indians and Mexicans, was aghast over what had transpired during the past twelve hours.

We killed a lot of greasers today. I bet we shot five or ten of the bastards for every Ranger who fell. They couldn't face our Colt revolvers with their lances and old muskets. Those damn little brown papists might wear fancy French uniforms, but they couldn't stop my men, my white men. But goddammit, we're the ones with our tails between our legs, skulking away from the enemy, hiding in the dark.

Just as bad, Callahan continued to wrestle over what to do when they reached the Rio Grande. *Do we resupply and ride back to fight again? Do I have enough men? Or, do we re-cross the Rio Grande to safety, and tell the people of Texas that we met the Mexican army and beat them in combat?*

What about the damned Apaches? Did we really punish them? Can we punish them if we ride back towards San Fernando? What about me? Do I go back to Texas having fallen short in the most important mission and biggest command of my life? What will the people think of James Callahan if we quit now?

Milo, grateful for Callahan's silence, let his own thoughts drift back to his friend Jesse and their adventures in this same region the year before. He thought about how much he and Jesse had depended on each other since he'd come to Texas.

How can I go back without Jesse's body? How can I face Malissa after leaving her brother's remains to the buzzards and Indians? Milo remembered the sight of the runaway slave leading away a brown horse carrying a Ranger's body.

Was that Jesse? Or Billy Clopton? Is one of them alive? Why would the Negro take a dead body? Why would he take a wounded Ranger? He hates us. I've got to go back and find him. But I was telling Will the truth. I can't leave Captain Callahan. Not now. Not yet.

Milo repeated his silent vow to Jesse and Malissa that he wouldn't return to Prairie Lea without going back, without making the effort to find the runaway Thompson and bring back either a body for burial or a living friend.

★

The battalion continued their moonlit ride until 3 A.M. when they reached the Rio Grande, just south of Piedras Negras. Captains Callahan and Henry rode side-by-side during the last segment of the journey.

"William, gather up six or eight of your boys and go visit the *alcalde* at his house. Tell him to surrender the town, that we are coming in at dawn and will gun down anyone who resists."

"The whole town?"

"Every damned building. Stables to whore houses. Even the church. Hell, especially the church. We need a man with Lieutenant Davant's telescope up in that bell tower as soon as it's light."

"What if the *alcalde* refuses?"

"Then we sack the town."

"What about the people living in the houses? Must be a couple of thousand of them. It's a big place."

"Tell him we'll not harm his people--if they open their doors and bring all the weapons in town to us. Remind the old goat that he lied to me about Colonel Langberg giving us a pass to San Fernando, and I ain't forgot." Callahan's mouth was a thin line of anger as he thought about how easily he had been lured into the Mexican colonel's trap.

"We need food and horse fodder, too," Henry added.

"Right. Tell him to bring food along with every gun and all the black powder in town."

★

Captain Henry returned within the hour, beaming. He could hardly contain himself as he strode up to Captain Callahan.

"Wait 'til you see what's in the old fort next to the *alcalde's* house. We now have artillery! Two cannons and one of them has two barrels. Like a giant double barrel shotgun on wheels."

"William, slow down. Start over." Callahan smiled. Already he had visions of resuming the expedition to San Fernando, this time with flying artillery to scatter the damned Mexican cavalry without his men even needing to use up their revolvers' ammo.

Captain Henry pulled out his flask of whiskey and sipped a bit to contain his excitement. "James, the fat old mayor is ready to hand over the key to the fort to you. A real iron key, big old thing. He wouldn't give it to me. Has to be you."

Callahan grinned at that, thinking back to his meeting with the *alcalde* just a couple of days before. "Good. What else?"

"The town folks are scared shitless of us. That's what. They're bringing in every old horse pistol and rusty musket in town."

"Food and fodder?"

"Yup. And the streets are full of people leaving town. Going ever' direction there is, some even going in boats to Eagle Pass. Like I said, they're scared of the *Tejanos Diablos*. Us, that is."

"Is the old fort a ruin, or might we defend it if needed?"

"Thick walls, some narrow windows. It's good enough that I think we should move right in this morning. Even if we just stay a few hours before we go back in to find the Apache camp. It's a roof for our wounded until we can get them back to Texas."

"Right. Let's go."

★

Ninety-nine Texas Rangers rode in a long two-men abreast column through the streets of Piedras Negras. Second Bugler Isaac Tanner, riding in the second rank next to First Sergeant McKean, held a Texas flag tied to a hastily cut willow sapling. Lieutenant Davant, in his role as the U.S. Army's observer, had questioned the propriety and prudence of flying the Lone Star banner while still in Mexico. Both Captain Henry and Captain Callahan had scoffed at his concern.

Callahan halted his battalion at the old stone fort and dismounted. He maintained a solemn countenance as *Alcalde*

Tijerina, bowed and held out the large old key before he stood aside and waved for Captain Callahan to enter the old stone building. Within minutes of completing his obligation to protect his people from the violence of the invaders, Tijerina was on the road heading south. He hoped to find Colonel Menchaca and the Negro who'd never returned his appaloosa mare.

The news of the cannons found in the fort, the prospect of resupply from Eagle Pass, and the absence of the Mexican cavalry had brightened Callahan's spirits. After instructing First Sergeant McKean to post sentries on the outer edge of town, and for Captain Henry to block the street intersections with ox carts, boxes, and timbers, Callahan himself stayed in the fort and took a pen to paper. Texas needed to know what he'd done the day before at the Rio Escondido.

In a sudden decision to remain in Piedras Negras and complete the two facets of his mission—to punish the Apaches and capture runaway slaves, Callahan penned a personal plea to the people of Texas to support his expedition, for patriotic volunteers to reinforce his battalion.

The captain wrote, *"Men of the frontier, come and help us. Let none come but those who will and can fight. If you come, come quickly; and come well prepared."* Callahan then wrote what he judged to be a detailed and accurate description of the battle the prior day.

Of the Indians involved, Callahan reminded his fellow Texans, *"Seminoles and Lipans are determined to scourge Texas with blood and outrage so long as they remain unchastised. Warriors of these tribes, including the celebrated Seminole chieftain Wild Cat gathered at the Little River to oppose us."*

He closed by stating confidently that his battalion, bolstered by more volunteers, would soon deliver an even stronger blow, punishing the Lipan Apaches a second time for their transgressions into Texas. Callahan did not mention his intent to pursue fugitive slaves. He sealed the letter in an envelope and passed it over to the adjutant.

"Lieutenant Kyle, you put that young courier fella on his race horse and get this letter to Rip Ford in San Antonio. Tell the boy to ride all night. Send a second mount so the lad can change out. I want Ford to read the letter first thing tomorrow and print it in his next newspaper."

"Yes, sir. Do I copy the letter first?"

"No time. I'll tell you what's in it after you get that courier on the road."

As soon as Lieutenant Kyle left, Captain Callahan summoned Lieutenant Davant.

"Lieutenant, I'm going to cross the Rio Grande in a skiff and go visit Captain Burbank. I'd like you to go along to verify what I have to tell your commander about our battle yesterday."

Davant took a deep breath, for he'd been wondering just what he would tell his commanding officer himself. "Sir, if I may ask, what is it you intend to say to Captain Burbank?"

"That we were on our way to find the Apache camp, with the foreknowledge and consent of Colonel Langberg, when we were treacherously ambushed by a large force of Mexican cavalry and infantry."

"Confronted or ambushed, Captain?" Davant looked dubiously at the older man. "The Mexican cavalry extended way past us on both flanks, but they never tried to surround us. Our path back to Piedras Negras was never contested. You could have withdrawn your Rangers without a battle. Yet you charged forward, vastly outnumbered."

"Damn right. Rangers don't turn tail and run from a pack of Frenchified Mexican peons pretending to be an army. And we busted right through them. We inflicted far more casualties on them than we took."

"Then you turned tail and ran back to Piedras Negras anyway." The memory of Jesse Gunn flashed across Davant's angry thoughts. "Leaving four Ranger bodies behind for the Indians to scalp and mutilate."

"Shortage of powder and balls for our Colts. And I regret leaving the corpses of my men. But you were there. You saw that they fell where we couldn't retrieve them."

Davant picked up on where the Ranger commander must be headed. "And now you're going to ask Captain Burbank for help ferrying your men and horses back to Eagle Pass. After fighting such a *gallant* battle at the Rio Escondido."

"Hell, no." Callahan glared at Davant. "My command is staying put, right here in Piedras Negras, until we are reinforced by more men. Men who hate the Apaches. Then I'll lead the battalion back to San Fernando to complete our mission. We'll attack and destroy the Lipan's camp, killing every damned Apache we see."

Taken back by Callahan's intention to stay in Mexico, Davant pushed. "Captain, what reinforcements? You now have less than a hundred Rangers. What difference will a few more guns make?"

"A letter is on its way this very moment. A letter that will be published in Rip Ford's newspaper in San Antonio. Then it'll be printed in newspapers all over the state. A call to arms from me. A call for patriots to reinforce my Ranger battalion with volunteers." Callahan walked to the narrow window.

"Within a few days, dozens, if not hundreds, of loyal armed Texans will start arriving. When we ride towards San Fernando next time, no damned Mexican army rabble will outnumber us or deter us. And we'll have flying artillery."

"If you mean those two little cannon relics in the old fort, you better look at them first."

Callahan grunted, suspecting that Davant might be right to question the condition of the cannons. The barrels were pitted and rusty, and one was only a barrel, with no carriage.

Davant continued, "Captain Callahan, I'll go with you to see Captain Burbank if you want. But if he asks me, I'll tell him that we fought a needless battle at the Rio Escondido. I'll tell him you lost four or five Rangers killed, two officers were seriously wounded, and most of your pack mules were scattered and taken. All in a reckless attack on a far superior Mexican force that blocked the road, but which left us a safe line of retreat back to the border. Back to the safety of Texas."

Callahan glared darkly at the young army officer.

"With your permission, Captain, I'll stay on this side of the river and see how I can assist Sergeant McKean. When you summoned me, I left him placing sentries around the perimeter of town. His eye for ground is not as experienced as mine. You can tell Captain Burbank that I did not accompany you because you were putting my West Point training to good use."

Callahan, disgusted with the defiant army lieutenant, muttered, "Stay then, and do what you want. Just get out of my sight." Davant started to leave, then blurted out a last caution.

"Captain, about that letter. I've no doubt you wrote a stirring description of a great victory over the Mexican army in their own country. The unexcelled bravery of your fine light cavalry. The devastating fire power of scores of Colt revolvers massed together. Unstoppable. Magnificent. Heroic."

Callahan looked sharply at Davant. "Yes, I did. Of course I wrote about our victory. It's what happened. It's true."

Davant nodded. "I'll give you that. I never imagined your hundred Rangers would be so ferocious in a charge. Even so, it will take a week to deliver your letter to the newspaper editors around the state and for them to print it. Whatever volunteers you entice to come here will have to muster and then ride over a hundred miles to reach Eagle Pass. Just how long do you plan to occupy and hold Piedras Negras? How long can ninety-nine Rangers defend this town when the Mexican army shows up with hundreds more *soldados*?" Davant drove home his point.

"You may be forgetting about Colonel Langberg, but he sure as hell hasn't forgotten about you. Langberg and the Mexican army don't cotton to armed invasions any more than you Texans do. He's coming. It may take a few days for Langberg to reinforce the battalions that we fought at the river yesterday, but he's going to arrive outside this town with an overwhelming force, just like Santa Anna did in front of the Alamo." Davant swept his arm in a big arc as he kept talking.

"One day soon, if you stay, you're going to look out and see a line of hard-bitten Mexican infantry arrayed in a big semi-circle around town, stretching from the river bank north of town, to the river bank south of town. The Rio Grande is still flooding, running fast and wide, blocking any galloping retreat to Texas. Five or ten *soldados* armed with muskets and bayonets for every one of your men. With nowhere for you to run, just like happened at the Alamo twenty years ago." Davant paused.

"I hope you and your Rangers can swim, Because if you can't, you're going to die here, and your bodies will be piled up and burned, just like your heroes at the Alamo. Every one of you."

Chapter 51

Town of Piedras Negras
State of Coahuila, Mexico
October 4, 1855

The wounded Rangers were shuttled to Texas in the two largest skiffs. The detail who'd stayed behind had kept a secure grip on the little boats, keeping them tied on the Texas side of the river This time the vessels were connected to the thick ferry rope that had been stretched across the river, and Rangers manned the oars.

Young private Benton was still unconscious. Captain Benton still nursed his own roughly bandaged mangled forearm and remained distraught over his son's head wound. Everyone who'd seen Eustace's eye socket assumed the young Ranger would die at any moment.

Captain Callahan rode in the last boat, sitting next to a Mexican saddle that was ornately decorated with silver. Captain Henry had found the hidden saddle and insisted it be immediately taken across the river with the wounded. Callahan expected his men would follow Henry's lead and empty every building in town of all valuables. That only concerned him if his enthusiastic Rangers become so distracted in plundering the town that they might fail to adequately blockade the streets. Regardless, Callahan said nothing as Captain Henry's sergeant carried the saddle to the boat. Callahan had ordered Henry to stay in Piedras Negras, to command in his absence. The task of fortifying the town was in Henry's hands, while he himself conferred with the commander of Fort Duncan.

★

U.S. Army Captain Burbank did not make Texas Ranger Captain Callahan wait. The fort commander had already heard rumors of a battle fifteen or twenty miles south of the border, and was eager to hear a first-hand report. Since Lieutenant Davant had yet to report back, Burbank thought who better than the Rangers' commander to give that report. When both officers were seated, Burbank spoke first, intending to immediately control the flow of the conversation.

"Before anything else, please take a look at this letter I received this very morning. It's from Colonel Menchaca of the Mexican army. He's the fellow who commanded the force that you fought yesterday at the Little River Why don't you read it out loud, so I can hear it again?"

Callahan read the short note, written in English in a flowing script. The Ranger captain's face turned darker in anger with every new word.

"Sir, take your American dogs out of Piedras Negras or I'll march in there and kill every one of them."

Callahan tossed the note onto Burbank's desk. The army captain picked it up and tore it in half. "He isn't much for courtesy between gentlemen, is he?"

Callahan muttered, "Mexican pig."

"American dogs—Mexican pigs, you're not much for genteel speech either." Burbank stood and dropped the letter onto the coals in the fireplace hearth. "The courier said he came from the Mexican camp at Villa Fuente near the Rio Escondido. Not far from where you fought. That means the Mexican cavalry can be at Piedras Negras anytime, and the foot soldiers by early afternoon. I imagine you're here to seek my assistance in ferrying your men back to Eagle Pass. There's no need to ask. You will have the army's assistance. I've already sent Captain Walker and a detail to the crossing. Moreover, a three-gun battery is limbering up right now to deploy overlooking your position on the Mexican side. The threat of my artillery should keep the Mexican soldiers from harassing you while we get your force back to Texas."

Callahan nodded, leaned back in his chair, and offered his own opening to the conversation.

"I left your Lieutenant Davant across the river. Turns out he's an old friend of my first sergeant. Together they're setting up our sentry posts on the edge of town and deploying the two cannons we found in the old fort."

This time Burbank nodded. "I've often wondered if the *alcalde* was sitting on any old artillery. Davant is a solid young officer. If he learned his lessons at the academy, he'll read the ground properly and place the pieces well."

Burbank knocked his pipe bowl on the edge of his desk, about to refill it. "How long do you think it will take for all your men to cross the river?"

"A while, as long as it's flooding. But that don't matter right now. My command is staying in Piedras Negras for a few days until more volunteers arrive. Then I'm going south again to attack the Lipan camp."

As Burbank stared in surprise at Callahan, the Ranger commander pulled a cigar from his vest pocket, bit off the end, and spit it onto the floor.

"We hurt the Mexican army riff-raff that ambushed us. Hurt 'em bad. My boys charged right through their ranks. We scattered them like quail before they ran for the hills. The Mexicans are stupid. They're still fighting the last war. Instead of modern firearms, they use lances, swords and old muskets. No better than the Indians that way. And just like the Indians, they couldn't handle the lead from our Colt revolvers. Like I said, that bunch of Mex soldiers are either dead or scattered like maverick cattle. I rode back to Piedras Negras to resupply. That's all."

Frowning at Callahan's wet tobacco on his office floor, Burbank's manner turned cold and his next words were blunt. "That's not quite what I'm hearing from others. Be that as it may, whatever happened at the Rio Escondido, I'm telling you to get out of Piedras Negras--today. You have no business there."

Callahan took the time to light his cigar and exhale a puff of smoke before he replied. "Captain Burbank, with all due respect, you are not the governor of Texas. You don't give me orders. I'm going to complete the mission assigned to me by Governor Pease by keeping my command fortified in Piedras Negras while we resupply and bolster our numbers with volunteers from San Antonio, Seguin, and Austin."

Burbank set down his pipe and leaned in, both elbows on his desk. "You realize that your Ranger battalion will be seen in Washington and in Mexico City as a military invasion force. Your continued presence across the border constitutes an act of war, Captain Callahan. The Mexican army will view your men as revolutionaries. They could legally execute every man in your battalion if they block your withdrawal and capture you. No different than Santa Anna and Goliad twenty years ago. You do remember Goliad, don't you?"

Callahan's thoughts tumbled back to his own narrow escape from the massacre at Goliad, while he stared at Burbank without replying. Seeing the Ranger commander wasn't going to answer, the army officer asked one more question.

"Why do you think your battalion will be reinforced? Has Governor Pease ordered another company of Rangers to Eagle Pass? I've not been informed of any such action."

Snapping back into the present, Callahan said, "I'll be reinforced because I've sent a letter describing our victory at the Rio Escondido to the newspaper in San Antonio. The letter issues a call to arms to the patriots of Texas to join my command so we can fully punish the Apaches for their depredations in Texas." Callahan leaned forward to emphasize his next comments.

"As you say, my command is now in a different country entirely. My battalion in Piedras Negras is Texas's only chance to avenge our ravaged women, and the children kidnapped by the Lipan Apaches." Callahan stabbed his smoking cigar at Captain Burbank.

"I'm Texas's only chance for vengeance because you won't do it. You're here. You have the soldiers. You have the artillery, but you give the damned Indians free rein to hide in Mexico. They think they're safe on the Mexican side of the Rio Grande." Red-faced, Callahan leaned towards Captain Burbank.

"But not this time. I ain't leaving Mexico until my battalion shows them and Texas and the goddamned U.S. Army that the Apaches ain't safe just because they can cross a damned river." Settling back into his chair to calm himself, Callahan continued.

"The newspaper editor in San Antonio is Rip Ford. He's an old Ranger captain and he'll publish the letter tomorrow or the next day. As soon as the word is out of my victory over the Mexicans, volunteers will muster and ride to my support."

The nonplussed army officer stared at his visitor. "You are delusional, Captain Callahan. I respect your fervor, the depth of your anger at the Indian raids. But I regret your failure to understand my position here. I do not give 'free rein' to the Indians. But neither do I have the men to guard every crossing spot across the Rio Grande." Burbank picked up his pipe again.

"As to your current position across the border, your plan will require no less than a week for any volunteers to learn of your call to arms, gather together, and ride over a hundred miles to Eagle Pass. And Colonel Langberg will not give you that week."

Callahan shook his head. "Mexicans move like molasses. Yesterday I routed whatever soldiers Colonel Langberg has. They won't be back in just a few days. No sir, yesterday's victory bought me at least ten days before the Mexican army will pose any threat at all. As I speak, Captain Henry is barricading every way into Piedras Negras. We are in a strongly fortified position. I know what I'm doing."

Burbank sighed deeply and played his final card. "Very well. You force my hand. My artillery battery will unlimber and remain here in Fort Duncan. I'll recall Captain Walker's support detail. You are on your own, Captain Callahan. May God have mercy on your men, because Colonel Langberg sure as hell won't."

Callahan stood, bristling internally. "You disappoint me, Captain Burbank. Your masters in Washington City have never seen what the Apaches do to white women, after they murder and mutilate their husbands. But you have. I expected more of you."

The Texan rubbed the end of his smoldering cigar on Burbank's desktop to extinguish it. "Now I'm going to look in on my wounded men, who your surgeon has kindly agreed to treat. One young Ranger took a spent ball in his eye socket. He was still unconscious an hour ago, but breathing. And that brave boy's father, Captain Benton, has a mangled arm from another Mexican musket ball."

★

Dr. Walter Doss, the same surgeon who'd treated Caroline Schmidt the year before, glanced at the rough-looking man who stood in the doorway. Dr. Doss's hands were covered in blood as he stooped over Ranger Lieutenant King, sewing together the long gash in his shoulder made by a slashing Mexican saber.

"You don't look injured. What do you want?"

"I'm the commander of these brave Rangers."

"Hmm. Captain Callahan, is it? Must have been quite a fight. Glad you made it back to the Texas side of the river. Did you punish the Apaches?"

"Some, but not enough. We'll be hitting them again soon."

Chapter 52

Town of Piedras Negras
State of Coahuila, Mexico
October 4, 1855

First Sergeant Milo McKean furrowed his brow and bit his bottom lip. He pulled off his hat and absently scratched his scalp. Milo was disturbed. He knew that Captain Callahan was intensely angry at the betrayal of the Mexican authorities. When the *alcalde* told the captain that the battalion would not encounter interference in their mission to punish the Apaches, Callahan had taken him at his word. Milo thought the captain had every right to be furious at the duplicity. And Milo was every bit as angry, the fate of Jesse and Billy Clopton gnawing at him every minute.

Nonetheless, when Captain Callahan told him to emplace the cannons discovered in the old stone fort as part of the fortification of the town, Milo had been surprised. After fighting a battle, taking casualties, and now painfully aware that the Mexican army opposed them, Milo had assumed Captain Callahan would order the ferrying of men and horses back to the Texas side of the Rio Grande. The first sergeant was unsettled by the captain's decision to hold the town until reinforcements from Texas arrived, and only after several more days of waiting, to ride once more toward the Apache village.

Milo fervently wanted the battalion either to return to Texas that very day, or to head out again towards the Apaches' camp immediately. Once back in Texas, Milo figured the captain would grant him permission to return alone to Mexico to search for Jesse. Or, if he failed to receive Callahan's approval, he'd go anyway. On the other hand, if the battalion rode further into Mexico today, back towards the site of their fight on the little river, he might return with Jesse's body, or perhaps find him still alive.

Milo tried to focus on where to put the cannons as a distraction to shake off his frustration, his mourning for his friends, and the uncertainty of their bigger situation. He squinted into the distance, unsure whether the double-barreled cannon would better be deployed behind the rock wall where he stood, covering the main road into the town, or a hundred yards to his left, covering the wide field he had just inspected.

"If you're scratching your head over where to put your wheeled cannon, I can tell you don't put it here." Will Davant said softly as he walked up. He gently patted Milo on the back. "Milo, I'm sorry about Jesse. I'm really sorry."

Milo nodded and knuckled one eye behind his eyeglasses to blot out the tear that was forming. "Billy Clopton, too. Goddammit. Why them two?"

"War. Randomness. Bad luck. All the same. No accounting for why them and not you or me or anyone else."

"I suppose. Will, you're a trained soldier. Did Captain Callahan do the right thing yesterday? And what about today? Why the hell ain't we either going back after the Apaches or going back to Texas? What are we doing trying to turn this whole town into a fort? We don't have enough men to defend every street corner, hold every house."

"We'll talk about that later, Milo." The West Point graduate looked closely at his friend.

"As Captain Callahan's first sergeant, you're right to mull over what happened. On the other hand, you're Callahan's right hand man. You're his fist if need be. Your job is to see that his orders, all his orders, are carried out—without question or hesitation. Did you do that yesterday?"

Milo nodded that he'd conscientiously performed his duties during the long day before.

"And are you doing that today?"

"Sure I--well, maybe not. I keep thinking about Jesse and Billy. About seeing that darkie Thompson leading away the horse with a Ranger draped over it. Hating myself for not going after him. Maybe I could've saved Jesse or Billy, or some other Ranger."

Davant put an edge in his voice when he replied quietly to his friend. "Sergeant McKean, you need to pull your head out of your ass. Right now. Billy and Jesse are casualties of war. Gone. Captain Callahan has given you direct orders. A hundred other Rangers are looking to you for their orders. And you have two cannons to place. You have no time today for mourning. Now, tell me why you want to put a cannon right here."

Milo took a deep breath, then pointed down the road. "The road. The foot soldiers will come down the road."

Davant nodded. "Which cannon? You have two."

"The one with two barrels."

Davant shook his head. "Put the other one here. Look how the road cuts through that dip in the ridge at least three hundred yards out. The Mexicans will funnel into that narrow gap before they deploy on this side of the ridge. The single-barrel piece can put solid shot balls right into the gap. Maybe even bounce the shot down the road. Catch 'em while they're in a column, take out three or four men stacked up behind each other with one ball. It must be demoralizing as hell to see the man next to you or in front of you lose his head or an arm or leg. The sort of thing that'll make a scared, nervous soldier turn and run."

Milo held up his hand to stop Davant from saying more. Raising his voice, he ordered the single-barreled artillery piece emplaced on the road, aimed at the gap, loaded with a solid ball.

Milo pointed to his left. "I'm thinking the double-barrel piece should be loaded with buckshot in both barrels and positioned to cover that wide field. I have a feeling that the Mexican cavalry will come from that direction. We'll wait for them to get real close before we fire it."

Lieutenant Davant nodded. Milo issued more orders. Soon both cannons were in position and wooden barricades were being built to mask their presence. Davant stayed to instruct the Rangers assigned to crew the two old artillery pieces. Milo left his friend lecturing about the geometry of bouncing solid shot and the deadly breadth of a canister of grapeshot. The horsemen turned artillery crewmen listened without interrupting their teacher, seemingly eager to learn how to load and swab out the cannon barrels. Davant was gratified to have their attention, but knew what they really wanted was a chance to fire the little cannons.

The first sergeant walked alone, turning corners almost randomly, working his way from the far edge of town, back to where the battalion's horses waited beneath the river bluff. Milo eyed two Rangers ahead of him leave a building, both men carrying burlap sacks over their shoulders. The activity was expected, as he'd personally relayed Captain Callahan's orders that the men search all the buildings to secure food and horse fodder. Milo understood that calling this theft 'foraging' was a smokescreen, since they had no intention of paying for the stolen supplies. On the other hand, Milo knew the *alcalde* had played a big part in the deception that led to yesterday's battle, and Jesse's and Billy's likely deaths. That made nything in the *alcalde*'s town spoils of war.

When the sack-carrying Rangers looked back at him, Milo waved to them. At the same time, he heard screams come from the house the pair had just left. Milo jogged forward, drawing his pistol. Before he could see through the open door, he heard cursing in English and more shrieks.

Reaching the doorway, holding his cocked revolver pointing forward, Milo took in the scene of a white man with his trousers around his knees holding down a Mexican woman on her back on a table. He stood between her legs, his hands pinning her shoulders to the table, his pelvis thrusting hard against her. Her skirt was pulled up over her waist as she flailed her legs in desperation. Noting instantly that the rapist was a Ranger he recognized, Milo reversed his pistol to grasp it by the barrel. He stepped forward and smashed the hand-grip solidly against the man's temple.

The assailant sunk to his knees and fell over. The woman rolled away and crouched in a corner, sobbing. Milo paused long enough to take off his hat and shrug in apology to her. Then he holstered his revolver and picked up a second Colt pistol off the dirt floor and stuck it in his belt. With a nod to the woman, Milo pulled the unconscious Ranger to his feet and slung him over his shoulder.

The sergeant hauled his limp burden the few blocks to the ferry landing, the rapist's bare buttocks pale in the morning sun. At the top of the bluff, he dropped the man to the ground. Seeing Corporal Ben Elam, a friend from Prairie Lea, Milo called for Elam to bring him a set of leg irons.

"Ben, I caught this turd with his prick in a Mexican woman. She was screaming and trying to fight him off, but he had her pinned to a table on her back. How about you put the leg irons on him."

"You bet, Milo. Should I pull up his trousers?"

"Nah. But wake him up and get him down to the boats. I want him taken across in the next skiff going over."

As Milo turned away, Elam casually kicked the unconscious Ranger in the testicles before he knelt to lock the shackles onto his ankles.

"Sergeant McKean, what the hell are you two doing to my Ranger?"

Captain Henry glared down at Milo and Ben Elam as he reined in his horse. "That's David Johnson and he's a private in my company."

"That man's a rapist. I caught him in a house ravaging a woman just a few minutes ago. I'm putting leg irons on him and sending him back to Texas."

"McKean, you have no authority over the men in my company. I'll deal with him my way. Put those shackles away."

Elam stood up and took a step away from Johnson who still lay unconscious.

Milo shook his head in reply to the mounted captain.

"Do like I told you, Ben. Put the leg irons on him."

"Don't do that, Ranger. I'm in command of the battalion while Captain Callahan is across the river. You *will* follow my orders. Both of you. Or I'll have *you* arrested and put in irons."

Milo stepped over to Corporal Elam and took the shackles from him. Without looking at Captain Henry, he knelt and clasped the iron bands around Johnson's legs, locked them and put the key in his vest pocket. When Milo looked up, he saw that Henry held his revolver, cocked and pointed at him.

"Captain Henry, in matters of fortifying and defending our position, I'll carry out your every order. But in this deal, I'm acting as the senior sergeant in the battalion, enforcing discipline like Captain Callahan expects. Johnson is a rapist who I personally subdued in the act. I carried him back here with his pants still around his knees. There is no question of his guilt. I'm taking him down to the boats to be ferried over and locked up on our side of the river. I will insist that he be appropriately punished for his crime. With your consent, or over your objection."

Captain Henry tried reasoning with Callahan's stubborn sergeant. "Didn't you say Johnson was in a Mexican house? Foraging, I gather. I suspect the Mex woman tried to interfere, and he was keeping her away."

Henry pointed his pistol at Milo's eyeglasses. "Hell, son, you wear spectacles. You misunderstood what was happening. Besides, it was most likely just a greaser whore he was messing with. All the decent senoritas and their mamas left town already. The only women still here are the whores trying to make a few pesos off our Rangers. Now release Johnson."

"Captain Henry, I didn't misunderstand a damned thing. I saw--through my eyeglasses--I saw the man's member stuck in a woman who was fighting like hell to get him off her. I'll see him lashed for his crime or at the very least, tarred, feathered, and riding a rail for a day."

Henry sighed and slowly holstered his revolver. "You go ahead, McKean. Enforce discipline. I ain't going to shoot Callahan's first sergeant. It'd take too much explaining. But we'll see what happens after we get back to Texas. This ain't over between you and me. No way am I going to let one of my men be tarred or whipped for roughing up a Mexican whore."

As the captain nudged his horse down the bluff, Ben Elam asked Milo, "You still want me to take Johnson to the ferry?"

Milo took a few seconds to think before he answered.

"Yep. It's the right thing. Mexican women deserve the same respect we give our own."

"Can Captain Henry stop Johnson from being punished?"

"Probably. Captain Callahan don't have much warmth in him for Mexicans, men or women. I'll report the rape to him, but I don't look for him to do anything while we're still on this side of the river. And as soon as we get back to Texas, the battalion is going to disband. We'll scatter all over the countryside back to our jobs and families. Ranger Johnson's crime is likely going to be ignored."

Corporal Elam looked down at Johnson who had started groaning.

"Well, he's already got a goose egg on the side of his head where you beaned him."

"And he's going to have blue balls where you put your boot toe. And the men will see him in shackles for a little while anyway. All that's better than nothing."

Chapter 53

Eureka
Settlement of Runaway Slaves
State of Coahuila, Mexico
October 4, 1855

Thompson looked down at the sleeping Ranger. He lay on his side, the rough horse blanket still covering him from thigh to chin. The black man nudged the white man's shoulder with his foot, prompting Jesse to twist on the ground, his arms instinctively reaching up to protect his aching head. Thompson nudged him again. After several seconds, the thin young man regained enough consciousness to groan and tentatively touch the crusted cut across his forehead. Raising his arm caused a sharp pain in the center of his chest, but the wounded man didn't open his eyes.

Reaching down, Thompson grabbed the tin canteen that lay next to the Texan's saddle. He knelt next to Jesse and let a trickle of cool water drip onto his forehead and face. Jesse sputtered awake, his eyes quickly focused, and he looked around in confusion. When he saw a Negro standing over him, he tried to sit up, but his chest pain and the weight of the iron leg shackles stopped him. He pulled at his unbuttoned shirt placket and with his chin tucked into his neck, he could barely see the dark brown and purple bruise in the center of his chest. Moving his head brought on another groan.

Jesse flexed his legs again and studied the shackles. He looked up at the black man who knelt by him.

"Thompson?"

"Never thought you'd see me again, did you?"

"Thompson?"

"No one but. And you my prisoner."

"Where am I?"

"Eureka. Where you be the onliest white man in miles and a camp full of black men is waitin' to slit your throat if I lets 'em."

"But the battle? Yesterday? A Injun hit me in the chest." Jesse touched his bruise.

"Yeah, an' then he sliced your scalp open to take your hair."

Jesse moved his hand to the top of his head, fingering a lock of hair, then touched his forehead. He flinched when he put too much pressure on the scabbed-over cut. "I still got my hair. Did another Ranger shoot the Apache before he could finish with me?"

"Nah. I shot him with your pistol." Thompson patted the pistol grip stuck in his belt.

"You what? You shot an Apache to save me?"

"Yeah."

"Well, I'm much obliged. I am. But, why? To put me in these leg irons? Why save a man just to turn around and shackle him?"

"No. I plan to trade you for a wife."

Jesse noticed his saddle and reached towards it, groaning with the effort. When Thompson saw his prisoner was trying to pull the saddle to him, he reached out and dragged it so the seat was behind the white man. Jesse eased his head onto the leather pad, sighing.

Covering his eyes with the back of his hand to block the morning sun, Jesse muttered, "Did you just say you're going to trade me for a wife?"

"Yeah."

"Well hell. You might as well shoot me now. What woman would come here?"

"A woman named Irene."

"A special Irene, or will just any Irene do?" Jesse groaned again as the chest pain squelched his bark of laughter at his own joke.

"Mistah Menger's cook in San Antonio. I'm gonna trade you fo' her."

"Me for a darkie woman cook. Is she a slave, Thompson?"

"Sho'."

"Mr. Menger don't care about me. He's never even seen me. And Irene is worth four or five hundred dollars to him. He won't trade her for me."

"I knows that."

"But you said trade me for Irene."

"After your friend Milo buys Irene from Mistah Menger."

Jesse reflexively raised his head so he could look at Thompson.

"Do you have Milo, too?"

"Nah, just you, and two brown horses and a pistol and a rifle and two saddles."

Jesse eased his head back to the saddle seat, head and chest both aching mightily. "And these leg irons," he muttered.

"You goin' to write a letter to Milo, like you and Milo did to trick me to the river. Only this letter won't be no trick. You fo' Irene. He goes to San Antonio and buys her. Brings her here and we swap."

"Thompson, Milo ain't a rich man. That's why we're rangering, for the pay. And that pay ain't enough to buy Irene."

"Maybe your pa and ma have money they'd give to get their son back."

Jesse snorted. "My family works a farm. I don't think Mr. Menger would trade Irene for a few bushels of corn."

"Mules? Horses? The farm land?"

"Thompson, I'm a growed-up man. My ma and pa got young'uns to raise. I'd never ask them to sell off their livestock or their land so you can have a wife."

"Then maybe Milo can talk Irene into running off to Mexico. Just leave one night with Milo like I done with Philip. Like ever' man in Eureka done."

"Philip--is he the tall really black darkie that Will shot in the river last year?"

"Yeah."

"Huh. He die?"

"Not yet. He gots him a Mexican woman."

"Why don't you do that? Get a Mex wife."

"'Cause I wants Irene, and I gots you to swap fo' her."

Jesse rolled to his side and pushed himself into a sitting position, trying to ignore the sharp pains in his head and chest. "You say you got two horses?"

Thompson nodded. "Yours and one more. You think Mistah Menger would trade Irene for the horses?"

Jesse looked past Thompson to where three horses were grazing.

"Is that white spotted horse the same one I saw the fat Mexican mayor riding?"

"That be the *alcalde*'s horse."

"Mr. Menger might trade a woman slave for that horse."

"Ain't mine to trade. I gots to take it back."

"Take him Billy's nag instead. Tell him his spotted horse got shot in the battle."

"Who's Billy?"

"The dead Ranger whose horse you took. Why were you at the battle, Thompson? Were you there to fight us Rangers?"

"I was back behind watching. The Mexican soldiers stopped me on my way back from here. I'd ridden on that spotted horse to warn the other Africans here that you might be coming to take them back into slavery in Texas."

Jesse replied in a voice he hoped sounded hurt. "We didn't come after you runaways. We came to punish the Apaches for their raids into Texas."

Thompson snorted in derision. "Then why those leg irons in the saddlebags? White mens don't take Injins back in chains. You kill 'em."

"Well, Captain Callahan said Apaches first, then if we saw any runaways..."

"Uh huh."

"The battle? I remember Billy falling off his horse when it hit the far side of a ditch we had to jump over. I got down to see to him. Then an Injun came at me...Then nothin' 'til now." Ranger Gunn gently rubbed the bruise on his chest. "Who won? Seems like we were doing good, except for that ditch that opened up in front of us."

"You white men turned and rode your horses to the creek flowing into the river. You all got off your horses and hid and kept shooting at the Mexicans and Apaches. In the fight with the Mexican horse soldiers you knocked a lot more men off their horses than they done you." Thompson pulled out Jesse's Colt revolver and hefted it. "The Mexicans' spears and swords wasn't a fair fight against your pistols."

"Are the Rangers still on their way to the Apache camp?"

The black man shrugged. "When I picked you off the ground and come here, the soldiers and you white men were still shooting at each other from both sides of the big field."

"I wonder if Milo is alive," Jesse said to himself as he laid back down. "What now, Thompson?"

"You write a letter to that Milo man." Thompson picked up both sets of saddlebags and dropped them next to Jesse. "I seen a bunch of letters tied together an' a writing stick in there somewhere."

"Yeah, I write to my family. Keeps them from worryin' over me." On the evenings when Jesse wasn't on sentry duty, he had written of his rangering experiences to Caroline Schmidt and his sister, keeping the un-mailed letters bundled together with his calico shirt.

"What do I write to Milo?"

"What we been talking about. That you be in chains at Eureka. That I, Thompson, will trade you for the woman Irene who cooks for Mistah Menger in San Antonio."

"But we also talked about how Milo's got no way to buy Irene. Besides, you don't even know where the Rangers are, or if Milo's still alive."

Thompson tapped the side of his own head. "He'll figure out a way, once he reads your letter. And your band of Rangers won't be hard to find. I'll just look for the buzzards circling in the sky."

Jesse grunted at that, suspecting it was true. "How you going to deliver the letter? You ride up to the Ranger pickets, they'll either shoot you or capture you."

"Philip's Mexican woman. She take it."

"Then send her on the spotted horse. Leave the appaloosa with Milo to trade for Irene."

"No. You write the letter now. Write the letter. No one here can read, so write what you want, but it's you fo' Irene. Sooner you write the letter, sooner I take it to Philip's woman, who take it to Milo. Longer you wait, maybe Milo go on back to Texas and forget you."

Jesse thought out loud as he spoke. "San Antonio is a long ride from Eagle Pass. Two days or more. Even if Milo can persuade Mr. Menger to make the trade, it'll take him a week or two to go, trade, and get back here."

Thompson nodded at the saddlebags. "Onliest food you gonna git is in there. It won't last many days. If you don't want to starve while you wait, write the letter now."

"How will Milo find you to make the swap?"

"Take Irene to a cantina in Piedras Negras. The sign over the door has three horse heads painted on it. Me or Philip be lookin' in ever' day just befo' dark."

Jesse wrote the letter. He wrote that the runaway slave Thompson recognized him and hauled him unconscious from the battlefield. He was now Thompson's prisoner, his ankles chained in the leg irons from his own saddlebag. He wrote that his forehead was cut where he was nearly scalped, and he was sore from a war club blow to his chest, but he would live.

Jesse tapped the end of the lead pencil on his knee as he pondered if he should write of Thompson's offer to trade him. The last thing he wanted was for Milo to set off on a fool's errand to rescue him. He could feel the comforting weight of the pocket pistol in the small of back. *I can get myself out of this pickle.*

Finally, Jesse decided it was too dangerous not to include the offer, in case someone did read his letter to Thompson. *If I leave out his offer to trade me for Irene, he might just shoot me dead with my own revolver.* So, he dutifully wrote that Thompson said he would swap Jesse for a woman slave named Irene who belongs to Mr. Menger in San Antonio. He finished by writing that Thompson or Philip—the tall really black darkie who was at the river with Thompson last year—would be watching for Milo at a cantina with three horses over the door in Piedras Negras.

The letter written, his forehead and chest throbbing, Jesse lay down again to think and rest. A few minutes later, Thompson came back from watering the horses and picked up the letter. He gazed at the paper before he folded it and stuffed it inside the crown of his battered hat.

"Thompson, if you leave me here while you take that letter to Philip's woman, the other darkies will kill me. You said so yourself."

"Huh. They might. Sho' 'nuf."

"Milo won't trade for a dead friend. Only a living one. Take me to somewhere else. Maybe where Philip lives with his Mexican wife."

"Huh."

"Thompson, it ain't just me that's in danger. It's you too. I got eyes. I can see that three horses and saddles, and three guns make you the richest man in Eureka. And I bet you ain't got any friends in this camp. Philip ain't here. You go to sleep, one or two of those men that been eyeballing us all morning, they may slit your throat and mine and then take your horses and guns and ride off somewhere south of here, rich men."

"Hmph." Thompson pulled a corn fritter from a saddlebag and bit into it. "Mexicans don't cook in grease like my ma and Irene do. I do miss cornbread."

"What about what I just said? Them men look plenty ready to kill you and me."

Thompson looked around at the dozen men lounging in whatever shade they'd found.

"All right. Tonight, after the sun go down, we ride to Philip's hut."

Jesse nodded, relieved, and believing that the road would offer him the chance to use his hidden pistol and escape.

"Now, you listen to me, white boy. I'm 'bout to walk over there and tell them men that I be givin' you my shotgun. That you gonna watch over me and the horses while I sleep. I ain't shut my eyes in two days. I'm gonna tell them that you shoot the first one gets close to me or the horses. That shot will wake me and I'll use this revolver to shoot any more of 'em who try to take what's mine."

"You giving me a loaded shotgun?"

"Do I look stupid? I run out of shot fo' that gun long time back. But they don't know that. You just stay awake or both our throats may look like yo' ugly fo'head."

Chapter 54

Road Between Eureka & Piedras Negras
State of Coahuila, Mexico
Night of October 4-5, 1855

D ark and cloudy. *The darker the better*, Jesse thought. He looked up at the clouds moving past the half-moon. He didn't have any idea where they were except on a road that Thompson said would lead them to Philip's hut. He hoped it would join the same road the Rangers had taken away from the border the day before.

Their sunset departure from Eureka had been watched by the men who continued to lurk around the edge of the clearing. Some sat in the shade of boulders, others lay under crudely built lean-to's or brush arbors. Jesse reminded himself that these were runaway slaves like Thompson—determined men who'd risked their lives to free themselves. Yet, now they were lethargic, staying in the primitive camp and accepting the chance of recapture by the Rangers and a return to bondage. Jesse found it baffling.

The Ranger still wore the leg irons, causing him to ride sidesaddle, precariously balanced, one leg in a stirrup the other one clumsily hooked over the saddle horn. He was glad Thompson had led him away from the battlefield draped over his own horse, a generally agreeable animal, tolerant of the lopsided weight on its back. The captive smiled thinking how differently the piebald mule would have reacted to him clinging to just one side of his saddle, the leg iron chain clanging against its flank.

Looking back at the dark silhouette of his captor riding behind him, Jesse said, "Thompson, I need to piss."

"Wet your pants. I ain't stopping."

"Don't you ever piss? Don't you need to relieve yourself?"

"Not now."

Jesse persisted. "Well, I ain't going to piss my pants. It makes me turn raw and itch down there. I'm stopping to take a leak. You remember that if you shoot me now, you'll never see Irene."

The voice from the darkness grudgingly gave in. "Hmph. All right. But hurry up."

"You'll have to lift me back on my horse like you did at Eureka. The damned shackles ain't helping. Why don't you take them off me?"

"Nope. The leg irons stays on. I'll boost you up in your saddle. but I ain't going to hold your pecker. Now get on with it."

Jesse unhooked his leg from the saddle horn and slid to the ground. "Was that something you did for Mister Smith? Hold his pecker while he peed?"

"No, and I didn't wipe his ass either, but I sure emptied his chamber pot every morning. Not something I miss."

Unbuttoning his trouser fly, Jesse made an effort to compliment his abductor, hoping to lull him into a sense of camaraderie. "You seem smarter than the other darkies I've talked to."

Thompson grunted. "Maybe that's because you wearing the chains and I've got the guns. Don't you know slaves act dumb so you white men will leave us be? Haven't you seen that *uppity niggers* gets the lash?"

Finished with his unneeded urinating, Jesse walked back to his horse, furtively pulling the hidden pocket revolver from the small of his back. "Yeah, I reckon so. But you still show a lot of brains, you got more sense than half the Rangers I been riding with for the past three months."

Thompson dismounted and walked up behind his prisoner. As the black man held out both hands to grab the white man's belt to hoist him up, Jesse twisted sharply at the waist and poked the cocked pistol into Thompson's chest.

"This one is loaded, not like your shotgun. If you live through this, remember that smart men always have a back-up gun somewhere."

Thompson dropped one hand to grab Jesse's Colt revolver from his belt, but the white man clamped his own hand on the pistol before the black man reacted.

Nose to nose with Jesse, Thompson calmly asked, "What now?"

"Now you get on your knees." The Ranger took a step back, pulling his revolver free from Thompson's waist belt. The black man knelt.

"Reach into the pocket where you got the key to the shackles and hold it out for me."

It was too dark for the two men to see each other's faces, but Jesse could see Thompson's eyes narrowing. "Befo' I do that, tell me if you're takin' me across the river. If that's your plan, kill me now. I ain't goin' back to be branded and pick cotton 'til I grow old and stooped. I been my own man fo' a year now. I ain't goin' back. Not Thompson. No."

Jesse let out a long breath as he admitted to himself that he respected the Negro who knelt before him.

"That ain't my plan, for two reasons. You saved my life when you draped me over my horse and took me away from the battlefield. I owe you for that. Second, I figure you earned your freedom when you shot the Apache that was trying to kill Will Davant last year. So I ain't taking you back to Texas. I'm leaving you right here. Now hold out the key to the leg irons. I need 'em off. I ain't no damned slave either."

Thompson held out the key. Jesse told him to sit down while he backed further away. The Ranger dropped to one knee and unlocked the leg irons with one hand, keeping the pistol pointed at the Negro.

Jesse tossed the shackles at Thompson. "Put those on, then lie down on your stomach while I lock them." The runaway slave did as he was told.

After painfully mounting his horse, sitting properly this time, feet in both stirrups, Jesse said, "I'm taking the appaloosa mare and my horse. I'm leaving the Ranger horse and your shotgun a mile or so up the road. You can walk in the leg irons. The key to them will be in the saddlebag. Maybe you can sell the shackles to a blacksmith and buy some powder and buckshot."

Standing up, Thompson asked, "You going to let me go then?"

"Ain't that what I just said? But don't follow me. Go to Philip's and stay hidden until you know Captain Callahan's Rangers are back in Texas. I know some of them boys are eager to collect a bounty for runaway slaves. Give it a month or so, and then you watch that three-horse saloon. You might find Irene there some day, if we're both lucky."

"You ain't takin' the spotted horse to the *alcalde*?"

"Hell, no. That fat bastard lied about the Mexican army leaving us alone. Piss on him. I'm going to sell his horse in San Antone and buy Irene like you want. Is that all right with you, *Mister* Thompson?"

"Yes it is, *Mister* Jesse. Yes it is."

In the dim light of the moon, neither man could see the grin on the other's face.

★

Jesse rode his own horse and led the appaloosa, staying on the road through the long hours of the night. When he reached the edge of a wide flat plain, he stopped and gazed at the sky. He easily found the Big Dipper, then looked farther beyond the end of the constellation's handle and decided which twinkling light was the North Star. The road bent, somewhat aligned with the star, causing Jesse to decide that staying on the road would take him into Piedras Negras. Wishing to avoid the town, he veered off the dusty wagon path and continued cross-country at an angle intended to take him generally east, hopefully still toward the Rio Grande, but south of the town.

As he rode, the young Ranger had decided he'd make for the river and look for a ford downstream of the town. Thompson had not been able to tell him who won the battle where Jesse was knocked unconscious and Billy was killed. But the runaway slave had been certain that the white men from Texas had dismounted and taken cover in a ditch by the river. Thompson didn't know what happened after that, and neither did Jesse. He had no clues whether the Ranger battalion had been captured en masse, or had beaten the Mexican soldiers and gone on to San Fernando after the Apaches, or had returned to Texas.

The one place Jesse absolutely knew he wouldn't find the battalion was the Mexican town of Piedras Negras. And beyond that, the one place Jesse did not want to take the conspicuous appaloosa mare was where its legal owner lived in Piedras Negras. So Jesse was heading back to Texas as furtively as he could.

At the first hint of dawn he dismounted and waited next to a boulder that was taller than the horses. Jesse kept the white appaloosa next to the rock, with his brown horse on the outside, hopefully blocking the mare's bright coat. He thought he could vaguely smell and hear the rush of the flooded river, but he marked it up to wishful thinking. When the sunrays of the new day revealed his surroundings, Jesse was glad he was on the west side of the big boulder, in its shadow. But he quickly saw his attempt to hide had otherwise been inconsequential.

He stood at the top of a long escarpment. Looking ahead he could see the brown ribbon of the Rio Grande and two towns, somewhat offset from each other, on opposite banks of the river a couple of miles away. While the boulder hid him from the south and east, he was exposed from the north and west, so that anyone searching the ridge from that direction would see him as soon as he moved, if not before.

Realizing that waiting any longer would only increase his danger, the solitary Ranger mounted and let his horse pick its way down the embankment to the edge of the fast-running river. He turned downstream and rode along the bank for what he guessed was two hours or more. Finally, he came to a prairie where the river spread broadly across the flat terrain. Tracks of horses led into the shallow water and were visible leaving the wide river on the Texas side.

Jesse nudged his heels into the flanks of his horse, entering the ankle-high current that flowed far beyond the normal channel. The two horses walked wide-eyed through the deepening water until at chest height they lost their footing and began swimming. Jesse pulled his Colt revolver and held it high over his head to keep the powder in the cylinders dry, and muttered a *halleluiah* that they only had to swim for a few yards across the deeply cut channel in the middle of the river. In a few minutes Ranger Gunn was back in Texas. Without hesitation, he turned left and this time at a canter that hurt his chest with every stride, he rode upriver towards Eagle Pass.

Chapter 55

Piedras Negras
State of Coahuila, Mexico
Eight A.M., October 5, 1855

The meeting took place in the *alcalde's* house. Sitting at the absent owner's long dining table, the four Ranger officers and First Sergeant McKean held corn tortillas in one hand and spoons in the other as they attacked the spicy bean and goat meat stew.

Speaking with a full mouth, Captain Henry complained, "Why don't Mexicans make bread instead of these flat things. They don't sop up gravy worth a damn."

"You call this gravy?" Lieutenant Burleson added.

Ignoring the banter, Captain Callahan looked at Lieutenant Kyle. "How many men we have on the Texas side of the river?"

Kyle pulled his small notebook and flipped through a few pages. "Fourteen. Officially."

"What do you mean *officially*?"

"I mean I don't have morning reports from the first sergeants, so I don't know if we lost any deserters last night."

Callahan raised his eyebrows at Sergeant McKean. "Milo?"

"Got the report right here, Captain. I can't account for three of our privates. We're spread out all over town. But every man's been assigned a post, and three fellas ain't at theirs."

"William?" Callahan glanced at Captain Henry.

"I'm still waiting on my morning report, too. With Benton and King both wounded, I'm leaning on Benton's first sergeant. He's slow."

Callahan wiped his mouth with his sleeve cuff. "Milo, put two pairs of good men patrolling the riverbank from horseback. If they see any Rangers trying to cross back to Texas, stop 'em. Block their way. Shame them. Lasso 'em, or shoot their horses if they have to. Just keep every Ranger here. We may need every gun during these days before reinforcements start reaching us."

"Yes sir. I'll do that now." Milo stood up and asked one more question. "What about the men who are stealing more than rations and horse fodder? I'm seeing men flaunting Mexican jewelry and wearing new serapes over their coats."

"Spoils of war. We may not get the chance to round up any runaway niggers, so I doubt the boys will be collecting any bounties. The *alcalde* betrayed me about the Mexican army. Hoodwinked me, the bastard, and he speaks for the whole town. So let the boys take what they can find."

Since he shared Callahan's opinion of the *alcalde's* deception, Milo accepted the captain's lack of concern over stolen property, but he felt compelled to mention one other matter. "I caught a Ranger raping a Mexican woman yesterday. I sent him across the river in shackles."

Callahan shoveled another spoonful of stew into his mouth and swallowed before he looked up at his first sergeant. "Captain Henry told me about that. Said the man got rough with a Mexican whore. Did he injure the woman?"

"Not that I saw beyond the obvious," Milo conceded. Then he added, "But she was screaming something awful. Not like any whore I've heard of."

"Well, whore or not, I've already ordered Johnson released and returned to duty. Like I said, we need every gun."

With a heartbeat's hesitation, Milo wordlessly nodded to Callahan, then walked out of the room.

"Testy, ain't he?" Captain Henry said, his mouth again full.

Callahan pushed back his chair and stood up. "You know, last year he rescued a white woman from an Apache camp not too far from here. He and his partner shot it out with the Indians and brought her out nekkid as a newborn. He's got a soft spot for women. Even Mexicans, I reckon. But he's a damned good first sergeant, and you make sure your Rangers keep their peckers in their trousers from now on."

The commander now addressed his adjutant, "Lieutenant Kyle, since Sergeant McKean is busy, would you round up a couple of good scouts to ease out of the town and find out if there are any Mexican soldiers near by."

"Yes sir. I have John Sansom and Cole McRae standing by. I thought you might want them to go on a scout. If you'll excuse me, I'll get them moving."

Ten A.M

Milo soon had four men from the Regulars patrolling up and down the riverbank to block any Rangers who might try to return to the Texas side of the Rio Grande without authorization. Then he went back to the edge of town to again inspect the placement of their two artillery pieces.

"Sergeant, the boys done named our artillery pieces," Corporal Elam stood next to Milo on the flat roof and pointed to his right.

"That one lashed to the wagon wheels is the Ground Hog." Looking left, he waved towards the open field. "The one over yonder with two barrels is Double Flirt."

Milo grinned and patted Elam on the back. "Good work. You seen Private Davant?"

Elam snorted. "You mean the army's spy?"

"Yup, him. That private stuff ain't fooled anybody, has it?"

"Nah, Milo. But we're glad to have him around."

"Me too. You seen him?"

"Sure, he's down there by the Ground Hog. He seems to have a special interest in bouncing a cannon ball down the road."

"I don't see him or his black hat."

"He's back in the shade working. He found a long rasp, and he's been filing the burrs and rust off the cannon balls, one at a time. He says even a little bad spot will spoil the accuracy."

Milo shook his head in admiration for his friend's attention to detail. Looking beyond the barricade he saw two riders galloping towards town, waving their hats. "Let's you and me get down to the Ground Hog and see what has our scouts racing each other back to town. I'll wager it's the Mexican army."

Sergeant McKean and Corporal Elam were standing next to Will Davant when Sansom and McRae reached the blockade that stretched across the road. With a nod of thanks, Sansom leaned down and held out the long brass telescope to Davant.

"Sergeant, I got to find the captain. There's hunerds and hunerds of Mescans comin' our way. Just like two days ago, musketeers on foot and mounted lancers."

McRae added, "We put the telescope on 'em and counted ranks 'til they got so close we was a-feared the lancers would see us an' come after us."

"How many ranks did you count, Cole?"

"Milo, them foot soldiers were four across on the road and I tallied up over a hundred rows of 'em. An' I could see more dust behind the ones I counted."

Sansom spoke up again. "The lancers and the riders with the carbines was walking their horses off the road a ways, lettin' their mounts graze while the foot soldiers marched. Sergeant, there had to be hundreds of horsemen. More than we fought at the river."

McRae was clearly excited and nervous. "I reckon it's time we all get back to Texas. Ain't any way, even with these cannons, that we're gonna keep all those soldiers out of this town."

"We'll see, Private McRae. You two go report to Captain Callahan."

Turning to Elam and Davant, Milo said, "Will, Ben here says you want to personally aim and fire the Ground Hog. You still got time to get back to Fort Duncan, if you go now, but once you start commanding a cannon crew, you may be stuck here."

Davant winked at Milo and patted the barrel of the squat cannon. "I bet this ugly hunk of iron can stop those *soldados* right there in the gap. Knock 'em down like ten-pins. Don't go worrying about me, First Sergeant McKean. Mama Davant's boy doesn't have a death wish. And how can I observe what to report to back to Captain Burbank if I leave now?"

"If you're sure. thanks. Good to have a trained artillery officer sighting this little beast. Ben, you best get over there to the other cannon. I think I'll stay here and observe our observer in action with his new toy."

Not thirty minutes later, Captains Callahan and Henry rode up behind the barricade. The two dismounted and called Milo and Will Davant into the shade for a status report. Milo pulled a hand-drawn map of the town streets from his vest pocket and laid it on a table.

"The two X's are where the two cannons are. We're here, with the Ground Hog aimed at the gap where the road cuts the ridge over yonder. The circled numbers are where I put squads of four Rangers on rooftops or behind barricades."

"Who's in charge of the artillery?" Captain Henry asked.

"Corporal Elam is commanding the crew of the Double Flirt over there where I figure the cavalry will come. Will here has the Ground Hog."

Captain Callahan glared at U.S. Army Lieutenant Davant. "Just spying for Burbank didn't sit too well in the saddle, did it Lieutenant?"

Davant grudgingly nodded in agreement to Callahan. "No sir, it didn't. Not when there's two artillery pieces involved. This is a lot more what I trained to do at West Point than tracking Indians across the prairie."

Callahan replied, "Glad that high-falutin' officer training school does one thing right."

Davant ignored Callahan's jab at West Point. "Sir, my point about not being able to defend the town still holds water. I heard your scouts' report. If there's more than five times our number of Mexican soldiers coming, we're stretched too thin to hold for long. You can see on Milo's map how spread-out our points of defense are. There's not one place around the perimeter of town where we have the firepower to stop a determined attack, except maybe where the two artillery pieces are. If I were you, I'd start crossing the horses and supplies right now."

The scowl that darkened Callahan's face didn't surprise any of them. He picked up Milo's map of their defenses and ran his finger from one circle to another, doing his own tally of the number of Rangers deployed.

"I only count fifteen squads out in town. That's only sixty men. Where's the rest?

Milo held up his hand and tapped each finger as he ticked off the location of the remainder of the Ranger battalion.

"There are eight men around each cannon. Four crewmen and four in support. That makes seventy-six Rangers deployed. Plus four Rangers patrolling the river to stop deserters, and four men on this side guarding the boats and ferry raft, and four men taking care of the horses and mules on this side. You two captains and two lieutenants, and me and Davant. That's ninety-four Rangers accounted for on the Mexican side of the river.

Captain Callahan handed the map back to Milo. "Sergeant, looks to me like you've done a good job of deploying the men. We'll see quick enough what our captured cannons can do when the greasers get here. I promised the governor we'd kill enough Apaches that they'd stop raiding. I still aim to keep that promise once more men get here from San Antonio. Texas will respond to my call. Meanwhile, we hold here."

Captain Henry slapped Callahan on the back, saying, "Damn right." Milo and Will Davant exchanged barely perceptible shrugs.

Chapter 56

Texas Riverbank of the Rio Grande
Near Eagle Pass
October 5, 1855

Private Gunn guessed the time was somewhere close to the noon hour when two riders across the river waved their arms to hail him.

Jesse recognized the two men as Rangers in his company. He reined in his horse, and waved his hat. "What are you two fellas doing on that side of the river?"

"On guard for deserters. Is that you, Jesse?"

"What?" Jesse couldn't hear over the sound of the fast-flowing water. He edged his horse closer to stand forefeet in the water. "Louder!"

"Jesse, we all thought you was dead."

"Well, I ain't. What are you two doing on the Mexican side? Where's the company?"

"We're watching for any chicken-shits who might try to run for home before the captain's ready. The whole battalion is forted up in Piedras Negras. Waitin' on more men from San Antone."

"I hear you, now. I'm comin' over. Is the ferry working?"

"Yeah, I think so. Glad you ain't dead. You collecting horseflesh now?"

"Hmph. This here mare is a long story." With another wave, Jesse nudged his horse towards town, pulling the appaloosa mare behind.

The river road ran past Fort Duncan. Seeing the army buildings caused Jesse to think about Caroline Hoffman--or Caroline Schmidt, or Caroline Hoffman Schmidt. Even a year later, Jesse was unsure what last name to attach to the young woman they'd rescued. Regardless what she called herself now, he wanted her last name to be Gunn—Caroline Gunn, Mrs. Jesse Gunn.

Jesse rode through the open gate of Fort Duncan, nodding to the sentry who stared at the rider with a look of unease. It didn't occur to Jesse that his slashed forehead made him look like a mounted dead man. The Ranger tied his horses in front of the infirmary. He glanced at the bench under the portico where one day last fall he and Caroline had watched bright streaks of lightning and talked through a thunderstorm.

When the door opened, Dr. Walter Doss looked up from the letter he was writing. His mouth was open ready to chastise whatever trooper had failed to knock and seek permission to enter, but he held his tongue when he saw it was another wounded Ranger, come for treatment.

The doctor did a double-take. "Bless my soul, if it isn't, isn't...Mr. Gunn, the savior and protector of Miss Caroline Schmidt."

Jesse took off his slouch hat and extended a grimy hand to the doctor. The physician looked down at the filthy fingers and with a mental shrug, grasped and vigorously pumped Ranger Gunn's hand. He tried not to stare at the young man's forehead.

"Are you with the Rangers, Mr. Gunn?"

"Yessir. I was knocked out during the battle a couple of days back. I got left behind. But a...a friend found me on the battlefield, and now I'm back."

Now looking intently at the blood-crusted scar on Jesse's forehead, Dr. Doss nodded. "That's a nasty knife cut on your face. Sit down here by the window so I can get the direct sunlight on it. What knocked you out? You fall off your horse?"

"No, sir. I ride better than that. I'd dismounted to see if my pard Billy Clopton was still alive, and a bad Injun punched me in the chest with a war club." Jesse touched his chest lightly.

"I see now. And then that bad Indian started taking your scalp as a trophy. Your friend stop him?"

"Nah, he was dead. But someone did, I reckon. Like I said, I was out cold."

"Hmm." The physician tenderly felt the long scab that stretched across the young man's forehead. He leaned forward and sniffed at the wound. "I don't think the cut is infected, but I'm going to wash it thoroughly. First, let me see your chest."

Jesse obediently took off his coat and vest, grunting when he moved his shoulders. When he pulled his shirt up to his shoulders, the large circular bruise centered on his white chest was vivid yellow, purple and dark red.

"This may hurt, I'm going to put pressure on your bruise to see if your sternum bone is broken." Dr. Doss pressed with his forefinger. Jesse gasped once, before he clamped his mouth shut.

"I suspect that you have a hairline lateral crack of the sternum, between your second and third ribs. My guess is the break doesn't go all the way through the bone, which is very fortunate for you. I'd like to wrap a tight bandage around your chest to restrict as much movement as possible." Jesse nodded and let the doctor pull his shirt off over his head.

"Your chest bruise reminds me of Mrs. Schmidt's bruises when you brought her in last year. Why don't you tell me how she's doing while I wrap you like an Egyptian mummy."

"Like a what?"

"Never mind. How's the young lady? Do you know? Have you seen her since she got home? You two seemed to be getting along when she left here."

"She was doing fine when I had Sunday dinner with her family last July. Right before I left for these three months of rangering with Milo and Captain Callahan."

"I'm glad to hear that. Abigail will want to know. She has fretted about that young woman's well-being since the day she left in the back of your buggy."

As Doctor Doss began wrapping a long cotton bandage around Jesse's torso, he talked about the rescued girl. "You know that she most likely will not be able to have children. When I removed the dead fetus, I couldn't be sure I didn't damage something crucial in her womb. Her surgery was the only time I've done such a procedure."

Uncomfortable with the doctor's information, Jesse said, "Should you be telling me that? Seems mighty private to me."

Standing behind his patient, Doctor Doss noted the pitted acne scars across the young Ranger's back. Without commenting on them, he used both hands to pull the bandage tight under the patient's armpit before he replied, "Yes, it is very personal. But since you're having Sunday meals with the girl's family nearly a year later, I'm betting you want to court her with marriage in mind."

"What if I do?"

"The *what* is that her womb may be damaged. Another pregnancy may be harmful to the fetus and to the mother."

"But you don't know that for sure?"

"No. I don't. But I do know that marriage means sexual relations between a man and his wife. And sexual relations invariably lead to pregnancies. Hold the bandage here, while I put a metal clasp on it."

Jesse held the edge of the cloth while Doctor Doss continued his verbal caution. "I'm just saying that after such severe abdominal trauma, and my lack of experience in removing the dead fetus, she may not conceive again, but if she does, the pregnancy could possibly be the death of her. The beatings, or my surgery, frankly, may have weakened a blood vessel that will eventually rupture under the pressure of a growing fetus. She might bleed internally, leading to her death. If you are sparking the woman, I thought you should know. Any man who marries a rescued Indian captive should have realistic expectations in that regard. You know the Apaches are not gentle with their white captives. She suffered and sustained long-lasting injuries, some we can't see."

Jesse grunted that he heard and understood.

"How is the young woman emotionally, if I might inquire?"

Sitting on the stool, Jesse puckered his lips in thought. "To me, she seems as good as you could expect. By the time we reached her home in New Braunfels she was talking to me about a lot of things, including her time with the Apaches. But what do I know? Caroline's mother won't let me talk with her without she's right there with us. I wish my sister could talk to Caroline and tell me what she thinks. Malissa is right smart about people."

The doctor smiled at that. He put Jesse's sweat-stained shirt on over the taut white wrap around his chest, and made the patient sit still while he cleaned the slash across his forehead.

"Thanks, Doctor. You treat many Rangers after the battle across the river?"'

"Only a handful. One poor boy lost an eye, and he's still unconscious. I doubt he will wake up."

At that moment a sharp crack of thunder interrupted them. Both men glanced out the open window at the cloudless midday sky.

"That a cannon?"

"Sounded like it."

"I gotta go, Doctor. If the battalion is still on the Mexican side, I need to get over there right now. But one more thing, can you help me get a box of cartridges for my carbine? Mine all got doused under water while I was swimming the river back to Texas."

Doss shook his head. "Our cartridges are all for the new .54 caliber Sharps."

Jesse grinned. "That's what I got. I lost my old gun during the fight with the Apaches. Caroline's pa gave me the Sharps after I brung her home. Even if her ma is stand-offish, he likes me."

An impressed Doctor Doss walked outside and called to a sergeant. He instructed the trooper to fetch him two boxes of carbine cartridges, quickly.

While they waited, the doctor said, "If you see Mrs. Schmidt again, please let her know that Mrs. Doss and I still think of her with affection."

Jesse grinned. "Doctor, I do surely plan on seeing her as soon as this rangering adventure ends." He rubbed at the acne scars on his cheek. "Caroline don't seem to mind my ugly face. She looks right past these scars. I reckon I can look right past something about her that I can't even see. Something that most likely ain't even a problem, 'cause you're a good sawbones."

The soldier returned with two boxes of cartridges. "I signed for them in your name, Captain. You may be charged for them." Doctor Doss shook his head in dismay at how nitpicky the army sometimes could be.

Handing the cartridges boxes to the young man, the doctor smiled dolefully and said, "Good luck, Ranger Gunn. Go with God."

Jesse paused in the doorway while he put on his jacket. "Sir, I'll take all the luck I can get, but I don't reckon to meet the good Lord over there. Across that river is a different place entirely. But I'll pass along your good wishes to Caroline when I do get back to God's country."

Chapter 57

Piedras Negras
State of Coahuila, Mexico
October 5, 1855

By happenstance, Will Davant was slowly scanning the ridgetop with his telescope when the first Mexican infantry skirmishers appeared. He collapsed the long brass tube and shoved it into the leather satchel that rested on his hip. Without speaking, Davant quickly tapped his crewmen on their shoulders, pointing at the ridge. While they each moved into the positions the army officer had drilled into them, Davant took the few steps to the small campfire, where he poked the coals with the tip of a slender willow branch wrapped in lard-soaked cloth.

Standing directly behind the Ground Hog, Davant sighted down the barrel for the hundredth time that morning. It hadn't moved. The iron tube still pointed straight at the gap in the ridgeline, elevated ever so slightly. Davant knew his aim was at best a good guess, since he had not been able to fire even a single practice round.

Fifty yards behind the line of red-shirted skirmishers, the four-abreast column of infantry appeared in the gap. Davant held his breath and waited, and waited, and waited, until the head of the column was well beyond the gap. Then he ordered the two Rangers on either side of the Ground Hog to pull back the big empty crates that had completely hidden the little artillery piece.

Saying nothing, he lit the fuse and took five steps back, keeping himself aligned with the cannon barrel. The young lieutenant hoped to note any left or right variances in the cannon ball's trajectory.

The first round ball fired from the Ground Hog sailed over the heads of the column of Mexican infantry. Nonetheless, the sight of the barricaded road and the sound of the cannon blast caused the *soldados* in the first few ranks to hesitate, reluctant to march into the open field. An officer mounted on a stately gray horse rode to the front and saw the cannon's smoke rising behind the roadblock at the edge of the town. He barked crisp orders to the sergeants and lieutenants to get the men moving forward again. With shoves and shouted threats, the front ranks of the formation were realigned. A lieutenant stepped to the front, lowered his sword and ordered them forward.

Will Davant was amazed that he could actually see the round ball pass over the Mexican column. He realized immediately that the black powder that had propelled the iron ball was old and weak--nowhere near the quality he'd used during the academy's artillery instruction. More importantly, he saw that he had poorly set the cannon's elevation. Irritated at himself, the army lieutenant was glad Captain Burbank had not witnessed this first errant effort. However, Davant was greatly pleased that the round ball had flown true, keeping a straight line, which is what enabled him to mark its flight.

He waved his arm for the crew to swab out the grime left from the first shot and push another linen sack of black powder to the base of the barrel. Another round ball was shoved down the tube to rest on the powder. Finally, a crewman pricked the powder sack with a slender steel rod poked through the vent hole in the barrel and inserted a fuse.

Davant ordered a Ranger to twist the elevation crank under the cannon barrel one-half turn down, while he stood behind the piece and gauged how far the barrel dropped.

"One more quarter turn, if you will." Satisfied, the commander of the piece waved his arm at the crewmen, ordering them to step back. Davant lit the fuse for a second shot.

The entire cluster of Rangers shouted and pumped their arms in the air when the cannon ball bounced just a few feet in front of the leading *soldados* and tore through the stomach of one luckless man. The iron ball next hit the soldier behind him in the chest. The round shot crushed his vital organs before ricocheting off and hitting a third man, fracturing his femur bone, before dropping onto the foot of a fourth soldier. The iron ball still rolled with enough momentum to injure the feet of yet more men.

This time the *soldados* ignored their mounted officer's futile haranguing to close their ranks and advance. Instead, the infantrymen, including their sergeants and lieutenants, scattered to either side of the road or turned to push through the soldiers behind them. While the formation was still in chaos with the leading ranks trying to escape further carnage and the more rearward ranks still marching forward, Lieutenant Davant sent a third cannon ball into the gap. More *soldados* fell, as the whole column buckled and dissolved into a disordered mob.

Captain Callahan, escorted by Lieutenant Kyle and Sergeant McKean, reached the roadblock in time to see the effect of the third shot. He quickly sent Lieutenant Kyle to share the good news with the squads of Rangers at the other fortified points and to tell them to hold firm. The captain and Milo made their way to the second artillery piece to observe what enemy it might be facing.

★

Captain Patino had nearly completed the deployment of his cavalry company across the far edge of the prairie south of the road. The noise of the three cannon shots encouraged him to order his troopers forward in a long single rank, nearly fifty men wide, about five feet between each horseman. He led the company from the center and dramatically lowered his sword arm to point at the town buildings. The lancers couched their spears and the carbineers held their short muskets at the ready as the line trotted forward. Midway across the field, Patino saw the barricade and the men behind it. He called for his company to charge the remaining two hundred yards at a full gallop.

Earlier in the day, Corporal Elam and Will Davant had paced off one hundred steps and planted a stick that stood a man's height, with a red rag tied to the top. Captain Patino rode past the stick, unconsciously wondering why it was there. An instant later Ranger Elam saw the enemy cavalry had reached his marker and lit the fuse on the right barrel of the Double Flirt. Its barrel erupted in flame. As soon as the smoke cleared and the crew rolled the little cannon back into place after its recoil, he lit the second fuse.

Two waves of thirty-six lead balls hit the charging Mexican cavalry. Four troopers were unhorsed as man and beast were hit by canister. Half a dozen Rangers armed with rifled-muskets fired a few seconds after the cannon. They accounted for two more casualties.

Captain Patino lay in the grass, his leg broken, trapped under his dead horse. The company sergeant twisted in his saddle and saw the gap in the center of their formation. He noted the riderless horses, including two wounded animals struggling to stand. He pulled up hard on his reins, calling out for the remainder of the company to retire. Patino struggled to pull himself free, but could not. In great pain and even greater dismay, the captain lay propped on his elbows watching his troopers retire, abandoning their charge after just one blast of cannon fire.

Callahan was grimly ecstatic. "Damn cowards. I knew they wouldn't have the balls to cross those fields under cannon fire. Ain't no greaser got a pair that big."

Milo was impressed by the damage inflicted by the canister. He nodded, greatly relieved he wouldn't be facing dozens of charging Mexican lancers.

The captain pointed at one fallen horse where a soldier was desperately trying to free his leg from beneath the horse carcass.

"Milo, see that man out there thrashing around under the horse. I think I see some gold braid on his jacket. Maybe he's an officer. Take a couple of men and go fetch him. Let's find out what he knows."

"Sir." Milo, Private Hynyard, and another Ranger jogged forward. They knelt by the horse and speaking Spanish, Hynyard told the angry Mexican cavalryman that he was their prisoner. Milo leaned forward and pulled a big flintlock horse pistol from its saddle holster and shoved it beneath his belt.

Hynard put his face just inches from the enemy soldier and pricked the man's chin with the point of his belt knife. "We're going to pull your leg free. And if you try to shoot or stab any of us, I'll cut your dirty throat. *Comprende?*"

"*Sí.*"

While Hynyard held his knife to the soldier's throat, the other two Rangers dug in their boot heels and leaned backwards as they pulled on the trapped leg. Finally, it slid out from under the horse carcass. The trio quickly half-carried the limping Mexican officer to Captain Callahan, under the protection of a dozen Rangers' carbines and shotguns intended to dissuade any heroic rescue by Patino's troopers. When they let go of their prisoner, the Mexican officer's twisted leg buckled, but he leaned against the barricade.

"Find out his name and ask him if he was in the battle two days ago," Callahan directed his interpreter.

The back and forth in Spanish between Captain Patino and Ranger Hynyard took several minutes. Hynyard turned to face Callahan and Milo with a face drawn tight in worry. The Mexican officer slid down the wall to take the weight off his injured leg.

"He says Colonel Menchaca has gathered all the soldiers in the state of Coahuila. He says there's over a thousand of them here already, surrounding the town, and more on the way. He expects another attack any time, with lots more soldiers. He says his cavalry company was just a scouting probe to see if we were still on the Mexican side of the river."

"Any time, huh? Well, we'll find out soon enough." Callahan looked out at the field where several corpses were still on the ground. "We got lots of gun powder. Tell him that."

Hynyard repeated the captain's words in Spanish. The Mexican captain made a curt reply, looking at Callahan while he spoke.

"Captain, he said he's glad you are so willing to stay and die."

Callahan spun around, drawing his revolver. "You little son of a bitch. The only one dying behind this wall is you, right now." As the Ranger captain cocked and pointed his pistol at the Mexican captain, Sergeant McKean stepped in front of the prisoner.

"No, sir. We don't execute prisoners of war."

"The hell we don't. Get out of my way, Milo."

"No, sir. Captain, please holster your Colt. This ain't our way."

Callahan's pistol didn't waiver from his aim. "Step aside, First Sergeant. That's an order."

"No, sir. You want to shoot somebody, go find the *alcalde*. He's the one who told you the Mexican army wouldn't oppose us. This man is a soldier, doing his duty, following orders, just like you and me are."

"He's an arrogant Mexican pig. He's probably one of the bastards who murdered hundreds of Texan prisoners of war at Goliad. Now, move aside, dammit!"

"No, sir. Look at him. He's too young to have been at Goliad twenty years ago. Besides, we're in his country, not Texas. It's time to cross the river, Captain. It's time to gather our men and get back to Texas. We can't hold this town for a week waiting on more men to answer your call to arms. If a thousand soldiers attack us, our eighty Rangers ain't going to stop them."

Callahan remained frozen in place, silent.

Milo tried once more to reach through Callahan's stubbornness and lifelong disdain for Mexicans. "Captain, our Rangers are spread out all over the edge of town. Our men are just pockets of resistance, not a real defense. Our artillery made 'em withdraw and caused a panic, sure enough. But that's just time enough to pull back to the river and start ferrying our men over. We can take the cannons with us. Present them to the governor as trophies. Hell, parade the cannons through San Antone and Austin and Seguin. Show the people back home what we did. What *you* did."

Milo thought he saw a crack in Callahan's determination to hold the town at all costs.

"Captain, you knew when it was time to bring us back here after the fight at the river. Even though we busted through the Mexicans and Apaches and killed a pile of them, you saw they had the numbers to overwhelm us. You decided a good commander protects his men by falling back when he must. It's time for you to do that again tonight – just like you did two days ago at the river."

Callahan squeezed his eyes shut and reopened them as if he were clearing his vision. With a grunt, he slowly uncocked his pistol and holstered it. "Milo, you should consider running for office. You can be good with words when you try."

"Yes, sir. Now I'm going to have this prisoner's hands tied and put him in the old stone fort. What are my orders after I do that?"

Callahan sighed deeply. "Pull the men back midway through town towards the river. Tighten up our defensive ring of guns while the Mexicans are still working up the nerve to attack again. Block the cross streets. Having to come at us down narrow streets instead of across wide fields will restrict how many of the bastards can reach us at one time. That'll work in our favor to even the odds." He paused. "And at dark we'll start ferrying the battalion back to Eagle Pass."

Callahan waited while Milo directed two Rangers to tie and escort the captured officer to the old stone blockhouse. As they walked away, half-dragging the sullen prisoner, the captain moved next to his first sergeant and spoke in a voice low enough that no one else could hear.

"Milo, what you did, jumping in front of my gun, was brave enough, but it was dumb. I mighta shot you. Not to mention a sergeant ain't supposed to defy his captain. Don't do that again, you hear me?"

"Yessir. I do. And I'm mighty glad you didn't plug me with your Colt."

Chapter 58

River Ferry at Eagle Pass, Texas
Two P.M., October 5, 1855

John Miers, an eighteen-year-old Ranger who lived in Prairie Lea, was on duty guarding the ferry rope on the Texas side of the river. A rider leading a spotted horse rode to the crossing, pulled a carbine from its scabbard, and slid off his horse. As the dismounted rider walked stiffly towards him, Miers' face lit up.

"Jesse? Jesse? Is that you? Are you a haint? I seen you get whacked by an Injun and crumple like a shot bird. Why ain't you dead? How'd you get here?"

Jesse Gunn smiled at the familiar face from home. "That Injun just knocked me out for a spell. When I woke up it was dark and I crawled off. Found a horse and made my way back here. Is Milo across the river?"

"Sure 'nuf, he is, Jesse. He'll be mighty glad to see you. What about Billy Clopton? Did he come back with you?"

Jesse shook his head. "No. He didn't make it. How do I get across?"

"Dang, I'm sorry about Billy. We was neighbors. Dang.

"How do I get across, Johnny?"

"We're hauling piles of food and fodder from over there. See the raft yonder across the river? It's about to come over. You can go back on it."

★

After waiting for the ferry for an hour, which gave him to time to add his horses to the other Rangers' animals tethered nearby,

Jesse Gunn stepped off the raft back into Mexico. He shook hands with more Rangers who'd believed he had died in the battle. He repeated his lie about being wounded and crawling off the battlefield.

No one knew where Milo was, other than somewhere in town. Jesse tucked his Sharps carbine into his elbow and went looking. As he walked through the narrow streets that seemed to randomly meander between rows of stick and mud hovels, Jesse wondered why the people who lived in such huts didn't improve them. He also was surprised that the streets were empty. *What happened to the Mexicans who live here?* He stopped where a cart with two huge, solid wooden wheels blocked an intersection and asked the three Rangers there if they'd seen Milo recently.

One of them pointed to his left where a pathway snaked away between two fences made of crooked upright sticks.

"The sergeant just went that way."

Jesse hurried along, aching with each step, until he rounded a bend and saw Milo walking ahead of him, going the same direction.

"I'm mighty thirsty. Can you point me to the closest cantina?" Jesse called.

Milo twirled, ready to berate some slacking Ranger. When he saw who was behind him on the path, his expression shifted from anger to disbelief and finally, to joy.

"Cantinas are all closed up, Ranger. Why ain't you at your post?"

Jesse grinned and kept walking as he answered. "Well, Sergeant, that's a wild story I was hoping to tell you over a whiskey. But since all the cantinas are shuttered, why don't I just stroll along with you and tell you a tale."

Jesse stopped a yard from his best friend, unable to continue his banter. Milo's eyes glistened behind his spectacles. He reached out and gently touched Jesse's scarred forehead, trying to bridle his emotions. Even so, when he spoke his voice cracked.

"Jesse, you really didn't need more scars on your face."

"Ah, Milo, Doctor Doss said this one is healing and will fade away. Mostly."

"Indian back at the river?"

"Yeah. Trying to lift my hair, but Thompson shot him before he could finish."

"I didn't know how I was going to tell Malissa and your ma. Damn, I'm glad to see you. Alive. I thought you was killed."

"Nearly. You should see the bruise on my chest. Doctor Doss bandaged me. Said my sternum bone got cracked when that Injun smacked me with his war club. Milo, ain't nothin' ever hurt so bad as my chest did when I woke up. Ever' breath felt like I was being stabbed."

"Oh, Jess, I'm sorry. But your chest will heal too."

"You look all right, thank God. What about Billy? Did you get to his body?"

"No. We rode back here at dark. We had to leave the bodies on the field. I sure ain't looking forward to telling his folks."

"Nah, I reckon not."

"Jesse, I know you ain't fit for real duty. But can you stand behind a barricade and shoot that Sharps?"

"You bet. I even got dry cartridges at Fort Duncan. But don't ask me to run anywhere."

While Jesse began to relate his experiences with the runaway slave, Milo led them to the barricaded road where Will Davant still commanded the crew of the Ground Hog. A crewman called out that Sergeant McKean was approaching, causing Davant to shift his gaze from the gap in the ridge where he suspected the Mexican infantry would reappear any time. The army officer recognized Jesse and saluted him when the pair stopped behind the cannon. Jesse blushed, but grinned at Davant.

"Will, what is this thing? Is it an old ship's cannon that got lost?"

"I don't know, Jesse. I've looked all over the barrel for some clue, but the only thing I've learned is that this little ground hog shoots straight, which is all an artillery officer can hope for. Now, where the hell have you been, my friend? We all thought you were killed back at the river."

"You remember Thompson, don't you?"

"Sure I do. The darkie that saved my hair last year."

"Well, he saved mine back at the river fight two days ago."

"Milo said he saw Thompson riding away with a body draped over a horse. That was you?"

"Yup. Knocked out cold, but breathin', because Thompson shot the Injun that was about to scalp me."

"Go tell. Are you joshin' me?"

"I ain't."

"But why? You can't convince me that darkie *liked* us."

"Hell, no. He saved my ass, then put me in leg irons. Here's the best part. He kept me alive as a captive so he could trade me back to Milo –for a wife. A slave woman in San Antone he met before he ran for Mexico."

Both Milo and Davant stared at Jesse, their faces showing confusion and disbelief.

Jesse nodded. "It's true. Nigger or not, he's a man, ain't he. Men want wives, don't they? I know I do, and Milo's been hound-dogging my sister. I bet there's some pretty Carolina belle pining for you back home, and you're thinking about asking for her hand. But you're stalling because you ain't sure Fort Duncan is a decent place for such a fine young woman."

Davant looked at Jesse with new respect. "Maybe. So how did you get here? Did Thompson let you go?"

"Hell no. I had a back-up pocket pistol he never found."

"You kill him?"

"Nah."

Davant patted Jesse on the shoulder. "Well, I'm real glad that's over."

"Me too, 'cept it ain't. I've got that spotted horse Thompson was riding. I'm gonna sell it back in Texas and buy that Irene slave woman and bring her down here to Thompson."

"You what?" Both Milo and Will gawked at their friend.

"Thompson saved my life. So, I'm going to fetch him the wife he wants when we're through here. Soon as my rangerin' hitch is done."

Milo held up a hand. "Whoa, Jess. That's enough for now. Our rangering hitch is still in deep water." Resuming his sergeant persona, Milo addressed Davant.

"Will, Captain Callahan says we're pulling back into a tighter ring around the ferry landing and we'll start hauling our horses and captured supplies back to Eagle Pass. I found the street corner where I want you to bring the Ground Hog."

Milo and Jesse left Davant to his task of moving the little cannon while they made the circuit of the other defended points around the edge of town. Milo gave the order to each corporal or sergeant in charge to pull back towards the river, to find defensive spots on either side of the town plaza.

Davant left one Ranger at the barricade with orders to hightail it back to the ferry at the first sight of a Mexican soldier, on foot or mounted. The Ranger sentry didn't have to wait long. With two hours of daylight remaining, a skirmish line of *soldados* appeared on the ridge crest.

★

The Ground Hog was loaded with grapeshot and aimed down a long street paved with river stones. Lieutenant Davant, armed with his Sharps rifle, had climbed a ladder to the roof of an adobe house on the far side of the street, half-way to the corner. When the first Mexican infantryman leaned around the corner to look down the street, Davant put a bullet in his chest.

The sergeant of the Mexican patrol immediately put his men to work with their bayonets, punching a hole in the wall of the building. Even if gouging their way through several walls slowed his progress, the sergeant intended to work his way down the row of dwellings until his men could dash across the street and kill the sharpshooter on the roof.

Three streets away, another platoon of *soldados* advanced four men abreast. They turned a corner, only to have one barrel of the Double Flirt fire grapeshot at them. Two men fell. Not knowing that little cannon had a second barrel, the lieutenant ordered his men to rush the cannon before the crew of Texans could reload it. The second barrel roared and three more Mexican infantrymen were hit. The lieutenant, wounded in the arm, yelled for his men to retire back around the corner to safety.

Once his arm was bandaged, the officer led his men down a side path to look for a way to bypass the cannon. He left one wounded soldier behind to warn anyone who followed them about the artillery around the corner.

After the second shot, Corporal Elam's gun crew pulled the Double Flirt several blocks closer to the river, to the far side of the main plaza, their last pre-arranged point of defense.

It took nearly half-an-hour for the first Mexican patrol to hack their way through three walls. Looking out from the safety of the building's front room, the sergeant saw an open door into the adobe house across the street. He didn't risk leaning out the window of the room where he stood to see if there were enemy soldiers further down the street.

While the Mexican infantry were knocking holes in walls, Davant had climbed down from the roof and rejoined the artillery crew. When the second Mexican soldier left the doorway to cross the street, Davant lit the short fuse of the Ground Hog. In the instant it took the fuse to burn down to the powder, two more *soldados* were in the open, crossing the cobblestones. The blast of grapeshot killed or wounded all four of them, including the sergeant. The corporal of the patrol ordered the remaining men to pop out of the door one at a time, fire quickly down the street, then jump back inside to reload so another man could take a hasty shot towards the cannon crew.

Immediately after firing the cannon, Lieutenant Davant ordered the Ground Hog dragged to the town plaza, near the river. Seeing that the Mexicans in the house were exposing themselves one at a time to fire towards the cannon, Davant lingered behind. He aimed his Sharps at the door and waited. Two seconds later, another *soldado* stepped through the door. Before he could point his musket, the U.S. Army officer squeezed the Sharps' trigger. The *soldado* fell. Davant quickly reloaded before he jogged after his cannon crew. When he reached the plaza, he waved at Corporal Elam and the crew of the Double Flirt as he ran to them.

"Ben, the Ground Hog is one street over to your right. I'm going back to the far side of the plaza to take a shot or two when the first Mexicans are a block away. I'll slow them down some. Don't shoot me when I run back." Corporal Elam nodded.

"Let me get back to the Ground Hog, then you shoot at the first group of Mexicans who try to cross the square. Then you listen for the Ground Hog, and after it fires, you shoot your second barrel. After that, get this baby down to the ferry. The captain doesn't want to lose her."

"Are there any Rangers out on our flanks?" Elam asked.

Davant nodded his assurance. "That was Milo's job, to pull back the other Rangers to either side of the square. You'll be protected long enough to shoot both barrels."

He hurried on to the other corner of the open plaza where his crew worked to load the Ground Hog. Davant spoke to the sergeant.

"I'm going back across the plaza to use the Sharps on the first Mexicans to get here. Don't shoot me when I run back. Don't touch off the fuse until I'm here. Corporal Elam is taking the first shot with one barrel of the Double Flirt."

Davant trotted back to the far side of the square and stopped behind an ox cart. He peeked around the edge of the tall wooden wheel and settled his rifle onto its top, ready to quickly align the front and rear sights on the first Mexican soldier to appear.

When the bullet punched through William Davant's coat between his shoulder blades and severed his spinal cord, he died before his Sharps rifle could clatter to the cobblestones. The Mexican scout didn't pull back his own rifle until he saw the hated *Tejano* collapsed on the ground. Only then did he lean back from over the edge of the roof to reload and congratulate himself.

Corporal Elam had watched Davant cross the square and hide behind the cart. When the army officer fell to the street and he heard the echoed crack of a rifle, Elam and a crewman sprinted to Davant. The pair lifted the corpse onto Elam's shoulder and the second Ranger retrieved the still-loaded Sharps rifle. Elam hurried as much as he was able under the weight of the U.S. Army officer's body.

The two Ranger cannon crews waited impatiently for the enemy. When the first red-shirted *soldados* appeared, Elam fired one barrel of grapeshot, again halting the Mexicans' advance. As Davant had directed, the crew chief of the Ground Hog waited until the Mexican sergeants prodded the musketeers to leave their cover and dash forward to overrun the cannon crew. The Ground Hog's cannon blast from the unexpected far corner of the plaza caught the attacking *soldados* in the flank, causing casualties and driving the others to dive for cover.

Corporal Elam lit the fuse of the Double Flirt's second barrel as soon as he saw a Mexican officer stand and wave his sword. This third blast of grapeshot ripped across the plaza, causing the Mexican soldiers to route, abandoning their attack. The crews of both cannons wheeled them as hastily as they could to the ferry landing.

Chapter 59

Piedras Negras
State of Coahuila, Mexico
An Hour Before Dusk, October 5, 1855

Captain Callahan and Captain Henry stood near the new trail the Rangers had worn down from the top of the escarpment to the ferry landing. Callahan did a double take when he saw Milo and Jesse limping towards him. "Private Gunn, we all thought you was killed back at the river fight."

Jesse was too tired to explain his travails. "Nah. Just banged up."

The battalion commander squinted at the blood-crusted scar on Jesse's forehead and put a hand on the young Ranger's shoulder. "I want to hear the whole story when we get home. For now, you take care of yourself. I was dreading facing your ma back at Prairie Lea." Looking at Milo, the captain asked, "You look to have a hitch in your get-along. You wounded?"

Milo shook his head. "Twisted my ankle jumping over a crate. Landed wrong. I'm all right."

Callahan nodded. "What's the situation up there in the town? I've heard cannons."

"I told both cannon crew chiefs to fall back about halfway to the plaza. Fire at the first Mexicans that show up, then head to the plaza and use grapeshot across the open square." Milo took a breath. "If our boys on the outer flanks keep the Mexicans from cutting off the cannon crews, we should be okay for a while."

"How long a while?" Captain Henry asked.

Milo shrugged. "Depends on how many Mexicans are attacking us, I suppose. You heard the Mexican cavalry captain say hundreds. Anyway, I told the cannon crews to bring the pieces here to take them across the river when the plaza gets too hot. But I ain't been to the plaza myself. I've been pulling our boys back from the outskirts of town. I got them split up on both sides of the plaza to shield the cannons."

Callahan chewed on his cigar. "Good, maybe the pistol and musket fire from the boys will drive them bastards right into our grapeshot again. That was good work out on the perimeter of town, Milo. Good work."

"One thing that ain't so good, Captain. Like I said this morning, the cold fact is that a lot of Rangers left their posts out on the edge of town. Some of the boys have been filtering back here, or maybe even crossing the river somewhere, in spite of our river guards."

Before either captain could question Milo's last observation, the cluster of officers and sergeants heard the rumbling of a cannon bouncing along the rutted, rock-strewn road leading towards the ferry landing. Following behind the Double Flirt, a Ranger led the little donkey whose panniers had been filled with packages of powder and grapeshot canisters. Stretched on his stomach over the panniers lay the corpse of William Davant.

"Looks like the crew lost a man," Captain Henry muttered.

"Ben, who's the casualty?" Milo called out.

"Lieutenant Davant from the army fort," Corporal Elam replied. "A Mexican sharpshooter got him from a rooftop at the plaza."

Jesse and Milo turned their heads to stare at each other. Neither spoke.

"Damn it! Captain Burbank will be steamed now," Captain Callahan said between clinched teeth, his cigar stuck in the corner of his mouth. "Elam, you send Davant's body across with the cannons right away."

Corporal Elam stopped next to the battalion commander. "Yes sir, I will. Captain Callahan, we sure enough killed some Mexicans today with both these little cannons. We slowed 'em down ever' place we stopped and fired a round. But sir, there are a lot of soldiers out there. I'd say it's time for all of us to get back to Texas. By now that market plaza is a piss-pot full of Mexican infantry. Only a few blocks away from where we're standing. It'll take 'em some time to get re-organized to push all the way here, but not all that long. Now if you'll excuse me, I'll get poor Davant and the Double Flirt onto the ferry barge."

Milo spoke up before Captain Callahan could. "Ben, you set up both artillery pieces in plain sight on the other side of the river, right near the ferry crossing. Aim them at a spot about halfway down the bluff. Fire the Ground Hog one time without a ball, just powder, as soon as you set up. Let the Mexicans know you're there, ready to defend the ferry landing. Then, if things get too close, you start shooting round balls over here. If it looks like we're being overrun and about to be captured, you load up with grapeshot and let her rip. We'll risk it."

Corporal Elam looked at Captain Callahan for his consent. Callahan nodded grimly. "Ain't none of us going to a Mex prison. Sergeant McKean got it right, Corporal Elam. Follow his orders."

Before he hurried away, Elam handed Davant's rifle to Milo. "There's probably some cartridges in the lieutenant's pockets. I forgot to look."

"No matter, I got twenty fresh army rounds," Jesse said. "Here's ten," he added as he handed a small cardboard box to Milo. "What say you and me go to work with these high-dollar guns Mr. Sharp so kindly made for us."

Milo straightened up and saluted Callahan. "With your permission, Captain, me and Jesse got some business back towards the plaza."

"You do that," Callahan replied, expecting both young men might not make it back to the ferry, but he wasn't willing to override their desire to avenge their friend. Callahan respected those feelings. As Milo and Jesse walked away, Callahan turned to face Captain Henry. Both officers' faces reflected the undeniable realization of how tenuous their toehold in Mexico had suddenly become. With an outer calmness he didn't feel, James Callahan pulled his cigar from his mouth and blew the embers until they glowed red.

"William, let's put the torch to this whole sorry greaser town. That'll push them Mex soldiers back out the other side and give us some light down at the river to finish our crossing. Since my first sergeant is busy with Lieutenant Davant's rifle, why don't you see to it."

Captain Henry whooped in agreement and yelled for his subalterns.

331

Chapter 60

Piedras Negras
State of Coahuila, Mexico
Near Dusk, October 5, 1855

Milo stopped at the water barrel that the Rangers had used all day to refill their canteens. "Here, Jess, a toast to your return from the dead." He handed the tin dipper to Jesse who filled it and gulped down several swallows before he passed it half-full back to Milo.

"Jesse, I...I'm really sorry about Will Davant, but I ain't going hunting for the soldier who shot him.

"What do you mean? What are we going to do?"

"We're going to join the last line of Rangers towards the plaza and help buy time to get more of our boys back to Texas. I'm going to use Will's rifle to shoot Mexican soldiers, but we ain't going stalking like we're on a deer hunt."

"Good enough, Sergeant Milo. Let's just do our duty, then get on that ferry ourselves and go home. To tell you the truth, I'm sore all over and been thinking about Caroline all day. I think I'm about done with rangering."

The pair left the water station and trudged towards the crackling of pistols being fired somewhere ahead. They both felt an urgency to join the few Texans who still held back the *soldados*, but Jesse couldn't bring himself to jostle his painful chest any more than he had to, and Milo wasn't about to leave Jesse behind again.

Milo knelt on one knee before he poked his head around the corner. Not far ahead he saw three white men lying on their stomachs behind a short barricade of rough-hewn timbers. A brass bugle tied to a rope lay across one Ranger's back. At the end of the street, Milo could see movement behind a two-wheeled cart with side rails. A musket flash appeared between the rails and a lead ball slamming into a timber made a soft but discernable pop. Only one Ranger answered with a shot from his revolver.

Milo raised Davant's rifle, blinked away a drop of sweat, and sighted on a spot of red between the cart's side rails. Jesse hurt too badly to kneel, so standing erect behind Milo, he aimed where the muzzle flash had been. Without any verbal cue, the two squeezed the triggers simultaneously.

Bugler Johnny McCoy turned his head in a panic to see who'd fired from behind them. "Sergeant McKean!"

"Stay down, Johnny. How many rounds you fellas have left in your Colts?"

"Only two or three each!"

While he reloaded, Jesse had been watching farther up the street they'd just walked from the water barrel. Without warning, he raised his carbine and fired in that direction.

"More coming from our left side, Milo. It'd be a good time to leave this corner."

Milo nodded and called, "Johnny, as soon as Jesse and me shoot again, you each run to us. Stay low."

Milo and Jesse fired at the cart again, and the three Rangers dashed to the corner. Two Mexican musketeers fired at the fleeing Texans. Jesse leaned against the wall and let his carbine slip down to rest the butt on the ground. Milo glanced at him, seeing Jesse's face was contorted in pain.

"You hit, Jess?"

"My shoulder. Hell's bells. But it's my cracked chest bone that's screaming at me."

Milo took a deep breath. "Johnny, you and Henry get an arm around Jesse and take him to the ferry. You may see Mexican soldiers anywhere, so don't holster your pistols. Zach, you take Jesse's carbine and cartridges. We'll stop at the next corner and slow them down again."

Zachariah Buggs raised his head and sniffed like a hound dog. "Sergeant, I smell smoke. I think the town's on fire." As if to verify Bugg's announcement, a Ranger on a frothing horse burst into their view coming from the fourth street that intersected the corner. Private George Tom reined in his skittish mare and held a flaming torch up to the edge of the straw roof of a house.

"What the hell, George?" Milo yelled at the horseback Ranger.

Private Tom looked down the street at the five Rangers on foot. "Sergeant, you all best get on down to the ferry. We're burning the whole town."

Milo was stricken with a sudden memory of the woman he'd almost saved from rape earlier. "But what about the people who live here?"

"They better be gone," Tom answered. Satisfied he'd lit the roof as if it were dry kindling, he pulled down the torch. Before he could kick his horse into motion, Bugler McCoy yelled for Private Tom not to turn left and not to go straight since there were Mexican soldiers up both streets. Nodding his understanding, Tom flung the blazing torch onto the roof of the building across the street, wheeled his horse around, and went back the way he came.

No more *soldados* appeared behind them. Milo assumed their enemies had fled from the fire by retracing their own paths to the open fields beyond Piedras Negras. By the time the five Rangers reached the water barrel, the town behind them was billowing thick smoke from dozens of burning buildings. Orange and yellow flames reached high into the air, bright red embers soaring even higher into the dark indigo sky, a display unmatched by anything the young Texans had witnessed before.

Milo felt the heat on his face and noticed snowflake-size pieces of ash floating down and settling on their hats and shoulders. He gazed in awe at the inferno before he ordered, "All of you, get on down to the ferry landing. I'm going to make sure we ain't left anyone behind."

Seeing that one section of the town was not yet aflame, Milo headed that direction. When he reached the old stone fort, four Rangers from Captain Henry's company were still loading sacks of grain and kegs of powder onto a cart, while one man with a shotgun stood guard at the corner.

"You boys the last ones up this way?" Milo asked.

"Far as we know. Our orders are to leave one keg of black powder and light a powder trail when we get down the street. So, watch where you're standing."

Milo glanced down and stepped sideways away from the line of grainy black dust he saw near his boots. "Right. Did you fellas release the Mexican officer or did someone take him to the ferry?"

A bearded Ranger laughed. "You nuts? He's still chained in there. I reckon his last shit will be while he watches that powder trail sparkin' its way to the keg."

Milo's face blanched under the grimy soot from the smoke, but he recovered before the others could see the anger on his face in the dim light. "Well, too bad for him. I come to tell you the captain said you gotta leave now for the ferry. Right now. Whatever you got on the cart, is good enough. You don't want to get cut off by the fire. Get goin' now!"

"Sure 'nuf." The bearded man called to their sentry, "Ethan, let's git."

"I'm Sergeant McKean of the Regulars, and I'll light the powder trail once you boys are down the street far enough," Milo added.

"Nope, Captain Henry said fer me to do it my own self. So you go on and finish your rounds, Sergeant, and we'll take care of our business here."

"Good enough then. One more thing. The Mex lancers killed my best friend at the river fight. I'm going inside to put a bullet in the balls of that cavalry officer in there. Let him hurt during his last few minutes."

"Hah! You don't reckon we roughed him up enough already? Just don't kill him. Captain Henry wouldn't like that."

"Don't worry. But don't light the powder trail until I come out!" Milo forced a guttural laugh. He walked through the open door and could barely see the shackled man in uniform slumped in a corner. The chain between his leg irons ran through a big ring set in the stone floor.

Milo drew his revolver and fired a round at the rafters overhead. Then he pulled a long iron key out of his vest pocket and dropped it in front of the prisoner, within easy reach. As soon as Milo appeared outside, the bearded Ranger tossed his lit cigar to the end onto the little mound of black powder about fifty feet away from the door. Milo ran past the sparking, sputtering powder trail to join them and helped push the cart towards the river. None of them were looking back to see the shadowy figure stumble through the doorway and stagger away. Milo was mightily relieved when they rounded a building corner, putting the blockhouse out of sight when the powder keg blew up and the old stone fort exploded outward, raining rocks in every direction.

Chapter 61

Piedras Negras
State of Coahuila, Mexico
Night of October 5-6, 1855

Beginning at dusk, with an unearthly backdrop of soaring flames, ash and smoke, Callahan's Battalion of Texas Rangers crossed the Rio Grande River to Eagle Pass. Ten Rangers armed with rifled-muskets and carbines crouched along the rim of the river bluff, under the watchful eye of Sergeant McKean. Although they remained in place for several hours, this last line of defense wasn't needed. The conflagration started by the torch-wielding Rangers served Captain Callahan's purpose better than even he had expected. The huge fire and smoke prevented any Mexican soldiers from passing through the town to the river. Even when the towering flames ceased streaking into the night sky, the heat from the scores of burning buildings obstructed the *soldados'* advance.

Captain Madero sought permission for his infantry battalion to attack one or both of the Texans' flanks by advancing along the riverbank. Colonel Menchaca quickly considered the proposal, but rejected it. He had no faith in the prospect of such an attack undertaken in the confusion of darkness. He also worried over the possibility of artillery fire from Fort Duncan and the two stolen Spanish cannons, which Menchaca suspected were now emplaced on the Texas side of the river. He would wait.

Ranger work parties hastily piled sacks of pillaged cornmeal, flour, and beans into the several small boats. These skiffs were rowed back and forth, ropes knotted to bow and stern, taut lines taken in and let out to keep the heavily loaded craft from being pushed downstream in the strong flood current.

The large ferry barge linked to a permanent heavy rope had carried the two old Spanish cannons to the Texas side, where

Corporal Elam quickly situated them to provide the threat of cover fire as the Rangers labored on. As sacks of stolen food were unloaded, they were stacked in front of the cannons to protect the crews from Mexican sharpshooters.

After the cannons, six skittish horses at a time were ferried across, usually with their owners holding their jackets over the animals' noses and eyes. Each round trip of the heavy square barge took nearly an hour.

The cart carrying casks of gunpowder and supplies from the old stone blockhouse was so heavy that a dozen Rangers had to use ropes to ease the cart down the steep escarpment to the ferry landing. Nervous Rangers hauled the kegs of gunpowder onto the ferry raft, while the food sacks were taken to Texas in the small boats.

Colonel Menchaca waited. By midnight, the burning timbers of the village were turning to hot coals and ash. At 1:00 A.M., he ordered Captain Madero forward.

Milo saw the silhouettes of the Mexican infantry coming towards his skirmish line. He kicked bugler Isaac Tanner awake. Three dozen of the Rangers' horses had not yet been loaded onto the ferry.

"Here come the Mex infantry, Ike. Sound the alarm right now!" Turner blew with gusto, the discordant notes reaching all the drowsy skirmishers and the men who still worked on the riverbank.

Captain Madero heard the bugle as well, and ordered his musketeers into a double-time advance. Milo saw the Mexicans were now jogging towards his ten Rangers, who constituted the rearguard of the battalion.

"Fire once, then hightail it down the bluff, onto the boats."

Six nervous Rangers led six horses, including Callahan's warhorse, onto the ferry barge. Three of the six men grabbed the thick rope to pull the raft across the swift black river for the last time that night. Nine of the ten Ranger skirmishers waded into the shallow water and scrambled into the three skiffs that floated there.

Milo waited on the muddy bank for all his men to climb into the boats. He held the loaded Sharps rifle at the ready, his eyes glued to the path down the bluff. He didn't want to draw attention to their location by firing, but he was prepared to slow down the Mexicans one last time.

"Come on, Sergeant, the other two boats have left already. We're all in but you."

Milo waded to the skiff, handed the Sharps to a seated Ranger and heaved himself up and into the boat. He looked over at the barge, barely able to see that it was low in the water with the weight of the horses and men.

"Hold that damned boat, Sergeant!" Milo twisted his head to see Callahan pushing his way through the water to the skiff. Sergeant and captain linked hands and Milo pulled him awkwardly over the gunwale. Callahan squeezed onto the bench seat next to Milo and stared at the ferry landing.

"Little late, aren't you, Captain?"

"Had to make sure the war horse got onto the ferry. Then I saw you standing there like a Spartan Hoplite at Thermopile and figured my place was with you holding a gun, not on that barge holding a horse's head."

As a Ranger pulled on the oars, the overloaded skiff, now without a stern rope to hold its course, swung sideways, rocking in the gurgling current.

Milo shook his head. "Captain, I don't have any idea what you're talking about."

"Don't matter. The Spartans all died at Thermopile, anyway. We didn't."

"Billy Clopton and August Schmidt and a few others did."

"Yeah, I hate that. Damned Mexican lancers."

After a few seconds of silence, Milo's curiosity of what his captain really thought about the last few days got the best of him. "Well, sir, we did it."

"Huh?" Callahan kept staring back at the ferry landing that was soon swallowed by the night. "Did what, Milo?"

"I ain't sure, Captain. We sure 'nuf raised some hell. Killed some Apaches."

"Not enough. We never reached that big camp August spied out."

"No, we didn't. But you're going to be famous anyway, Captain."

"Huh."

"No, I mean it. Wait 'til all these boys muster out and start talking about what they've been up to. About Callahan's great Ranger expedition into Mexico. You're going to be the hero of the newspapers."

"Huh. Maybe so." Callahan lapsed back into silence, then said loudly, "Maybe so. I think I'll light up my last cigar."

Chapter 62

Eagle Pass, Texas
October 6, 1855

Milo walked straight from the rowboat to join Corporal Elam by their artillery pieces. As soon as he confirmed that the two little cannons were loaded and an alert sentry was on duty, Milo sat with his back to a sack of beans and slept through the few hours until dawn.

When the Ground Hog fired its first shot of canister across the river, Milo jerked upright and blinked a few times in confusion. Fearing they were under attack, he twisted around, but saw only the mist-shrouded river below them.

Captain Callahan's gruff voice penetrated Milo's mental fog. "Up and at 'em, Sergeant. That blast was just a reminder to those greasers that we still got teeth. Officers' call in O'Kelly's Saloon in ten minutes. I want you there, too."

Corporal Elam left the small campfire the artillery crews had kept burning all night and handed Milo a tin mug of hot coffee and a rolled-up tortilla stuffed with mashed beans.

★

The three captains sat around the table while the lieutenants and sergeants leaned on the bar. The dark circles under Captain Callahan's eyes were in counterpoint to his upbeat demeanor as he gave instructions.

"Lieutenant Burleson, I'll be needing a complete inventory of the food stuffs we brought back. Don't forget the sacks that are piled up in front of the cannons."

Captain Henry asked, "And what do you have in mind for all that food, James?"

"Lieutenant Burleson is going to sell all he can to the commissary officer at Fort Duncan. Then he and a detail are going to haul the rest of it to San Antonio and sell it to the army supply depot at the Alamo, or sell it in the market if he has to. We didn't have a chance to round up any runaway darkies, so we'll divide up the money from the food among the men when they muster out."

"Sounds good," Henry said as he sipped whiskey poured from the bottle Mr. O'Kelly had set on the table.

Captain Benton, his left arm bandaged from hand to shoulder and resting in a sling, asked, "What about our wounded boys?"

"They're going to San Antonio with Lieutenant Burleson. Nate, you can go with Eustace or stay with the battalion, your choice. A new letter from the governor was waiting on me here. Governor Pease is ordering us back to Fredericksburg to patrol until the boys' enlistment term runs out on the nineteenth, two weeks from now."

"I'll stick with Eustace. He ain't woke up yet, but he's breathing better."

"All right. William, you'll lead all three companies to Fredericksburg."

Captain Henry nodded. "What about you, James?"

"I'm leaving this morning for San Antonio. I'm going to stop and talk to Rip Ford, so he'll have our story right when he prints it in his newspaper. Then I'm reporting to the governor in Austin City so he'll hear the truth about what we done. After that, I'll head out to Fredericksburg to join you for the mustering out. Lieutenant Kyle will be going with me to file our written reports and handle the pay vouchers for the men."

Milo spoke for the first time. "We left nearly thirty saddled horses across the river. I'm not sure we can mount every man, even on mules."

Callahan drummed his fingers on the table while he considered that problem. "Lieutenant Burleson, once Milo gives you the names of every man without a horse, see if you can buy enough army nags to mount them all."

"And saddles," Milo added.

Callahan grunted and nodded. "But don't trade sacks of food for the horses or saddles. Use state payment vouchers. Anything else?"

Lieutenant Burleson asked about the two captured cannons.

Callahan rubbed his jaw. "Well, Texas don't have an army any more. And the U.S. Army artillery is all modern rifled pieces now. I have in mind to haul them to San Antone with the wounded and put them on display for a spell. Maybe in front of the Alamo."

Everyone nodded in agreement, and Burleson said he'd see to buying horses.

With a stutter of reluctance, Lieutenant Kyle said, "In spite of our posted guards along the riverbank, when we got back to Piedras Negras, I saw a few men swimming across the river, holding onto logs. Deserting. The current would have taken them downstream a ways before they landed, and they may have walked back here to Eagle Pass. Or they may have hiked off in some other direction. Sergeants, I need a morning report within an hour, with the names of the Rangers you can't account for."

Glad that the adjutant had not overlooked the deserters, Milo again mentioned the men who had abandoned their duty stations around the perimeter of Piedras Negras the day before.

"Captain, yesterday morning I put four Rangers at every post around the edge of town. I bet at least one in four left those stations and spent the day rooting through empty houses looking for anything valuable."

"Then it's a good thing that Lieutenant Davant and Corporal Elam's cannon fire drove the Mexicans back. Milo, I'm not asking you to dig out which men didn't stay where you put them. Some of the boys may have given into the temptation, but ain't none of them cowards. The fight at the river proved that. Things worked out all right. Let it be."

Milo gave it one more try. "Captain, walking up here, I seen Rangers wearing rings on ever' finger and silver trinkets around their necks. Earlier, I passed one Ranger carrying a Mexican saddle that was damned near covered in silver."

Callahan was unfazed. "I saw Captain Henry's sergeant with that saddle myself. Must have been the *alcalde's*. I wonder if that fat little bastard is still alive."

"Spoils of war," Captain Henry said as he swallowed the last of whiskey.

"I know that," Milo said. "But I'm telling the Regulars to stash the jewelry in their pockets until they get home, and not to flaunt it around town today. A lot of folks whose homes we burned down somehow crossed the river and are in Eagle Pass now. Some Mexican woman might see one of our boys wearing her favorite necklace and tell her husband to take it back for her. We don't need any knife fights."

"Milo, sometimes you do fret over the damnedest things," Callahan said as he stood up and patted his first sergeant's shoulder. "My gallant Hoplite."

Chapter 63

Fort Duncan, U.S. Army Post
Eagle Pass, Texas
October 7, 1855

Jesse had spent two nights and the day between them lying on his back in bed in the Fort Duncan infirmary. He had refused the laudanum offered by Dr. Doss to ease his pain, but the doctor had insisted on rewrapping his tight chest bandage.

Eustace Benton and Lieutenant King occupied the other two beds. Benton was still unconscious, but King and Jesse spent hours trying to piece together everything that had happened since they first reached Eagle Pass ten days ago.

During the second morning, Milo came in looking haggard.

"The battalion is heading back to San Antonio today. I came to fetch all three of you invalids."

"To hell with that invalid talk. You bring my horse saddled?" Lieutenant King blurted.

"Tied out front, Lieutenant." King immediately sat up and looked around for his clothes.

"You may have to boost me up into my saddle, Milo," Jesse said, making a feeble attempt to sit upright. "Between my shoulder and my chest, I ain't movin' too good."

Milo pulled Jesse up and swung him around so his feet were on the floor. Milo grabbed Jesse's boots from under his bed and knelt down to push the worn footwear over his friend's socks.

"I'm thinking you won't be on a horse for a while yet, Jesse. Doctor Doss said the smooth ride of a buckboard with springs is how you need to travel home. And Eustace has to have a place for us to stretch him out."

"And where you going to find a buggy with springs and how would you pay for it?"

"Doctor Doss is renting me his. He says he won't miss it for a while since there really ain't anywhere to take his wife around here, unless'n they go all the way to San Antone."

"Am I ever going to ride out of Eagle Pass on my own horse? And how are you going to pay that buggy rent?"

Milo grinned. "Now that's the beauty of it, Jess. I ain't payin' the buggy rent. Captain Benton and your daddy are going to split the cost. Your pa just don't know it yet. But he'll pay half. You watch. Your ma and Malissa will turn on him if he tries to wiggle out of it."

"Gee, thanks, Milo. he'll have me behind a plow 'til I'm thirty to pay him back."

"Ain't that what you're planning to do anyway?"

"Well, I was giving some thought to learnin' the gunsmithing trade. From Mr. Hoffman."

"And leave Prairie Lea? Leave your folks?"

"Milo, think about it. Whenever it is that Caroline agrees to marry me, whenever it is her ma lets her, that is, I can't ask her to move to Prairie Lea where her dead first husband's family lives now. I can't do that."

"Well, New Braunfels is just a day's ride from Prairie Lea. I reckon that'll do for Sunday dinners ever now and then." Milo handed Jesse his coat and gun belt.

Milo dropped his voice so only Jesse would hear. "I got a serious question. What about the old *alcalde's* appaloosa mare? You still hell-bent to trade that spotted horse for the slave woman in San Antone so Thompson can have a wife?"

Jesse settled his battered hat on his head. "Yup, I am. I promised, and I owe that darkie for saving my hair and my ass."

"Good, because I already told Doctor Doss we'd be bringing his buggy back ourselves, with a woman."

Chapter 64

Menger's Boarding House
San Antonio, Texas
October 11, 1855

Jesse's shoulder wound still ached, but as long as he didn't hurry himself or carry heavy things, his cracked sternum didn't hurt too much. He had surprised himself by sitting in a rocking chair on the porch of the boarding house most of the day before. He'd thought that after the long ride in the buckboard from Eagle Pass to San Antonio, he would be eager to start the final leg of his journey home to Prairie Lea.

It didn't occur to the twice-wounded and scarred young Ranger that the contentment he'd found in the rocking chair stemmed from being the center of attention all day, answering questions and retelling the tale of the great Texas Ranger raid into Mexico. Between the sessions with curious visitors and newspaper reporters, Jesse left the rocker long enough during the afternoon to disassemble and clean Lieutenant Davant's Sharps rifle.

He and Milo had swapped Jesse's carbine for Davant's longer army-model Sharps, since the shorter carbine was easier for Milo to carry while mounted. Milo had then loaned his old English-made muzzle-loading rifle to Private Buggs for the last two weeks of their stint in Callahan's Ranger Company.

Jesse worked on the rifle at the high table in the backyard of the boarding house. He hummed church hymns to himself while he scrubbed the small metal pieces with a fine wire brush and then carefully oiled each part before reassembling the weapon.

He watched the cook with sidelong glances as she prepared the evening meal. In the course of her work, she began making a pie, standing at the end of the same table where he had the rifle parts arrayed on a cloth. She had not spoken to Jesse. In addition to her normal reticence to speak to any white man, the knife scar on his forehead and the acne scars on his cheeks made her uneasy. When he quit his off-key humming and spoke to her, she involuntarily jumped.

"Is your name Irene?"

"Yes, suh."

"Irene, you are the first African woman I've ever spoken to. May I ask you something?" Irene nodded nervously as she poured flour, shortening, and salt into the bowl.

"Do you remember a young man named Thompson?"

"Thompson, suh?"

"Thompson. A slave owned by Mr. Smith from Austin City who stayed here last year."

"Long time ago, last year. Thompson, you say?"

"Thompson."

"He dead, this Thompson? You say he *was* owned by Mistah Smith." She put both hands into the bowl and began kneading the mixture.

"Nah, he was alive when I saw him two weeks ago in Mexico."

Irene nodded at this news. "I mighta seen a black man here last year who go by Thompson."

Jesse smiled, trying to put the black woman at ease. The smile only made her more tense, for she'd learned when white men grinned her way, it signaled that they intended to violate her.

"Well, Irene, this Thompson wants to marry you. Does that sound like the same man?"

Her hands went still in the bowl of dough. "Yessuh, it do. Dis Thompson took a hankerin' to me. But I told him he an' me be slaves, so don't be talkin' such talk."

Jesse leaned his elbows on the edge of the table. "Irene, if I bought you from Mr. Menger and took you to Mexico to marry Thompson, to live together in Mexico as man and wife, would that make you happy?"

Irene snorted. "Happy? What do a slave know about *happy*? That be a white man's word."

"You'd be a free person in Mexico. Not a slave. A woman not owned by anyone."

She took her doughy hands out of the bowl and wiped them on her apron, trying to believe what this odd, ugly white man was saying.

"No bounty hunter come after me, put me in chains and take me to an auction house?"

Jesse shook his head. "I can't swear that no bounty hunter will ever see you in Mexico and try to kidnap you. But Thompson will be there to stop him."

"How did Thompson get to Mexico?"

"He took off with another runaway slave named Philip. They stole three horses and rode south. Philip lives near Thompson with his Mexican wife and their baby."

"Even if you have the money to pay Mistah Menger for me, why you do that?"

"See this scar? Thompson shot the Injun who was trying to take my hair. I owe him for that."

Irene fought the skepticism she felt, but said, "I heard wit' my own ears Mistah Menger turn down three hunerd dollar fo' me."

"That's a lot of money. It sure is. That man must have taken a hankerin' to you, too."

"He be a white man that own a fancy rest'rant an' want me bakin' pies all day."

"Well, Irene, I got a fancy spotted mare and a fancy army rifle that may tempt Mr. Menger."

"More'n three hunerd dollar?"

"We'll see. That is, if you want me to make the offer to Mr. Menger. Do you?"

"How I get to Mexico, and how I find Thompson?"

"I'll take you in a buckboard. Me and my friend Milo. But first I'll take you home to teach my ma and sisters how to bake pies worth three hundred dollars."

Irene sprinkled flour on the tabletop and set the ball of kneaded dough in the middle. She picked up a rolling pin and started pressing the dough into a flat disk.

"Mistah Menger like three mugs of beer befo' bed. Maybe you offer him the swap afta' he drink two."

"I'll do that tonight."

★

To Jesse's surprise, an affable William Menger agreed to trade Irene for the appaloosa mare. In explaining his reason to his displeased wife, he reflected that the colts thrown by the spotted mare could be sold as yearlings, just a year or two old, whereas any off-springs of Irene would have to be fed and housed for a decade before the first sale. Since the price of a spotted colt was roughly the same as a ten-year-old slave, he could increase his profit by a factor of five or more, and ride one of the most prized horses in San Antonio. He promised to buy another Negress who his wife could teach to bake a good pie. Besides, he added, these days his paying guests were more interested in the beer from his cellar than the pies from her kitchen.

★

Jesse handled the reins of the buckboard while Milo rode Buck alongside. Irene refused to sit on the bench seat next to Jesse. Instead, she made herself a comfortable nest in the wagon bed behind the seat. The trio had left San Antonio after Irene made a last hearty breakfast for the seven men and three women who had slept at Menger's Boarding House the night before. In a parting act of defiance, she left the tall stack of dirty dishes on the worktable in the open air kitchen and let the stove fire burn to ashes. Her possessions consisted of a second dress Mister Menger had bought for her to wear when she helped serve meals to a full house.

The Gunn family greeted Milo and Jesse with gusto, the bear-hug Malissa gave her still-healing brother leaving him gasping in pain. While Mr. Gunn pumped Milo's hand, Jesse's mother ran her finger across the knife scar on her son's face and touched the dark stain where his coat was patched. She dabbed her eyes with her handkerchief before she ordered Jesse to bend down so she could kiss his forehead. Malissa went onto her tiptoes to plant a furtive kiss on Milo's cheek, a quick act her parents studiously ignored.

Since Jesse hadn't needed to include the Sharps rifle in the trade for Irene, he'd sold it for fifty dollars to another guest at the boarding house. When Milo arrived from Fredericksburg with their pay for three months of rangering, the pair went shopping. After they jointly selected items for each member of the Gunn clan, and a new bonnet for Caroline Hoffman, Jesse surprised Milo by adding a set of three pots and two frying pans to the pile of gifts on the store counter. His explanation was three words: "For Irene's kitchen."

In the late afternoon, Jesse and Milo used sawhorses to support a plank tabletop under the shady canopy of an oak tree. Irene covered the temporary dining table with a sheet pulled from a bed. She topped the make-shift tablecloth with two candlesticks from the mantle and a cluster of late-blooming weeds stuffed into a glass. Then she made dinner, including two fruit pies. When she appeared on the porch to serve the meal, she wore a clean black dress with a white collar. The family bit back big smiles, trying to maintain the decorum of the occasion. Jesse couldn't help but think about the mourning dress he had refused to buy for Caroline. Afterwards, over the token objections of Jesse's mother and sister, Irene cleared the table and washed every plate and piece of silverware.

Chapter 65

New Braunfels, Texas
October 13, 1855

The next morning, Milo, Jesse, and Irene left Prairie Lea, headed to Eagle Pass by way of New Braunfels. When the buckboard reached Hoffman's Gunsmith Shop, Jesse insisted that Irene go in with them.

Herr Hoffman greeting them with his usual blunt demeanor. "*Herr* Gunn, welcome back, but you know I do not approve of Negro servitude. Why is that woman here with you?" Jesse's reply perplexed the middle-aged German immigrant for just a moment.

"This here is Irene. She is betrothed to Thompson, the runaway darkie we went after for Mr. Smith last year.

"The Negro you could not find? You are now taking the elusive Negro a wife? Is this a ploy to capture him?"

"No, Mr. Hoffman. It's not a trick to capture Thompson. He's now a free man in Mexico, and me and Milo are escorting Irene there, so as they can get hitched and open a place for hungry folks to eat a bite—in Mexico, that is."

"Why do I suspect that Mr. Smith is unaware of Irene, and unaware of Mr. Thompson's whereabouts in Mexico."

Milo answered with a tiny shrug, "You suspect right, sir. And we'd like to keep it that way."

Herr Hoffman grunted before he looked at Milo. "And how are your spectacles working, Mr. McKean?"

"Well, they're scratched some, but you see I'm wearing them."

Hoffman smiled and said, "If you hand them to me, perhaps I can polish the scratches out of the glass."

While the gunsmith studied the spectacles, Jesse said, "I brought a gift for Caroline. And I'd like her to say hello to Irene.

She used to cook at Menger's Boarding House in San Antonio. That's where Caroline spent a day recovering on our way here last year. She met Irene there."

Caroline's father nodded as he applied a drop of oil to the lenses of the eyeglasses and held them to a foot-pumped spinning contraption to which a small cloth was attached. "My wife will have heard us. She'll call for you when she's ready."

The three travelers stayed only an hour with the Hoffmans. Milo bought a brass flask of powder, a bag of buckshot and a tin of German priming caps for Thompson's wedding present. *Herr* Hoffman was amused that Thompson still had Mr. Smith's shotgun.

With her mother by her side in the family's parlor, Caroline smiled when Jesse handed her the bonnet wrapped in brown paper. In a strained voice, she acknowledged Irene and wished her well in her upcoming marriage in Mexico. *Frau* Hoffman invited Jesse to Sunday dinner when he returned from Mexico.

After the travelers left the Hoffmans' living quarters and Milo and Irene waited at the buggy, Jesse mentioned his interest in learning the gunsmithing trade, maybe from Mr. Hoffman. With a raised eyebrow, the third generation craftsman answered in a word. "Perhaps."

★

The unlikely trio reached the border town without incident after what seemed an endless trip to all of them. The only bright spot were the breakfasts of eggs Irene insisted be bought in San Antonio and the stews of vegetables and jackrabbits shot by Jesse during the day.

On October 26th, with the buggy and horses secure in a stable, Milo paid a Mexican who spoke no English to row them across the Rio Grande in his skiff. When they stepped out of the boat, Jesse pulled a folded paper out of his coat pocket. He motioned for Milo and Irene to stop walking. Unfolding the paper, Jesse Gunn read the words printed on the paper.

I, Jesse Gunn, of Prairie Lea, Texas, do hereby grant the African woman Irene Thompson her life-long freedom from bondage.

"Malissa put the words together, but I wrote and signed it in my own hand, and Milo and my pa both witnessed it. It's a legal document—as long as you don't go back to Texas." Jesse held out the paper to Irene, who stood speechless with emotion.

"You might say thank you, but don't hug me. I'm a betrothed man. Or will be. Someday."

The sack of pots and pans slipped from Irene's grip with a clatter as she accepted the paper. She whispered a soft "Thank you" to Jesse before she knelt on the muddy ground, and openly weeping, thanked the Lord.

They walked up the rutted path to the top of the bluff and looked out over the charred remains of Piedras Negras. Somehow, the church bell tower still stood, perhaps saved by the openness of the cemetery that surrounded it, or because no Ranger had ridden among the graves to toss a burning torch at the tower. However it came to survive the inferno, the damaged structure reminded Milo of a solitary blackened finger jutting towards the sky, the centerpiece of a circle of desolation.

Milo came out his reverie first. "It's all gone. We knew it would be, but standing here, seeing this, I..."

"Where's the town? How will I ever find Thompson?"

"They moved it. Look over yonder. Follow the river." Jesse pointed to a small cluster of huts that lined the river about a mile away. "They're rebuilding upstream."

"What about the three-horse saloon?" Irene asked, her normal composure evaporated, replaced by a voice full of apprehension.

Just as suddenly, Jesse's confidence came through. "What's the first business that opens up in a new town?"

Before Milo could answer, Jesse continued, "Not that. The other first business. In Texas, a saloon. Here, a cantina."

The three walked towards the new town.

Before they found a cantina, they spied two black men who were at work adding bundles of straw to the roof of a small building. The two men straddling the rafters cautiously watched the trio of strangers walk closer to the half-built structure. There was a tense moment when Philip recognized Milo, the man he'd confronted in the river the year before. As Philip reflexively reached for his belt knife, Thompson put his hand on that of his friend, signaling him to wait.

Milo also recognized Philip and crossed his arms over his chest and tucked his hands into his armpits, away from his pistol. He hoped the gesture would reflect his friendly intent. Jesse just put his hands on his hips and grinned. Neither spoke.

Thompson looked down at the slender woman wearing a yellow turban and smiled broadly before he called, "Is that Irene's pots and pans in the sack? Sound like it."

Irene's eyes lit up and her smile matched Thompson's as she replied, "Is that Thompson's new eatin' place? Look like it."

Chapter 66

On the Road to San Antonio
From Eagle Pass
October 17, 1855

After the buckboard was returned and the rent paid to Doctor Doss, Milo and Jesse started the long ride back to Prairie Lea. After a comfortable hour of silence, Jesse asked his friend a question.

"Milo, I didn't want to talk about this in front of my family, or even Irene, but are you planning to sign on for another stint as a Ranger? You did good as Captain Callahan's sergeant. He may want to lead another company of volunteers next year, now that he's famous. He might make you his lieutenant next time."

Milo rode without answering, until he finally said, "I reckon not. I think my days of rangering are behind me. I owe Captain Callahan a lot. Yes, I do. I'll be planting a crop on my own land next spring, thanks to him. And now I can ask for Malissa's hand."

Jesse interrupted to say, "It's about time."

Milo stroked his beard as he ignored Jesse and thought about his future and James Callahan, who had been his gruff mentor and his captain for the past three months.

Jesse didn't notice Milo's inattention as he continued. "I asked Mr. Hoffman to take me on at his gunsmith shop. I got a knack for it."

"You got a knack for Caroline, that's what you got."

"Well, sure, but it's more than that, Milo. I'm good at taking things apart with tools, like you're good at building things with tools. But, back to rangering, I confess I won't miss weeks of sleeping on the cold hard ground. Or the rain and mud, or the heat and dust."

"Me neither, Jesse, but there's more to it for me."

Milo glanced at his friend to see if he was listening. "It's the Captain and men like William Henry. Sometimes I think Captain Callahan and Henry are bedeviled by their hate for everybody who don't look like them or talk like them, or even dares to disagree with them. They've both been fighting Mexicans and Indians their whole adult lives. After all those years of warrin' and chasin' hostiles, there's an anger down inside both of them that boils over too often."

Talking more to himself than to Jesse, Milo concluded, "Ain't neither of them the sort of man I want to be for Malissa. Or for me. After all, I expect there'll be a looking glass in our house someday."

Epilogue

First Sergeant Milo McKean

Milo bought the piebald mule from Captain Callahan. In the spring of 1856, the flatulent animal pulled the plow when Milo broke ground of the first fifty acres of the McKean farm. Milo and a family of hired Scottish immigrants named Mason seeded, hoed, and picked the first crop of cotton.

On October 6, 1856, Milo and Malissa were married in the Methodist Church in Lockhart, a building which Milo had helped to build.

In 1861, Milo enlisted in Story's Company of Confederate cavalry recruited in Lockhart. The other recruits knew of Milo's service as First Sergeant of Callahan's Ranger Expedition into Mexico, and elected him to serve as Second Lieutenant. The company was assigned as Company K of the 36th Texas Cavalry Regiment, where Lieutenant McKean served under the command of Colonel Nate Benton.

After the war, Milo continued to farm and prosper. Malissa took sick and died at the age of forty-four, leaving Milo with six children, four still living under his roof. Within a year, he married Gretchen Schmidt Elam, who was Ben Elam's widow, the Ranger and Confederate veteran having died in an accident at Reed's Cotton Gin.

Gretchen and her three children moved into the McKean farmhouse, to which Milo added another bedroom for himself and his new wife.

Private Jesse Gunn

In November 1855, Jesse became *Herr* Hoffman's apprentice. In December 1856, after two years of mourning her first husband, and two months of chaperoned courtship, Caroline and Jesse were married in a Lutheran Church in New Braunfels.

In October 1857, Caroline died from a hemorrhaging artery during the birth of her stillborn son. Caroline Hoffman Schmidt Gunn was laid to rest in the church cemetery in New Braunfels to the left of her first husband, Josef. To her left, a tiny wooden casket holds the remains of blond-haired Milo Luther Gunn.

During November and December 1857, a depressed Jesse and his friend Milo constructed a small two-room building on Market Street in Lockhart. In January 1858, Jesse opened his own gunsmith shop. The painted sign over the door read *J. Gunn the Gunsmith.*

During the Civil War, Jesse only opened his gun shop on Saturdays. Monday through Friday were spent supervising the production of rifles in the new Confederate armory in Prairie Lea.

Thompson

Since the only churches on the Mexican side of the river were Catholic, Thompson and Irene married by jumping the broomstick, an age-old slave custom performed in secret when a young couple were forbidden formal marriage by their masters.

Thompson and Irene lived in the rebuilt border town of Piedras Negras. The small adobe building that began as a single-room unnamed café was added onto when baby Jesse arrived. Irene insisted they move from their tent next to the open-air kitchen, into a sleeping room under a real roof. More babies and more add-on rooms followed during the next decade.

Thompson traded the double-barreled shotgun for a Colt revolver that he wore conspicuously in a belt holster. During the first few years, the occasional armed white man known to be a bounty hunter would appear at the door to Irene's cafe. Thompson made a point to personally serve a plate of food and then lean against the wall with arms crossed, gazing at the customer until he paid and left. After the first bite, the meal was usually left uneaten, since Irene knew when to replace black pepper with stone-ground rat pellets.

Even after the Civil War brought an end to the South's *peculiar institution,* and Juneteenth became a celebrated holiday for African-American Texans, Thompson slept with his pistol within reach, and Irene kept a sharp butcher knife under the edge of their mattress.

In 1868, the couple moved their family and their café across the river into Eagle Pass, where for another twenty-five years the *Cocina del Appaloosa* served dishes inspired by Mexican, African-American and Anglo cuisine.

Irene welcomed being called Mrs. Thompson, however, Thompson himself never took on a second name. He believed too many freed men were burdened with the unwelcomed names of men who once owned them.

Afterword

There is certainly a mystique attached to the Texas Rangers of the 1800's. To this day, the Rangers enjoy an aura of being the tough good guys. Yet, the untrained volunteers during the years of Texas' early statehood surely were men with lesser or greater flaws, like every one of us.

The moral compass that guides present-day Texas is not the same as in 1855. African-Americans are no longer an enslaved people. We are not in an ethnic war for contested land with Mexico, as we were during the entire adult life span of James Callahan. We are no longer trading savagery with Native Americans, in the vicious undeclared war that lasted thirty years beyond Callahan's death.

Regardless how American society has changed over the past 160 years, in the middle years of 19th century, Texas was a violent, unforgiving place to live. It was a frontier region where Hispanics and Anglos fought for dominance, Native Americans fought for survival, and African-Americans were chattel who tried by the thousands to escape Texas, running for sanctuary in Mexico. Texas was in a time and place where the Rangers' brutal violence toward all enemies was not only accepted, but lauded as necessary.

★

James Callahan remains a puzzling figure in Texas history. His reputation has ebbed and flowed with the tides of time. Following his raid into Mexico, he was loved by the people for his exploits across the border, but also criticized as being excessively reckless for torching the town of Piedras Negras and displacing 2,000 people. Callahan's decision even to stay in Mexico after the cavalry battle was questioned by his own Rangers, and the looting of Piedras Negras by the undisciplined Ranger battalion is noted in several primary sources. For twenty years afterwards, politicians and diplomats dealt with the international backlash of the raid, with the U.S. Government eventually paying $50,000 in damages to 150 citizens of Piedras Negras.

James Callahan moved his family to a cattle ranch near Blanco. His new fame as a Ranger captain followed him, but so did recurring rumors that the recent foray into Mexico had a second unsavory purpose: to recapture runaway slaves and bring them back to Texas. The odd vignette of his shooting to death a hired Negro slave came from two newspaper accounts published shortly after the killing and his move to Blanco.

An old acquaintance from Seguin, Woodson Blassingame, rented land from Callahan near Blanco. Blassingame's older son Calvin worked with his father, and his younger son Luther had served as a private on the Rangers' raid into Mexico. For reasons never publicly revealed, James Callahan felt the Blassingame family had disrespected the Callahan family. Perhaps the perceived slight involved the rumors about capturing runaway slaves in Mexico. Perhaps James Callahan's anger was more personal, involving romantic improprieties between members of the two families.

Whatever the root cause, on April 7, 1856, just six months after leading the Ranger battalion into Mexico, James Callahan and two friends rode to the Blassingame house to defend the honor of his family. All three men were armed. From horseback, Callahan called for Woodson to come outside. A blast of buckshot fired from a window hit Callahan square in the chest, killing him. One of Callahan's companions died from gunfire an instant later. The other friend escaped, rushing to Blanco to report the shooting to the sheriff.

Woodson and Calvin Blassingame were arrested for murder. Within a week, as word of Callahan's death spread, a crowd of fifty enraged men dragged the father and son from the cabin where they were being held under guard. While the two Blassingame men protested they had fired in self-defense, the mob shot them to death in the street.

Regardless of the murky facts of the expedition into Mexico, the citizens of Texas did not forget the enigmatic Ranger Captain. The people remembered that without help from the U.S. Army, Texas' own Rangers, led by Captain James Callahan, had avenged the far-flung settlers who had suffered from vicious Indian depredations for twenty years. Even if few Apaches were killed during Callahan's raid to punish them, the expedition made the point that Texas had the resolve and the fangs to strike like a rattler if provoked enough.

In spite of all the questions that swirled around James Callahan's life, nearly eighty years after he was buried in Blanco, Texas, his remains were honorably moved to the Texas State Cemetery in Austin, and a county was named for him during the Texas Centennial celebrations.

★

Captain William Henry's reputation as a fighting man was so enhanced by the Callahan Expedition that the voters of San Antonio elected him to the position of sheriff in 1856. In 1859, Henry joined the company of Ranger Captain William Tobin to put down the border insurrection led by the *bandito* Juan Cortina.

In 1862, yearning for an appointment to command a new company of Confederate soldiers being raised in San Antonio, Henry instigated an argument with William Adams. The quarrel, begun on the main plaza of the city, devolved into a gunfight in which William Henry was mortally shot. The subsequent investigation concluded that Adams killed Henry in an act of self-defense.

Captain Nate Benton was present when his son Eustace woke from his three-day coma. Although Eustace lost his eye, he recovered from the grievous wound. Eustace's mother, the Captain's wife, died in 1861, whereupon Nate Benton soon organized a company of mounted volunteers. The company became Company B of the 36th Texas cavalry in the Confederate army.

Benton received a promotion to lieutenant colonel of the regiment and in April 1864 lost his arm in battle in Louisiana. After the war, Benton remarried and settled in Seguin. He was elected county judge, but served as a school teacher during the era of reconstruction when Confederate veterans were disallowed public office. Benton died of illness in 1872.

Historically, William Menger was a brewer and operated a boarding house before he opened the famous Menger Hotel in San Antonio just a block from the Alamo.

Rip Ford was a well-known Ranger and newspaper editor. The July 4th celebration at the Magnolia Hotel in Seguin occurred, complete to the interruption of Senator Wilson's speech. Sadly, Methodist pastor John McGee and his murdered son Jouette played their roles in my novel as they did in real life.

The unfortunate Billy 'Easy' Clopton was an ancestor of the present-day pastor of my Methodist Church in Lockhart, thirty miles from Seguin. Ranger Clopton did die when his leaping horse failed to clear an irrigation ditch during the cavalry battle at the Rio Escondido.

William Davant was in fact a U.S. Army lieutenant stationed at Fort Duncan located on the Rio Grande River. Davant was the son of a North Carolina plantation owner, and was a recent graduate of West Point. He is recorded in army records as drowning while wearing civilian clothes and assisting Callahan's Rangers cross the flooding Rio Grande. I amended his role and the manner of death to contribute to a more exciting story.

The Ground Hog and the Double Flirt cannons are mentioned in the primary sources. They were used with effect in the Rangers' aborted defense of Piedras Negras. The portly town *alcalde*, but not his appaloosa mare, is portrayed as recorded by witnesses.

This novel is historical fiction. Milo McKean and Jesse Gunn are fictional characters who are inspired by two real men who were friends, then brothers-in-law--Constantine Connolly and Jesse Holmes. Connolly served as Callahan's first sergeant during the raid into Mexico.

Poor Caroline Hoffman Schmidt Gunn is fictional, as is her father and her father-in-law. Thompson and Irene, Philip and Juanita, and the piebald mule are all fictional.

The characters of Benjamin Smith and Malissa Gunn are based on recorded family histories. The Negro-Seminole chief Black Cat and the Mexican army officers Colonel Menchaca, and Captains Madero and Patino are named in the primary sources.

The title *A Different Country Entirely* is a quote from Frederick Law Olmsted, the famous architect who designed New York City's Central Park and the Boston Commons. In 1854-55, Olmstead and his brother traveled with a guide on horseback across Texas, writing a travelogue for a northern magazine. I think Mr. Olmsted's four-word description of Texas is apt.

In 2013, author Philip McBride completed his first novel, **Whittled Away,** a Civil War story about the Alamo Rifles, a Confederate infantry company.

McBride's next three novels, published between 2014 and 2016, comprise the trilogy about Captain John McBee of the Fifth Texas Infantry Regiment, CSA. –**Tangled Honor 1862**, **Redeeming Honor 1863**, and **Defiant Honor 1864**.

A Different Country Entirely is McBride's first novel set in Texas in the early days of statehood.

McBride has also co-authored a nonfiction history book, **Texans at Antietam**, published in 2017, and since 1999, he has contributed over eighty articles to the Camp Chase Gazette, the national magazine devoted to the hobby of Civil War reenacting.

McBride is a retired teacher, high school principal, and public school district administrator. He is an avid student of the Civil War and Texas history, and a compulsive reader of military historical fiction. He and his wife Juanita live in Lockhart, a small farming town in central Texas.

The author welcomes comments or questions about **A Different Country Entirely.** He may be contacted at:

ptmcbride49@gmail.com.

McBride publishes regular blog posts about writing his books, his family, history, and other topics that prick his interest.

http://mcbridenovels.blogspot.com/